Aileen Armitage is ▮▮▮▮▮▮▮▮▮▮▮▮▮▮▮▮
She began writing w▮▮▮ ▮▮▮▮▮ ▮▮ ▮▮▮▮ ▮▮
give up work in the outside world and in 1988 she was
the winner of the Woman of the Year award. She is
also the author of *Hawksmoor*, *A Dark Moon Raging*,
Touchstone and *Hawkrise* and the *Chapters* series of
novels, *Chapter of Innocence*, *Chapter of Echoes* and
Chapter of Shadows. Her most recent novels, *The
Jericho Years* and *Cedar Street*, are also published
by Corgi. She is married to the author, journalist and
broadcaster Deric Longden.

Also by Aileen Armitage

THE JERICHO YEARS
CEDAR STREET

and published by Corgi Books

The Dark Arches

Aileen Armitage

To Wendy
Sincere good wishes

Aileen Armitage

CORGI BOOKS

THE DARK ARCHES
A CORGI BOOK : 0 552 14453 3

Originally published in Great Britain by Bantam Press,
a division of Transworld Publishers Ltd

PRINTING HISTORY
Bantam Press edition published 1996
Corgi edition published 1997

Copyright © Aileen Armitage 1996

The right of Aileen Armitage to be identified
as the author of this work has been asserted in accordance
with sections 77 and 78 of the Copyright Designs and Patents
Act 1988.

All of the characters in this book
are fictitious, and any resemblance
to actual persons, living or dead,
is purely coincidental.

Conditions of Sale
This book is sold subject to the condition that it shall not,
by way of trade or otherwise, be lent, re-sold, hired out or
otherwise circulated in any form of binding or cover other
than that in which it is published and without a similar
condition including this condition being imposed on the
subsequent purchaser.

Set in 10/12pt Century Old Style by
Hewer Text Composition Services, Edinburgh.

Corgi Books are published by Transworld Publishers Ltd,
61–63 Uxbridge Road, London W5 5SA,
in Australia by Transworld Publishers (Australia) Pty Ltd,
15–25 Helles Avenue, Moorebank, NSW 2170
and in New Zealand by Transworld Publishers (NZ) Ltd,
3 William Pickering Drive, Albany, Auckland.

Reproduced, printed and bound in Great Britain by
Cox & Wyman Ltd, Reading, Berks.

To those friends who generously gave me the benefit of their time, knowledge and expertise: Ian Augustus, Bridie O'Connell, Jack Rosenthal, Helen Sutcliffe, Susan Wood, and especially my husband Deric Longden my love and grateful thanks.

PART ONE
1959

Chapter One

Mr O'Byrne evidently didn't know his shirt-tail was flapping out over his prodigious backside as he waddled across the shop to the door, turned the sign round from 'Open' to 'Closed' and rattled down the blind. Rosa pretended not to notice, busying herself flicking the duster along the shelves between the packets of sugar and flour.

'Another day done, thanks be,' he muttered.

She could hear his deep, wheezy breathing as he emptied coins from the till and stacked them on the counter. He always counted the day's takings before stowing them away in a canvas bag to carry home. Not that it was ever a massive amount – no-one in Clondarra earned and spent enough to make any shopkeeper's fortune.

From the corner of her eye she caught sight of Joe's dark head as he peered out from the stockroom and glanced up at the clock on the wall. Mr O'Byrne spotted him too.

'Don't be minding the time now,' he growled, unfastening his apron strings. 'There's still the last orders to go out before ye knock off. And Rosa—'

Rosa turned. 'Yes, Mr O'Byrne?'

'The counter's all sticky here from the jam. Be sure and give it a good wash down tonight.'

'I will.'

She could hear Joe slapping around in the back room whistling softly to himself, and she smiled. They'd planned it this way, Joe and her. Always prompt at six on a Saturday, never a moment later, Mr O'Byrne emptied the till and left for home. And Saturday nights Rosa had to stay late to clean the shop. If Joe dallied long enough over the orders he'd still be here when their employer left. That way they would have the empty shop to themselves for a whole half-hour before she had to lock up and drop the keys through the boss's letter-box.

She watched as Mr O'Byrne pulled on his overcoat. Why couldn't he move his great body a bit faster and get the hell out of there? At last he lifted the latch and the doorbell clanged.

'Rosa, don't forget to lock the back door behind Joe.'

'I won't.'

'And remember to turn off the lights.'

'I will.'

'Now drop the latch again behind me.'

She hurried across, only too eager to shut out the sight of his bulk and turn to Joe's warm young arms. She'd been aching for them all day long. It had been a terrible torment to watch the muscles in his back, firmly outlined under the taut shirt, and steel herself to keep her hands off him. There was magic in Joe Clancy's touch, in the feel of him and the glow of his sea-green eyes.

No other boy in the village could match up to Joe Clancy, and it wasn't only his looks. He was a stranger from the far north, where they spoke with a rougher voice than hereabouts. Not that Joe was rough; on the contrary he'd always been gentle and kindness itself to her. Oona was more than a little jealous, but even to her sister she'd not yet confided the one fact about Joe which made her a little uneasy.

She leaned against the stockroom doorway, smiling as he came back in from the yard.

'How many have you still to do?' she asked.

'Four,' he answered, coming towards her with outstretched arms, 'but they're all in Fancy Lane. They can wait.'

The tweed of his jacket pressed roughly against her cheek and a button dug deep into her breast, but Rosa was only aware of the smell of him, sweet and sticky from effort, and of the touch of his lips against her neck. He spat out a long strand of her hair and she heard his murmured words against her ear.

'Will I take ye to the flicks tonight?'

'I can't, Joe, really I can't.'

'Back row – double seat?'

The dearest seats in the house – it hurt to say no. 'Sorry,' she murmured, 'like I said ...'

'The coffee bar then?' he went on persuasively. 'I'll let ye choose the records on the jukebox.'

He treated her like a queen. She shook her head sadly. 'Mammy won't let me go near those places. And she certainly wouldn't let me go on my own.'

'Ye'll be with me. Ah, come on.'

She loved the cajoling tone in his voice, but it was no use. 'She doesn't know about you,' she whispered. 'I haven't told her yet.'

He groaned and broke away from her. 'Are ye a babby still? Ye're eighteen, for Christ's sake!' he growled. 'Old enough to be married.'

The dull anger in his tone hurt. Rosa nuzzled up against him, stroking a coaxing fingertip down his cheek. 'Don't blaspheme, Joe. I'll tell her soon,' she promised, 'but 'tis not an easy thing to tell her.'

'I want to walk out with ye, see more of ye,' Joe grumbled; 'not have to make do with odd minutes we snatch in the shop.'

'So why are we wasting time?' she said softly, snaking her arms around him and drawing him close. 'Turn off the lights and let's make the most of the next twenty minutes.'

Thomas Lane, its narrow cobbled width bordered on either side by a row of tiny two-up-and-two-down cottages, had never seemed so long as Rosa made her way home. On the little bridge spanning the culvert a couple of scrawny chickens clucked in irritation and scattered out of her way.

Through open doorways the smells of supper-time filled the evening air. The scent of boiled bacon and cabbage drifted from the Leahys', something with onions from the Lynches'. Judging by the pungent smell of peat smoke from the McBrides' they must have the chimney blocked by birds nesting there again like they did last spring. From the Colgans' came the succulent aroma of frying ham. No wonder they had the door standing wide open.

'Leave the door open and let the whole village have the benefit.' Mammy always said the same when they cut a great slice of ham from the cured side of pork. Yesterday it had been fish as always on a Friday, and Saturdays it was mutton – either shepherd's pie or cottage pie. Rosa's stomach rumbled in anticipation. Maybe after, when they'd all settled down over a big pot of Mammy's strong black tea, she'd bring up the subject of Joe. If she could wait that long …

Rosa stared fixedly at the bowl of shamrock wilting on the window-ledge while she waited apprehensively for Mammy's reaction. St Patrick's Day had come and gone, but Mammy never had the heart to throw out the blessed shamrock until it had dwindled to a withered brown mass.

Her mother's lips were still compressed into a tight line as she bent to lift the large dish from the oven and place it on the checked tablecloth, then began dolloping out spoonfuls of shepherd's pie. Oona sat opposite Rosa moodily picking at her fingernails, unaware of Grandma Sheridan's scowl. Daddy Kerrigan's expression was hidden behind his evening newspaper.

Mammy spoke warily. 'So who is he then, this Clancy fellow? I know of no Clancys in the village.'

Before Rosa could answer her sister cut in. 'New people down the west side, Mammy – they came to live in old McCafferty's cottage last year after he died.'

Grandma Sheridan stopped sucking her teeth and looked up sharply. 'McCafferty dead?' she exclaimed. 'God rest his soul. Why did nobody tell me?'

Rosa cast her sister a warning look, but she took no notice as she dipped a tentative fork into the shepherd's pie and added airily, 'They came from away up north.'

Mammy glared distrustfully. 'Up north?' she repeated. 'Whereabouts? I hope to God he's a good Catholic boy like Desmond.'

Rosa saw Daddy Kerrigan's anxious glance and lowered her eyes. 'He's not,' she said quietly, 'he's a Protestant, but it makes no difference.'

'No difference?' Mammy stood, spoon in hand, as she slapped the last plate down in front of her mother-in-law. 'Did ye hear that, Timmy-Tom? May the saints preserve us! Would I see a daughter of mine marry a Proddy-dog? Not while there's breath in my body!'

Rosa tried to keep her voice level. 'I'm not talking of marrying him, Mammy. I only want to walk out with him.'

'And what's walking out if not one step on the way? Why couldn't ye pick a good Catholic boy like Oona's gone and done? She'll be well set up when she marries Desmond.'

Oona's smile oozed complacency as she laid her fork aside. 'Daddy would turn in his grave,' she remarked.

'Indeed he would,' growled her mother. 'I'll not hear another word said, do ye hear me? Not another word about this Clancy fellow.'

Rosa bit her tongue. Daddy Kerrigan cleared his throat and spoke for the first time in his soft Cork accent.

'Ah, go easy on the girl,' he murmured. 'She only wants a bit of company to go to the pictures. Ah sure, there's no harm in that.'

Rosa darted him a grateful look. Her real father was no more than a three-year-old's hazy memory, but Daddy Kerrigan, mindful always of being only a stepfather, had always understood and taken her side.

Mammy scowled. 'Ye'd spoil the child, so ye would, Timmy-Tom, but I'll not have her hobnobbing with a Protestant boy,' she retorted. 'We'd be the talk of the village. There must be a million good Catholic men in the south of Ireland and she has to go for a heretic! No decent Catholic girl should dream of insulting her faith or her family that way. 'Tis more than flesh and blood can bear. She'll not see him again.'

'I have no choice,' said Rosa quietly. 'He works in our shop.'

Grandma Sheridan pulled a strand of meat from between her teeth. 'Are ye going to let the child talk to ye that way, Deirdre?' she demanded, her voice barely discernible as she masticated noisily. 'Ye'd best get yourself off down to Confession tonight, my girl, and repent of such wicked behaviour.'

'Indeed she will.' Mammy was still making rumbling sounds in her throat as she speared a lump of mutton and chewed savagely, then, seeing Oona push her plate away, she turned her attack on her elder daughter.

'And what's wrong with that pie?' she demanded. 'That's best neck of mutton. Your nan is managing it all right.'

'Nothing's wrong at all,' Oona smiled sweetly. 'I just want to lose a bit more weight so I can fit into my wedding dress. It's not long now.'

Mammy sighed. 'God willing,' she murmured, then added sadly, 'though the Lord alone knows why I should be glad. With my other children all gone and left me there'll only be Rosa here on her own.'

Daddy Kerrigan wiped a blob of mashed potato off his spectacles with a corner of the tablecloth and replaced them on his nose. 'And me,' he reminded her gently as he picked up his newspaper again. 'I'll be here.'

The church was dark but for the glow of a sprinkling of penitential candles near the altar. The sweet smell of incense still lingered in the air as Rosa crouched in the pew, hands clasped in prayer, waiting for Oona, the last of the repentants, to come out of the confessional box. She'd hung about till the end, reluctant to go in.

Oona emerged at last and knelt beside her. 'Ten Hail Marys he gave me,' she whispered. 'I'll be done by the time ye get out. Go on now.'

Taking a deep breath Rosa entered the pitch-dark of the confessional and knelt, making the sign of the cross.

'Bless me, Father, for I have sinned.'

Beyond the grille she could hear the priest's breathing, and even before he spoke she knew by the whiff of Irish whisky which drifted through to her that it was Father O'Flynn. At least he wasn't so severe as Father Nolan.

'Tell me what sins you've committed, my child.'

She kept her voice to a whisper, in the hope he wouldn't

recognize her. 'Disrespectful to my mammy ... spoke harshly to my sister ... kept a penny change when a customer didn't pick it up ...' Oh God, he'd recognize her now!

'Anything else, my child?'

Rosa hesitated. It didn't seem right to confess how she felt about Joe – it wasn't a sin, surely, to love? 'Love thy neighbour,' the Commandment said. Even so, her conscience couldn't be entirely clear and clean again if she didn't speak ...

'I've fallen in love, Father.'

'Ah, I see.' The slurred voice fell silent for a moment, then spoke again. 'And do you have lustful thoughts about this boy?'

'Yes, Father.' Her voice was tinier still now, barely a hiss in the dark.

The priest exhaled a long sigh, thick with whisky fumes. 'Oh, the torment of the flesh,' he murmured, 'but we must strive to overcome these sinful thoughts, my child. To yield to temptation would lead to far worse torment in hell. You must be strong and put such thoughts from your mind. Pray to Our Lady that you may be as pure and chaste as herself.'

Rosa said nothing. 'Go now and say ten Hail Marys and I'll grant you absolution,' he said. 'Now say the Act of Contrition with me.'

'Oh my God, I am sorry and beg pardon for all my sins ...'

Ten Hail Marys – the same as Oona. Rosa couldn't help wondering just what her sister had confessed. As they left the church together she glanced at her face, half-hidden under the flowered headscarf. There was no way of telling whether she too had kept to herself a sin she didn't dare to confess.

'Oona.'

'What is it?'

'Is it a mortal sin not to confess a sin to the priest?'

Oona pulled off the headscarf and tossed back her long black hair. 'Not if ye forgot, it isn't.'

'But if ye didn't forget, what then?'

Oona stuffed the headscarf into her handbag. 'Don't go bothering me with your silly questions,' she snapped. 'Ask Father O'Flynn.'

They took a few paces more. 'Have you ever done it?' Rosa asked.

She heard the click of her sister's tongue and saw her quick look. 'Done what? What are ye on about?'

'Not confess something. What did you think I meant?'

Oona quickened her pace. 'Let's get a move on or I'll be late – Desmond won't wait all night.'

Rosa hurried to keep up with her. 'Where are you going with him?'

She saw Oona's face turn to her, pale in the lamplight. 'That's no business of yours.'

Rosa couldn't contain her curiosity. 'I've seen the two of ye down by Delaney's farm. I hear tell some couples go into the barn there.'

'And what if they do?' demanded Oona. 'Been there yourself, have ye?'

'I have not,' protested Rosa. 'Not yet.'

'Anyway,' Oona went on, 'very soon now we'll not have to find a private place at all, once we're married.'

'You'll get no privacy in the Reillys' house. Packed out like sardines, they are. How many brothers and sisters does Desmond have?'

Oona stopped and turned. 'Listen,' she said quietly, 'not that it's any business of yours, but I'm not going to stay in that house for long. Desmond and me, we have other plans.'

17

'Move to a place of your own, do you mean?'

Oona nodded. 'I know Mammy would like me to stay within her beck and call, but that's not for me. When I'm not around she'll have to get used to it.'

'You're moving out of Clondarra,' Rosa breathed. 'Where to?'

Oona pursed her lips. 'All in good time. Now ye keep this to yourself, do ye hear, or I'll flay the hide off ye, so I will. I'm telling ye no more so hold your whisht and bother me no more with your questions.'

Rosa fell silent as they walked on. So Oona did keep secrets to herself. Sinful ones? Who could tell?

As they neared the Tudor, the only cinema Clondarra possessed, Rosa could see the line of bodies snaking away down to the hardware shop on the corner. At once her thoughts leaped back to Joe. She scanned the faces in the queue, hoping like mad she wouldn't spot him with some slender-waisted girl at his side, laughing up at him, her hair all silky and her skirts flouncing out over layers of net underskirt. Rosa longed to have a skirt like that, but Mammy didn't hold with such frippery.

'He's not here,' said Oona shortly, 'so ye can stop looking.'

At the corner of the main street she stopped. 'Off home with ye now,' she said tersely. 'See ye later.'

She turned and began walking away. Rosa called after her. 'Will we be going to Communion in the morning?'

She saw Oona's airy wave of the hand. 'Why not? We got absolution, didn't we?'

18

Chapter Two

Rosa stood looking out of the window. Heavy globules of rain clung, quivering under the eaves. If only it had stopped raining heavens hard before Mass ended she could have walked down the glen again, just as she did last week when Oona went off with Desmond to talk to the priest about the sacrament of matrimony. Joe might have been down there again today, wet-haired and eager, waiting for her ...

Behind her she could hear the whirr of Mammy's old sewing-machine and the occasional muttered words of irritation when the thread kept snapping. She was still at a loss to understand why her daughter could conjure up no enthusiasm for the matching frocks she was making for the wedding, both squeezed out of five yards of emerald green satin.

'It's fine stuff,' she averred, 'even though I got it cheap in the market. The fellow told me he can't get enough of it.'

'People will know they're home-made when we're both wearing the same,' Rosa pointed out. 'They'll think we can't afford new.'

Mammy shook her head firmly. 'After five weddings in the family ye're lucky to be having a new frock at all.'

'A nice new hat then,' Rosa persisted. 'I can't go bare-headed in church and a headscarf's hardly smart enough for my sister's wedding.'

She had a fleeting vision of it; a huge picture hat, like they wore in the films, with a trimming of flowers or feathers. Mammy thought for a moment.

'A half-hat,' she pronounced at last. 'I've a bit of petersham and with the leftover scraps of satin I could just about manage a half-hat. And God willing,' she added, 'the weather will be better than this on the day or the colour could run.'

The hat lay now beside Liam's photograph on the sideboard, and propped behind the silver frame stood his latest letter. Every month without fail the letter with its American stamp arrived, always signed 'Your loving son Liam' and always enclosing a few dollars for Mammy.

They'd all got away, all but Rosa. Liam and Deirdre both now on the other side of the Atlantic, Dominic settled in his good job in the distillery up in the city and married to a Dublin girl, Shelagh married to a Kerry farmer, gone as fat as a sow and perfectly happy producing more piglets every year. And now Oona ...

Mammy's voice cut in on her thoughts. 'Ye'll write and tell Liam and Deirdre all about it after the wedding,' she said. 'Oona has a fine hand but 'tis ye who'll have to do all the writing once she's gone.'

'I might not always be here,' Rosa murmured. 'You could write to them yourself. They'd like that.'

'Me?' Her mother's voice was sharp. 'Won't I have enough on my hands? Haven't I to see to Kelly's chickens and all? Surely to God ye can see I'll need help to look after the others.'

'There'll only be Daddy Kerrigan now – and Dominic the odd times he comes down from the city. And Grandma can help.'

'Never ye mind her. She's getting too old to be much help now. I need ye here.'

20

Rosa pouted. 'I could go off somewhere too. I could get married.'

Her mother stared, aghast. 'Get married?' she echoed. 'And ye the youngest daughter? Ye'll stay home and do as I say. Don't Daddy and me need to be cared for when we're old?'

She turned away, muttering to herself as she slapped the lid on the sewing-machine and stowed it away in the cupboard. 'Whatever are ye thinking of, child? Didn't I stay and care for your Grandma Reilly till she died?'

Rosa stared out through the rain-spattered glass, visualizing the years of blankness stretching ahead, years of experiencing life only at second-hand through random letters:

'How are things with you? Nothing much is happening here ...'

Rebellious anger stirred in her. Mammy had been lucky – when she escaped she'd still been young enough to marry and bear children, but I don't want to waste my life trapped here. I want to be with Joe. I want to savour again the thrill when I lie in his arms, even in the wet grass. She smiled as she recalled Oona's warning when she'd finally plucked up the courage to tell her.

'Don't look to me for sympathy if you catch pneumonia – or worse,' she'd said darkly. 'You should have more sense.'

'I know. I'll make sure to keep dry in future.'

'You dope. You know what I mean. Take precautions.'

Beyond the misted window-pane something moved. Rosa cleared a patch with her fingertips and recognized the girl walking down the lane.

'I'm going out for a while, Mammy,' she said. 'I need a breath of air.'

Her mother came to join her at the window. 'Has the rain stopped? Ah look, there's Maggie Malone.'

'I'll catch up with her,' said Rosa, grabbing her coat, 'maybe go for a walk on the common.'

Mammy nodded. 'You do that,' she said approvingly. 'She's a nice girl, from a good family. Being in service at the Riordans' has given her nice manners too. Ye wouldn't catch her messing with a Protestant fellow.'

By rights, with her ripple of blond hair like a cascading waterfall and her eyes a deeper brown than Mr Regan's spaniel, Maggie Malone should have been the prettiest girl by far in Clondarra. But nature had not played fair with her. Her nose veered off to the right, and those trusting brown eyes were set just a little too close together. To compound nature's failings, the left eye turned in as though trying to burrow under the cock-eyed nose in search of the right eye. But she was a sweet and gentle girl for all that. Rosa hurried to catch up with her.

'I haven't seen you in weeks, Maggie,' she remarked. 'The Riordans been keeping you at it?'

'Not specially.' Maggie's tone was dull. Rosa searched her face. It too wore a dull disinterested look

'I haven't seen you at Mass either,' Rosa ventured. 'Have you been poorly?'

'No.'

Rosa stopped walking and tugged at Maggie's arm. 'What's up? Something is, I can tell.'

'Nothing.' The voice was thin, plaintive. 'I can't tell you.'

Maggie sighed and slumped down on the grass. There was dejection and utter helplessness all about her. Ignoring the wet grass Rosa knelt beside her.

'Who can you tell if not me?' she murmured. 'Come on.'

Maggie exhaled another deep sigh before answering. 'Father Nolan says I'm a terrible sinner, doomed to hell-fire.

22

He won't have me in his church any more. Never again, he says.'

Rosa gasped. 'No Mass, no Communion? Dear God, what have you done?'

Visions flicked through her brain – the church collection box stolen and rifled, the waspish Mrs Riordan battered or even murdered. Maggie's tear-stained face looked up at her.

'I've just found out – I'm in the family way, Rosa. Up the junction good and proper.'

Rosa sank back on her haunches, trying to absorb the news. Of all the girls in Clondarra, who would have guessed that Maggie Malone ...

'For pity's sake don't tell anybody,' Maggie whimpered. 'If Daddy finds out he'll take his belt to me.'

'He wouldn't do that – not to a girl who's ... expecting.'

It was hard to say the terrible word. Then the next question leapt to mind. Who was responsible? Maggie had no boyfriend that she knew of. She'd kept him very quiet.

'Your fellow – does he know?' she asked.

Oceans of loneliness welled in the reply. 'I have no fellow. I'm on my own.'

Rosa held her tongue. There must have been someone once, but not any more. The swine, leaving Maggie to face the music alone.

'I'm going to get away before they find out,' Maggie said dully. 'When I get enough money together I'm going to buy the boat and go to me sister Kitty's in England. She'll look after me.'

A sudden idea seemed to strike her. She grasped Rosa's hands between hers. 'Why don't you come with me?' she breathed. 'You've always said you'd like to get away from Clondarra – why not come with me to England? Kitty tells me the place is loaded with opportunities for young people like us.'

For a moment the dream beckoned and Rosa held her breath. Then the vision of Mammy returned. With her away up the country, often for days at a time, choosing birds for Kelly's, the big provisioners in the city, bringing them home to pluck and prepare, she really did need help to mind Daddy Kerrigan and the old lady.

'I can't,' she said sadly. 'I'd love to but I can't.'

Maggie's hands fell away from hers. 'I'll miss you,' she murmured. 'It'll be good there – Kitty says you can earn three times as much as you can here. Think of it – we could be rich.'

Rosa said nothing as she got to her feet. For an unmarried girl with a baby earning a living could never be easy, especially in a strange land.

'I can't stay here,' Maggie muttered. 'I've got to get away before it shows.'

Rosa nodded. 'I suppose so. Unless you marry the fellow.'

Maggie got up abruptly. 'That's out of the question. I'll buy the boat – get a one-way ticket to Liverpool. I've got a pound saved up – I only need another ten shillings.' She linked her arm through Rosa's. 'Not a word to anybody, swear on your eternal soul.'

'I promise.'

Maggie snuggled closer. 'And if you should change your mind about coming with me . . .'

Only Grandma Sheridan was in the house when Rosa returned, fast asleep in the rocking-chair, her mouth agape as she wheezed and snored. Outside in the backyard voices, Oona's and Mammy's, were raised in argument. Rosa hung back, unwilling to be drawn in.

'Given up your job now, with the wedding only a week away?' Mammy was shouting. 'I thought ye were to work until the first baby came along?'

Rosa squeezed carefully behind the rocking-chair and crossed stealthily to listen at the window. Oona was clearly in no mood to brook any opposition.

'So I will, but not here. No more stocking factory for me, Mammy. Like I said, I'm off to Australia with Desmond just as soon as our visas come through.'

From here Rosa could see their angry figures; Oona standing before her mother, hands on hips, Mammy seated on an upturned crate, a newly killed chicken stretched across her aproned lap. She sat silent for a moment, but her compressed lips and the fierce, deft movement of her fingers as she snatched feathers from the bird's breast spoke of her fury only too well. The setting sunlight glinted on her wedding ring, and in her dark hair a stray white feather quivered in the evening breeze then fluttered silently to the cobblestones.

'Ye're leaving us then.' Mammy's flat tone showed the first sign of resignation. 'Going to the other side of the world where we'll never clap eyes on ye again.'

'Yes.' Oona's tone was quietly firm.

'So it'll have to be Rosa.'

Oona shrugged. 'It was anyway. She's the youngest.'

'Ah well,' sighed Mammy, 'she's certainly no need to be thinking of marrying now. I hear tell that Clancy boy is up to no good anyhow.'

Oona snorted. 'She's not that pretty anyway so it's no loss.'

Rosa drew back angrily. What right had they to determine her life for her? For two pins she'd go out there and tell them about Joe.

25

'*We won't tell a soul, sweetheart – this is our secret, just between you and me.*'

She'd promised Joe so it must remain a secret yet a while. Rosa bit her lip and turned to creep away. Grandma Sheridan snored herself awake with a start.

'Holy Mary, I wasn't sleeping, Deirdre, only resting my eyes. Is it time to peel the spuds now for the dinner?'

By mid-morning the shop had fallen quiet. Rosa had heard Joe rattling in and out of the back room, but so far she hadn't set eyes on him. Mr O'Byrne glanced at the clock then pulled off his apron.

'Now 'tis gone quiet a while we'll have that cup of tea, Rosa, and while the kettle's boiling I'm just nipping down the pub for some sixpences for the till. I'll not be long.'

The moment the doorbell clanged behind him Rosa hurried into the stockroom. Joe appeared at the back door and Rosa smiled at him shyly.

'I'm sorry I couldn't get to meet you, Joe. Did you wait in the glen for me?'

He nodded. 'Till I was soaked to the skin.'

'Oh Joe! I'm sorry!'

He busied himself with the boxes on the floor. 'You can show me how sorry next time,' he muttered, and she dimpled with pleasure. So he still wanted her. 'But you had time for Maggie Malone,' he went on. 'I saw the two of ye on the common.'.

Rosa started. 'You saw us? Then why didn't you come and speak to us?'

He shook his head. 'Not while ye were with her. I wanted ye on your own, didn't I?'

He shunted the boxes with his foot then picked up the largest, whistling as he carried it out to his bicycle.

Disappointment filled her. He could have snatched a few more moments alone with her until Mr O'Byrne got back. She sidled across to the doorway, leaning nonchalantly against the frame. He didn't look up as he heaved the box into the basket.

'Maggie tells me there's an old woman down the south side tells fortunes for sixpence,' she remarked.

'So?' He still didn't look up.

'Wouldn't ye like to know what the future has in store for you, Joe?'

He threw a long leg over the crossbar. 'Not what some old biddy thinks I might have. I'd rather make my own future.'

Rosa felt a glow of admiration. He sounded like the young hero of the films, the small-town boy who goes out and, against all odds, carves his fortune and that of his home-town sweetheart who remained true to him despite the wily wooing of the rich middle-aged merchant. She knew how the girl would respond.

'Oh Joe, I'm so proud of you,' she breathed. 'If all the world should turn against you I'll still believe in you.'

He stared at her for a second then swung the bike around to face the yard gate. 'I'd better get this down to Mrs Delaney,' he muttered, and rode off unsteadily over the cobblestones.

The trouble with Joe was, you never knew where you stood with him. Did he care about her the way she did about him? Was there a future for the two of them? Maybe the fortune-teller would know. She'd have to find the opportunity to sneak down there alone. If what she was beginning to suspect was true, there was all the more reason ...

*   *   *

27

The opportunity came when Mammy sent her down to the village to fetch pins and cotton from the haberdasher's. Half an hour of freedom. Rosa was panting by the time she'd hurried up the rutted lane to the dilapidated little cottage. A wizened old face peered out at her curiously.

'Have ye a minute to spare?' she asked the old woman breathlessly. 'I'm sorry to trouble you but—'

'No trouble at all, girleen,' wheezed the woman. 'Sure I've all the time in the world.'

The air in the cottage was filled with the odour of stale cabbage and tom-cat stink as the old woman led her inside. Rosa crossed the leathery palm with a sixpence. The old woman sat, knees widespread, as she peered closely at Rosa's palm for a moment, then straightened her bent back.

'What is it ye wish to know, child?' she asked.

Rosa took a deep breath. 'Will I ever marry or am I to stay a spinster all my life?'

The old woman clicked her tongue. 'What kind of foolish talk is that for a young girl? God love ye, child, there'll be an engagement ring in your hand before the end of the year, so there will.'

'An engagement ring?' Rosa echoed faintly. 'Are you sure?'

'Sure as eggs is eggs. I see that ring as clearly as I see your face now, a gold band with three stones, and come Christmas you'll hold it tight in your hand.'

Engaged by Christmas? And it could only be to Joe Clancy! Joy surged in Rosa's breast. Then there'd be no need to confess about Joe and her. And what was more, marriage would mean escape from Mammy, escape from a lifetime of servitude to a possessive mother.

It seemed as if her feet touched only gossamer clouds as she walked home. And was the music in her ears really only the church bells ringing for vespers in the distance?

Chapter Three

'Do you want to hear what she told me, Joe?'

They were reaching the upper end of the glen, where a low bridge spanned the hollow, carrying the dusty road out of Clondarra towards the town. Joe was tugging her hand, leading her under the shelter of the arch beneath the bridge.

She hadn't intended to tell him, but she couldn't bear to hug it to herself any longer. And here, in the close darkness of shadows under the arch, so cosy, so intimate, it might just give him the nudge he needed.

'No. I don't give a damn what that cracked old dame had to say,' he muttered, pulling her close. 'Why waste time?'

She covered the hand reaching for her buttons. 'Joe.'

It was only a gentle reproof but he took it badly. 'Girls!' he exploded. 'Ye're all the same – teases, the lot of ye. All come-on and no action. Ye promised to show me how sorry ye were.'

'I already did, Joe – twice.'

His voice softened to a purr. 'And ye liked it, didn't ye? Come on, Rosa.'

Those dark eyes looked so earnest and eloquent when he pleaded, speaking her name so softly. And he'd promised to be careful. And truth to tell, it was rather nice. And maybe afterwards he would say those magical words.

* * *

He didn't. He hardly spoke at all as they made their way back along the bank of the culvert towards the village. Rosa hurried to keep up with him.

'My sister's getting married on Saturday.'

He grunted.

'I don't suppose you can come, it being our church?'

'Don't be daft.'

Nearing the first cottages where the street lamps began he mumbled something.

'What did ye say, Joe?'

'We'd better split here so nobody sees us. See ya, kid.'

He strode away down the lamplit street, leaving her filled with a sinking feeling of disappointment. He could have given her a fonder farewell after what had just happened – the young hero in the films would have said something more romantic than just 'See ya, kid,' wouldn't he? The hero would murmur something about Fate tearing us apart, but only for the moment. Soon, very soon ...

Still, maybe he'd been a bit off-hand, but he'd shown concern, not wanting to embarrass her by being seen with him, hadn't he?

Under the first lamp she paused to inspect her skirt carefully, then took a pocket mirror from her bag and checked her hair. It was crucial to remove every wisp of grass which might give the game away. So far as Mammy was concerned she'd been with Maggie Malone tonight. May God forgive her for the wicked lie, but once confessed she could banish it from her conscience.

Joe was out on his rounds and Mr O'Byrne was just about to slip away into the back room to savour the freshly brewed pot of tea when Rosa caught sight of the figure waving through the shop window. Maggie Malone's white face peered anxiously through the glass.

31

Mr O'Byrne growled. 'I wish to God people wouldn't handle the goods that way,' he muttered. 'I put those tomatoes out cheap because they're soft. Go and see to her, Rosa, while I drink my tea.'

He lumbered away. The doorbell clanged as Rosa went out onto the pavement. Maggie was clutching a tomato in her fist, her squinty eye staring.

'Rosa – I'm going crazy.' The word hissed out in a low voice, and it was clear she was near the edge. 'Mrs Riordan's given me the sack. Now how in God's name am I to get the money I need? I need it quick. I still haven't enough to get away.'

Rosa deliberated. 'I've a bit put by under the mattress. How much do you need?'

'I've just about enough for the boat, but there's the train fare to Dublin, to the North Wall dock—'

'I'll have enough to cover that, I'm sure.'

'And another shilling or two for the train from Liverpool to Hawksmoor—'

'We'll manage, you'll see.'

Maggie's voice trailed away miserably. 'And then there's the abortion ...'

Rosa started. 'Abortion? What are ye talking of, girl? Ye can't do that! 'Tis a terrible sin.'

Maggie shook her head, staring at the tomato in her hand. 'It's the only way – Kitty will know someone – she'll sort it out for me once I get to England.'

Rosa felt herself grow hot. 'No matter who she knows – it's wrong, it's wicked! You can't kill a baby!'

Maggie's face reddened. 'It's all very well for you,' she snapped. 'You're not the one in trouble. How could I get a job with a baby to mind? And what about the child? What kind of life will he have with no father to his name?'

'Then tell the father,' Rosa retorted. 'It's his responsibility too.'

Maggie shook her head fiercely, her long hair swinging around her shoulders. 'That's out – he won't have anything to do with it. It's up to me now and I've decided.'

Rosa fell silent for a moment. There seemed nothing she could do except help with money.

'I can't talk now, Maggie,' she murmured. 'Meet me tonight after work.'

'OK. I'll be down the glen when you finish.'

'But I tell ye this,' Rosa added as she reached for the door handle, 'if I had a child I'd hang on to it till death, so I would. I'd never let it go.'

She saw the tears in Maggie's eyes, the juice of the tomato dribbling down redly between her fingers, and wished to God she'd held her tongue.

It seemed an odd gesture of fate that just when Maggie was in need of money Mrs Murphy should let a shilling of her change fall, unnoticed. When she left Rosa had put the pound note safely away in the till before she spotted the shilling, lying on top of the sack of potatoes. Mr O'Byrne was out in the yard taking charge of the morning delivery of fresh eggs from the farm.

Her first impulse was to run out after Mrs Murphy, but already the tall widow had disappeared from sight. Rosa stood uncertainly on the pavement, looking this way and that. She couldn't leave the shop to go searching in the cobbler's and the post office, the draper's and the chandler's. She looked down at the gleaming coin in her hand. It was little enough to the wealthy widow whose dead husband had once owned the brewery, but to Maggie Malone ...

She tucked the coin away in her apron pocket and went back into the shop. After all, if anyone should come enquiring after it, sure she was only minding it for the moment, wasn't she?

The clock on the wall chimed six. Mr O'Byrne waddled across to turn the sign around on the shop door and went back to empty out the coins from the till onto the counter.

'Well now, Rosa, ye can be on your way,' he murmured, 'but tell me, didn't ye want this Saturday off for your sister's wedding?'

'I do. I asked if it would be all right.'

He nodded as he stacked a pile of florins. 'So it will, so long as ye see to the cleaning.' He began sliding shillings deftly off the counter into the palm of his hand.

'I'll do it tomorrow night,' Rosa promised, 'before I go home. All shining and clean it will be for ye on Saturday.'

He grunted. 'That's all right then. Away home with ye now.'

Maggie was waiting on the bank near the bridge. She looked a small and desolate figure, sitting on the grass with arms curled around hunched knees. Rosa sank down beside her and pressed the shilling into her hand. Maggie looked up at her, enquiry in her dark eyes.

'A gift from heaven,' said Rosa. 'I'll see what I can manage to go with it. Will ye be at Oona's wedding?'

Maggie shook her head gloomily. 'I can't go in the church – but I'll come to the shindig after, if that's all right.'

'Do that. They'll be in the pub all night and half the next day as well. Drunk as lords they'll be so no-one will notice us.'

She stayed hunched on the grass as she watched Maggie scramble away up the bank. She looked around in the growing gloom. Just over there, under the shadow of the bridge, lay the private place which knew her secrets. It seemed odd to be here without Joe, without his strong

34

arms about her, his muttered words in her hair. Those wild and wonderful moments, they were sheer heaven, but over the last few days they'd given her cause to fret. Not just the sin of it now …

She hadn't seen him to talk to alone today. Somehow Mr O'Byrne was always within earshot and whenever he slipped out Joe was just leaving on another delivery. Maybe if she could let him know that on Saturday night, with the family all drinking heartily to Oona's happiness, she might have the chance again to slip away down here. Maybe she ought to tell him then what was beginning to prey on her mind.

Tomorrow. She'd have to find the opportunity to snatch a word with him since it would be her last day at work this week. Sure, he'd hang around after the boss left once he knew she'd be cleaning. If she plucked up the courage to tell him he'd probably be able to set her mind at rest. Joe was a man of the world.

Promptly at six on Friday evening Mr O'Byrne closed the shop and left with the takings. Rosa hurried out through the stockroom into the yard. Joe was just chaining up the bicycle. He gave Rosa the briefest of glances.

'I'm off,' he said. 'See ya.'

Rosa held out a hand. 'Joe – I wanted to talk to you.'

He was already striding towards the gate. 'Tomorrow,' he said over his shoulder. 'I'm in a hurry.'

'I won't be here tomorrow,' she called. 'The wedding—'

'Monday then.'

And he was gone. Rosa turned miserably back to the cleaning.

There was no joy in putting on the emerald-green frock with the matching half-hat next morning. Oona was fluttering about like an excited humming bird, twisting this way and that as Mammy adjusted her white dress and arranged the veil over her shoulders. Rosa was relieved that they were both too occupied to take notice of her. As a rule her mother's eagle eye would spot in a moment that she was off-colour.

It grew worse during the service. She watched Desmond's dark suit, strained tight over his brawny shoulders, as he spoke his vows, pledging his all to Oona. If she concentrated on the pinstripes running down his spine maybe she could banish the feeling of nausea which kept threatening to overwhelm her. It was nerves, of course it was, with the eyes of all the village centred on the Sheridan family on their special day. And the reek of incense on an empty stomach. There'd been no chance of breakfast in the hurry to get ready on time. That's all it was.

At last the service came to an end and the newly-weds walked arm in arm out of the church. Thank God. Now for a breath of fresh air. Rosa walked behind Mammy and Daddy Kerrigan as they made their way outside.

The tall figure of Doctor Reilly stood outside in the sun, his hat between his hands. He shook hands with her parents and then glanced down at Rosa.

'Hello, young lady,' he smiled. 'You look a mite peaky. Now if you were the one receiving the benefit of holy matrimony today I'd be wondering.'

Rosa coloured as she saw her mother dart him a puzzled look. Please God she wouldn't suspect. 'I'm fine,' murmured Rosa. 'Never been better.'

The doctor cocked his head to one side. 'Possibly a touch of anaemia,' he surmised. 'Call round and see me and we'll give you the once-over.'

'She will indeed,' agreed Mammy. 'First thing Monday.'

Oh Lord, thought Rosa as the flurry of rice and confetti

whirled over the happy couple's heads, now there's no way out.

'She'll demand to know what Doctor Reilly says,' Rosa told Maggie as they sat together in a corner of the pub yard. From inside the taproom came the sound of lively fiddle music, raucous laughter and tuneless singing. Grandma Sheridan's shrill voice rose above the rest.

'And what are ye worrying about?' asked Maggie. 'He'll give ye iron pills same as he did my brother and ye'll be fine.'

'Because I know I'm not anaemic,' Rosa replied quietly. 'I'm late. A week late.'

In the half-light she saw Maggie's jaw drop, and then she sat silent for a moment. 'Well ye're a dark horse and no mistake,' she murmured at last. 'I'd no idea ye had a fellow,'

'Neither does anyone else,' muttered Rosa. 'Not yet. I don't know what I'll do.'

'Ye don't know for sure then?'

'I will on Monday. And if I am up the creek, God help me. Mammy will kill me.'

'And him – the fellow – what about him?'

'I'll tell him, once I know for sure.'

The stocky figure of Wacky Phelan staggered out of the taproom and stumbled across the cobbles towards the outside toilet. Maggie craned her neck to peer at Rosa's face.

'Will he marry ye?'

Rosa watched the distant figure fumbling for the latch. 'I'm sure he will,' she murmured.

Not for the life of her could she bring herself to tell Maggie about the engagement ring before the end of the year.

*　　*　　*

37

Doctor Reilly looked serious as he removed the stethoscope from his ears and laid it aside.

'Will I tell your mammy for you?' he said kindly.

'No.'

She hadn't meant to sound so abrupt. It was the shock of hearing her worst fears confirmed. A baby. A small being already beginning to grow inside her ...

'Ye'll face her with it yourself then?'

'Maybe. I don't know. I haven't taken it in yet.' Rosa looked up at him anxiously. 'Ye won't be telling her, will you?'

Doctor Reilly shook his head and patted her hand as he rose. 'Ye're not the first girl this has happened to, Rosa,' he said quietly. 'It may seem like the end of the world right now, but don't worry. I'll take good care of you.'

The house seemed quiet without Oona, but Mammy was still full of the wedding and noticed nothing amiss. Rosa watched her as she chattered on excitedly to Daddy Kerrigan.

'Did ye see the hat on her, Daddy? 'Twas more like a chocolate box, I swear. But she knows how to enjoy herself, so she does. Seven port and lemons down her – I know, I counted them – and before the priest had even sunk his first whisky.'

If she knew, thought Rosa, she'd soon give up black-guarding Mrs Kilroy. She'd go crazy thinking how the village would soon start gossiping about her. Rosa played the scenario over in her head:

'Ye're what? I don't believe it – ye're no daughter of mine, hawking yourself around like a common Cork whore. Get out of this house and bring no bastards here ...'

That's the way it would end, for sure, even if she had a gold band on her third finger. And Joe, a Proddy-dog for a father – no, Mammy would never in this world accept that. Alternative plans had to be made.

38

There was more money than she thought saved up in the tin box under her mattress when Rosa came to count it. Enough to help Maggie out as she'd promised, but now things were different. Rosa laid a hand on her stomach. A baby on the way. Good God, how could she have been so stupid? And after all Oona's warnings too?

Joe would have to be told before anyone else. Only then could she make plans, know how much money was needed. A wedding dress, perhaps – but could she still be married in white? White was for virgins, not for fallen girls like herself and Maggie Malone. Poor Maggie – she hadn't even the chance of a husband.

She had it all clear in her mind how she would break it to Joe, down in the hollow under the arch while they lay close, his arms about her. She'd find the chance to whisper the words in the shop, arranging to meet tonight.

But Joe wasn't in the stockroom next morning and the bicycle was still chained up in the yard. Rosa looked at Mr O'Byrne's chubby face.

'Where's Joe?'

'Off sick,' the shopkeeper said tersely. 'He won't be in today so I'll have to do the damned orders myself.'

Rosa's heart sank. Not that she'd been looking forward to seeing the shock on Joe's handsome face, but this was only delaying matters. She hoped it was nothing serious.

It was mid-afternoon and Mr O'Byrne had gone, breathing heavily as he pedalled the bicycle away up the road. Rosa looked up as the doorbell clanged and saw Joe's tall figure blocking the light.

'Joe! I thought you were sick.'

He planted his feet astride, his hands deep in his pockets. 'Not me,' he said jauntily. 'I went after a job in town. That's what I came to tell the boss – I've got it; start tomorrow.'

There was a broad smile on his face and Rosa bit her lip before she spoke. It had to be said now.

'Joe, I'm up the creek – expecting.'

She saw the smile fall away, the frown replacing it, and the redness spreading across his cheeks. 'It's right,' she murmured. 'I've seen the doctor so it's right.'

'Expecting?' The word rapped out like a bullet. 'Ye stupid bitch.'

Rosa almost reeled backwards in shock. 'It's yours, Joe – you're the father.' It was all she could manage to say.

'Don't give me that,' he snapped. 'It could be anybody's.'

Anger began to ripple. 'What do you take me for?' she demanded. 'Aren't ye the only boy I've ever known?'

She saw the lip curl, the face she'd always believed so handsome suddenly taking on a hard and heartless look. 'Ye mean ye want me to carry the can,' he said mockingly. 'Marry ye and take on the two of ye, millstones round my bloody neck, just when I've the chance of a lifetime. No dice, sweetheart. Do ye think my family would let me wed a Papist?'

'No more than mine would like me marrying a Protestant,' Rosa countered, 'but we should do what's best for the child.'

'Do as ye please, Rosa, but count me out. Tell Mr O'Byrne I won't be back.'

The doorbell clanged behind him. Rosa stood clutching the edge of the counter to stop herself swaying. Thank God no-one else was about. Shaking, she went through into the back room and slumped on a chair and, despite herself, the tears flowed.

She loved him so much. Every night since she first met him she'd dreamed of him. The two of them walking through the meadows hand in hand, fondly watching their children picking flowers, showing them how to make daisy-chains. Joe teaching them to swim in the brook.

Sod Joe. He'd never meant a single word he'd said. He'd wanted her body and that was all. How could she have been so stupid? Even if she wanted to there was nothing she could do to force his hand. No-one had ever seen the two of them together. Without him she was in a devil of a mess. Once again the tears began to fall. Those strong arms would never encircle her again ...

But what the hell? He'd brought her nothing but a load of trouble and once the chips were down, he'd scampered off like a rat from the barn. He'd be no use at all to her or her child, she told herself fiercely. She'd be a damn sight better off without a weak and selfish man like Joe Clancy. But it was hard to think of it, struggling alone, and the tears began to fall once more.

Her thoughts were cut short when the doorbell clanged again. Brushing the tears away she hurried back behind the counter. The widow Murphy stood there, raising her nose to sniff around imperiously. She was accustomed to being served by the boss.

'Mr O'Byrne not here?' she asked.

'He's out on an errand, madam. Can I help you?' said Rosa.

The older woman eyed her suspiciously. 'Ye've the signs of too much drink on ye,' she remarked. 'Pale as a corpse ye are. Weddings are no excuse for not being fit for work.'

''Tis not the drink,' said Rosa. ''Tis the bad humour I'm in.' She shouldn't have said that, but having started, she ventured rashly on. 'Is there a man alive who's not weak and selfish?'

She expected a sharp reproof from Mrs Murphy, but instead she saw the widow's knowing nod. 'Indeed so,' she murmured. 'I've often wondered the same. The only

41

thing Mr Murphy did to humour me was to die while I was still young enough to enjoy his money. Now then, have ye a jar of that Dundee marmalade in stock?'

The shop was busy most of the afternoon, and with the boss out delivering Rosa had little chance to mull over her quandary. It was only as she trudged homewards that she had time to think again.

What choices lay before her now that Joe refused to have anything to do with her? Not that she'd have him now, even if he begged on bended knee. It was funny how quickly a dream hero could melt into a weak-kneed louse. Right then, what was left? Tell the family and hope they would back her. An unpleasant prospect since it would inevitably lead to much shouting and screaming, accusation and recrimination. Who would be the best one to start with? It was a pity Oona was gone to Desmond's. Rosa shrank from the thought of telling Mammy. Not Grandma Sheridan either – she was away with the fairies and wouldn't understand. Maybe Daddy Kerrigan – he'd be shocked, but he'd never yet failed to take her side.

Or the other alternative – tell no-one, go away out of Clondarra and manage alone. After all, Maggie Malone was planning to do just that. Mind you, she had a sister in England to run to. My sisters are even further away.

I'm trapped, just like that dragonfly I saw in the glen, caught in the spider's glistening web, struggling its beautiful life away. Joe laughed when I set it free, saying it had only the day to live in any case so I was wasting my time.

And suddenly Rosa felt filled with fierce determination. I will not waste my life just because of you, Joe Clancy. I'll have a good life, and my baby too. Somehow I'm going to find a way to see that it happens.

42

Halfway up the hill she caught sight of the girl crossing the field. 'Maggie!' she called. 'Maggie!'

She was breathless by the time she'd run through the thick tangle of grass. 'Are ye still planning to go to England?' she asked.

Maggie nodded. ''Tis the only way. I'll be sad to leave ye, Rosa, and Clondarra too.'

'But there's opportunities over there – you told me.'

'I know, but Clondarra's the only home I've known. If it wasn't for that lousy Joe Clancy I'd stay here for life.'

Rosa felt the pit of her stomach give way. 'Joe?' she echoed. 'Joe Clancy?'

Maggie gave a rueful smile. 'I hadn't meant to tell you. It just slipped out. If it wasn't for him—'

Rosa clutched her arm. 'Tell me, would your sister find room for the two of us, do ye think? Just for a while, till we find work?'

Chapter Four

It was strange how, once the decision had been made, Rosa felt a kind of feverish frenzy take over. To hell with the two-timing Joe Clancy. Now everything was geared towards running off with Maggie to a new life.

There was no need to tell Mammy anything at all yet. But just as soon as she had enough to cover both her own fare and Maggie's she'd break it to her then. In the meantime Mammy would expect her two pounds ten shillings a week as usual and that was most of her three pounds' wages gone.

Walking home one evening she saw figures emerging from the church. Of course, the novena Father Nolan had spoken of from the pulpit last week. She watched the last of the figures fade away down the street, then she pulled a headscarf over her head and went in through the arched doorway.

'Please God, help me,' she prayed as she knelt alone in the echoing emptiness of the church. 'Let me get away before they find out about the child. They couldn't bear that. Let me find the money soon.'

He must have been listening. As she rose from her knees a fragment of white glowed in the gloom under the pew and she bent to pick it up. A folded piece of paper. She unfolded it and smoothed out the creases, then gasped. A ten-shilling note!

It must have fallen, unnoticed, from the plate during the

collection, an offering from one of Clondarra's better-off inhabitants. It belonged to the church – it would be thieving to take it – and yet, it had come at the very moment she'd prayed for help.

Rosa looked up at the stained-glass window above the altar, the robed image of Christ etched there in blue and gold, His hands outspread in benediction.

'Sweet Jesus, 'tis only a loan, I swear,' she breathed. 'Ye heard the prayer of a sinner and You answered. One day I'll repay You, I promise.'

Mammy switched on the wireless five minutes early so as to be sure of catching the news. Grandma Sheridan clearly liked the music which crackled out of the old set for she began beating out the rhythm on the table with her spoon. Specks of mashed potato flew everywhere and, with a sigh, Mammy took the spoon away from her.

Rosa took a deep breath. 'I'm going away,' she said quietly. 'I'm going to work in England.'

'England? That ye will not!' snapped her mother, wiping a blob of mashed potato from Grandma Sheridan's chin with a tea towel. ''Tis blasphemy even to think it. Whatever are ye thinking of, in God's name?'

'I'm thinking of making a life for myself, that's all.'

'A lone Catholic girl in that heathen country? God knows what might happen to ye. No, I'll not hear of it.'

'I won't be alone, Mammy,' Rosa persisted quietly. 'I'm going with Maggie Malone.'

Her mother looked up at her, startled. 'Mrs Malone's willing to let her child go to that heathen place? I can hardly credit that.'

The thought was clearly clouding her resistance. Rosa waited. Her mother finished feeding Grandma and put the bowl down.

'Anyway,' she went on, 'ye're needed here, not like Maggie.'

'Would ye have her go alone to a heathen country?' Rosa persisted. Grandma Sheridan's eyes closed and her head drooped onto her chest.

'Don't be brazen,' snapped Mammy. 'That's no business of mine and 'tis none of yours either – 'tis her own mammy must decide that. I'm telling ye, ye're stopping here.'

Rosa braced herself. 'No, Mammy. I'm going with her. I've already bought the boat.'

Her mother's jaw dropped open 'Ye've done what?'

'I'll be off to Dublin this Friday.'

She saw her mother's startled stare, followed by a look of fury.

'Ye'll do no such thing,' she roared, planting her hands on her hips. 'Dear God, how did I deserve such disobedience?'

'I'm going,' said Rosa, 'and that's all there is to it.'

Mammy's eyes were popping from her head. 'And have your head turned by those evil folk? Ye, in your ignorance, made a fool of, maybe turned into a trollop and carried off into white slavery? Ye hear tell of all kinds of wicked things happening to girls like ye and Maggie Malone. Would ye have me die of worry and shame?'

'You've no need to worry,' Rosa said soothingly, 'I know how to take care of myself, and I'll send money home regular. Maggie's sister says the money is very good in England.'

'I don't give a damn about the money,' Mammy exploded, then crossed herself rapidly. 'I'll not have a child of mine defy me this way.'

Grandma Sheridan awoke with a start and began singing in a loud, shrill voice: 'If you were the only boy in the world, and I was the only girl ...'

'Hold your whisht,' said Mammy; then as Grandma's head

drooped again she turned back to Rosa. 'Just ye listen to me – ye're the youngest, with your duty to us and all. Ye'll not leave this house, not till the day ye're carried out feet first, and there's an end to it.'

Rosa headed for the narrow wooden stairs leading to the upper room. 'I'll go and sort my things to pack,' she murmured.

'That won't take long,' Mammy shouted after her. 'If ye insist on leaving here against my will, ye're no child of mine. Ye'll not take a single thing unless 'twas bought and paid for with your own money.'

Mammy said no more till Daddy Kerrigan came home from work. Rosa could hear her rumbling in the room below.

'Did ye ever hear the like, Daddy? A child of eighteen. I don't want to let her out of my sight. She's too young – she's no experience at all of the world.'

Rosa could visualize Daddy Kerrigan's mild blue eyes creasing at the corners as he tried to placate her. 'Ah, don't be hard on the girl,' he said. 'She's a woman grown now – ye can't be robbing her of the chance to make something of herself.'

'I won't have her answering me back in that brazen manner! None of the others defied me like that!'

'Ah, she's a mind of her own, that one,' murmured Daddy Kerrigan. 'So like her mother. So much life in her.'

Mammy growled. 'I don't care. She's not going, and that's an end to it.' .

Mammy, her square-boned face still set implacably, refused to come down to the railway station to see the girls off. But Daddy Kerrigan managed to slip out of work to be there as the train drew in.

'Here,' he muttered to Rosa as Mrs Malone engulfed

47

Maggie in a huge embrace, 'I'm sure ye can make good use of this.' He pushed a couple of pound notes into her hand. Her eyes stinging with tears, Rosa could only nod her thanks. She looked up at him anxiously.

'And Mammy?' she asked.

He squeezed an arm around her shoulders. 'Ah, don't ye go fretting about her. Pay no heed to her harsh tongue – she'll come round. Just give her time. Now be good, and be happy, child.'

Leaning out of the window, Rosa could see his cheerful wave only hazily through her tears as he receded into the distance. Bless the man. He'd never breathe a word to Mammy about any of this – if only she could appreciate his gentle kindness.

Rosa and Maggie both sat silent, staring out over the fields as they slipped by the window. The grass had never looked greener or lusher than it did now after the rain. Throughout the journey up to Dublin they hardly exchanged a word but Rosa felt sure that Maggie too was thinking of the man she was leaving behind, the man who had betrayed them both. Blast him. He was receding into the past now, along with the cobbles and cottages of Clondarra. She would think of him no more.

Drown him under those murky waves, she thought as she stood on the deck, staring down at the dark grey swirl of water in the ship's wake. She was still barely able to believe the adventure had really begun. The rich green of home was receding into the mist, and ahead lay only a vast open space. Funny how home had never looked so beautiful as it did today.

The rumble of the ship's engines drowned out thought, but the gusting wind up here and the roll and sway of the deck was infinitely preferable to being down below where Maggie still sat. Steerage tickets were all they could afford;

a seat on a slatted bench below deck where the noise was horrific and the stench of vomit unbearable. Never mind, thought Rosa, gripping the rail, the wind slapping her hair into her face, it's only for the moment; once we set foot in England a whole new life will begin. In fact, four lives, Maggie's and mine and the two yet to be born. God grant it will be a good life.

Maggie's pale face appeared at Rosa's elbow. 'I don't feel at all well,' she muttered. She looked distinctly green. 'In fact I feel lousy. I'm beginning to wish I'd stayed at home.'

She still looked fragile when the boat finally docked and a straggle of wan passengers filed down the gangway to the dockside. Rosa caught her breath, staring in amazement at the huge grey buildings surrounding the dock, taller and more impressive even than those she had seen in Dublin. So this was Liverpool, the gateway to the magic of England.

'What do we do now?' whispered Maggie.

'Follow the others,' replied Rosa.

One by one they clambered aboard a rickety-looking bus which, they were told, would take them to Lime Street and the train. As the bus rattled on the shops grew larger, the buildings taller, until Rosa found herself staring at a brilliantly lit shop as long as the whole stretch of Clondarra's main street. A moment later the bus deposited them in the railway station, a bewildering mass of platforms and framed timetables, uniformed guards and porters.

They found the right platform and the train for Hawksmoor, then slumped, overwhelmed, into corner seats. A middle-aged man came into the compartment and sat down heavily. He smiled at Rosa.

'Where you off to, wack?'

Rosa frowned, not understanding. 'Pardon?'

'Leeds, is it, or York? Where you heading for?'

Maggie chipped in. 'We're going to my sister Kitty's,' she said, 'in Hawksmoor.'

He looked puzzled, then fell silent. His words were hard to make out, thought Rosa. Maybe he was finding hers just as hard to understand. Was it going to be just as difficult to understand the English everywhere?

The man was pleasant enough. He handed down their bags when at last they reached Hawksmoor and wished them well. The guard at the ticket barrier told them the way to Trinity Street where Kitty lived, and as they walked up the long hill Maggie picked out the tall terraced house.

'Jesus, 'tis a fine place,' she murmured. 'I'd no idea Kitty lived so grand.'

As she knocked at the door Rosa set down her bag and looked up. It was indeed a grand house, twice as tall as the cottage at home with its extra floor above the bedrooms. The door opened and a buxom woman stood framed against the light. She threw out her arms and drew Maggie inside. Rosa followed them into the hallway, heavy with the odour of cabbage and carbolic. The woman, unmistakably related to Maggie with the same hair the colour of flax and dark brown eyes, scanned her sister's face in concern.

'Holy Mother of God, what the devil ails ye?' she demanded. 'Ye look terrible.'

'She was seasick,' Rosa explained. 'She'll be all right when she's slept.'

'To be sure,' said Kitty. 'The two of ye must be jaded after the journey. It's a hot meal and bed for the both of ye right now.'

She opened a door under the stairs and led them down a flight of stone steps into a basement kitchen. A kitchen underground? Whoever heard of such a thing? And the supper – that delicious smell in the air – where was it coming from when there was no pot over the fire?

50

Kitty explained. 'I have a gas stove,' she said proudly. 'See, the pan is steaming ready on the hob.'

Rosa stared in awe at the ring of flame magically burning under the pan, but she was too exhausted to marvel.

When she awoke in the morning in the big high bed in the attic she thought for one sleepy moment that the warm body next to hers was Oona, and then recollection returned.

Maggie looked much better. The colour had come back to her cheeks and the light to her eyes. She lifted her nose and sniffed.

'I swear I can smell bacon frying,' she murmured. 'I'm starving.'

Kitty was bustling about the kitchen serving breakfast to two burly men. She seemed to have a fancy for blue and orange, thought Rosa as they sat down, judging by the patterned linoleum on the floor and the flowered overall covering her ample body.

'Meet my husband, Ted,' Kitty said brightly as she put mugs of hot tea before the girls, 'and this is Mike, one of my lodgers. The others are off to work.'

Rosa nodded shyly. Mike pushed back his chair and stood up. 'I'm off to work too now,' he said gruffly, and clumped away up the stairs.

Ted leaned his elbows on the table. 'Well now, Maggie, what are you planning to do?' he asked. His voice sounded strange to Rosa, with a funny accent, and harsher than the soft tones of his wife. Still, he was English.

'Find work as soon as we can,' replied Maggie. 'Know of anything?'

Ted rubbed his still-unshaven chin. 'Aye, well, I hear there's vacancies for weavers up at our place,' he said. 'Noisy work, but it's well paid.'

'That'll do us,' said Rosa. 'Who do we see?'

Ted scraped back his chair and stood up. 'I'll have a word with the overseer and let you know what happens.'

Rosa stood looking out of the attic window, down over grey slate roofs, grimy streets and blackened mill chimneys. So much filth, so unlike home.

'Doesn't it make ye want to take a bucket of soapy water to it?' she murmured. 'Everywhere in this town is black with filth.'

Maggie smiled as she draped a jacket over a hanger and hung it on a hook on the low beam running across the room. 'No matter,' she said contentedly, 'tomorrow we're going to start earning money here. I never thought it would be so easy. Ted only had to say the word to the foreman.'

Rosa turned. 'Hey, that's my hanger – there's only four – two each, remember.'

'It's my Sunday-best jacket. I always hang it up.'

'Then you'll have to put several things on one hanger, same as me. Tell me something, you haven't told Kitty about me, have you?'

'The baby? No. Did ye want me to?'

'I do not. The word could leak back home. Anyhow, she's enough on her plate worrying about you. With luck I'll have moved on before it shows.'

Maggie ducked under the beam and blew the film of dust off the surface of a small chest of drawers. 'Ye know Kitty's finding out about somebody for me,' she murmured.

'I do.' Rosa was aware that her voice sounded stiff.

Maggie opened the top drawer and laid her Bible and rosary carefully inside. 'Ye could do the same, Rosa. We'll soon have the money and Kitty could fix it.'

'No,' snapped Rosa, 'I'm going to keep my child. Promise me you'll not say a word to Kitty.'

Maggie sighed. 'OK. I promise. But I'll soon be sorted out – I'll never give a thought to Joe Clancy again. It would be good if ye too were able—'

'I've told you,' Rosa cut in sharply, 'nothing on earth will ever part me from my child. He has no father – he's mine.'

Maggie shrugged. 'Ye never told me who the father was,' she remarked. 'Are you going to tell me?'

Rosa hesitated. 'Are you sure you want to know?'

'If ye'll tell me.'

'Only swear you'll never mention the name again.'

Maggie came close, touching her arm. 'I swear.'

Rosa took a deep breath. ''Twas Joe Clancy.'

She waited for Maggie's reaction; the look of shock, the cry of despair. But for a moment there was only silence and Maggie's face showed no sign of shock. At last she nodded and squeezed Rosa's arm.

'I guessed as much,' she murmured. 'Come on, the lodgers should be home by now – will we go down and see if supper's ready?'

During supper seven men came and went from Kitty's laden table. Apart from Ted there were Mike and Mick, Paddy and Shamus, and two Englishmen whose names Rosa did not catch. Paddy, the little wiry fellow, evidently had a mind to tease the girls. As Kitty lifted a pan to bring to the table he nodded in the direction of the cooker.

'Blow out the light, Maggie girl,' he said. 'No point wasting fuel.'

Maggie rose obediently and crossed to the cooker. As she bent to blow the ring of flame the men began to laugh. Maggie blew again, to no avail. The men were holding their sides laughing. Kitty wagged an admonishing spoon.

'Ah, don't be tormenting the girl,' she scolded. ''Tis cruel to trade on her ignorance. Ye knew no better yourselves when ye came. Sit ye down, Maggie, and eat your supper.'

''Twill be the same for a while, I reckon,' said Rosa in the privacy of the attic room. 'Being in a foreign land – there's a deal we have to learn.'

'Like the way they talk,' said Maggie. 'I can't understand a word.'

'No more can I,' said Rosa, 'but it will come.'

'At least they're friendly,' murmured Maggie as she slithered down under the blanket. 'Really nice people. Everybody calls me love.'

Rosa yawned. 'I wonder why people yawn when they're tired?' she murmured sleepily.

'How in the world should I know?' replied Maggie.

'Somebody once told me it's because you need more oxygen. Why would we need more oxygen to go to sleep?'

Maggie groaned and buried her face in the pillow. 'Go to sleep, Rosa, and don't be bothering me with your idle questions. We've to be up again at half-six.'

The muffled voice tailed away into silence.

The noise in the weaving shed made Rosa's head spin. Above the roar of the machines and the clatter of the spindles it was impossible to make oneself heard. The other women seemed to have learned a way to communicate by shrieks and sign language, but the effort of trying to shout above the racket made her throat sore and her head throb like the machines. By the time she and Maggie trudged home they were almost too exhausted even to eat Kitty's hot stews.

'But ye've got to keep your strength up,' she protested, then added to Maggie, 'specially you.'

The first week seemed never-ending with so much to learn and all the time the noise threatening to murder the brain. Back home in the evening the girls were scarcely aware of the bustle of activity, Kitty forever cooking in huge pans to feed the other lodgers, washing and ironing.

At last pay-day came. The two girls could hardly believe their eyes as they sprawled on the bed, fanning the notes out on the flowered quilt.

'Eleven pounds,' breathed Maggie. 'It'd take me nearly a month to earn that at the Riordans'. I've never held so much money in my hand before. We're rich!'

'We have to carefully plan what to do with it,' said Rosa thoughtfully.

'We'll be able to drink coffee in Field's like the posh ladies,' Maggie sighed dreamily. 'We'll buy new clothes. How much will we send home?'

Rosa thought for a moment. 'Maybe we won't send any, not this time. We've Kitty to pay for our keep and there's other stuff we need. We'll send a pound or two next week.'

Maggie looked dubious. 'What'll we do with it?'

'First we'll buy some new bloomers and chemises – I hear there's nice ones in that big Woolworths shop in the high street – and then we'll hide the rest – under the mattress. Come on, get up off the bed.'

Saturday afternoon they stood in front of the stall laid out with an array of ladies' underwear. Rosa surveyed the face of the girl behind the counter, pale and superior-looking, watching as Maggie fingered the fabric.

'What'll we say?' Maggie whispered. 'If she don't understand me – and I don't know if they call these bloomers here or not.'

'We'll not call them anything – or the chemises either,' Rosa replied firmly, then she turned to the girl. 'Two of these, please, and two of these.'

The assistant packed them up and took the money without a word. The girls fled outside.

'Just wait,' exclaimed Maggie in delight. 'Soon we'll be able to afford those lovely ones with the lace edging. Still, that Paddy won't be able to mock me when I hang these out on the line.'

Rosa made sure Maggie didn't see when she slipped one of the precious ten-shilling notes into the collection box at Sunday morning Mass.

'Thank You for the loan, Jesus, and thank You for making me able to repay it so soon. I'll make this a good life You've given me, I swear I will.'

Maggie was in a happy mood. She'd received Communion again at last and no vengeful thunderbolt had struck her down.

Kitty came back from church with news. 'I've been talking to Mrs Laycock – she's told me about somebody who can help ye, Maggie. It'll cost five pounds.'

Maggie looked up at her eagerly. 'I have it – where is she, this woman? When can I see her?'

'No names, no pack drill,' Kitty answered. 'I'm to take ye there on Tuesday.'

'Are ye sure ye won't come with me, Rosa?'

Maggie sat on the bed, surrounded by money. She looked up, searching Rosa's face. 'Of course I will if you want me to,' said Rosa.

Maggie shook her head. 'Ye know what I mean – get rid of it?'

'We've been through all that. No,' snapped Rosa, 'now drop it.'

Maggie sighed, fingering the banknotes. 'It's all going to work out right, isn't it? I told Mr Clayton I can't take any more of that noise in the weaving shed, so he says he'll move me to the mending room next week. Everything will be fine then, won't it?'

On Tuesday morning Rosa set off alone in the grey dawn for work. Kitty's voice still rang in her ears.

'Tell Mr Clayton that Maggie's took sick – a touch of the flu, tell him – she'll be back in a day or two. No more than that.'

All day Rosa felt anxious as she tended her loom, for once oblivious to the racket. If anything the clattering machines served only to emphasize the turbulence of her thoughts.

She shouldn't have let Maggie go to that place without trying once more to stop her. What if they caused her pain? What if they did her some damage? Kitty had confided to her privately that it sometimes happened.

'And what's more,' she'd added, 'it's a man she's to see, not a woman. But I haven't the heart to tell her that.'

A voice bellowed in her ear. 'What's up with thee, lass? You've not got your mind on your work.'

Mr Clayton wagged a reproving finger and walked on by. I should have told her it would be a man doing the operation, thought Rosa angrily. She'd be frightened enough today as it was. I'd have gone with her only Kitty felt just the two of them was enough.

'Oh please God, take good care of Maggie.'

*　　*　　*

The minute the factory hooter sounded for the end of the shift the workers hurried out into the street. Rosa fled downhill, home towards Trinity Street.

The house was empty, no sound, no smell of cooking or steaming washing to break the silence or show signs of life. It was still too early for Ted or any of the lodgers to be home from work, but Kitty was hardly ever absent from the basement kitchen. Only the smell of damp and lingering gas hung in the air.

The fire in the big open grate was no more than a pile of grey ash. Rosa picked up the poker and raked the embers and added more wood, then watched the flames begin to lick the edges.

Ted was the first to arrive home. His rugged face wore an anxious look as he hurried in.

'I got a message at work – Kitty said to fetch you straight up to the infirmary.'

'The hospital?' Rosa felt her stomach turn over. 'Oh my God! Maggie!'

Kitty was sitting, head bowed, on a bench in the hospital corridor, her cheeks blotchy with tears. She buried her face in Ted's rough jacket.

'I should never have let her go to that foul place,' she sobbed. ''Tis all my fault!'

'How is she?' demanded Rosa. 'Can I see her?'

'I could hear her crying out in there,' Kitty whimpered, 'I wanted to go to her but the door was locked – I couldn't see what he was doing to her. If I'd known ...'

'Where is she?' cried Rosa. 'I want to see her.'

Kitty turned a ravaged face to her. ''Tis no use – ye're too late,' she sobbed. 'The doctor said she hadn't a hope – she'd been butchered.'

Rosa's knees buckled under her. 'Butchered?' she whispered, sinking onto the bench. 'You're not telling me she's – dead?'

Kitty buried her face in Ted's chest. 'Not twenty minutes ago,' she howled, 'and I couldn't get the priest here in time!'

Chapter Five

Maggie dead. The fact was too huge, too unbearable to take in. Rosa could register only disbelief and a gaping, aching emptiness under her heart. And inside that gnawed another emotion: guilt. If only she'd tried harder to persuade Maggie not to go through with the abortion ...

Lying alone in the big high bed was the worst time. Twice during the night Rosa awoke and stretched out an arm, expecting to feel Maggie's comforting warmth or hear her deep regular breathing, only to find a cold empty space, and she wept.

From here, caught in the patch of moonlight on the far beam, she could see Maggie's Sunday-best jacket still on the hanger. She hadn't the heart to shift it. Such a young life snuffed out, such a lovely natured girl. It was so cruel, so wrong. Tears burned Rosa's eyelids till sleep came.

The house seemed even darker and danker after Maggie had gone. The long gloomy corridors and sombre rooms with their bottle-green dados and brown paint seemed to exude gloomy misery, as if the house too mourned. The dizzying round of work in the deafening roar of the factory where thought was impossible was infinitely preferable. And when the hooter sounded Rosa was in no hurry to return home. She walked slowly through the town centre, unaware of the brightly lit shops and oblivious to the bodies hurrying to catch buses home.

It was a scent which brought her back to reality, the delicious aroma of freshly ground coffee. Rosa looked up. She was outside Field's coffee-shop, the meeting place patronized by the well-off ladies of the town. Rosa plodded on, memory flooding back. Walking past here on pay-day last week, Maggie excitedly clutching her pay-packet.

'Did ye ever smell such a smell in your life? We'll drink coffee in there, Rosa, you and me. 'Tis sixpence a cup, they tell me, but we'll treat ourselves.'

'Why not? Will we do it now?'

'No, wait – once I've sorted out this bump – we'll dress up and put on lipstick and come down here to swank like the fine ladies – just to celebrate.'

Under the viaduct, where no-one could see, Rosa slowed her steps and pressed her forehead against the cold stone. Anger mingled with her grief. I'll go to Field's for you, Maggie, she swore to herself. If ever a life deserved celebrating it was yours; lovely even with your squinty eye. I'll go to the coffee-shop and drink for the two of us, and there'll be no finer lady there than you.

There were few mourners in St Bridget's church the day of the funeral, and fewer still huddled in the drizzling rain to watch the coffin being lowered into the soggy earth. Kitty managed with effort to remain composed though white-faced as Ted cupped her elbow. In the days that followed she spoke little, and it seemed to Rosa as if she were deliberately avoiding her. She still busied herself cooking mountains of potatoes, cabbage, brisket and bacon joints, but her step had lost its bounce and she no longer sang Irish folk-songs as she worked. Rosa often tried to catch her eye, to talk to her, but to no avail.

How Kitty explained her sister's death to her family back home in Clondarra Rosa did not know until an unexpected letter arrived from Daddy Kerrigan. Mammy must still be feeling sore; nothing would induce her to pick up a pen to her renegade child, Rosa thought as she slit the envelope. The sheet of paper, jagged at the edge where it had been torn from a notebook, looked as frugal as the words scrawled upon it.

Dear Rosa,

We heard the news about Maggie Malone. They said it was bronchial. Your mammy says she should never of run off like that. She should of stayed home. Mammy and me put a shilling in the box to have a mass said for her soul. Her mammy is very lonely now Patrick is gone for a priest. Your mammy is sure it was the good Lord's punishment for running out on her duties. Hoping this finds you as it leaves me.

Your loving Daddy.

Rosa sighed as she refolded the letter. Mammy's reproach was clear – only wicked, wilful girls ran off to England, and misfortune was their just reward. If only she knew that the same fate could well have befallen her daughter.

Rosa came home from work to find Kitty in the kitchen, her hands deep in a bowl of flour. Ted, sunk in the fireside chair, nodded a greeting over his newspaper. Rosa peeled off her jacket and draped it over a chair back.

'Look,' she said quietly, staring fixedly at the checked oilcloth covering the table, 'I'm not wanted here, am I? I'll find myself another place if you want.'

Kitty avoided her gaze and carried on pummelling the pastry. Rosa watched the specks of flour flying over the oilcloth. Ted lowered his newspaper.

'Nay, not at all,' he said gruffly. 'You're a good lass.'

'I know you don't want me.' Rosa persisted. 'And I understand why.'

Kitty pursed her lips and shook her head, but still didn't speak.

Ted cleared his throat uneasily. 'It's not you, lass,' he muttered. 'It's only that you remind her so much of Maggie. Nothing more.'

Rosa nodded. Before long the coming child would begin to show, which would only make matters worse. That settled it, she decided. She had to move on.

'I'll sort something out,' she murmured. 'Just as soon as I can.'

She picked up her jacket and went up the stone stairs, aware that neither husband nor wife was going to argue.

The next day Rosa gave in her notice at Blamire's mill. After all, she couldn't face Ted every day. He mustn't see her grow thicker and guess the truth.

Mr Clayton was very kind. The foreman shook his head sadly when she broke the news. 'I'll be right sorry to lose you, lass,' he said. 'You're a good worker. Found another job, have you?'

'Not yet. I'll find one.'

He rubbed his bristly chin. 'I've no doubt you will, and I wish you well. And if you should change your mind ...'

It was one of the girls in the canteen who gave Rosa a timely cue. She sat across the table, chattering animatedly to her friend.

'I hear tell they're looking for folk down at the bus depot,' she mumbled around a mouthful of mashed potato. 'Good rate of pay too. How do you fancy being a clippie?'

Her mate shook her peroxided curls. 'Have to gab to folk all day long while you give out tickets? Not me, thanks very much. I'd rather have a bit of peace while I work – no need to think.'

Rosa still felt leaden inside as she made her way down to the bus depot. The malodorous smell of sulphur from the chimney-stacks hung in the air, not sweet and homely like the scent of the turf fires of home. Everything about this land was alien and unfamiliar, from the strange way the people spoke to the curious food they ate. For a moment a wave of homesickness welled over her, but she banished it quickly. A new life, she reminded herself – it could only begin here.

She came away from the depot feeling rather more cheered. 'A couple of days watching another conductor to see how it's done, then you're on your own,' the inspector had said. 'Clock in Monday morning and we'll kit you out with uniform then.'

And that was all there was to it. As she was coming out of the main entrance a pretty girl in a conductress's uniform was just clocking on. She eyed Rosa curiously.

'You starting here?'

Rosa gave her a smile. 'Monday. All I need now is a room to rent.'

The girl cocked her head to one side. 'You're Irish, aren't you? You talk like my friend Nora.'

'I am.'

The girl gave her a thoughtful look. 'As it happens I know of a place,' she remarked. 'It's nowt special but at least it's cheap. And it's not too far to walk into work at four in the morning. There's a lot of Irish folk living thereabouts.'

'Is that right? Then I'd be glad of the address.'

Dusk was falling when Rosa found the little cobbled backstreet. The landlady seemed a cheerful soul, with crisp grey hair and bird-bright eyes. 'Come on in, love,' she invited, stepping back to let Rosa in. A delicious scent of fresh-baked scones filled the air as she led her upstairs.

'There's just the back room now,' she explained. 'The front one's taken.'

She opened the door to a small room and stood back while Rosa surveyed the narrow bed and fading wallpaper.

'You're in work, are you?' she asked mildly.

'I start on the buses on Monday.'

'A bus conductress?' she repeated happily. 'Oh, that's nice – it'll make a change from students. Ever since my husband died I've had students, usually a young man from the Tech, you know. They're no company – you never know what time they'll come home.'

It would do fine for the time being, thought Rosa. After all, she'd have to make plans sooner or later about where to have the baby. At the doorway she turned to the woman.

'Friday then,' she said. 'I'll move in after work. By the way, I'm called Rosa Sheridan. What is your name?'

The woman dimpled. 'It's Clancy – Mrs Clancy. I'm not Irish but my husband was – he came from Wexford. See you Friday evening then.'

It was ironic, thought Rosa as she walked carefully round a puddle. To travel so far only to find a home with a landlady with the one name which never crossed her lips.

Kitty broke her silence to offer to help Rosa pack her few belongings together. She stood staring out of the attic window at the rows of mist-damp roofs.

'Ted's brother's coming to stay a while,' she said gruffly. 'I'll need to get the room ready for him.'

Words still seemed to come hard to her. Rosa could sense it was painful for her, being in this room. Kitty tried hard to sound natural.

'It's rough down there where ye're going – will ye be all right?' she asked.

'I will – there's Irish folk there,' Rosa assured her.

Kitty took down Maggie's jacket from the beam and gave a deep sigh. 'They don't know back home – I didn't want the whole of Clondarra ballyragging her name.'

'I won't say a word,' said Rosa. 'Not to anybody.'

Kitty turned to clear out the chest of drawers. She stood looking down at the pathetic little collection of Maggie's treasures, the jar of Pond's vanishing cream, the battered Evette lipstick from Woolworths, the tiny blue scent bottle labelled 'Evening in Paris'. Then, with a trembling hand, she picked up Maggie's Bible and rosary. For a moment she looked down, trickling the string of white beads between her fingers.

'I remember this well. Maggie had it for her first Holy Communion,' she muttered. 'Such a good girl she was. She never knew the meaning of sin.'

Then suddenly she thrust the rosary into Rosa's hand. 'Here, I know she'd want you to have this,' she said gruffly, then hurried from the room.

Work on the trolley buses was not quite so easy as it had looked while she was observing, Rosa discovered. It wasn't just a matter of collecting fares and giving out tickets and change in return, but of learning the routes, being able to call out the name of each stop, jumping off the bus to drag out the long pole to switch the overhead trolley pole from one electrified line to another, and worst of all, trying to make the money in the satchel balance up at the end of the day with the number of tickets sold. Any deficit, they told her, would be deducted from her wages.

Passengers varied, some pleasant, some not, from the early-morning grumpies to the late-night happy revellers, but at first they were all hard to understand until gradually her ear grew attuned to their strange flat voices.

Setting off to walk to the depot at four in the morning to take the first bus out at a quarter to five meant early to bed at night. And late shift meant finishing after midnight and getting home at one. Split shift was the best, she decided, doing four hours in the morning and another four in the evening which left the middle of the day free, but whatever shift she did, it was exhausting work.

'You want to get out for a bit, love – come down the pub with me,' said Mrs Clancy. 'Do you a world of good.'

'Thanks, but I'm not really a drinker.'

'Happen not, but you'd meet folks – your own kind. I don't like to see a girl your age stuck indoors all the time. It's not natural.'

Rosa smiled. 'Don't worry about me – I meet lots of people all day. Anyway, I want to write home tonight.'

Rosa put down the pen and re-read what she'd written. She'd made no reference to Daddy Kerrigan's letter, just in case Mammy didn't know he'd written.

Dear Mammy and Daddy,
    All is well here. It was a very sad business about Maggie and I miss her badly, but I have a good job on the buses and new digs which are very nice so you've no need to worry about me. I hope both of you and Grandma Sheridan are well.

Rosa chewed the tip of the pen. What more could she say? Not a word of the truth; how she felt desperately alone without Maggie, unable and unwilling to make new friends, fearful about the coming baby. No, half-truths would have to suffice. And she was damned if she'd confess to the priest;

in fact, she felt too angry with God for His injustice to go into the church any more. A kind God would not have let Maggie die, not like that.

Rosa folded the sheet of paper, pushed it into an envelope, licked the edge and stuck it down with a clenched fist.

Daddy Kerrigan wasn't long in replying, but his letter made it clear that Mammy was preoccupied with her own problems.

> Mammy and me went down to Cobh to see your sister Oona off on the boat to Australia last Wednesday. God knows if we'll ever see her again. Your mammy cried a lot because she says it's very lonely here now. It would be nice if you was here. Thank you for the money. Mammy has some lovely plump birds she bought in to rear for Kelly's for Christmas. She says she could do with a hand when it comes to the plucking. Dominic says he won't be able to come home for Christmas and Shelagh won't be here either as she's expecting again. Mammy wonders will you be home at Christmas?

No chance, thought Rosa. As the newest recruit at the depot she'd already been told she'd be put down on the rota for full-time Christmas duty.

'Never mind, lass,' the inspector said cheerily, 'you'll get some time off in the new year to make up.'

In any event, thought Rosa, if she went home they'd soon spot her condition. After all, her waist had thickened out and she was sure she'd felt a faint fluttering in her stomach the other night. She wouldn't be able to ignore this coming child much longer.

By the time Christmas came Rosa was only too aware that her growing girth was making climbing the stairs to the top deck ever more of an effort. Not only that, but the greasy paper left behind by the hungry fish-and-chip eaters which had once smelt so tantalizing now seemed to leave a nauseous stink which made her feel distinctly queasy.

Christmas Eve was exhausting, the bus packed to bursting point all day with excited last-minute shoppers and rowdy revellers at night. But on Christmas Day the bus was almost deserted. The ticket rack strapped to her waist remained almost untouched and Rosa was able to sit and rest.

She cleared a patch on the misted window and gazed wistfully out as the bus glided through empty streets, past stop after stop. Everyone else in the world was at home with their families. She could visualize them laughing and smiling as they exchanged presents around ornamented Christmas trees, sitting around the table laden with turkey and roast potatoes and plum pudding. There'd be noise and happy laughter, smiles and hugs. She'd never felt so alone, so shut out in her life.

At the terminus Ben, the burly driver, stepped down and went off for a smoke. Rosa took out the cards she'd been keeping in her pocket; one with robins from Mammy, another with a coach and horses in the snow from Shelagh, a jolly Santa from Dominic, a golden bell with holly from Liam and Deirdre in the States. Nothing from Oona though – that was strange. She loved sending cards for every event. Still, Australia was a long way off – maybe she'd forgotten the post took a long time to arrive.

She held the cards close to her chest and the tears fell. Her child was going to miss his family too.

'Ready?'

Ben's burly figure stood at the doorway.

Rosa sniffed back the tears and nodded. 'Ready.'

*　　　*　　　*

She relaxed on the back seat near the door, her feet propped on the opposite seat as the bus glided on. Finally it stopped and she looked up in surprise as a young man climbed aboard. He grinned as she swung her feet down to let him pass. He was tall and broad in the shoulder and moved with easy grace, just like her brother Dominic. He took a seat and dug in his pocket for coins.

'The Junction, please,' he said. His voice held a warm friendly sound, strong and full-bodied like his build.

'Threepence,' said Rosa, and added as she handed over his ticket, 'Do you live round there?'

'Sometimes. When I'm in Hawksmoor. Why?'

She shrugged. 'I used to live in Trinity Street, with a family called Pearson. Know them?'

He chuckled, a happy sound which matched his good-humoured face. 'Too right I do. Ted Pearson's my brother. I'm spending Christmas with them.'

'Ted and Kitty? Oh!' Rosa pulled her stomach in hard. He mustn't notice, mustn't tell them. 'Please send them my good wishes,' she said. 'Tell them – tell them Rosa is doing fine.'

'Rosa?' he repeated. 'A pretty name for a pretty girl.'

She felt the colour blushing her cheek. 'Ah, go on with ye,' she quipped. 'You fellows are all the same.'

The bus was racing on past every stop. Too soon it pulled up outside The Junction pub. With his amiable smile and easy manner she was reluctant to let him go.

'Your stop,' she said. 'Happy Christmas.'

He stood on the platform, looking down at her with a smile. 'And to you, Rosa. And a happy new year. Maybe we'll meet again.'

As the bus pulled away he ran alongside it. He was nimble for a big man, thought Rosa. At the corner he waved and turned off down the street. What the devil had Kitty said his name was? Whatever it might be, he'd certainly brought the first glow into her day.

Rosa slept late on New Year's Eve. She didn't hear the tap at the bedroom door. As she opened her eyes the first thing she saw was Mrs Clancy's face bending over her.

'You awake, love?' the old lady enquired. 'I don't like disturbing you when you was on late turn last night, only the postman's just brought you a parcel and I thought you'd like to know.'

Rosa sat up, rubbing the sleep from her eyes, while Mrs Clancy drew back the curtains, letting the daylight stream in.

'It's got an Australian stamp on it,' the landlady went on. 'My nephew collects foreign stamps.'

She hovered for a moment, curious, then closed the bedroom door behind her. Rosa blinked down at the packet, small and tightly sealed. It must be from Oona – making up for missing Christmas.

But the letter wrapped round a small box inside was not in her sister's neat hand. It was brief and to the point, signed Desmond.

My dear Rosa,

I am very sad to have to break bad news to you. I've just finished writing to your mammy. Oona had a terrible accident last week. She wasn't used to the traffic here in Sydney. The taxi driver says he never saw her ...

Rosa's stomach was already shrinking in apprehension before she read on:

She died in hospital the next day. She will be buried here on Friday so I know you cannot be here. The

71

last thing she said to me was that she wanted you to have her ring, so here it is. Wear it in her memory ...

Rosa's hand trembled as she opened the little box and saw the gold ring with three small stones lying on the velvet pad, and her stomach turned to ice.

She had a sudden vision of the wizened old fortune-teller back home in Clondarra.

'Believe me, ye'll have an engagement ring in your hand before the end of the year.'

Chapter Six

In the chilly air of the little back bedroom Rosa sat alone, her aching feet immersed in a bowl of warm water. She'd been too exhausted when she came home from work even to draw the curtains, and now she could see the snowflakes settling silently on the window-panes. Downstairs she could hear Mrs Clancy trying to teach her new budgerigar to speak.

'Come on now, Mickey, there's a good boy. Merry Christmas,' she kept repeating, over and over, in a high-pitched voice. 'Merry Christmas.'

The budgie's only response was more shrill chirping, but Rosa could hear the landlady keep doggedly on. She'd been so excited when she brought it home.

'For a bit of company,' she'd said.

'Talking about company. What about the other lodger?' Rosa had asked. 'You said you had somebody in the front bedroom though I've never seen or heard them.'

Mrs Clancy shook her head. 'No, Mrs Holyoak's not here very often, but she pays the rent regular as clockwork. She's a real lady, is Mrs Holyoak.'

Through the window the noise of merrymaking down in The Dog and Duck rose and fell like waves on the shore. At times the jocular shouts gave way to arguments and brawling, to the accompaniment of a woman's shrill cries, but before long the rancour gave way once more to laughter and song.

Life was going on just the same as always, Rosa thought: noisy and energetic, but she had no wish to join in. It seemed somehow sacrilegious that the world neither knew nor cared about what had happened. First Maggie, now Oona, both snatched from life before their time – maybe Mammy was right after all about God's punishment for running off.

Stop it, she told herself angrily as she towelled her feet dry. You've got to think ahead, plan for this baby. Those vague flutterings in her stomach were becoming more pronounced movements every day. Already the waist buttons on her skirts would no longer reach the buttonholes. The minute she came home from work she always changed quickly into her old dirndl skirt; the gathered fullness did wonders to hide the bulge even if the waistband did ride an inch or two higher than it should.

'They must be feeding you well down in yon canteen,' remarked Mrs Clancy. 'You're putting on a bit of weight.'

'It's the fine meals you cook for me,' replied Rosa. 'You feed me up like a turkey cock, so you do.'

The landlady's eyes brightened. 'Well, I've no-one else now, so it's nice to have you and Mickey to see to. Makes all the difference.'

Rosa bought a yard of elastic from Woolworths and sewed a loop on each buttonhole. That solved that problem, but that was only the beginning.

What about the time when the truth became obvious? An unmarried mother, here under her roof – it would be a terrible shock to Mrs Clancy and cause her dreadful embarrassment. She couldn't expect her landlady to be involved in anything so shameful as the birth of an illegitimate child. She'd have to move on, and soon. But where? Who would accept her once they knew of her condition?

From years of habit Rosa made the sign of the cross,

put her hands together and bowed her head. 'Jesus, I don't think You've played fair,' she whispered, 'letting Maggie and Oona die like that. That was cruel of You. Now I've got no-one to talk to but You. Help me to find a way to have my baby safely and give him a good life. It's the least You can do. I don't mean to be rude but You have been a bit unfair lately. I'll be a good mother, I promise You.'

From down in the alley at the back of the house came the sound of a man's staccato laugh, followed by a woman's giggle. Rosa lifted her head to listen. Footsteps crunched along the frosted cobbles and stopped. The giggle subsided into soft moans of pleasure. Rosa could visualize the two of them, locked together in the crisp night air.

'PS Jesus keep an eye to that girl out there,' she murmured. 'Don't let her make a fool of herself like I did.'

She was alone in the house as she pulled on her uniform to go off on the afternoon shift. Mrs Clancy had just popped down to the corner shop for a pound of dripping. She had a fancy, she said, for toad-in-the-hole for supper.

'That all right with you, Rosa?'

Rosa stared, imagining a dish of the squirming green things down in Clondarra's bog. 'I don't know it,' she murmured doubtfully. 'Will I like it?'

The landlady beamed. 'You're in for a real treat, love. I got some lovely beef sausages—'

Rosa smiled to herself as she cleared away a patch of the delicate frost-tracery on the window-pane. It was so beautiful – it looked just like the lace on Oona's wedding dress. She brushed the thought away and looked up at the leaden sky. There was still more snow to fall.

She pulled on her overcoat and went out onto the landing. At the top of the stairs she stopped and stood back in surprise. A woman was climbing the steps towards her, a woman much older than herself but not so old as Mrs Clancy.

'Good afternoon,' said the woman. 'Filthy weather.'

She must have let herself in, for she pushed a key into the lock of the front bedroom door and went inside, leaving a whiff of fragrant scent behind her. Before the door closed Rosa had a swift glimpse of a green quilted bed and a vase of dried honesty on a chenille-covered table under the window.

So, she mused as she went out into the street, that must be the other tenant – what did Mrs Clancy say her name was? She certainly looked a well-off lady with her smart coat and fur-lined boots, her gloves and neat little hat. Now why would a well-dressed woman like her be renting a room in this lowly part of town?

The snow crunched sharply underfoot and Rosa could feel the damp cold striking up through the soles of her shoes. She'd give her eye-teeth for a pair of little fur-lined boots like the lady on the stairs, but there'd be other more pressing items to buy before long. Snow like this never lasted for more than a few days back home in Clondarra but Mrs Clancy said it was different over here.

'Sometimes it gets so deep you have to dig your way out of the house,' she said darkly. 'You should have seen it back in forty-seven – high as the rooftops it was, and still lying on the ground at Easter.'

Easter. By then Rosa would have found a place to go. Soon she'd have to scour the advertisements in the *Examiner* for a second-hand pram and a cot. Just a little pram, not a big coach-built one. If this rotten weather continued she could make do with a cheap pair of wellington boots.

'I saw your other lodger today,' Rosa told Mrs Clancy that evening over the toad-in-the-hole. 'Is she still here?'

Mrs Clancy raked the last lurking piece of sausage out from under the tunnel of batter. 'Mrs Holyoak? No, she's gone home. I didn't see her meself,' she said with a shake of the head. 'Keeps herself to herself, does Mrs Holyoak.' The landlady glanced around, then added confidentially, 'Only knew she'd been when I went in there to do a bit of dusting like I always do of a Wednesday. Not that she makes a mess, you know. Tidy soul – she even keeps a pair of slippers here so as not to mark my lino and she always leaves everything just so.'

Rosa frowned. 'She has a home of her own yet she comes here? What on earth for?' she queried.

Mrs Clancy shrugged thin shoulders as she cleared away the dinner plates. 'It's not for me to ask, love, but I have a fancy she's not all that happy up there in Edgerton. No more would I be. Snobby lot up there. Think they're the bee's knees because they have big houses and money.'

'But not Mrs Holyoak?'

'Dear me no,' replied the landlady, doling out slices of apple pie. 'She's a real lady. It's not as though she's meeting a gentleman friend here – not so far as I know at any rate and she'd be hard put to keep it from me. And even if she was, my view is, if she wants a spot of privacy down here now and again, who am I to pry?'

'She has no visitors then?'

'I never hear voices.'

'What does she do up there then? Listen to the wireless?'

'There isn't one. So far as I know she just sits there. Lonely soul, I think. Lord knows what thoughts go through her head. Then she goes home.'

Rosa was still pondering about the mysterious Mrs Holyoak as she undressed for bed. What did she do in that room next to hers, she wondered as she ran her hands down over her bulging stomach? Play patience? Do some sewing or embroidery – something which had to be done secretly as a surprise for one of her family?

So it might be that Rosa was not the only one of Mrs Clancy's tenants with a secret to hide. Curiosity was still nibbling as she settled down to sleep, but it faded when she remembered tomorrow. Tomorrow she was going to visit Field's coffee-shop, just as she'd promised Maggie. And to honour Oona at the same time she would wear her ring.

She couldn't help the tingle of anticipation as she threaded her way through the shoppers in Westgate. She'd prepared carefully, brushing her skirt and coat till not a speck of dust remained, pressing the one good blouse she owned and polishing her shoes with all the care usually reserved for going to church. She felt a little self-conscious about the make-up; Mammy would have considered her, with the lipstick and dusting of face-powder, no better than a loose woman, but Mrs Clancy had been impressed.

'Eeh, love, you do look smart. You should get dolled up like that more often.'

She felt conspicuous too in the half-hat, the one Mammy had made for Oona's wedding, but it was essential. No lady worth her salt would be seen in a smart café like Field's without a hat.

The delicious aroma of freshly ground coffee drifted tantalizingly to her nostrils even before she reached the doors. She walked inside, past the confectionery counter laden with buns and cakes, meringues and tarts, towards the stairs with all the nonchalance of a woman accustomed to this way of life. As she reached the top step and took in the rows of neat, white-draped tables she could feel a quiver inside. It took effort to walk sedately to an empty table in the bow-fronted window.

From the safety of her seat she surveyed the other customers as she peeled off her knitted gloves. She was right – every woman there wore a hat, with the exception of the smiling girl in the middle with her mother, and she was clearly only about fourteen. The gentleman with them wore a beautiful black overcoat like old Mr O'Casey, the undertaker back home, and the lady's little finger stuck out as she raised her cup to her lips. Rosa looked around. Another one over there – was it the done thing to stick out your little finger? It looked damn silly; she'd be blowed if she'd do it.

She sat listening to the tinkle of china teacups on saucers and the gentle hum of conversation until a waitress came to stand by the table, a girl about her own age. She looked incredibly smart in her black uniform with a frilly white apron and cap, but her eyes seemed to see nothing. She stared over Rosa's head.

'What can I get you, miss?' she asked dully.

Rosa put down her handbag on the chair beside her. 'Two cups of coffee, please. And some cakes – fancy ones, with icing on.'

The girl wrote something on a pad without a word or even a raised eyebrow, and Rosa felt a prick of disappointment. She'd been looking forward to this moment, rehearsing how she'd insist that she wanted the two cups at the same time and not one after the other.

The girl came back and placed a tray on the table. The collection of cakes looked mouth-watering, especially the meringue with the cream oozing out. The waitress placed the two cups of coffee on the linen tablecloth, then paused. Rosa looked up. The girl was staring fixedly at the ring glistening on Rosa's left hand. For the first

79

time there was a gleam of interest in the dark eyes. The girl recollected herself.

'I'm sorry,' she said awkwardly. 'Your friend late, is he? Have I to keep that coffee hot?'

Rosa couldn't help the slight smile. 'No need,' she replied softly. 'She'll not need it hot where she's gone.'

'This one's for you, Maggie.'

Rosa popped the last delectable morsel of meringue into her mouth. She'd given up the battle of trying to tackle it with the little fork like the other ladies were using because the damn thing only crumbled and spurted cream everywhere. It was far easier, and neater, to use her fingers.

She closed her eyes. Washed down with the now-tepid second coffee the meringue melted on her tongue and slid effortlessly down her throat. As she opened her eyes again she caught sight of the man by the cash desk and stared.

He had his back towards her, but there was something about the size and build of him that was familiar. Tall as a stable door he was and very near as broad in the shoulder, with a shock of wavy dark hair almost touching his coat collar.

He turned and the breath caught in her throat. He was the man on the bus that day she'd been so homesick – the man who'd brought a glow of warmth to her Christmas Day. Ted Pearson's brother. Surreptitiously, over the top of the menu card, she watched him standing there awkwardly, looking about him until a waitress led him across to a vacant table. Rosa smiled to herself. He looked as out-of-place here as she felt, but he was a fine-looking man, not handsome like the film stars, but with a strong and kindly face. Dan, that was his name. Dan Pearson.

As he pulled out a chair he looked around the room and his eyes met hers. She saw the look of half-recognition as

80

he paused, and she coloured up and quickly looked away. By the time she dared to glance again in his direction he was seated, scanning the menu.

It was stupid to feel so embarrassed and awkward when in truth she was delighted to see him again. She'd give anything to have him sit here and talk to her. But even as the thought crossed her mind a young woman appeared at the top of the stairs and came across the room to join him. He stood up, smiling, as she took her seat.

Disappointment filled Rosa. She picked up the bill, gathered up her handbag and gloves and moved calmly over to the cash desk. As she paid she took care not to look back. The sooner she got out of here the better. He would not see the bulge, not with that pretty girl to feast his eyes upon.

Thoughts of the burly Dan Pearson still lingered in Rosa's mind as she unlocked the door and let herself into Mrs Clancy's. Mickey uttered a couple of shrill squawks in greeting then turned back to the job of pecking at the hard lump stuck between the bars of his cage. A pair of worn slippers left warming on the hearth made it clear the landlady was out.

Of course, thought Rosa as she removed the half-hat in front of the mirror, it was her afternoon for the whist drive up at the Liberal Club. Nothing on earth would induce her to miss that. In a game of whist or solo Mrs Clancy had the rare knack of being able to remember every card played.

'I can recall who played which card, in what order they fell, and who trumped what in every round,' she used to say proudly. 'I may not always be able to recollect what day it is, but you can't fool me where cards is concerned. Me dad were just the same.'

Coat and hat draped over her arm, Rosa headed upstairs.

At the top she almost started out of her skin. A pair of fur-lined boots stood before her, and above them a tall slim figure blocked her way. She looked up into the stern features of Mrs Holyoak.

'If you have a moment,' the woman said quietly, 'I'd like a word with you.'

And with the authoritative manner of a woman accustomed to being obeyed, she turned and led the way into her room.

Chapter Seven

Once inside the room Mrs Holyoak closed the door and indicated the one chair alongside the table.

'Please sit down.'

Rosa stared at the chair, a Victorian dining chair upholstered in a similar shade of green to the quilted bedcover, and hesitated. Even under the dusting of make-up Mrs Holyoak looked lined and tired. She must be Mammy's age – no young woman, not even a pregnant young woman, took a seat when an older woman stood.

'I don't mind standing,' Rosa murmured.

'Sit down,' repeated Mrs Holyoak, and squeezed her way past the bed to stand looking out of the window. Rosa perched reluctantly on the edge of the chair. It was a relief to get the weight off her feet.

'My name,' said the woman, 'is Greta Holyoak. What's yours?'

'Rosa Sheridan.'

For a time Mrs Holyoak stood in silence. Rosa waited. However curious she was it would be rude to pursue the conversation before Mrs Holyoak was ready. She shivered. It was cold in here. For two pins she'd put her coat on again. Mrs Holyoak was still wearing hers, a good wool one with horn buttons, and a blue silk scarf at the neck which matched exactly the blue of her hat.

Rosa began to grow restless. She watched the woman's

slender hands as she fingered the dried flowers in a bowl of pot-pourri on the table, releasing a delicate scent of lavender which filled the room.

'Put your coat on if you're cold,' said Mrs Holyoak.

Gladly Rosa slid it round her shoulders. 'There's an electric fire,' she pointed out. 'Shall I switch it on for you?'

The older woman gave a slow smile and sank onto the edge of the bed. 'I've only to feel the cold and it brings it all back to me,' she murmured. 'The old days – the good old days.'

Rosa frowned. This was a woman who evidently had everything – probably even those fancy central-heating radiators in her fine home – so why should she willingly suffer the cold?

'Bare feet on the icy linoleum, icicles hanging from the cistern in the outside privy,' murmured Mrs Holyoak. 'You forget, in time.'

'It's no fun,' snorted Rosa. 'Chilblains on your toes, hands so blue with cold you can't count out pennies without dropping them. What's the fun in that?'

'I never said it was fun. It brings back memories, that's all.'

Rosa fell silent. Either the woman was unhappy or she was mad. But why on earth had she asked her in here? There must be something.

Mrs Holyoak stood again and crossed to the window. Beyond the window-panes evening was darkening the sky over the slate roofs. 'Recalling happier times makes one feel more at peace,' she murmured, 'reaffirms one's concern for humanity. I want to do my bit.'

She turned from the window to meet Rosa's gaze. 'And I believe you are in need of help, my dear. Am I correct?'

Rosa gave her a sharp look. She knew, all right. 'What makes you think that?' she said defensively. 'I'm OK.'

84

Mrs Holyoak cocked her head. 'You're Irish, Catholic? Alone in a strange land? Do you have any relatives or friends here?'

'No.'

The stern face softened into a smile and she glanced down at the ring on Rosa's hand. 'I take it he jilted you,' she said sadly. 'You poor child. Do your father and mother know of your condition?'

Rosa bit her lip. 'My father's dead; when I was three.'

'And your mother?'

'She's married again now.'

'And does she know? Will she help you?'

Rosa looked away. 'No.'

The woman sighed. 'You aren't prepared to tell her?'

'I can't,' Rosa exploded. 'It would kill her! She'd never be able to hold up her head in Clondarra again!'

'I see.' Mrs Holyoak folded her hands in her lap. In the fading light Rosa could see the gleam of emeralds. 'So what are you planning to do?' Mrs Holyoak asked quietly. 'Do you want this child?'

Rosa glared. 'What are you suggesting? An abortion?'

'Is that what you want?'

'That I do not!'

Mrs Holyoak nodded. 'Just as well, since it's far too late, I think. When are you expecting?'

'About two months.'

'Have you booked in at a maternity home?'

Rosa looked down at her hands. 'No.'

The older woman sighed. 'You can't just ignore it in the hope it'll go away. Plans have to be made. Do you have money?'

'I can manage. I have a job.'

'And after? How will you work then?'

The woman was beginning to annoy her, forcing her

to face issues she'd prefer to ignore. 'I don't know,' she muttered. 'Something will turn up.'

Mrs Holyoak gave a dry laugh. 'Ever the optimist,' she murmured, then reached down to pull open the drawer of the table. She took out a large jotter pad and a fountain-pen, unscrewed the cap and began to write. 'I want you to take this address,' she said as she wrote, 'and keep it by you.'

She tore off the sheet and waved the ink dry, then handed it to Rosa. Rosa squinted down at it in the gloom.

'It's a small private home you can go to,' explained Mrs Holyoak. 'No, don't worry about expense. I have a personal interest in the place so there'll be no question of cost.'

For a moment Rosa held the paper in her hand before folding it and putting it in her bag. The woman eased herself to her feet. Rosa stood up, clutching her hat and bag.

'I'm very grateful,' she said quietly. 'You have no need to help a girl you don't know from Adam. You're very kind.'

'Ah well,' sighed Mrs Holyoak, moving towards the door, 'that's what we're put here for. Those of us who are showered with blessings should share them with the less fortunate, I feel.'

She held the door open. As Rosa made to pass her she laid a hand on Rosa's arm. 'Just one thing – don't mention a word of this to anyone – not Mrs Clancy or anyone.'

'Oh no, to be sure I won't,' Rosa exclaimed. 'I don't want anyone to know – I didn't even mean to tell you.'

Mrs Holyoak smiled. 'But I'm glad you did, my dear. Believe me, it gives me more pleasure than you know to be able to help.'

Happiness glowed in Rosa all evening. She heard Mrs Holyoak's footsteps patter down the stairs and out into the street long before Mrs Clancy came home.

'And do you know,' Mrs Clancy exclaimed, still in her coat as she bent to examine the casserole cooking in the range, 'that Miss Pargeter,' she rumbled, 'she's no idea, no more than this pot-holder, how to play whist! Three times she revoked; kept pretending she didn't understand.'

Mrs Clancy straightened and drew a small knitted square from her coat pocket. 'I ask you, how can anyone not know you have to play a spade if everyone else does?'

'I don't know.'

'Ruined the game, she did,' grumbled Mrs Clancy. 'It ought to have been progressive whist and then someone else would have got the worry of her for a bit. So I didn't win this week. Got the booby prize, we did – another blessed pot-holder and I've already got seven.'

She threw the knitted square on the table and peeled off her coat. As she pulled on her overall and fastened it she threw a question over her shoulder.

'So Mrs Holyoak's been in again, has she?'

Rosa started. 'How did you know?'

'Footmarks in the hall. Did you see her?'

'Just for a minute,' said Rosa, then added casually: 'she seems very nice.'

The landlady set about laying the table. 'Oh, she's nice all right, but I reckon she's not a happy soul. Sits up there by the hour, she does. I can't complain that she burns my lecky 'cos she doesn't. No light, no fire on. Must be to get away from him, I reckon. Mr Holyoak's a terrifying fellow in the court, they tell me. Shouts everybody down.'

'In the court?'

'He's a lawyer, you know – boss of Holyoak, Brett and Fenton; big office in the high street. Big man in Hawksmoor. Bet he doesn't recognize what a saint he's got, all the charity work she does. Must be hard for a refined woman like her living in the same house with a fellow like him.'

'It must,' agreed Rosa.

Mrs Clancy lifted the steaming casserole from the oven and placed it in the middle of the table. 'There now,' she said contentedly as she lifted off the lid, 'that'll warm the cockles of your innards.'

Someone left a glossy magazine on the back seat of the bus. During the ten-minute break at the Outlane terminus Rosa flicked through the pages.

HAPPY NATURAL CHILDBIRTH. The headline caught her eye. She scanned it quickly, growing more astonished by the minute. At least she'd know what to watch out for now: regular contractions in the small of the back, it said, a dull ache – definitely not pains – and possibly the waters breaking first. Funny, she'd felt tiny limbs kicking out in the night, but had no idea that the baby was surrounded by a bag of water. Good job this magazine had come her way. Even though she wasn't much of a reader she should have thought of borrowing a book from the library.

Ben climbed back into the cab and gave a quick bip on the horn to indicate it was time to go. Rosa laid the magazine aside and gave an answering double ring of the bell, and it was just as the bus began to slowly move away from the kerb that she felt a strange sensation low in her stomach. It felt like cramp, but a few seconds later it was gone.

The second time it happened was just before they reached the Waterloo terminus. An elderly woman needed a hand with her shopping bags as she lowered herself gingerly down the step, and as Rosa straightened the cramp gripped her guts again. It could be colic, but she usually only suffered from that after eating baked beans.

By the time the shift ended Rosa could feel the sweat breaking out on her forehead. The cramps were coming faster and harder now, at times so severe she felt sick. She sat in the depot, trying to concentrate on ticket numbers, trying to make them tally with the money in the bag, but her head was beginning to swim.

'You look rough,' said Ben as he clocked off. 'In fact you look proper poorly.'

'Stomach ache,' said Rosa. 'It's bad.'

'Whisky and hot water – that's what my missus always prescribes,' he replied cheerily. 'Never fails.'

It was at that moment that the truth dawned. Rosa could feel the trickle, and felt at the same time astonished and overwhelmed. The baby – he was on his way! It was too soon!

She saw Ben was staring at her, puzzled by her silence. 'You all right, lass?' he asked. 'Can I do owt?'

Pull yourself together, Rosa urged herself – get to the home. She groped in her pocket for the piece of paper Mrs Holyoak had given her.

'Ben,' she said gruffly, making a huge effort to sound controlled, 'will you ask in the office if you can ring a taxi for me? As quick as you can?'

'Course I will,' he said, hurrying to the office door. 'Where's it to take you?'

She looked down at the paper and the blurring words written there. Another wave of pain crashed over her. 'Shelley,' she whispered. 'I'll tell him the address on the way.'

After being bundled out of the taxi and into a building with interminable white-walled corridors Rosa could remember little. She felt as though she were being hurtled along on some relentless train journey, plunging into tunnels of blackness and pain, emerging briefly into the light of consciousness only to lurch once more into oblivion.

Eternity and pain seemed all there was. She had a hazy

recollection of cool hands on her forehead, of someone clamping something over her face which she tried to fight off.

'Gas and air,' a hollow voice said. 'It'll help you.'

But nothing helped. Eternity stretched on, and then suddenly came release. Thank God. It was over. Dimly she heard thin cries, like a rabbit caught in a snare.

'You have a baby girl,' someone said. 'She's perfect.'

Baby girl ... baby girl. The words hammered through her numb brain. That's my baby, my daughter, come far too soon. A girl – funny, I always thought of it as a boy. A perfect girl. Weakly Rosa raised her head.

'Let me see her, please.'

They laid a tiny, towel-wrapped bundle in the crook of her arm. She stared down at the tiny face surrounded by a fuzz of downy fair hair, the diminutive, quivering mouth and the biggest, bluest eyes she had ever seen. They seemed to take up half her face, like the china doll Oona would never let her play with. A minute fist protruded from the towel. Rosa slid her finger through it and it gripped on tight.

'Just look at her fingernails,' she whispered; they're perfect.'

The nurse smiled. 'You did a good job, even if she did come a bit soon. Have you thought of a name for her?'

Name? Rosa stared down, bewildered. She hadn't thought about names for a girl. The little fist drew her finger close. She watched in delight as the tiny mouth found the knuckle and began to suck. This child was perfection in every way, as beautiful as an angel. Rosa smiled and lay back.

'Angela – that's what I'll call her. Like a little angel.'

The nurse came with a cup of tea. 'Now give me the baby and I'll take her to the nursery,' she said.

Rosa clung to the bundle. 'I want to keep her with me,' she protested, but the nurse was firm.

'She'll be better off in the nursery where we can keep an eye on her,' she said.

Rosa felt a leap of alarm. 'There's nothing wrong with her, is there? She'll be all right?'

The nurse shook her head. 'Nothing's wrong at all, don't worry. It's just that premature babies need to be watched over for a while and you deserve some rest. You'll see her again soon.'

Reluctant as she was to see her beautiful child taken away, Rosa handed her over, then lay back and sank gratefully into sleep.

When she awoke it was dark and it took some moments to acclimatize her eyes to the gloom. Dimly she could make out other beds in the ward, but their occupants were no more than unseen, deeply breathing ghosts. Apart from a distant wail the place was silent. It must be the middle of the night. No-one would bring the baby to her now. She'd have to wait until morning.

Mrs Clancy – the poor woman would be worried stiff wondering what had happened to her. Somehow she must get a message to her in the morning – find some way of explaining her absence without giving the reason. It was going to be tricky now finding a place to live as soon as she got out of here. She'd been stupid, leaving things so late. Baby Angela had caught her on the hop, but she'd have to think of something.

The woman in the next bed gave a loud snore which startled her into life. Rosa heard her sniff.

'You awake?' came a whisper.

'Yes,' replied Rosa.

'I could kill for a smoke – got any fags on you?'

'Sorry, no.'

There came another sniff. Rosa leaned on her elbow. 'Do they bring the babies in the morning?' she asked.

'Six o'bloody clock for the first feed,' came the answer. 'Not even a dog-end?'

'What?'

'Cigarettes – oh, never mind,' the woman groaned. 'With any luck Bill might remember tomorrow.'

Within moments she was gently snoring again.

Before dawn the lights snapped on and a different nurse arrived, bearing bundles of squealing babies. One by one she distributed them to yawning mothers while Rosa waited eagerly. The last bundle deposited, the nurse stood looking around, hands on hips.

'Where's my baby?' asked Rosa. 'You haven't brought mine.'

The nurse frowned down at Rosa's name card. 'Yours the prem, delivered last night?'

'That's right.'

'Not to be brought in, that one.' She turned away to the next bed.

Rosa was bewildered. 'Why not? She must be hungry by now.'

'She'll be fed, don't you worry,' replied the nurse cheerfully. 'Now then, Mrs Drake, is he taking the nipple this time?'

Rosa's neighbour gave a thin, apologetic smile. 'I don't think he's quite got the hang of it yet.'

Her uniform creaked as the nurse seated herself on the edge of the bed. Rosa saw her wrinkle her nose.

'I'm not surprised,' she said severely. 'I wouldn't want to latch on to all that nicotine, either. Come on now young man, I reckon you'll just have to get used to it.'

*   *   *

Visitors for the other mothers came and went. Rosa buried her face in the pillow until they'd gone. By late evening she was growing anxious, and when they brought the babies in for the last feed of the night she accosted the nurse.

'There's something wrong with my baby, isn't there? I know there is.'

'Rubbish,' retorted the nurse. 'She's prem, that's all.'

'Then why can't I at least see her? Can I go down to the nursery?'

There was a crackle of starch as the nurse bent to read Rosa's notes pinned to the end of the bed. She straightened, shaking her head.

'Why not?' demanded Rosa. 'I haven't seen her since she was born.'

'It's too early for you to get out of bed. Give it a day or two.'

The nurse marched briskly away to the far end of the ward. 'It's no use arguing with them,' sighed Mrs Drake in the next bed. 'Little Hitlers, the lot of them.'

'We'll see about that,' muttered Rosa. 'First thing tomorrow. I'll tell them I want to see Mrs Holyoak.'

'You can tell her yourself,' said Mrs Drake. 'She'll be doing the rounds after elevenses.'

As they sipped milky morning coffee Rosa sat up in bed watching the ward doors, willing the tall figure of Mrs Holyoak to appear. It was cruel keeping her from her newborn daughter. The sooner she got this sorted out, the better.

The doors swung open, admitting a short, black-robed figure with a clerical collar. He paused to speak to the nurse seated at her desk, then headed deliberately down the ward towards Rosa.

'Mrs Sheridan? I'm Father Anderson,' he said softly. 'May I sit down?'

He pulled a chair close to the bedside and drew out a rosary from his pocket. 'Let us give thanks for your safe delivery,' he said smoothly, 'for you know, a woman is never closer to death than she is in childbirth.'

Rosa found her voice. 'How do you know about me – that I'm a Catholic?' she demanded. 'No-one knows.'

The priest smiled. 'You had a rosary in your handbag.'

'You looked in my handbag?' repeated Rosa. 'Why?'

He shrugged. 'You were delirious, they said. They had to – they didn't even know your name.' He touched cold fingertips to Rosa's hand. 'Don't be angry, my dear. Don't be guilty of the sin of pride. The good Lord brought you safely through your ordeal and you should be grateful.'

Rosa fell silent. Indeed she was grateful. Now she had the most beautiful child in the world.

'And you mustn't let the sin of pride stand in the way of your future – or your child's future,' he went on softly. 'You must be prepared to make sacrifices.'

'Oh I will,' breathed Rosa. 'I'm going to do everything I can for her.'

The priest nodded. 'Good. Would you like us to pray together now?' He fingered the black rosary beads. A vision of Maggie's white rosary leapt into Rosa's mind.

'No thanks,' she answered. 'I'd rather pray alone.'

'Very well,' said the priest, stowing the beads away in his pocket. 'Just remember to hold fast to your resolution, my dear. Spare no sacrifice and the reward of Heaven will be yours.'

Barely ten minutes elapsed after the priest had gone before the ward doors opened again and Rosa saw Mrs Holyoak accompanied by a senior-looking woman in uniform. She pointed to Rosa's bed.

'Very well, Matron,' Mrs Holyoak said, 'leave it to me now.'

Rosa sat up eagerly to greet her visitor. She was clearly of some importance in this place. Now the problem could be quickly resolved. Mrs Holyoak stood by the foot of the bed, the pearls at her throat glowing softly against the dark dress.

'Now, my dear,' she said calmly, 'you and I have matters to discuss.'

There was something in her tone, the stiff and formal way she stood, hands folded before her, which made Rosa think of the old days at school when she was called before the headteacher, and it gave her an uneasy feeling of apprehension.

Mrs Holyoak took a step closer. 'This is not going to be easy for either of us, I fear, but we have to think of what is best for the child.'

Chapter Eight

'What is it?' asked Rosa. 'Something's wrong, isn't it?'

Mrs Holyoak walked round the side of the bed and seated herself slowly on the chair Father Anderson had recently vacated. 'First of all let me ask you – Mrs Clancy knows nothing, does she?'

'No.'

'Then let me set your mind at rest,' said Mrs Holyoak, neatly rearranging the pleats of her skirt. 'I sent word to her that you'd been called away – indicated some illness and someone you had to look after and that it might be some time before you return. Since you said you don't plan to go back there I can arrange to send for your things later. We couldn't have the poor lady worrying about you.'

'No, to be sure. But listen,' said Rosa urgently, 'what about my daughter? They won't let me see her. Something's wrong, I know it. They're hiding something from me!'

Mrs Holyoak smiled. 'Dear me, what a vivid imagination you have! No, I assure you, there's nothing wrong, nothing at all. But we do have to talk about her future.'

Rosa looked down at her hands clasped on the counterpane. Oona's ring reflected the stark ceiling lights. 'I'll look for work after a while,' she murmured. 'I can get by until then.'

Mrs Holyoak's gaze rested on the ring. 'How? Sell your

bits of jewellery? That won't keep you going long. What kind of work would you do?'

Rosa shrugged. 'Shop work, maybe – I'm used to that.'

'And what could you do with a child while you're working? No, my dear, that's impossible.'

Rosa felt her hackles rise. 'Domestic work then – a live-in job where they'll let me have her.'

Mrs Holyoak's laugh sounded like a tinkling bell. 'Servants are a thing of the past, Rosa. The choice is between working or bringing up a child with no money at all.'

'I've got to work! I have no choice!' Rosa exclaimed.

'Exactly,' agreed Mrs Holyoak, 'so a child is an encumbrance. The solution is to allow someone to look after her and really care for her in a way you could never afford. That's the sensible thing to do.'

'Give her up?' breathed Rosa. 'Give up my daughter to a stranger? Never in this world! She's mine, and I'm keeping her!'

'To go without?' asked Mrs Holyoak quietly. 'When she could have the very best of everything? Don't you think that's being selfish, Rosa? You should be thinking of her, not yourself.'

'I am thinking of her!' Rosa exploded. 'How could you even suggest it? Nobody else could love her like I do.'

Mrs Holyoak spread her hands, smoothing down the folded pleats of her skirt. 'You've only seen her for a few seconds,' she said drily, 'and as a matter of fact I do know some people who would love her – who're just longing for the chance to show how much they could care for her. They're very well-off people who'd give her a good home, the best food and clothes, the finest education money can buy. She'd want for nothing. Could you bring yourself to deny her that comfort?'

Rosa stared at her, unable to believe what she was hearing.

Mrs Holyoak patted her hand then stood up. 'I'll leave you to think it over, my dear. I'm sure you'll come to the right decision, for her sake. I'll call again and see what you've decided.'

Rosa felt the colour rush to her cheeks, the blood pound in her ears. 'No need to wait till then,' she cried. 'I'm telling you now – she's my daughter, mine, and you'll not give her away to someone else like she was a Christmas parcel! I'm grateful for your help, Mrs Holyoak, but you're not damn well taking my child away from me! I'd kill anyone who tried to touch her!'

Rosa could barely see the woman walk away through the red mist dancing before her eyes. From the next bed came Mrs Drake's low growl.

'Told you – little Hitlers, the lot of them. You can't win.'

'I will,' fumed Rosa. 'She'll not take my baby.'

Mrs Drake sighed. 'Aye, that's what Vera said, but she gave in in the end. She had no choice.'

'Vera?'

'Tall girl, end bed, left yesterday. Mind you, I think she was glad in the end. Meant her parents would never find out. Most of the mothers here are unwed or else they're hard-up. That's how they get them for adoption. Charity, my foot. It's a roaring good business, I reckon.'

Rosa stared at the woman, for the first time taking in her drawn face, the haggard look about her eyes. 'You knew this,' she asked, 'and still you came here?'

Mrs Drake gave a weary smile. 'It's my seventh. My husband walked out six months ago and left me with nowt.'

'I saw a man at your bedside, the man who brought cigarettes.'

'My brother,' explained Mrs Drake. 'He's a good lad.'

'But your baby,' Rosa said incredulously; 'how can you bear to part with him?'

Mrs Drake shrugged her thin shoulders. 'I've hardly seen the kid and the money'll come in useful, I can tell you, with six more at home to feed.'

Rosa considered for a moment. 'Well,' she said at last, 'I'm not giving up my baby and that's all there is to it.'

'Aye,' said Mrs Drake in a tired voice, 'that's what Vera said, but it's a different matter when you have nowt.'

She turned over to sleep. Down the ward someone switched on a transistor radio and Rosa could hear Cliff Richard singing about his living doll.

'Cut it out,' called the nurse's voice. 'Some of the patients are trying to sleep.'

'And that is why she satisfies my soul—'

The radio snapped off and the ward fell quiet. Rosa's tears trickled silently into the pillow.

Over the next few days Rosa's conscience was wracked with torment. She wanted her baby desperately, but was she, as Mrs Holyoak had said, being selfish to deny her the right to a comfortable life? And what was it the priest had said about being prepared to make a sacrifice?

Saints had gone to heaven for their noble self-sacrifice, but she was no saint, God knew. Mrs Holyoak was wrong – maybe she had only glimpsed the baby for a few seconds, but in those moments a surging torrent of love had poured from her, a flood of exultant feeling like Mrs Holyoak could never have known or she couldn't have demanded such a price from her. But if she took the baby with her when she left here, there was no chance of getting work, no chance of giving the little one the kind of life she deserved. Mother of God, what was she to do for the best?

Questions tumbled in her brain, questions she wanted to

put to Mrs Holyoak. Maybe these people would foster the baby, just as a short-term measure until she could afford to take her back. Maybe it would only be for a little time, a few months, and the baby would never be aware.

On the sixth day Rosa was allowed out of bed. She was sitting in the day room with Mrs Drake when Mrs Holyoak opened the door. She stood there in silence, holding her handbag and gloves before her, while Mrs Drake quickly stubbed out her cigarette and stood up. She put the dog-end into her dressing-gown pocket and, murmuring apologies, left the room. Mrs Holyoak took her seat. Now Rosa had a chance to put the question about fostering.

Mrs Holyoak shook her head. 'I can make no promises, I'm afraid, but if you sign the papers saying you're willing to let these people care for your baby ...'

Rosa saw a gleam of light. 'Can I talk to them, these people?' she asked.

'No, my dear. That's not the customary thing to do. We have to observe the formalities in these matters.'

'But how can I be sure I can get her back when I can afford to?' Rosa persisted. 'Is it written in the papers?'

'As I told you, I can give you no guarantees. But if you want to guarantee security for your child ...'

'I don't know,' said Rosa miserably. 'I don't know.'

Mrs Holyoak rose and began pulling on her gloves. 'Well, think about it. You'll be leaving in a couple of days. The papers are here.' She tapped her handbag. 'When you've decided, they'll be with Matron in her office.' At the doorway Mrs Holyoak turned. 'Oh, and by the way, I've left thirty pounds with her. That'll help to get you started on your new life.'

Rosa didn't look up. 'Thirty pieces of silver,' she murmured, after Mrs Holyoak had closed the door. 'The price of a life.'

Rosa could not sleep. They still hadn't brought the child to her and her breasts were sore, but she hardly noticed while her brain was in such tumult.

Love or duty? Should she give her baby away to enjoy a better life than she could ever give her, or do as nature dictated and keep her only to struggle? The first choice was unnatural, but the latter was selfish, or was it?

Who was Mrs Holyoak to judge? Her motives seemed less than honourable – if what Mrs Drake had said was true, she must be making money out of providing babies for people. Childless people, poor things. But why should she give up her child?

Because otherwise she'd be obliging the baby to live in poverty, having to do without all the luxuries she could enjoy in that other life. Oh God, what was she to do for the best?

She fell at last into a fretful sleep. At six the next morning the lights snapped on and the nurses began carrying in wailing bundles and distributing them among the mothers. Once again, her baby did not appear. A strange quiet calm came over her.

'Where's my baby?'

The nurse's eyebrows rose. 'Now then, Mrs Sheridan,' she scolded, 'you know very well—'

'I'm not Mrs Sheridan and I want my baby.'

The nurse's patient tone was irritating. 'If you're uncomfortable we'll bring a breast pump in a moment. Right now as you can see we're very busy.'

'No need,' said Rosa. 'I can see to myself.'

Throwing back the covers she got out of bed and made

for the door. The nurses, occupied in attaching small mouths to nipples, took no notice. They would think she was on her way to the toilets to express the milk herself. They'd be too busy for the next few minutes to check on her.

She found the nursery at the far end of a corridor. Through a glass window she could see the rows of cots stretching, two by two, down to the distant window. She let herself in quietly and closed the door.

Three babies still lay in their cots, two sleeping and one wide-eyed with curiosity. Rosa's heart leapt at the sight of her. She knew at once this was Angela. She had no need to read the paper pinned to the foot of the cot.

The huge blue eyes watched her as she bent over the crib and Rosa felt her heart spill over at the sight of those trusting eyes and the downy lashes curving on her cheek. How could I bear to part with you, she thought as she touched the soft skin and marvelled at the miracle. Grown inside me all these months, my own flesh and blood, and maybe a tiny part of my soul lies in you too. You're part of me – to give you up would be like tearing off my own leg. Yet for you I want all that is good and wonderful, I want your life to be filled with happiness.

She couldn't help it. Pulling back the covers she scooped the baby up in her arms. As she did so she caught sight of a card pinned to the cot above the baby's head ...

'Designated.'

That was a long word – what did it mean? Special, that's what it ought to mean. She looked down lovingly at the diminutive face, the eyes now drooping with sleep, and bent her head to kiss the downy cheek.

'Gentle Jesus, meek and mild, look upon this little child ...'

Her silent prayer was suddenly cut short as the door opened and a young nurse came in. She hadn't seen this one before. She looked at Rosa, curiosity in her eyes.

'Hello, what are you doing in here?' she asked. 'Don't you know it's out of bounds for mothers?'

'Seeing my child,' said Rosa. 'I haven't seen her for days.'

The nurse came forward, frowning as she took the bundle from Rosa's arms. 'You must have agreed to adoption,' she said, laying the child back in the crib.

'Not yet I haven't,' protested Rosa. Not yet? Why had she said that?

The nurse turned her gently about. 'I'm afraid I'll have to ask you to leave, Mrs Sheridan. Risk of infection, you know. Very dangerous for the babies.'

Rosa glanced back for one last glimpse of Angela, her eyes now closed in sleep then, unresisting, she let herself be led away.

It was lonely in the day room after Mrs Drake left. Rosa sat, fully dressed, flicking through the pages of a magazine. The senior nurse walked in briskly.

'Right, Mrs Sheridan,' she said brightly, 'doctor says you can go home this morning. If you'd like to get your things together then come with me down to Matron's office ...'

Matron sat sipping a cup of coffee behind a large desk, looking every inch as severe as Mr O'Toole in the old days back at school. Rosa was fascinated by the spectacles suspended on a gold chain about her neck. She'd never seen glasses on a chain before.

'Feeling well, Mrs Sheridan?'

'Very well, thanks,' said Rosa warily.

'Good. Mrs Holyoak has brought your things from your landlady's.' Matron waved a hand towards the bag by the door. 'And I hope you have reached your decision.'

The spectacles swayed as the woman bent to lay down her cup on the desk, then she glanced at her fob watch. 'If not, you have five minutes,' she went on.

'Five minutes?' echoed Rosa.

'Before the people come. The ones you were told about. Is your child to have a good life or not? It's up to you.'

A movement beyond the window caught Rosa's eye. A maroon car, big and expensive, swept by in the drive and pulled round the conservatory towards the main door. Matron saw it too. She signalled to the nurse, who left the room.

'Three minutes,' said Matron, pushing papers across the desk. 'You've only to sign ...'

She unscrewed a fountain-pen and held it out. Rosa hesitated, her heart pounding under her ribs. 'Will I ever see her again?' she whispered.

The matron shook her head. 'A new life begins here, for her and for you. A godsend, my dear. Don't be foolish, or you'll always regret it.'

Rosa was trembling and near to tears. 'I can't,' she murmured. 'She's mine. I sneaked into the nursery yesterday so I could hold her in my arms —'

Matron nodded. 'So I understand. Only it wasn't your child. Nurse told me she found you cradling Mrs Whitaker's little boy.'

She hadn't recognized her own child? Rosa felt as though she'd been stabbed. She stared down at the papers swimming before her. It had to be done. I owe it to her. May God forgive me.

Laboriously, through the blur of threatening tears, Rosa signed her name. She watched as the matron checked the signature and then nodded.

'Very good. Now take this.'

She held out a long white envelope. The thirty pounds, thought Rosa as she took it, the thirty pieces of silver ...

'Now pick up your bag and let me see you to the door.' Taking her arm the matron led her from the room. She turned Rosa left, towards the back door, just as a nurse hurried past carrying a bundle towards the front. Rosa turned and stared. The last sight ever of my child, she wept inwardly, and she is going one way down the corridor while I go the other.

'Tell them her name is Angela!' she called out after the nurse's retreating back, but the stolid footsteps did not slacken.

'Come on,' said Matron, tugging her firmly by the arm. 'No looking back.'

PART TWO
1968

PART TWO

1968

Chapter Nine

Rosa dried the last of the supper dishes and stacked them away in the cupboard. Now, at last, she could get out of the scullery and go and sit down by the fire. Her footsteps rang hollow on the stone-flagged floor, making the little house seem even more empty and desolate.

Now she could read the newspaper, or tune in to the play on the radio, but truth to tell she was far too tired to concentrate. Instead she lay back in the fireside chair and closed her eyes.

The fatigue which threatened to overwhelm her was not the result of effort, she knew. It was Christmas approaching which gave her this crushing sense of weariness. It happened every year, ever since that day ...

She wrenched her mind away from the memory. The pain still lay too deep inside her, a pain she'd never been able to confide to anyone. Not even him. It seemed that the pain and the guilt would remain with her for ever, her cross to bear, and hers alone.

Think of other things, happier things. Remember the night you finally plucked up the courage to go and see Kitty again. Remember how she welcomed you in, open-armed and crooning with delight ...

'Come in, come in – sure ye're a sight for sore eyes, so ye are! Ted – just look who's here!'

Remember how you looked up at the tall figure coming

down the stairs and how your breath caught in your throat. From below, in the gloom of the hall, he looked like a giant silhouetted against the naked light-bulb, filling the staircase with his height and breadth.

'*Ah, ye haven't met my brother-in-law, have ye? This is Dan Pearson.*'

Dan. A dreamy smile touched her lips. Like a god, he seemed, his rugged face gentling into a smile as he held out a huge hand to engulf hers. He'd held on to it tight, a searing current seeming to pass between them as Kitty went off in search of Ted. And that was the start of it all ...

Only one thing had marred the magic, and the ache still lingered as it always would. God grant that she knows the kind of love I would give her if I could, and that happiness fills her days.

The child sat alone in the summer house, knees blue with cold pulled up under her chin as she stared out over the white expanse of lawns. The snow looked beautiful, only the track of her own footsteps down from the house marring its surface. It had been such fun listening to the crack of the sparkling snow underfoot, the softness underneath making it look for all the world like a cream fondant.

The footmarks ended in a crazy whirl around the snowman which stood there, facing her, his head slightly lopsided on his squat body and the dried-up leaves for eyes fluttering in the chilly wind so that he had the eerie appearance of winking at her.

She was fed up with trying to build him unaided. It was much more fun when Daddy helped her to build snowmen. But he wasn't too well Mother had said, and hadn't to be bothered when he came home from work.

Blue shadows were deepening under the elm trees. It must be getting near teatime. She looked down at her gloves, the new leather ones Mother had bought last week. She'd be cross that these too were now soaked. It would be no use trying to dry them out herself – they'd probably just crack on the radiator like the others did.

'Lucy! Where are you? Come in this minute.'

Mother's distant voice trailed down the length of the garden. So she was back from the bridge club. It was no use. She'd have to go in and get told off. Lucy sighed as she uncurled herself from the bench and slowly retraced her tracks up the length of the garden.

She changed her shoes and washed her hands in the cloakroom before going on through to the kitchen. Little Graham was already sitting up at the table, a napkin around his neck as he spooned soup into his mouth. Mother stood in front of the new electric cooker, stirring a spoon in a pan and Lucy knew by the smell that it was oxtail once again.

'Washed your hands, dear?'

'Yes, Mother.'

Mother came to the table and set a bowl of soup in front of her. 'You haven't used the nailbrush,' she remarked, looking down at Lucy's hands. 'I can see grime behind your fingernails. No,' she added as Lucy rose to leave, 'eat your soup while it's hot. You can have another go at them after tea.'

'I'm going to be in the play,' said Graham. 'Teacher picked me.'

'That's very good, dear,' said Mother, 'but don't wave your spoon about, there's a good boy. You'll get soup on your new shirt.'

'What play?' asked Lucy.

'The school nativity play,' said Mother. 'Graham is to be the first wise man. Very appropriate.'

'So Mother's going to make me a box of gold to

111

carry,' said Graham triumphantly. 'Better than anybody else's.'

Lucy looked at her mother. 'Real gold?' she asked.

'Don't be silly, of course not,' Mother retorted, wiping down the Formica counter she was so proud of. 'He can have my gilt trinket box, and I'll fill it with some of those chocolate coins, the ones covered in gold paper. Like we put on the Christmas tree.'

'And I can eat them after,' said Graham. 'I can eat them all up.'

Lucy said nothing. She didn't begrudge her little brother the sweets even if he could be a little horror at times, but she couldn't help recalling when she'd been cast in the school nativity play herself, when Mother had been horrified at the thought of having to kit her out as a citizen of Bethlehem.

'Teacher says we only need a sheet to drape round us,' Lucy had tried to tell her, but Mother had only grown more agitated. 'A sheet? Does Miss Lane realize what I had to pay for good linen sheets?' she'd raged. 'I'm not having them trailed around on dirty school floors.'

It had been embarrassing trying to explain, but in the end Miss Lane had found an old sheet from somewhere. Mother hadn't even come along to see the play. She'd been too busy on sports day too and hadn't seen Lucy winning the egg-and-spoon race.

'Lucy!'

She looked up, startled. Mother's accusing finger was pointing at her chest. Lucy looked down at the brown stain on the front of her school blouse.

'Just look!' exclaimed Mother. 'Why can't you be careful? Your six-year-old brother doesn't make the mess you do!'

Lucy looked across at the smug smile spreading across Graham's chubby face and felt the anger burn in her throat. For two pins she'd have hurled the soup at him.

'As soon as you've finished get that blouse off so I can put it in to soak. I don't know,' Mother sighed, 'I work my fingers to the bone to give you a beautiful home and lovely clean clothes. It's a good job we've got the new washing-machine, that's all I can say.'

She trailed her fingers lovingly across the white enamel front of the machine, set neatly among the Formica-topped cupboards of the new fitted kitchen she was so proud of. Lucy had seen her, her face aglow, bringing her bridge friends into the kitchen.

'You haven't tried an electric oven?' she'd say in surprise. 'My dear, they're wonderful, so clean and easy to use. I wouldn't be without mine now.'

Mother was helping Graham down from his chair. 'When you've taken your things off, Lucy, you can get yourself ready for bed. Make sure you have a good wash. I'm taking Graham for his bath.'

'It's not bedtime yet,' Lucy protested. 'It's only—'

'Never mind that. After I've given Daddy his dinner I'm going to a committee meeting so you can be ready for bed. You can have a read if you like.'

'Can I ask Daddy to read me a story?' Lucy asked hopefully. Those were treasured moments, alone with Daddy. He had a gentle voice, and he always had time to listen.

'No, dear,' said Mother. 'He'll be tired when he comes home. He'll need a rest.'

Lucy fell quiet. She knew Daddy was a builder – 'the biggest and best in Leeds,' Mother said – so he must be tired after carrying all those heavy bricks around all day. Still, she'd miss those quiet moments alone together while he read to her until her eyelids drooped.

'Can I have a story?' piped up Graham. 'I like stories.'

Mother patted his shoulder. 'I'll tell you one while you have your bath. Come on, Lucy, what are you sitting there for? I told you I'm in a hurry.'

The grown-ups were talking in the dining-room when Lucy came down for a glass of milk. She could still hear their voices murmuring as she put her foot on the first step of the stairs to climb back up to bed.

'. . . another pair of gloves absolutely ruined,' Mother's voice complained. 'I honestly don't know what I'm going to do with her.'

Lucy paused to listen. So she'd found them draped along the skirting-board in the cloakroom. They were supposed to be hidden from view, behind the lavatory.

Daddy murmured something. Mother wasn't pacified.

'I'm not being hard on her, Theo. It's just that one hopes that a good upbringing will make up for her background, but it doesn't seem to be working. I know it's only little things in your eyes, but to me they're symptomatic – I can't help worrying.'

Daddy's voice was a little louder this time. 'We chose her, remember. We didn't have Graham then, Dorothy. We'd given up hope – we might never have had him.'

'Graham's our own flesh and blood,' Mother protested. 'We don't know what's in Lucy's genes.'

'No matter what her background,' Daddy said sternly, 'she's our daughter.'

Lucy began to tremble. She didn't understand their words, but it sounded as if Mother didn't really want her. What would happen? Would she send her away? No, she reassured herself as she climbed back into bed, Daddy wouldn't let her go. Daddy loved her, just as much as she loved him.

*　　*　　*

'I mean,' Dorothy Challis persisted, 'is it good for Graham?'

Theo pushed his dessert plate away with only the slightest trace of irritation. 'Dorothy, we've been over this a thousand times. What on earth are you worrying about? A poor parent isn't a contagious disease, you know. They're fine, both of them, both kids to be proud of.'

Dorothy scowled. 'I do wish you wouldn't use slang words, Theo. It doesn't set a good example to the children.'

He noticed the way she laid emphasis on the last word, but chose to ignore it. Dorothy was never happier than when she could pick on some minor error to correct.

'However,' she said briskly, laying her napkin aside and rising from the table, 'I haven't time to pursue this conversation right now.' She began stacking the dishes into a pile. 'If I don't get to the Guild committee meeting early they'll perhaps try to start without me and get themselves into a dreadful mess.'

'I'm sure they would,' he murmured, reaching for the coffee pot. Give her her due, she was at home organizing others, whether they wanted it or not. She was pretty efficient at it too, but he'd much rather she was sorting out a bunch of her women cronies than scheduling his evening for him. A quiet read of the paper, maybe a restful programme on the television accompanied by a tot of whisky – that was his idea of relaxation. After yet another hectic day in the office going over the plans for the new development a man deserved a rest.

Dorothy was loading dishes onto the tea trolley. 'It's the final preparations for the Christmas Fair, you see,' she went on, then stopped and held a finger in the air. 'Which reminds me, could you take the afternoon off either tomorrow or the next day, no later than Thursday? I want you to drive me into town; go round Schofields or Lewis's to get the children's Christmas presents.'

'I thought we were taking them to the grotto to see Santa on Saturday.'

She gave him a pained look. 'We can hardly buy their presents while they're there, can we? I've made a list – Graham wants a cowboy outfit and a bicycle, but I think a bicycle is too dangerous at his age.'

Theo shrugged. 'Not if it has stabilizers. What about Lucy?'

'Oh, a doll, I expect. She talks about a nurse's uniform, but I hardly think that's suitable. We must encourage her to set her sights a little higher than that.'

Theo smiled. 'What about Graham being a cowboy then?'

Dorothy glared and snatched up his coffee cup. She didn't seem to notice it was still half full. 'Don't go in to look at the children,' she said as she wheeled the trolley to the door, 'you'll only disturb them. Oh, unless you hear Graham cough. His linctus is on the bedside table, but don't give him more than one teaspoonful.'

Theo looked up in mild surprise. 'I didn't know he had a cough,' he remarked.

His wife glowered. 'How could you? You're at work all day. No, he coughed a couple of times this evening – it's just as a preventative, that's all.'

Theo rose stiffly and made his way to the lounge while Dorothy disappeared into the kitchen with the tea trolley. He could hear her clattering the dishes into the new stainless-steel sink. She fussed too much over the boy, he mused as he picked up the evening paper. Mollycoddled him. Getting him into a good boarding-school would be the best thing that ever happened to the lad. Teach him how to take care of himself; make a man of him. Lucy, now she was different. Quiet and deep that little miss. She had her head screwed on.

Theo's gaze lighted on the green exercise book lying on the coffee-table and he reached down to pick it up. 'Lucy Challis, Class 3.' He flicked over the pages, a smile curving his lips. She left it there on purpose for him to see. He found it: the red-ink comment from the teacher appended to the last piece of work.

'Very good, Lucy. A.'

She'd be so proud, he thought, letting his gaze run over the neatly written piece of work. She was a trier all right, filled with quiet determination. There was grit buried deep in her bones, and she hadn't inherited that from either him or Dorothy.

The door opened and Dorothy breezed in, already in her hat and coat and pulling on her gloves, smoothing them down finger by finger. 'Cheese and crackers ready on the kitchen table,' she pronounced. 'I'll see they get through the agenda sharpish so I shan't be late tonight.'

She was turning to go. Theo held up the exercise book. 'Have you seen Lucy's homework?' he asked. 'It's really very good. She's a bright kid and no mistake.'

'Oh, she's bright enough,' said Dorothy drily as she opened the door, 'considering.'

He must have dozed off, because when he woke the television announcer was relaying the late-evening news. She'd be back any minute. If he was going to have a quick glimpse of the children he'd have to make it quick.

Theo eased himself up and tossed back the last drop of whisky still in his glass, then rose stiffly and made for the door. As he climbed the stairs he swore under his breath. They seemed to become longer and steeper every day. A man his age shouldn't have to strain like this to get upstairs – it must be rheumatics – what else could make his limbs feel so painfully fragile and unwilling to work? Thank God he didn't have to spend much time these days outdoors in foul weather. He'd come a long way from those laborious days of hod-carrying and cement-mixing. At least he'd made Dorothy proud of his success and been able to give his family a good life.

His family. Gently he pushed open the door of Graham's nursery and by the subdued glow of the night-light he could just make out the little face, eyes closed in sleep and a thumb jammed into his mouth. So far the habit hadn't deformed his jaw the way Dorothy feared. She was paranoid about the child, far more finicky than she'd ever been with Lucy.

Lucy. '*It's the Latin word for light,*' Dorothy had said proudly when they first brought her home. '*She's brought a light into our lives.*'

And so you did, he thought, looking down on the child's sleeping face, the tumble of fair curls. A wave of tenderness washed over him. You brought light into our barren lives – and then the miracle happened. When Graham came along we could hardly believe it. Maybe your sunny little face melted something in Dorothy. He couldn't help himself. He bent to place a gentle kiss on her forehead.

She stirred in her sleep and he drew back, though he half hoped she would waken. Then he could savour again the pleasure in those deep-blue eyes, the way she'd throw her arms about his neck and squeeze him so hard he could barely breathe.

Whatever it was you gave us, Lucy, he vowed, I'll always give thanks for you.

Chapter Ten

Greta Holyoak caught a trolley bus back into town. She could have taken a taxi as Reginald kept telling her she should, but to be honest she preferred being among people. This way she could eavesdrop on their conversation, and feel as though she were really part of them.

'How do, Fred. How's the missus? Got over her poorly leg now, has she? ... Aye, glad to hear it. Soon be running up Scapegoat Hill again, she will, chasing them rabbits for your supper.'

And the home-going shop-girls, chattering happily about the evening still ahead. 'Did you get that new lipstick to match your frock? ... He did what? ... You jammy devil. Where's he taking you then? ...

It was good to feel life going on around her, thought Greta, to feel again the buzz of anticipation and excitement which seemed to be so lacking in her own life. As a rule she found pleasure in going out to the maternity home where all those new little lives were beginning, but not today. Matron's obduracy had cast a decided shadow over the day.

'I'm sorry, Mrs Holyoak, but this is the way I've always done it. I see no reason to change my methods now.'

'You know the committee of management made the decision at its last meeting, Matron. The motion was carried unanimously.'

'If you'll forgive my saying so, the committee doesn't have

to run the place. Even though you yourself call in here regularly you don't know the daily problems.'

'You were present at the meeting, Matron; you had the chance to air your views and explain.'

She could still see Matron's stiff back, the starched cap perched on her iron-grey hair and the set line of her thin lips. *'I repeat, Mrs Holyoak, I do not intend to change my routine. It's worked well for the past fifteen years and I see no reason to change now.'*

'I'm sorry you feel like that. As chairman it is my duty to report your attitude to the board. Won't you reconsider?'

Every line of Matron's square body had still expressed stubborn truculence. *'You can tell the board if they think they can run this place any better than me, they're welcome to try. That's all I have to say.'*

Such a pity, thought Greta. With Christmas only days away the air ought to be suffused with goodwill and happiness, not charged with bitterness. The home had been set up to make birth a happy experience, especially for those unfortunate girls who'd fallen by the wayside. Rejected by their families, most of them, they found a haven at Wood Lea. And if she thought they were unable to cope with a child, she'd done her level best to find good homes for the poor little mites.

The bus was nearing the town centre. She glanced at her wrist-watch. It was still early – she didn't want to go back to an empty house, not yet. If she walked along New Street she could call at Kaye's, the draper's, and get that new shirt and tie for Reginald. Not that he'd appreciate it, but she had to buy a present for him to unwrap on Christmas morning. And after that? A cup of tea in Field's or Silvio's, maybe, but she might risk being buttonholed by one of Reginald's colleagues' wives or worse still, one of his clients. She could catch a bus down to Lockwood –

yes, an hour alone in Mrs Clancy's front bedroom watching the world go by would do her a world of good.

Mrs Clancy put down her pen as she heard the key in the front-door lock. It must be Mrs Holyoak – nobody else had a key to the house these days, apart from Stanley, that was. She hurried to open the living-room door before Mrs Holyoak disappeared upstairs.

'Hello,' she said brightly, 'I thought I heard you. I must say, I hadn't expected you to come again this side of Christmas.'

Mrs Holyoak smiled. 'It was just a whim, Mrs Clancy. I fancied being alone for a bit.'

'And so you shall,' agreed Mrs Clancy, 'only I was just about to brew up. Fancy a nice cup of tea?'

Mrs Holyoak shook her head. 'I wouldn't dream of troubling you—'

'No trouble. Come in and sit yourself down.' Mrs Clancy turned to plump up the cushion in the fireside chair. 'Dearie me, just look at this fire,' she murmured. 'It needs a good talking to. I just can't get it to draw today. The wind must be coming the wrong way.'

She pulled off the outer sheet of last night's *Examiner* and placed it over the fire opening. Mrs Holyoak stood silent, watching the flames begin to glow through the paper. As the newsprint began to scorch Mrs Clancy snatched it away.

'There, that's better,' she sighed, crumpling the paper into a ball. 'Now, let's get the kettle on.'

'Please don't bother for me,' said Mrs Holyoak.

Mrs Clancy looked up anxiously, reluctant to let her go so soon. With her old chest playing up so much these days she didn't get out as often as she used, and apart from the Co-op insurance man few people called.

'I just wanted to let you know you have the place to yourself now,' she said with an apologetic smile. 'My other tenant left last week and I'm not thinking to take anybody else.'

'I see.'

'Only I'm not as young as I was, you know, and it's not as though I need the money. I can manage quite well on me pension.'

She saw the startled look which leapt into the other woman's eyes. 'Oh,' exclaimed Mrs Holyoak, 'you mean you'd prefer me to give up my tenancy too? Of course, if that's what you want, only I've been very—'

'No, no, not at all,' Mrs Clancy cut in, waving her hands. 'That's not what I meant at all! Dear me, no. It gives me pleasure to have a lady in the house. You stay as long as ever you want.'

Mrs Holyoak smiled. 'I'm glad to hear you say that. You've no idea the sense of space and peace that little room affords me. I'd hate to be without it now.'

'And you shan't,' averred Mrs Clancy, 'not till they carry me out feet first. And even then you could perhaps come to some arrangement.' She pointed to the letter lying half written on the chenille-covered table. 'I was just writing to our Stanley – he's my nephew, you know, the only family I've got left. He lives down in Macclesfield. We don't have much contact with each other as a rule, but seeing as it's Christmas . . .'

She would have gone over to the chest of drawers and taken out the album of faded photographs to show her a picture of Stanley, but she could see the distant look on Mrs Holyoak's face.

'I'm sorry,' she murmured, 'I'm keeping you. You've no doubt things you want to get on with.'

She felt a little forlorn as she watched Mrs Holyoak climb

the stairs. With a sigh she turned back to the letter. Stanley wouldn't write back – he never did.

A feather fluttered down to settle on the notepad. Above her head the budgie began to cheep and then suddenly, loud and clear, he squawked, 'Merry Christmas.'

Mrs Clancy craned her neck round to look up at the bird and smile. 'Eh, Mickey love,' she murmured, 'I know I grumble a lot about me aches and pains, but it's a good job I've got you.'

Reginald Holyoak stayed out until quite late, and Greta was grateful. She'd only had to put up with his acid comments for a comparatively short time over dinner before he had to hurry out again to one of his endless council committee meetings, so for once peace lay over the elegant house he'd chosen, as befitted his standing, he said, as senior partner in Holyoak, Brett and Fenton.

It was a beautiful house, right enough, but it gave her little pleasure. There were two Greta Holyoaks; one was a capable, efficient woman who immersed herself in charitable works, and the other a poor faded little mouse of a woman whose confidence drained away the moment she stepped through the front door.

Reginald had done that to her. Over the years he had gnawed away at her self-esteem until, in his presence, there was very little of it left.

She hated this house. It was far too big for two middle-aged people with no family and the very devil to keep clean with only part-time help three mornings a week. With all his outside interests, home for him was a place to sleep and be serviced, but for Greta the cold here struck deeper than the icy lino in Jubilee Terrace.

'Oh, by the way,' he'd thrown back over his shoulder on his way out, 'I've asked Brett and his wife to dinner on Christmas

Eve. And I suppose you'll be expecting something in the way of a Christmas present, though God knows, Christmas has little significance for me. Maybe you could make a list so I don't need to waste my time. Something useful, I thought, gloves or a scarf maybe.'

Nothing feminine, nothing to make me feel special, she thought sadly as the door slammed behind him. She bent to switch on the television. You wouldn't dream of buying me a flimsy nightdress or a bottle of perfume. I'm not a woman to you, not since I failed you. I'm a household appliance, as useful as the toaster or the Kenwood Chef; something which makes life run that bit more smoothly, nothing more. I see to it that your shirts and suits are immaculate for your court appearances, I entertain your dinner guests with charm and grace, but beyond my function as the ideal housewife I don't exist.

She sat in the deep armchair where he usually sat. On the small screen ballroom dancers twisted and pirouetted in a swirl of organza but she paid no attention. In front of her on the coffee-table lay the sheets of coloured tissue-paper intended for wrapping up Reginald's gift: the shirt and tie from Kaye's, but when the programme finally came to a close they still lay untouched.

'*Christmas has little significance for me.*' Greta gave a brittle laugh. That was not true. Christmas held a terrible significance for them both. A sudden urge came over her. She pushed the tissue-paper aside and rose from the chair.

There was a slightly musty smell up here in the loft, but at least it wasn't damp for the old blanket covering the trunk was as dry as a bone. Greta held the candle higher. Cardboard boxes full of papers lay everywhere, mostly ancient office records Reginald felt obliged to keep though most of them dated from his father's days. Vases, jugs, horse brasses –

relics of the past she'd never brought herself to throw out – all of them covered in layers of fluffy dust.

'Don't know why you hoard all that junk,' Reginald often grumbled. 'Hangover from your days of poverty, I suppose. Don't throw anything away in case it might come in useful.'

He liked to torment her about her youth, the days when she used to live in a terraced house only a couple of streets away from where Mrs Clancy now lived. It gave him pleasure to point out the difference between them: she the daughter of a railway guard while he was son and sole heir to Archibald Holyoak, solicitor. If she sometimes did something which brought a scornful smile to his face, he would remind her.

'I suppose we can't expect any better from a girl from the back streets of Lockwood,' he'd sigh. *'Can't think why I saddled myself with you.'*

'You know very well why you did, Reginald.'

'And I've been paying for it ever since.'

She pulled aside the blanket and lifted the lid of the trunk. Her wedding dress, the tulle embroidered with seed pearls, and under it a small tissue-wrapped parcel. Laying the candle aside she folded back the layers with reverence. There it lay, every tiny stitch immaculate. Tears pricked behind her eyes.

'Greta! Where are you?'

The sudden, peremptory voice startled her. She leapt up in panic, dropping the package, and at the same moment catching her foot against the candle. It fell and rolled across the wooden floor. She stared in horror as a heap of papers burst into flame.

'Greta? Are you up there?'

She stood transfixed as Reginald's head appeared through the trapdoor, silhouetted against the sheet of fire now

126

threatening to devour the cardboard boxes. She saw his jaw sag.

'Good God!' he exclaimed, and then suddenly he was pushing her aside, grabbing the blanket from the floor and swamping the flames with it. Moments later nothing remained but a haze of black smoke, and on the floor a tiny smudged christening robe.

Reginald straightened and turned to her. 'Downstairs, Greta,' he said in that grim tone she knew so well. 'I think we have some talking to do.'

It was the same old ritual, thought Greta as she sat, head bowed, listening to his tirade. They'd gone through this argument a thousand times before and it never got them anywhere. Round and round in circles, the same old worn phrases '... biggest mistake of my life ... shackled to a moron ... never should have taken a halfwit from the slums ...'

It was no use pointing out, yet again, that she was no halfwit; she'd had a decent education. She'd got her qualifications in shorthand and typing, hadn't she? How else would she have worked her way up to become his father's secretary?

She'd been taking shorthand notes the first time Reginald came into the office. She'd seen the way he watched her, the way he just happened to be hanging around outside when she finished work for the day.

'I should never have let you seduce me,' he rumbled. 'Thought you'd done well for yourself, didn't you, ensnaring the boss's son?'

'It wasn't like that, Reginald, you know it wasn't.'

'And then getting pregnant so I had to marry you.'

'I didn't make you. It was your father who insisted.'

Reginald groaned. 'The worst turn he ever did me, just because he lived in hope of a grandchild. My mother knew better – she said I'd live to regret it.'

127

Greta hung her head. 'It wasn't my fault, Reginald. It was fate.'

He turned to her, and she saw the lip curled in a sneer. 'You couldn't even give birth properly. You've never done anything right – a dead son, you gave me. A dead son.'

He rolled his eyes towards heaven as if in search of an explanation. How could any woman be so stupid? 'It killed my father', he muttered, 'when he learned you couldn't have any more.'

No matter how many times he'd said it, it still cut her to the quick. Greta felt the tears begin to form. Reginald poured himself a whisky.

'Useless, that's what you are. And now I find you trying to burn the damn house down.'

'I'm sorry,' she said miserably. 'It was an accident – you made me jump.'

Reginald's glass paused on its journey to his lips. 'That's right,' he hissed. 'Blame me. Can you never accept responsibility for your own ineptitude? What the devil were you doing up there anyway?'

'Nothing. Just looking.'

How could she explain to him? Just to look at the little robe she'd prepared so lovingly in the days when she still felt loved and needed, to look at it because it was Christmas, the anniversary of the day the inert little creature had slid from her body, looking for all the world as if he were only sleeping?

Charles, she'd called him in her mind, but Reginald had given no name when it came to registering the death. The light had gone out of his eyes after that whenever he looked at her.

He slapped the whisky glass down. 'It's late,' he said gruffly. 'I have to be in court in the morning. We'll talk about this tomorrow.'

It made no difference, she thought as she levered herself out of the chair. They'd only go over the same old treadmill again, round and round like a trapped hamster, getting nowhere.

As she reached the door of the lounge she heard Reginald go into his room and slam the door. She sighed. If it wasn't for that little bedroom in Lockwood and her work at Wood Lea she'd go crazy.

Rosa lay awake in the big bed, listening to the night sounds of the street.

By the light of the lamp shining in through the uncurtained window she could see her breath rising in a steam in the icy air.

Out in the night a tom-cat on the prowl made a dismal howling sound, a dog barked in answer, and a lone pair of feet clattered along the cobblestones past the house.

Soon those cobbles would probably vanish, she mused, along with so many other old features of the town. Hawksmoor was changing fast, hardly recognizable nowadays as the town she and Maggie had viewed, wide-eyed in amazement, when they first arrived here from Clondarra.

All over town rows of terraced houses such as this had vanished in a pile of rubble, only to resurface as huge tower blocks of flats. Even the old cinema whose back-row double seats held such warm memories was gone. Huge buildings like the new civic centre and police station had risen just beyond the shopping centre, and an enormous ring road now circled the town. Old was giving way to the new civic pride everywhere; it couldn't be long before this part of town too suffered a change, and the thought saddened her. It was so much like home here, a friendly, close-knit community of every nationality under the sun – English, Irish, Polish, Indian, Jamaican – it would be a terrible shame to split them up and send them away.

She heard a sound downstairs and closed her eyes. She heard boots clatter to the floor in the little vestibule, creeping footsteps on the stairs, and then the door creaked open.

'Rosa? You awake?'

She lay still and said nothing. She could smell the Guinness on his breath.

'Rosa.' His voice was low and charged with urgency. She wouldn't give in, not when he'd promised not to go near The Fleece.

She felt him slide into bed beside her, hunching across until his body curved around hers. Like spoons, she thought, and tried to ignore the feelings he stirred in her as his hand slid across her and hugged her close.

'You promised,' she muttered. 'You broke your word.'

'It was only a couple, love – I met Fred Brook.'

She prised his hand away and rolled over to face him. 'You're hopeless, Dan Pearson,' she said into the darkness. 'Whatever you promise, you haven't the strength to resist.'

She heard his smile as he pulled her close. 'But you love me, Rosa, don't you? Like I love you.'

Within those big arms, cradled against his hard muscular body, she felt safe. Maybe it was only an illusion, but on a cold winter's night there was comfort in the strength of him.

'You good-for-nothing,' she murmured, 'I must be the biggest idiot in the world.'

Chapter Eleven

Dorothy had taken the children down into Leeds on a shopping trip. Theodore Challis settled down in his armchair to watch a bit of football on the television. Even though Dorothy was still grumbling about the pine needles on the carpet, Christmas was well and truly over and the new year launched.

It had been a good Christmas, he reflected. Dorothy had produced an excellent table, well up to her usual Marguerite Patten standard, and the kids had clearly enjoyed their presents, the cowboy outfit, the nurse's uniform, the big doll and the Lego. Graham had got his bike with the stabilizers after all, and Lucy was thrilled with the new swing.

'When can I play on it, Daddy?'

'Soon, lovey. I'll get it fixed up for you.'

He'd get one of the men on to it as soon as the snow cleared, set it in a concrete bed for stability. 'Near the kitchen window,' Dorothy had ordered, 'where I can keep an eye on the two of them.'

She'd been in a particularly hectoring frame of mind ever since she discovered at the Guild's first meeting of the new year that she'd been thrown off the committee. It seemed a shame, after all the energetic work she'd done for them, but he was willing to bet her overbearing manner had become too much for them.

'I won't go there again,' she declared. 'That's it, if they

don't recognize a good organizational brain when they've got one, well, they don't deserve me.'

'There's always the Housewives' Register,' Theo tried to soothe her. 'You once said you'd like to try that.'

She wouldn't listen. 'They want to discuss anything but the home,' she said dubiously. 'And no more charity work for me either – charity begins at home.'

It was cosy watching Leeds United in the warm comfort of the lounge, thought Theo. In the old days he'd have been down at Elland Road, but not any more. The weather was still too wintry for his aching limbs, that biting wind still blowing in from the east. Moreover Dorothy objected strongly to his being seen on the terraces.

'A man in your position, Theo – I mean it's just not dignified.'

He'd never liked sitting in the stand. If he had to sit down he might as well do it at home. Maybe later, when the warmer weather thawed his aches away, when Graham would be old enough to appreciate the game. Man and son, rattles in hand – yes, he'd like that. For two pins he'd dig out his old rattle now, drape his old white scarf about his neck and cheer from his armchair, but he could guess what acid remarks such schoolboyish behaviour would draw from Dorothy.

The lads were playing well; that new inside left had magic in his feet all right. For a time Theo sat riveted, and then gradually his eyes began to feel heavy. He must have fallen into a doze, for the next thing he knew the children were leaping all over him, eager to tell him about their outing.

'We got new pyjamas', Graham said proudly, 'with teddy bears on.'

'In the sales,' explained Dorothy. 'Only a little more than half price.'

'We've both got the same,' said Lucy. 'Teddy bears.'

'Don't grumble,' said her mother. 'You should be grateful you got new pyjamas at all.'

'I'd rather have had the book,' said Lucy. Theo could see her crestfallen look.

'What book?' he asked.

'It wasn't suitable for children,' said Dorothy crisply. 'It was about first aid. Rather unpleasant pictures, I thought.'

Theo couldn't help smiling to himself. Anything which wasn't meticulously scrubbed and sanitary was displeasing to her finicky taste. She herself always looked as fresh and wholesome as Doris Day, like the woman in the advert on television for 'hands that do dishes can feel soft as your face' with some product or other.

'You didn't buy any books then?' he asked.

'Oh yes I did,' she countered with a broad smile. 'I got Elizabeth David's new book. You know, the expert in Continental cookery. I remember how much you enjoyed the food at that new Italian trattoria – I thought I'd have a go at it myself.'

That evening Theo read his newspaper while Dorothy sat poring over her new book.

'I shall have to go shopping, maybe to London,' she pronounced as she laid the book aside. 'Elizabeth says we need things like a garlic press and a Sabatier knife – I doubt I'll find those in town.'

Theo lowered the newspaper. 'A what knife?'

She brushed the question aside. 'And I think I'll start a herb garden – chives, tarragon, rosemary – that sort of thing.' She rubbed her hands together. 'I'm really looking forward to this,' she enthused. 'Oh and spices too, I mustn't forget those.'

Theo sank deeper into his armchair. So now she had a

new guru in this Elizabeth David, a new passion which might supersede the Ruth Morgan and Marguerite Patten books which had governed her kitchen for years. Still, Dorothy was right – he had enjoyed those Italian meals.

'So maybe I can look forward to a spaghetti Bolognese soon?' he said mildly.

Dorothy shook her head firmly. 'Elizabeth says it's very difficult to eat spaghetti properly unless you're very skilled. Imagine what a mess the children would make. No, vermicelli or some other small pasta to start with, perhaps, with a nice Neapolitan sauce.'

'Vermicelli?'

'Elizabeth says it means literally little worms, but I'm sure it's not as bad as it sounds.'

Theo sank back behind his newspaper. She didn't make it sound very appetizing, but he was prepared to withhold judgement. She wasn't a woman to settle for anything until she'd got it exactly the way she wanted.

Dorothy sat gazing into space, her chin cupped in her hand. 'How about giving Lucy elocution lessons?' she said.

Theo stared. 'What's brought this about?' he asked. 'She speaks well enough.'

'Only I've been thinking,' Dorothy went on, 'remember her birthday, when we had Mrs Drake's little granddaughter here for tea?'

He remembered the child well, a prim little madam with her hair screwed up tightly in ribbon-tied bunches. She wasn't one of Lucy's school friends but the child specially chosen for the day by Dorothy, the grandchild of the wealthy widow up the road. Dorothy wouldn't rest until she'd got the old lady to agree to give up her precious Sophie for the afternoon.

'Didn't she talk nicely?' Dorothy said, with that fond

tone in her voice which conveyed her admiration. 'Beautiful diction – such a contrast to Lucy.'

'She talks like that because she comes from Surrey,' Theo retorted. 'There's nothing wrong with Lucy's speech.'

'It reflects on the family,' said Dorothy calmly. 'I mean, in your position. You're a man of standing now with your fleet of lorries and all those men working for you. You're not just a small-time builder like your father.'

'There's no call for airs and graces all the same,' muttered Theo. 'She'd only be a laughing stock at school with a prissy voice like that Drake kid.'

Dorothy gave a sigh. 'Oh well,' she murmured, spreading her hands in resignation, 'I've done my best. If you're satisfied with her hoydenish ways—'

Irritation prickled in Theo. She was a good mother but for her habit of forever finding fault with the child, suggesting she was, at best, only a second-rater. 'Leave her be,' he growled. 'There's nothing wrong with her.'

Dorothy smoothed down her skirt and stood up. 'If you say so, dear. Cheese and crackers?'

He watched her leave the room, and knew by the firmness of her tread that this was only the opening gambit of her campaign. Like the pasta, she wouldn't leave the child alone until she'd got her the way she wanted her.

Rosa fetched the washing in off the line in the backyard. It was no use; none of it had dried. In fact, most of it was stiff as a board, frozen solid in this bitter weather.

'Don't know why you bother hanging it out,' said Dan, munching a slice of toast. 'Waste of time.'

'Because you don't like it draped on the clothes-horse round the fire,' Rosa retorted, 'so where else is there?'

He cocked his head to one side, frowning in thought.

He was a handsome fellow, she reflected, even if he was always under her feet.

'How about me knocking up one of those ceiling things for you?' he asked. 'Would that help?'

She smiled. 'A ceiling rack? That would be wonderful, Dan.'

He stood up at once, wiping toast crumbs from his mouth with the back of his hand. 'Right,' he muttered, 'I've a bit of timber in the shed might do the job. Just need a couple of brackets then and a bit of rope.'

He was good at knocking things up, as he put it, thought Rosa, just as she was adept at finding bargains. From the day when, after a whirlwind courtship, he'd asked her to marry him, they'd made a good team. She'd been the one who'd rushed around the estate agents until she found this place to rent; and she'd been the one who'd unearthed in junk shops the pieces of furniture they needed most. Dan had been the one to clear the drains and mend the roof, to put up shelves and cupboards, to paint and paper the little house until it became a home – he was a marvel with his hands.

'Brawn, that's what I was born with, not brains,' he used to joke. 'That's why I needed to marry a clever woman like you.'

He was a good man none the less, she thought, good-humoured and kindly, willing to do anyone a good turn. And he was generous to a fault; he'd give his last sixpence to a crying child in the street, but he'd gone too far that time when he refused promotion.

'Nay, Rosa,' he'd explained with a schoolboy's gruff embarrassment, 'I couldn't take the ganger's job when Jim Roberts has been with the firm twice as long as me. I told them give him the job – and they did.'

'But why, Dan?' she'd argued. 'We could have done

with the extra money – specially if we want to start a family.'

'I told you, love. Jim deserved it, that's all. Anyway, we have enough for now.'

That had been five years ago, and no baby had happened along. In the early days of their marriage, when Dan had talked of his dreams for the future with his family around the table, she'd often bitten her lip and wondered whether this was the time to tell him. But she never had.

Time was, when she used to think of Angela a thousand times a day, wondering where she was and what she was doing, but the speculation had gradually diminished to a dozen times a day, and nowadays it was maybe twice a week. But every time it brought with it, not only the yearning to know, but also painful pangs of guilt. I should never have let her go. I should have kept her with me. Dan would have understood.

But the passage of time had made it difficult to speak. It wouldn't be easy now for him to understand. He'd question, naturally, why she'd kept silent for so long. God grant we have another child soon to take the place of the one I wickedly gave away.

So every time Dan took her in his arms she felt a traitor. She loved him so much – there ought to be complete openness between them, but there was one area of her life he knew nothing about. The trouble was, he seemed to sense something was wrong. He spent far too much time – and money – these days down at The Fleece.

'I'm just off for a pint, love – thirsty work digging all day.'

She couldn't argue with that. It was energetic, working on the new motorways. Sometimes he'd have to go away down to the Midlands for the week, then he'd be home again, all weather-beaten and his muscles hard as rock, open-armed and wreathed in smiles.

'Come on, Rosa lass,' he'd murmur into her hair, 'let's make that baby.'

It meant so much to him. Push the dark thoughts away out of your head, she told herself, hold him close, and pray to St Anthony that this time, God willing ...

Reginald Holyoak felt restless. There was that old familiar feeling stirring which he knew from experience would not go away until he did something about it.

He walked through to the kitchen. Greta was sitting at the table writing something on a notepad. She looked up and gave him a gentle smile. 'Just writing my list of jobs for tomorrow,' she said.

Her tone of apology irritated him. Come to think of it, she irritated him. So did her provincially well-off twin set and pearls and her mild-mannered inconsequence. Why couldn't she be a real woman, with a mind and will of her own? Why couldn't she wear something more original and dramatic? His thoughts began to stray, and the old familiar hunger was back again.

'I'm going out,' he said curtly. 'Don't wait up for me.'

She gave him a look of mild surprise. 'I thought you had no more meetings this week,' she said.

'No – this is just tidying up a few loose ends, that's all,' he muttered. 'Got to be done.'

'And it's always you who does the tidying up,' she said amiably. 'Really, Reginald, you drive yourself too hard at times. Let someone else do it now and again.'

'This is something I have to see to myself,' he said gruffly, and picking up his car keys he turned and left the kitchen.

* * *

He knew exactly where he was heading. And he knew exactly what it was he sought. Not here in Hawksmoor, obviously; it had to be out of town, but it was only a half-hour's drive to the remedy he needed.

Dark Arches, they called this place, and he could understand why as he drove through the gloomy subterranean hollow under the railway tracks. Positively Dickensian it was down here; one could visualize the vagabonds and pickpockets Fagin would have nurtured. It was a fitting area for a lady of Madame Zara's undoubted skills.

He parked the car well away before he knocked at her door.

'Well hello,' she purred. 'Long time no see. Come in. I wasn't expecting anyone tonight so you'll just have to wait till I'm ready.'

He had to sit on a hard chair in the dingy little sitting-room while she went into the bedroom to prepare, but it was worth the wait. She was wearing the black leather gear tonight and she carried a whip. He felt his insides churn in wild anticipation. She'd ridicule him – just for a little while – and then she'd tie him up.

'Reginald.'

He stood up, his whole body quivering and subservient. 'Yes, mistress?'

She pointed the whip magisterially into the bedroom. 'Inside.'

God, she was magnificent! He shambled past her, his brain eddying in delight. This was going to be a night to remember.

Greta finished writing her list and sat clicking the pencil against her teeth. Poor Reginald – he was clearly in an edgy mood tonight. Maybe it was the unfinished council work, or more likely it was the prospect of that approaching court case of Mr Oldroyd's.

Reginald had agreed to handle it – a solicitor can't very well turn down a request to defend his bank manager against a shoplifting charge, especially when the accused is also his close friend. He should have let someone else handle it, but that was Reginald all over, a glutton for hard work. Precious few solicitors in Hawksmoor would be out tidying up council business on a night like this. And he'd stick at it till past midnight if necessary to get it finished – he'd done it before, though not so often lately. Tonight's bit of work must be important.

She dropped the pencil and notepad back in the cutlery drawer and headed up the staircase. How smooth and satisfying the mahogany banister felt beneath her fingertips, as smooth as a young girl's skin. Once her skin used to feel just as firm and sleek.

She passed Reginald's room and went into her own. In front of the cheval mirror she undressed and surveyed her reflection wistfully.

From the bottom drawer of the dressing-table she drew out the filmy nightie she'd treated herself to in the sales. She draped it over her naked body, and smiled. A diaphanous covering hid a multitude of sins. One of the glossy magazines this week said that a man under stress often needed more sex in order to unwind. What a pity Reginald never read magazines.

Sighing, she refolded the nightdress carefully and put it away in the drawer.

Chapter Twelve

'You've been married for how long, do you say?' asked the doctor.

Rosa sat on the edge of the hard chair, clutching her gloves tightly between her hands. 'Six years now, doctor, and still no sign of a baby. And it's not as though we've been – you know, doing anything. I'm a Roman Catholic so I wouldn't anyway.'

'Your husband too – is he a Catholic?'

She lowered her head. 'No, it's a mixed marriage, but he wouldn't try to stop it – he desperately wants a family. That's why I thought if I came to you ...'

The doctor nodded. 'Well, let's see what we can do. If you'd like to go into the examination room and strip off.'

Rosa dressed quickly and came back to sit down before him. He was busily writing something on a pad. When he finally laid down his pen she searched his face eagerly.

'Well,' she said, 'am I all right?'

'So far as I can tell you're in perfect working order,' he replied with a smile. 'We'd need further tests to be absolutely certain, but I can see no apparent reason why you shouldn't conceive.'

Rosa bit her lip. 'A further test, you say,' she murmured. 'What would happen?'

'I can arrange for you to see the gynaecologist at the

infirmary – you need only spend a day there,' the doctor replied. 'But why didn't you tell me you'd already had a baby?'

Rosa caught her breath. 'How do you know?' she breathed. 'Nobody knows about that.'

He gave a knowing smile. 'My dear, I am a doctor. The signs are there.'

She felt the agitation fluttering in her chest. 'You won't tell my husband, will you? Oh God, if he found out ...' She could feel the panic rising.

The doctor patted her hand. 'No need to worry, my dear. Confidentiality is part of our contract. Whatever is said in this room remains here and will not be repeated, I assure you, so you need have no fear. Was it before you were married?'

Rosa looked down, twisting the gloves in her hands. 'I was young and foolish. I knew no better.'

'And the baby? Where is it now?'

I wish to God I knew, she thought. She swallowed the hard lump in her throat and answered softly. 'I had her adopted. They promised me she'd have a good home.'

He nodded. 'That was probably wise in the circumstances.'

'So if I had one baby, why haven't I had any more – that's what's puzzling me.'

'And that's what we have to find out,' the doctor rejoined. 'Now, I've written a letter to the consultant. They'll send for you soon to come in for those tests. Then we'll know better where we stand.'

Every day Rosa watched anxiously for the postman bringing the vital letter. It was imperative Dan shouldn't find out. If he insisted on coming with her and the gynaecologist let anything slip about Angela. No, it didn't bear thinking about.

He'd usually left for work before the post arrived, but the morning she looked out of the window and saw him chatting to the postman her heart nearly stopped. Suppose he handed Dan the mail – suppose that letter was amongst them ...

It wasn't. It finally arrived at a timely moment when Dan was gone for a few days, working on a motorway a hundred miles away. Rosa scanned the wording quickly looking for the date for the appointment – in a week's time, it said, when he'd be gone again. She tucked the letter away safely where he wouldn't see it. She felt shifty, furtive, but it had to be done if she were to solve this problem.

As a rule Dan never enquired about what had come in the post, but for some odd reason it was one of his first questions when he arrived home on Friday night. Rosa was ironing at the time, wishing for the thousandth time that they could afford a steam iron.

'Anything interesting happen while I was away?' Dan asked. 'Anything in the post? We haven't won the pools or owt?'

Rosa spat on the hot iron and watched the ball of spit run, hissing, off the edge. 'There was a gas bill,' she answered quietly, 'and it won't be long before the electric comes too.'

He lost interest and asked no more. Paying the bills was her department. Dan was always the first to acknowledge that he was hopeless at budgeting the family finances; handing over his pay-packet to her was the end of his responsibility. He was happy to let her allot the money to bills, rent, insurance and housekeeping. Then he only had to budget his spending money. And she couldn't help noticing that more and more of it these days was winding up in The Fleece – and no doubt in other Midland pubs near his motorway. Still, she comforted herself, if these tests were

143

to sort out her problem, surely it would resolve Dan's at the same time.

Mrs Clancy let herself into the house and as she put the key away she saw the letter on the mat. She bent with difficulty to pick it up, then, breathing heavily, dumped her shopping bags gratefully on the living-room table. If she just sat down on the chair for a minute to get her breath back she'd feel better. Then she'd go through and put the kettle on for a nice cup of tea. Yes, she'd feel a lot better with a hot cup of tea inside her.

'As long as I've got me health and strength,' she used to say cheerily, 'I can look after meself.' She didn't want no busybodies coming in to clean up after her or fetch her shopping. But now, at seventy-seven, it took more out of her going down to the shops than she cared to admit to anyone. Still, with spring nearly here the weather would soon get warmer and the going would be easier.

'Merry Christmas. Merry Christmas.'

She glanced over at the budgerigar's cage and shook her head. 'Eh, Mickey lad, I do wish you'd learn to say summat else,' she sighed. 'What are we going to do with you, eh? What are we going to do with you? Just 'cos it's freezing outside – it'll soon be Easter, you know. Happy Easter, Mickey. Happy Easter.'

She became aware of the letter lying on the table under her hand. She picked it up and peered closely at the postmark. She couldn't be certain without her spectacles, but it looked like Macclesfield and her heart lifted. So Stanley had written back after all.

'Dear Auntie,' he wrote in his big, sprawling hand, 'thank you for your letter. Sorry I haven't written back earlier but we've been very busy.' A pity he didn't say what they'd been doing; she'd have loved to hear how they passed their days, he and that pretty Carole. With no children to see to; did they play golf or tennis, or did they perhaps go abroad for their holidays like so many young couples nowadays? She read on to the next paragraph:

'I think it's a very good idea to make a will as you mentioned. It simplifies all the messy procedure, not to mention the expense, of probate. It also avoids any possible argument, though I think I'm right in saying I'm actually your only living relative now, aren't I?'

You are, lad, you are, and well you know it, she thought sadly. All my family gone before me, and all my Alf's too. If only we'd had children of our own I wouldn't need to set so much store by you, Stanley. I haven't even set eyes on you since I gave you my Royal Albert dinner service when you got wed.

'It's very easy to make a will,' the letter went on. 'You could, as you say, write your own on a will form and get someone to witness it, but it's better to get it done legally. You don't have to feel embarrassed. Just go along to a solicitor and he'll sort it all out for you. Just tell him what you want and he'll do the rest. It needn't cost very much.'

Mrs Clancy refolded the letter, laid it aside and rose weakly to go to the scullery. It took the mention of my will to make you write to me, did it, Stanley?

A mist was swimming before her eyes as she filled the kettle. She felt strangely weak today, as if someone was syphoning the lifeblood out of her. She'd never felt so vulnerable.

Or so desperately alone.

Reluctantly Lucy peeled off the nurse's uniform and tugged on the teddy-bear pyjamas. She looked up anxiously into her father's eyes.

'Will you read me a story tonight, Daddy?'

She saw the crinkles at the corners of his eyes deepen and knew she'd won. 'Not tonight,' he replied, and her heart sank, 'only you hop into bed, lovey,' he went on, 'and see what I've got for you.'

She scrambled eagerly into bed and pulled the covers up over her knees. 'I'm ready, Daddy. What is it?'

She watched, wide-eyed, as he took his hands out from behind his back and held out a package. 'This is our secret, just between you and me, sweetheart,' he whispered. 'Don't tell your mother.'

She could feel her heart pounding in anticipation as she tore open the brown-paper bag, then she let out a cry of delight.

'It's my book! The one I saw in the shop! Oh, Daddy, thank you!'

He sat down on the edge of the bed beside her. 'So I did get the right one then? Thank goodness for that.'

She let the book fall on her lap and curled her arms about his neck. 'You're the best daddy in the world, and I love you.'

He hugged her close. She could feel the bristles on his chin scraping her cheek. 'Well that's all right then,' he said gruffly, 'only remember, it's our secret, just you and me.'

Lucy was glowing. It was a wonderful conspiracy. To share a private secret with the person you love most in the whole world is terrific, something only the two of them could share.

Spring was clearly on its way. The crocuses were in bloom at last and Dorothy insisted that it was time the garden was tidied up after the winter. Obligingly Theo went out to fork over the patch she'd marked out for her herb garden.

He was lost in his own thoughts when the kitchen door opened. Dorothy came striding down the path towards him.

'What's this I found in Lucy's cupboard?' she demanded.

Theo straightened up. She was holding out the first-aid book at arm's length as though it might infect her fingers.

'Oh, that,' he said, slamming the fork into the earth once more. 'Yes, I thought it might be a good idea, seeing as Lucy's got her heart set on nursing. It's not a bad way to start.'

Dorothy tucked the book under her arm. 'Well really, Theo,' she exclaimed, 'are you determined to undermine my authority? After I told her she couldn't have it? How do you expect me to control that child if you give in to her all the time?'

'Like I said,' replied Theo, not pausing in his digging, 'if she's going to be a nurse—'

With a click of the tongue, Dorothy cut in. 'We'll see about that,' she muttered. 'She can do better than nursing if she's to be a credit to us, so I'd be obliged if you didn't go encouraging her like that.'

'If it's what she's got her heart set on—' Theo began.

'Never mind what she wants!' stormed Dorothy. 'I'm not having that child override me just because she knows she can twist you round her little finger. The cunning little minx, she knows how to play the weaker one off against the other, but she won't win, I'll see to it that she doesn't.'

'She knew nothing about ...' He began. But Dorothy stamped away up the path and Theo sighed. Two strong-minded women in the same house; one day the sparks would be sure to fly between those two.

Mrs Clancy lay in bed listening to the distant peal of the church bells. Sunday morning, it must be, for the only other time the bells could be heard was on a Wednesday evening when they did their practice.

Sunday morning. She ought to be up and about by now,

147

pinning on her Sunday-best hat to go to church. She'd never missed since Alf passed away, only that time she had shingles. Nasty, that was, but she'd hardly ever felt poorly since.

Not till now, that was, and even now it wasn't so much feeling poorly as feeling dead-beat. Not an ounce of strength left in her. Well, maybe just for once she'd allow herself the luxury of a lie-in. There was nothing that had to be done today. Thank goodness she'd got that trip to the solicitor's over and done with.

She had toyed with the idea of going to Holyoak, Brett and Fenton, just because of that nice Mrs Holyoak who came now and again, but she'd thought better of it. By all accounts Mr Holyoak was a fearsome man to deal with and that Mr Smythe in the high street had been very pleasant and helpful so that was all right. The will business was all sorted out now, so Stanley should have no problems.

I'm glad. I don't want to think about that any more. I don't want to think about anything. Funny how your brain can get tired out too. Even lying down here I feel proper whacked.

What was that? She lifted her head to listen. Mickey – of course – he hadn't been fed yet. He'd need his seed topping up and fresh water in his little bowl too. Oh dearie me, there was nothing else for it. She'd have to go down and see to the little fellow, then she could sleep.

Easing herself out of bed and pulling on the sleeves of her dressing-gown had never been so strenuous, but she struggled to do it, then made her way slowly down the stairs, clinging to the banister. By the time she reached the hallway her heart was pounding in her chest and the blood was roaring in her ears. For a moment she had to stand still, leaning against the door jamb, until she could fight off the rising waves of dizziness.

At last she levered herself upright and felt her way into the living-room. The dizziness was coming back, swamping her; she clutched at the table, felt the chenille cover slip away in her hand. She couldn't breathe; she sank to the floor, struggling to draw breath, but her lungs seemed to have no power to work. Terror seized her as the blackness closed in around her ...

There was no sound now in the room but the gentle peal of distant bells and a bird chattering to himself in his cage.

'What are we going to do with you, eh? What are we going to do with you?'

On Monday morning Rosa could not get to the doctor's surgery fast enough. Today, he'd said, he'd have the results of the tests from the infirmary. She let herself in through the iron gate and walked quickly up the gravel drive, round the back of the big house to the lean-to surgery built on at the rear.

'Doctor's ready for you,' said the nurse.

Rosa could feel her heart fluttering as she walked through the carpeted passage into his office. The doctor waved to her to sit down, then glanced through a letter in his hand. Rosa took a deep breath, waiting for him to speak.

'Well, it's good news, Mrs Pearson,' he said cheerfully. 'They could find nothing wrong at all. There's no reason why you shouldn't have more children, no reason at all.'

Rosa looked up at him dubiously. 'What are you saying, doctor? That it isn't my fault?'

'Exactly, my dear,' he replied amiably. 'As I thought, you're in perfect working order. If you haven't conceived in six years, then if the trouble doesn't lie with you, it must be your husband.'

'Oh Lord!' she whispered. 'What am I to do?'

'Don't worry,' the doctor said in a reassuring tone, 'that's not the end of it. We can do more tests. It's possible we can help him. It may be that he simply has a blocked tube, though I must warn you, it's equally possible he could have a low sperm count, in which case he could never father a child.'

The words plunged ice into Rosa's heart. She gazed up at the doctor's kindly face.

'But let's look on the bright side,' he went on. 'Would you like to ask your husband to come and see me?'

'I don't know,' she muttered. 'If you think there's a chance ...'

The doctor shrugged. 'I can promise nothing. All I can tell you for certain is that it's not you who's infertile, my dear. It's your husband.'

'Not you who's infertile – it's your husband.'

All the way home the words hammered in Rosa's brain. How could she possibly break the news to Dan? She could visualize his face now, the blank stare of incomprehension, then the haunted look of despair.

He would never agree to tests to prove his virility. He wouldn't have it questioned. His manhood meant so much to him – the men he worked with looked up to his superior size and strength. He wouldn't be proof against the insults they might hurl at him if ever they found out.

'He fires blank bullets ... no lead in his pencil.'

Oh no, he couldn't bear that! He'd never be able to cope with the disappointment, to live with what he saw as his failure. Oh God, what on earth was she to do?

Chapter Thirteen

Dorothy Challis felt good as she presided over her Sunday tea table. With her new bouffant hairdo and her full-skirted pearl-grey linen dress matched with the new pearl stud ear-rings she felt as crisp and attractive as any of the model housewives in the television adverts.

She surveyed the room proudly, the pale spring sunlight enhancing the high polish on the furniture, the gleaming brasses and ornaments she'd shone up so lovingly. Her gaze came to rest on the pretty tablecloth she'd embroidered herself in her early married days and which had been such a talking point that time the Guild committee meeting had taken place in her home. She recalled how she'd revelled in their admiring compliments with a dimpling show of modest pleasure.

'You did this yourself, Mrs Challis? My, how clever you are with a needle, such intricate stitches.'

Theo looked a little tired, she thought. Ignoring Graham's outstretched hand she passed the plate of home-made cakes to her husband.

'Your first choice, Theo. Do try one of my sponge cakes with angelica on.'

'No thanks, dear,' he replied mildly. 'Maybe later I'll have a slice of fruit cake.'

Disappointed, she offered the plate to Graham. He had

no hesitation in selecting the largest cake. Then she turned to Lucy, and frowned.

'Sit up straight, for heaven's sake,' she reprimanded the child. 'In my grandmother's day her mother used to make her sit with a poker down the back of her frock to keep her straight. Maybe I should do the same with you.'

The girl looked up at her with wide unblinking eyes and made no move to take a cake. Dorothy put the plate down. Very well, miss, she thought. You can do without. I'll have no dumb insolence from you.

She smiled at her husband. 'Theo, don't you think it would be a nice idea to invite the Blakes to a little dinner party one evening? And maybe that couple we met at their house? I've got a wonderful new recipe I could do, and you might be able to pick up some business from him.'

Theo looked surprised. 'Business?' he repeated. 'I don't need any more business.'

She shook her head reprovingly. 'Tut-tut. I can remember when you had to beg for work. Never look a gift horse in the mouth.'

'That was years ago. Right now I've got as much as I can handle with local authority work. Anyway, I thought I heard them say they were going to invite us.'

Dorothy smoothed out her napkin. 'I know, but I think I'd prefer to ask them here first.'

He looked baffled. 'But why?'

She shrugged. 'Well, that way I can set the lead. If I do my *coq au vin* it'll be up to them to try and match up, won't it?'

'I see.' She could swear there was a hint of a smile on Theo's lips. He knew how much it meant to her, maintaining her reputation for *haute cuisine*. She'd seen the *coq au vin* on television, before the Cradocks took over and started doing their ambitious roast sucking pig menus. That was going a little over the top.

152

Graham looked sweet in his new pullover. She watched Lucy thoughtfully as she stirred sugar into her second cup of tea. She looked almost angelic with her pink frock and shiny blond hair. Maybe she could be a little more generous about spending time on the girl. After all, she'd spent nearly two hours helping Graham with his jigsaw this afternoon. Maybe she could teach the girl some basic cookery.

She smiled brightly across the table. 'How would you like to make some jam tarts with me, Lucy? We'll have to scrub your hands clean, of course, or we'll end up with grey pastry, and we don't want that, do we?'

Three pairs of eyes stared at her. She turned to her husband. 'Well,' she said defensively, 'cooking's a useful skill for a girl. She can only catch a husband if she can cook.' She saw Theo's eyes widen. 'I mean, just look at the adverts on television,' she argued. '"Oxo gives a meal man-appeal." Appeal to a man – that's what it's all about.'

'No thank you,' said Lucy quietly.

Dorothy turned to her. 'What?'

The child looked her straight in the eye. 'No thanks. I don't want to make jam tarts with you. Or anything else.'

Dorothy stared in amazement. Theo cleared his throat. 'Talking of cooking, dear, those herbs you want planted, the ground is ready now if you'll just tell me what you want to put in. Sage, was it, or mint?'

With a click of the tongue she rose at once to fetch paper and pencil. If she didn't write it all down for him he'd be sure to get it wrong.

Dan came in from the yard, his hair spattered with flecks of white. He'd been whitewashing the outside privy he now used as a store shed. Rosa held up the teapot invitingly.

'Cuppa?'

153

He dropped the pail on the scullery floor and came to her, taking hold of her by the shoulders.

'What is it, lass?' he said quietly. 'Something's bugging you, I know.'

She looked up into his grey eyes and found it hard to hold his candid gaze. 'Whatever makes you think that?' she said lightly, trying to break away. 'Don't let that tea go cold.'

He was having none of it. His grip tightened on her shoulders. 'Never mind the tea – tell me what's on your mind. You've been funny ever since I got home. Is it money?'

She shook her head. 'I wish it was. I could sort that out.'

'Well what then? Tell me.' She could hear the irritation in his tone. She'd put it off long enough; it was no use trying to keep it from him any longer.

'I went to see the doctor,' she said quietly. 'I had some tests.'

She knew the moment she'd spoken that she'd put it badly, for she saw the alarm which leapt into his eyes. 'No – there's nothing wrong,' she blurted. 'I'm not ill.'

'Then what, for God's sake? Why did you go?'

She prised his fingers gently away, searching for the words. 'About the baby, Dan. To see why we haven't got one.'

He sank down on the kitchen chair, silent for a moment, then he began easing off his boots. 'I see. What did he say?' he murmured.

She took a deep breath. 'He said it wasn't to be, but it wasn't the end of the world if a couple—' She broke off momentarily. She'd been about to say 'were infertile' but the word seemed too harsh. 'If a couple are childless,' she hurried on.

154

Dan snorted, his head still bowed. 'Not to him, maybe. He's probably got a few.'

She touched a finger to his shoulder. 'Does it mean that much to you, Dan?'

He looked up into her eyes and she could see the depths of emptiness there. 'A man should have a family,' he muttered. 'It's what he goes out to work for, to look after and provide for.' He glanced back at the big deal table behind him. 'If you knew how often I've seen 'em in me head, all sitting round this table ...'

She could swear his eyes were misting with tears. 'There's other things to work for, Dan,' she said urgently. 'We'll find other things; we'll make plans. We won't let it be the end of the world. Here, drink your tea.'

Dan sighed wearily and took the mug. 'Did he say what was wrong, why we haven't had a baby?' he asked.

This was it, the moment she'd been dreading. Rosa refilled her own mug and sat down. 'Yes,' she said quietly, crossing her fingers behind her back. 'It's me; I can't. It's my fault.'

May God forgive me for the lie, but it's meant well. For a time Dan sat silent. All Rosa could hear was the slow tick of the clock on the mantelpiece. Then Dan looked up, his grey eyes filled with sadness.

'You know, lass, I wish you hadn't gone,' he murmured. 'While we knew nowt we could still go on hoping. As it is ...'

Something plummeted in Rosa's stomach. She'd done the wrong thing after all. She hadn't been able to spare him pain. Then he reached over and took her hand.

'It doesn't matter, love,' he said gruffly. 'We've got each other, and that's all that matters.'

Rosa felt empty. He'd said the right words, but somehow they had a hollow ring ...

* * *

Greta Holyoak felt flustered and ill at ease. If there was one thing she always tried to avoid it was open antagonism, and yet the management committee's meeting this morning at Wood Lea had been nothing short of open warfare.

The other committee members had had their knives in Matron for some time now because of her resistance to their wishes, but Greta hadn't expected them to come out so blatantly hostile as they did today. She'd tried her level best to smooth things over, trying to play the mediator, and it would have been a very delicate balancing act if she could have pulled it off.

As it was, they had rounded on her, insinuating that she'd been implicated in some kind of shady conspiracy with Matron, and their angry accusing tone had bewildered her.

'What are you saying?' she'd asked. 'I don't know what you're talking about.'

'You deny knowing what was going on? You worked closely with Matron on a daily basis, and you expect us to believe she got away with it for all these years without your ever beginning to suspect?'

'Suspect what?' Her knees had trembled. Whatever it was, she resented the imputation against her integrity.

They'd shown her a letter. 'And this is not the only complaint. We've come to learn of many more such incidents.'

Matron, it seemed, had been taking money from adoptive parents for years in return for finding a child for them. Greta had sworn she knew nothing, and gradually they'd quietened.

'Though you must admit it does seem odd that you sometimes gave money to these girls,' they said ... 'Matron told us so.'

'From my own pocket, I assure you – I felt sorry for them.'

In the end she'd managed to convince them, but whether it was through her shining transparent honesty or because Reginald Holyoak was a powerful and potentially dangerous man, she'd never know.

They'd called in Matron then and given her a summary dismissal. She'd blustered, but she didn't argue for long. It wasn't easy for her to explain away the gleaming new car outside in the drive, not when the committee knew exactly what salary she earned.

So Matron was now packing her bags, and, since the committee had invited Greta to be a member of the interviewing panel to choose her successor, it seemed that they were prepared to soldier on as before.

Still, the morning's turmoil had left its mark and Greta felt drained. She needed a little peace, alone, to think over calmly what had come to light, to get over the anger that had seethed in her when she realized how that wily woman had been exploiting those poor girls. As much as £200 they said she'd taken for a baby! And to think she'd been doing it all this time, slyly, right under Greta's nose! Instant dismissal was too lenient a punishment for a woman like her, but the committee might yet institute proceedings. And what about all those girls who'd unwittingly sold their babies ...

The peace of Mrs Clancy's for an hour – that's what she needed in order to unwind.

Greta picked her way with care across the cobbles of Jubilee Terrace until she reached the safety of the flagged pavement. Her heels weren't exactly high but high enough to cause her ankles to go over on the uneven surface. The Lord alone knew how the young women of today coped with cobblestones in those pencil-slim stiletto heels.

As she neared the door of number seven she dipped into her handbag for the key. She was just fitting it into the lock when the door suddenly opened, and a young man in a grey overcoat stopped as he was about to step out.

'Good afternoon,' he said with a polite smile. 'Can I help you?'

She felt confused. This was the right house, wasn't it? 'I was just going in,' she said. 'I have a room here.'

'Ah yes,' he said. 'Mrs Holyoak, isn't it? Mr Mellor told me about you. Do come in for a moment.'

For a moment? Mr Mellor? Greta followed the young man into Mrs Clancy's living-room. Despite the spring sunshine filtering in through the lace-curtained window the room was cold. The fire was unlit and the air held a dank musty smell of disuse. A budgerigar chirped spasmodically in a cage in the corner, but there was no sign of Mrs Clancy.

'What's happening?' she asked the young man. He peeled off his gloves and laid them on the table.

'You don't know, do you?' he said quietly. 'Mrs Clancy has passed away. The house now belongs to her nephew, Mr Mellor, and he's asked my firm to put it on the market.'

Mrs Clancy dead? Greta sank on the chair. 'Oh dear, I'm so sorry,' she murmured. 'Such a kind lady.'

'I'm sure,' said the young man, 'but you can see Mr Mellor's position. If the house is to be put up for sale, it must be with vacant possession and, of course, your contract was with Mrs Clancy, not Mr Mellor.'

'Merry Christmas,' squawked the bird. 'What are we going to do with you?'

'Of course, I understand.'

'So if you have any of your possessions in the house it would be wise to remove them as soon as possible so I can complete the inventory. We've been given instructions to

158

auction all of the deceased's furniture and effects. Everything is to be sold – unless the new owner wishes to purchase any of them which, in view of their age, is very unlikely.'

'I suppose so,' murmured Greta.

'Except the bird,' he said, jerking a thumb towards the cage. 'A neighbour has been feeding it but it will be sent to the RSPCA to find it a new home.'

Greta sat, head bowed. It was hard to assimilate: Mrs Clancy gone; an unknown nephew, the new owner, anxious to get rid of everything that remained of the old lady. It was cruel. But the hardest prospect was her own loss; the privacy and peace of that little room were gone for ever. It didn't bear thinking about.

'How much?' she asked quietly.

The young man looked startled. 'I beg your pardon?'

'How much is Mr Mellor asking for the house?'

She saw the flicker of surprise on his young face, swiftly replaced by a veiled look of caution. 'Well, we're recommending fifteen hundred,' he said tentatively, and then hurried on in a brisk professional manner.

'After all, there may be cheaper houses to be found in this neighbourhood,' he admitted grandly, 'but this fine little house does have the benefit of a small back garden, not a yard, and it has an indoor bathroom, not to mention a large loft which is ripe for conversion, if need be, for family occupation—'

Greta was no longer listening. Fifteen hundred. There was more than enough in her private account. Throughout all the years of their marriage Reginald had always been generous with the monthly allowance he made her.

'Call it a dress allowance or what you will, but it's very important to me that my wife always appears well-dressed, well-shod and with your hair and nails immaculate. Money's no object – just see to it that no-one can ever find fault.'

She looked up. 'I'll have it,' she said.

The young man stared. 'Excuse me? Did you say—'

'I'll have it,' she repeated firmly. She watched his expression change slowly to delight. He could never have made an easier sale in the whole of his short career.

'Subject to survey, I take it?' he murmured.

'Of course. Now would you like to tell me the name of your firm?'

Rosa sat on the edge of the bed, peeling off her stockings. Dan was already in bed, his hands curled behind his head.

'Dan, we ought to talk about plans for the future,' she began. 'We agreed we need more money—'

'No,' he said briefly. She looked round to see his expression.

'You don't know what I was going to say.'

'I don't want you going out to work. I'm the bread-winner.'

She could see by the firm set of his lips that he meant it. 'OK,' she agreed as she climbed into bed, 'so let's make other plans. What about you going into business on your own?'

He stared at her in blank amazement. 'Me, set up on me own? You're joking. You know what they say about Yorkshiremen, born and bred – strong in t'arm and weak in t'head.'

'Your brother did,' she pointed out. 'Kitty and he plunged all their savings into that lorry and just look at them now.'

Dan groaned. 'Aye, Ted's always had more guts than sense. He could have lost the lot.'

'But he didn't, that's the point. It's getting to be a good haulage firm now. They're far better off than when he was in the mill.'

'Being me own boss isn't for me, Rosa. What the devil could I do?'

He sounded defeated already. She shrugged. 'General building work – you can turn your hand to anything. If you had a little van—'

'I'm a road-digger,' he retorted. 'Digging's all I'm qualified for. Oh, I can drive a JCB, but that's it. Builder indeed!'

'I meant general property repairs; fences, drains, plastering, that sort of thing. And you're a damn good bricklayer.'

He made no comment. Another idea struck her. 'What about woodwork?' she urged. 'You've made some great stuff for us.'

'You're talking tripe,' he said irritably, rolling over to switch off the light. 'What would I want with being boss of my own business, with all them books to keep and all? You know me – I won't write a letter unless I'm forced to. I'd never keep on top of the paperwork, let alone the work itself.'

She snuggled up against his broad back. 'I'd help you, Dan,' she said persuasively. 'I'd enjoy being your partner.'

She felt his back stiffen against her touch and knew it was no use. 'Well what about asking Ted to take you in with him?' she whispered in a last attempt. 'That'd be something.'

'Can you see me collecting me wage packet off me own brother of a Friday night?' he growled. 'Nay, a man's got his pride. Now leave me be, Rosa lass. You go ahead and run summat if you like, but leave me in peace.'

For a time she lay silent in the darkness. It was useless; he'd never take on the responsibility. He had no aspiration, no desire to get on. It was as if the disappointment over the baby had finally robbed him of any last vestige of ambition he'd ever had. It wasn't fair to push him beyond the limits of his capability, but on the other hand she couldn't let it rest there.

'Then I'll have to think of something else,' she whispered. 'I'll find something.'

His only answer was a groaning sound, halfway between assent and a snore.

Chapter Fourteen

Greta Holyoak could hardly contain her excitement as the secretary led her in through the door marked 'Edwin Smythe, senior partner'.

The tall, balding man behind the desk took off his gold-rimmed spectacles as he rose. 'Good morning,' he said genially, indicating the chair opposite. 'Do sit down.'

Greta took a seat and waited until the secretary had closed the door behind her. Mr Smythe sat down and took up the papers in front of him. 'Mrs Holyoak,' he said pensively. 'Are you by any chance related to—'

'Reginald Holyoak – I'm his wife,' said Greta quietly. 'And that's why I need to ask you – will you keep my business confidential? I do not wish to involve my husband in the matter I've come to see you about.'

She saw his eyebrows arch, but he smiled. 'Of course, provided the matter does not affect him. If it were a personal matter, such as separation or divorce—'

'It's nothing like that.' She cut in. 'I want to buy a house.'

'I see.' He drew a sheet of paper towards him and took out a gold-tipped fountain-pen from his inside pocket. 'Then you'd better give me some details. Address?'

'Number seven, Jubilee Terrace, Lockwood.'

* * *

It had afforded her infinite pleasure just to say the words, thought Greta as she headed for home. It made her feel as if the house were already hers, and she revelled in the proprietorial feeling. And now she'd been assured that Reginald need never know, she could hug the wonderful secret to herself.

Not that Jubilee Terrace was hers yet. In her ignorance of such dealings she'd believed it would be only a matter of handing over the money and taking possession of the deeds, but Mr Smythe said it would take a few weeks.

'There are certain legal aspects to look into,' he said, 'before the conveyance can be completed, but it should prove quite straightforward.'

He hadn't seemed at all curious about why a woman married to a well-known and well-to-do solicitor should want to buy a humble little house in the poorer part of Hawksmoor. But then, perhaps he already knew that Holyoak's wife was involved in charity work and the purchase could have something to do with that. At any rate, he'd asked no awkward questions.

She was going to have that house, come what may. Just as it was.

'I understand the vendors are prepared to auction or sell off the whole of the contents at a nominal sum,' she'd told Mr Smythe as he showed her to the door. 'Please make an offer for the lot.'

The solicitor smiled as he shook her hand. 'I think at this price they may well be willing to include the furniture. Just leave it to me. I'll ring you when there's any news.'

'Oh no! Don't telephone!' she said in alarm. 'Write – it's safer that way.'

Theo sat absently munching his toast while he read the morning paper. He'd already heard the main items of the day's news upstairs on the transistor radio while he was shaving, but it was good to read it in more detail in the *Yorkshire Post* ...

Around him the normal activity of a weekday went on. Dorothy was spreading honey on Graham's slice of wholemeal bread. Lucy, looking as neat and appealing as a chorister in her school uniform, was chomping cornflakes with enthusiasm.

'Don't make so much noise when you eat,' Dorothy reprimanded her. 'It's not ladylike.'

The child looked up with a frown. 'I can't help it. Cornflakes are noisy.'

'Don't answer back,' said Dorothy primly. 'Just do as I say.'

'Good gracious!' exclaimed Theo. 'Have a look at this.'

He handed the newspaper over to his wife. She licked sticky fingers and dried them on her apron before taking the paper. She peered at the column he indicated, then drew in her breath sharply.

'Seafield Junior School,' she whispered. 'Why, that's—'

Theo wagged an admonitory finger and she read on in silence. There was a hollow look in her eyes as she handed back the newspaper.

'I think I met that Mrs Bamforth once at the uniform sale,' she murmured. 'Poor woman.'

Too late she realized her mistake and her fingers flew to her lips. Lucy looked up with a smile.

'Atkins, Bamforth, Brook, Challis, Dickinson ...' she chanted. 'We've got a Clare Bamforth in our class. The others don't play with her 'cos they say she cheats at sums, but she doesn't. I like her.'

Dorothy busied herself wiping Graham's chin. Theo looked down again at the newspaper.

Clare Bamforth, the nine-year-old girl missing since Monday evening, has not yet been found. She was last seen leaving Seafield Junior School and heading towards Shaw Wood. Police are intensifying the search, extending the area to cover the quarry and ponds. A man is helping ...'

The paper trembled between his fingers and as he lowered it he caught sight of Dorothy's blanched face.

'Teacher missed out Clare Bamforth yesterday,' said Lucy. 'I know because I know the register by heart. Maybe she's gone away.'

Dorothy was still pale as she gathered up the plates. 'Perhaps we'd better keep the children at home,' she muttered through tight lips. 'Take no chances.'

Theo saw Lucy look up hopefully at the prospect of an unexpected holiday. He shook his head. 'No point – they'd have to go in sooner or later,' he remarked. 'Besides, they've got him, it seems.'

'Only a man helping with enquiries, it says,' his wife retorted. 'It's not bound to be him.'

Lucy was singing softly to herself, nodding her head in rhythm to the words. Theo laid the newspaper aside and stroked the thick plait lying over her shoulder.

'I don't think there's any need to worry,' he said reassuringly, 'not so long as someone keeps an eye on them.' He rose from the table. 'Come on, kids, let's be having you. I'll take you in the car today.'

At that moment Graham sneezed, so loudly that his whole body convulsed. Dorothy seized hold of his shoulder.

'Listen,' she said anxiously, 'he seems to be coming down with a cold. Maybe he should stay home today.'

Theo shook his head. 'That's not like you,' he murmured; 'giving in.'

Dorothy reddened. 'I'm not giving in,' she protested. 'You know how colds play havoc with his chest. No, it's bed with hot lemon and honey for him. Lucy can tell his teacher. Go and get your coat on, Lucy.'

'Spivey, Turner, Wallace, Wood,' the child chanted, and scampered out into the hall. Theo hesitated in the doorway.

'What about teatime?' he asked.

Dorothy frowned. 'What about it?'

'Fetching Lucy home. I don't finish till five-thirty.'

Dorothy shrugged. 'I suppose I could ring and ask Mrs Wallace, though I don't know her terribly well ...'

'Do,' said Theo tersely as he closed the door, 'Like you said, take no chances.'

Theo drew up at the school gate and turned to Lucy.

'Now promise me you'll wait for Mrs Wallace at teatime,' he said gravely as he reached across to open her door.

'I will, Daddy.'

'Nobody else, mind you, not unless you know them.'

'Promise. Cross my heart and hope to die.'

He watched her skip away across the school yard, fingering the warm damp kiss on his cheek. She was wonderful, this child, all that a man could wish for. Bright, enquiring, curious about everything. That trusting look in her wide eyes could melt your heart, yet at the same time she could appear far more knowing and worldly-wise than many a grown woman.

Maybe that was what Dorothy saw at times and distrusted. Maybe she sensed a threat; something had to account for the way she clearly favoured Graham. At one time he'd put it down to the fact that the boy was their own flesh and blood, but that didn't make sense. She'd idolized Lucy as a baby, the godsend come to fill a gaping hole in their otherwise perfect life. And she hadn't suddenly put

167

the child aside when Graham came along two years later. It had been a slow and imperceptible change, so subtle he hadn't become aware of it until recently.

But it was undeniably there, a kind of prickling resentment of all the child did and said. Nothing pleased Dorothy any more. But how could he broach the subject without putting her back up? He could visualize her now, her back stiff and her face indignant.

It ought to be aired, but he doubted whether he would ever do it. Was it worth the contention which would inevitably follow, the accusation that he obviously favoured Lucy over his son.

Peace at any price? Well, not exactly, perhaps. He could, from time to time, gently point out when he felt that Dorothy was being unfair to the girl. In her own quiet way, bless her, Lucy tried so hard to please. But she might not always be so amenable. Beneath that quiet exterior lay a hint of latent fire. God knew what genes she'd inherited. Maybe one day that fire would erupt if Dorothy pushed too far.

Theo swung the car off the road into the muddy entrance to the site. Through the windscreen he could see the foreman waiting on the steps of the site office, clipboard in hand. By his stance Theo could guess the reason; the eagle-eyed architect was querying the plans again. Not following the fine detail of the specification. What had he spotted this time? Was it the aggregate, or maybe the wall ties? The fellow couldn't seem to grasp that sometimes substitutions had to be made according to the circumstances. Flexibility, that was the keynote. What did Maitland and his cronies know about it? Blooming architects, locked away in their ivory tower blocks – it took a man with his years of experience out there in the field, to recognize that sometimes prudent compromise was the only sensible solution.

Theo sighed and stepped out into the squelching mud, all thoughts of Lucy and his wife forgotten.

Greta Holyoak couldn't wait to wave her husband off to work. The letter in her pocket, the one she had not laid before Reginald at breakfast, was burning a hole in her apron pocket. Addressed to her in neat typescript, it had to be from the solicitor.

Her hand trembled as she tore it open and scanned the contents.

... search reveals that there is a tentative plan at present under consideration by the Planning Committee to redevelop that area of Lockwood bordered to the north by Mafeking Street ...

Mafeking Street – where she'd been born and reared. Biting her lip, Greta read on.

... which would, of course, include the property you are proposing to purchase in Jubilee Terrace. Until such time as the committee reaches its decision it would clearly be unwise to continue with this matter ...

Oh no! She sank onto the dining chair. Could they really do what Mr Smythe said, compulsory purchase, forcing people out of their homes whether they wanted it or not? It was too cruel, doubly cruel to see her dream shattered like this!

But the decision had not yet been made, he said. Planning? Reginald was chairman of that committee. He must know about the scheme – maybe he could influence the vote. But why should he? He knew nothing of its significance for her. And even if he did, he'd probably only laugh.

She poured out a cup of lukewarm tea and sipped it dejectedly. Such plans she'd had: put in a tenant to keep the place warm and aired, a nice young family, perhaps, who would leave the little bedroom free for her, but perhaps it was too late. Like so much of old Hawksmoor, the cramped rows of old cottages might soon be pulled down to make way for new tower blocks. There was nothing she could do to influence the committee's ruling.

With a sigh she stood up. She'd make one last sentimental journey to her old stamping ground. And in the meantime she'd keep her eyes and ears open.

Dorothy Challis hugged the telephone close to her ear, twitching with excitement.

'You must have heard,' she said breathlessly. 'It was in the paper. No? Well it seems the poor child hasn't been seen since she left school on Monday. They've got a man in for questioning, but they haven't found the child yet. I mean, two nights now ...'

It was gratifying to hear the gasp at the other end of the line. 'So you see why it's important to pick the children up,' she went on. 'I'll take my turn tomorrow if you could manage today. I don't know whether we can count on Mrs Finch to take her turn ...'

It was even more gratifying to hear Mrs Wallace's opinion of Mrs Finch, which, surprisingly, was not dissimilar to her own. And if the conversation led on for the next twenty minutes to a mutual agreement over the failings of the school and other parents, it did no harm. In fact, she thought as she went to fetch the duster and polish, it was rather pleasant to find another woman of discernment.

Even while Greta tried to balance the accounts with Wood Lea's new matron she couldn't get the house out of her mind.

Whatever she was doing, images of drab Lockwood streets kept intervening, disrupting her thoughts.

Dammit, she thought as Matron closed the ledgers and stowed them away in the cupboard, if the area was to be demolished, she'd promised herself one last bout of nostalgia, walking the streets of her childhood, indulging in bitter-sweet memories. One day soon, before the demolition men moved in.

Today, she thought – why not? Spring sunshine lay soft over the valley; even smoke-grimed Lockwood would be enhanced by its balmy warmth.

She shook hands with Matron at the front door. 'I'll see you on Tuesday,' she said, then turned to set off down the drive. Today Greta Holyoak would go in search of the young Greta Kaye for whom life had once spread out a glorious vista of hopes and dreams.

Rosa emerged from the indoor market into the sunlit square outside the library. It had taken time to find the material she wanted for the new cushion covers, not like the old market they'd pulled down and where she'd known exactly where to find everything.

This passion for new was all very well, but it saddened her to see all the old Victorian buildings with their wrought iron and cosy familiarity disappear. It was as if Victorian meant worn out and useless, but that old market would have stood for years yet. Like Dan said, they knew how to build in those days.

She shifted the heavy shopping bag to the other hand as she made her way uphill towards the high street. So OK, maybe Hawksmoor wasn't her native town, but she'd grown fond of the place over the years, familiar with its stolid strength and the gritty resoluteness of its inhabitants. She felt at home here, and felt a proprietorial pride in the town. Just don't let those planners rob it of its distinctive personality.

She paused at the entrance to one of the old arcades they hadn't yet touched, and on an impulse turned into the wrought-iron entrance. Overhead a vast glass dome arched over a parade of small shops and the spring sunlight falling through its dusty panes steeped the arcade in suffused light, enhancing the warmth of the old mahogany window-frames and glinting on the brass fittings.

Neglected it might be, but the sheer unheeded beauty of the place took her breath away. Few people evidently came in here for many of the little shops had blanked-out windows or gaping voids with only dust and dead flies on display. One shop, however, stood out, a green-glossed frontage bearing the words 'A. Kadinski, Grocery and Provisions' picked out in white.

She still needed cheese. Why not buy it here? It might be a bit dearer than elsewhere, but she had an urge to buy in this quaintly gracious oasis.

The doorhandle had a satisfyingly solid feel and the bell tinkled softly as she went inside.

The memories were crowding in on Greta as she walked past Victoria Street's huddled houses towards Mafeking Street. She could see them still, the old neighbours who'd always been there in a crisis, the tallyman calling of a Friday night for his dues while Dad's wage packet was still intact. There'd always been creditors, the debt-collectors, the shopkeepers who wouldn't let the slate run up any higher. Life for her parents, God rest them, had seemed to consist largely of juggling money to keep afloat. It had become easier for them when first Hilda and then she herself had started work, but the habits ingrained in her from her earliest days had stayed with her always. Even now, in the days of financial comfort, she couldn't help being a saver rather than a spender.

She paused by the viaduct as another memory leapt into her mind: Hilda. How she'd hated her sister when she found her here, under the shadow of this arch, kissing Bob Berry. To have your first boyfriend stolen away by a scheming flirt of a sister had been heartbreaking. She'd been forced to lie next to Hilda in the back bedroom, feeling the hatred and anger spill over against the figure lying next to her in the double bed. Hilda hadn't even wanted Bob Berry; she'd gone off with that fair-haired Terry from Millsbridge the very next week and married him a year later.

Greta looked up. From here she could just see the house. Twenty Mafeking Street. The house which had contained all her hopes and fears for the first twenty years of her life, until she met Reginald Holyoak. She wondered who lived there now, were they happy, and did they know about the planned redevelopment?

A middle-aged woman in an apron sat on a rickety chair outside the house next door, basking in the warm sunshine. It couldn't be young Mrs Tasker who came there as a newly-wed, could it? Greta smiled.

'Good afternoon,' she said politely. The woman looked up, shielding her eyes against the sun.

'Don't I know you from somewhere?' she asked.

Greta spread her hands in apology. 'I don't live round here,' she said, 'though I used to, years ago – at number twenty.'

The woman cocked her head to one side, then nodded. 'It's got to be Greta Kaye 'cos I know Hilda went off to Australia. Well I never, who'd have thought it, and you such a skinny little thing in them days?'

Greta chuckled. 'That's true. I just wanted to have a look at the old place again.' She hesitated. She wondered if the

173

woman knew anything of the plans afoot. She didn't want to alarm her.

'They've made a lot of changes to the town since those days,' she commented. The other woman nodded.

'Aye, and there's talk of them doing summat here and all,' she muttered. 'Folks are saying they want to pull this lot down but I tell you this for nowt – they'll not get me out. They'll have to carry me out feet first.'

Greta nodded towards number twenty. 'Do you know who lives there now?' she asked.

'Course I do. Mrs Kadinski and her son.'

'Do you know her well?'

'Aye, I do. Her and her husband when he was still living. Known 'em since they came here with their little lad just after the war. Worked in our mill, both of 'em, till they got a bit of brass together and opened the shop. Nice place, that shop, but it's not doing so well these days. Alex hasn't much of a head for business, not like his dad.'

'That's the son?' said Greta.

'Lovely lad is Alex. Can't figure why he never has a girlfriend, good-looking fellow like him.' The woman raised a finger. 'Eh, it's coming back to me now – you was the one married yon lawyer fellow, didn't you, him as is a councillor? They say he might be mayor soon.'

'Well yes,' Greta admitted, 'it's possible.'

The woman folded her arms across her chest. 'Well just you tell him from me that while there's breath in my body I'll fight him and all his pals on the council. They'll not shift me.'

'You're right,' agreed Greta. 'There's no reason why you should move.'

The woman nodded grimly. 'Aye, Betty Tasker is staying put. No matter what he might be cogitating, nothing and nobody's going to make me budge from here.'

*   *   *

174

Dorothy flourished the *Examiner* under Theo's nose the minute he came in from work.

'Have you seen this?' she demanded. 'They found her – in Leicester of all places.'

Theo paused, his coat half shrugged off his shoulders. 'Leicester? Who?'

'The Bamforth girl – she'd run away, seemingly, because she'd been told off about something. Did you ever hear the like?'

Theo hung his coat on the hook. 'So she's safe after all,' he murmured. 'That's a blessed relief. Lucy got home all right?'

Dorothy took a clothes brush from the drawer in the hall table and began brushing the sleeves of his coat. 'Mrs Wallace brought her and the *Examiner* at the same time. Nice woman, that Mrs Wallace. I've asked her round for coffee next week.'

She put the brush away and went to stand at the foot of the stairs. 'Come along, children,' she called out. 'Daddy's home.'

Theo could hear feet pattering above as he made his way into the living-room. Dorothy followed him, tut-tutting to herself.

'What a wicked thing to do,' she muttered. 'What a dreadful child that Bamforth girl must be.'

Behind her Theo saw Lucy's face in the doorway. 'Upsetting her parents like that,' Dorothy went on, 'just because she'd been scolded. Wicked, that's what she is, utterly disgraceful.'

'She isn't,' said Lucy quietly, 'she's nice.'

Dorothy shot the child a furious glance. 'Just goes to show how little you know, madam,' she snapped. 'From now on you're to have nothing to do with her, you hear?'

Theo saw the child's face redden and her jaw jut. 'Why not?' she asked. 'She's my friend.'

'Because I say so,' said Dorothy tartly. 'No argument – from now on you'll keep well away from her.'

'I can't,' said Lucy, her solid little body seeming to plant itself more firmly on the carpet. 'You've got to stick by your friends.'

Dorothy's face turned white with anger. 'Upstairs this minute, madam,' she commanded. 'Stay in your room till I tell you.'

For a second the child glared back, then she turned and marched out of the room. As she climbed the stairs Theo could hear her muttering to herself.

'She's my friend and I like her, and I don't care what you say.'

Chapter Fifteen

'... Hawksmoor Town two, Leeds United one.'

'Damn!' Theo's fist thudded the table in vexation. Dorothy looked up from her knitting and cast him a disapproving frown.

'Language, Theo,' she murmured. 'The children ...'

He couldn't help the ripple of irritation. The children were outside in the garden while she sat there placidly, her fingers busily flying through that ever-growing grey mesh.

'A pullover for Graham,' she'd told him last night. 'With his chest he needs warm woollies.'

She was completely ignorant of the importance of this result. United had already been knocked out of the Cup and now their hopes of the League were growing fainter by the minute. They could surely have beaten Hawksmoor, even away.

He'd hear more about this when he went down to the site on Monday morning. The lads who travelled in daily from Hawksmoor knew his obsession with United and they wouldn't be able to resist the temptation to taunt him.

'... Wolverhampton Wanderers three ...'

'Turn that transistor off,' Dorothy cut in, laying aside her knitting. 'I want to put the television on.'

No point listening to the rest anyway. Despondently Theo switched off. He should have been in Hawksmoor to cheer the boys on. He felt disloyal, not being there when they needed every ounce of encouragement they could get.

Next week, he vowed. No work problem on earth would prevent him going down to Elland Road next week. Dorothy would object, of course. She'd say he was putting football before her insistent requests for a utility room.

'Taking off muddy shoes in the kitchen isn't good enough,' she kept saying. 'There's space enough for a nice little extension and I could have the washing-machine out there too. You could do it at weekends.'

All because this Mrs Wallace she'd recently befriended had a utility room. If you didn't have one you were nobody. At that moment he heard the back door open and the children came running in. Dorothy shrieked in alarm.

'Shoes!' she cried as they appeared in the doorway. 'You've got half the garden on them! Just look at the floor!'

Lucy took Graham's hand and led him out to the kitchen. Dorothy flung her husband a scathing look as she stood up.

'See?' she said. 'Utility room.'

Saturday afternoon was the busiest time of the week in Hawksmoor and Rosa had to line up impatiently in the queue for a trolley bus home. She could barely wait to tell Dan about her brainwave.

It had come to her while she was talking to that nice Mr Kadinski in his shop. Such a selection of teas he stocked, every kind from Darjeeling and Assam to Chinese and Earl Grey and even herbal teas. And no less than five different kinds of brown sugar. And his coffees – the mere scent of the beans was enough to drive you mad with yearning for a cup.

Mr Kadinski hadn't been in sight when she first went inside, but he'd evidently heard the bell because he appeared at the top of the cellar steps, shirtsleeved and dusty, carrying a wooden crate. He apologized as he set it down.

'It being quiet, I thought I'd fetch up some stock,' he explained. 'Not many folk come in this late of a Saturday.'

His voice was gentle, she noted, with just a hint of Polish hidden amongst the Yorkshire vowels. She watched him brush the dust off his sleeves, shake out his jacket and pull it on. He'd be about Dan's age, not quite as tall but equally broad in the shoulder and his eyes creased with kindliness at the corners.

'That coffee smells grand,' she'd said shyly. 'You ought to sell cups of it. You'd do a roaring trade.'

He smiled. 'Good idea. You want to do it?'

She looked around. 'You've no space.'

'Happen not,' he agreed, 'but there's upstairs if you fancy it. Same size as here. Now, what can I do for you?'

He'd clearly put the thought aside as a mere pleasantry, but as she stood in the bus queue Rosa couldn't put it from her mind. You could get five, even six small tables in that space. Of course you'd need room for brewing up, but it could be done. If he supplied the teas and coffees, she could specialize, appeal to the connoisseur – she could beat Field's and Silvio's for choice. But what kind of rent would he ask? Could she take enough to pay her way?

Questions burned in her brain, but she must talk it over with Dan before anything else. At last the bus came in to sight.

For once Reginald appeared to be staying in tonight. As she carried dishes into the kitchen to begin the washing-up Greta could hear him in the hallway. He was evidently making a telephone call. She had no intention of eavesdropping but once she heard the words 'Swan Lane redevelopment' she couldn't help stopping to listen. She set the tray down quietly on the kitchen table and went to stand just behind the open door.

'Compulsory purchase orders the minute the resolution's passed,' she heard him say. 'It's high time we got rid of those slums.'

Then he fell silent for a time. His colleague evidently had quite a bit to say. She heard Reginald gasp.

'How did you learn that? ... Are you sure? ... In that case we'd best call a meeting ... No, of course I wasn't offered anything, but that's not the point. I'm not going to let that bastard Metcalf get away with it. Tonight, usual place. The sooner we get this moving the better.'

She heard the receiver slam down and moved quickly back to the sink. Reginald's face was thunderous when he came in.

'Everything all right?' she asked mildly. She knew better than to mention the plans. He glowered at her.

'No, it isn't,' he snapped. 'I'm going out.'

Hands deep in soapsuds, she sighed as she heard the car pull out of the driveway. He wouldn't be back before midnight. Whatever it was this Metcalf fellow had done to anger him, one thing was clear, he was anxious to hurry the Lockwood plan through. And that would mean the end of Jubilee Terrace and Mafeking Street. Even putting aside her own dream, it was a crying shame, dislodging people like Betty Tasker. Those people down there had a right to protest. They ought to organize a petition.

Reginald Holyoak had a good look around the bar of the George Hotel to make sure there were no familiar faces before he went to join the sparse-haired man with a moustache in the corner. He draped his coat over the back of a chair and sat down.

'So where did you hear this about Metcalf?' he asked.

'Hinchliffe,' the other man replied. 'He's always reliable.'

'Should know what he's talking about,' muttered Reginald, 'being in the same firm. He reckons his boss slipped Metcalf a backhander to get his tender accepted?'

'A hefty one too, by all accounts. Soon as it's passed in Planning he's going to get it through Housing. At the moment it seems like an even split so he'll use his casting vote. Drink?'

'Not now. Got to keep a clear head.'

Reginald rubbed his chin. Using his casting vote was no more than he himself had planned to do, but to see that preening bastard Metcalf come out of it with a well-lined pocket was more than flesh and blood could bear. And what was more, the way things were going Metcalf was in the running for mayor like himself.

'Can it be proved?' he asked.

The other man shook his head. 'Doubt it. Hinchliffe's not going to lay his head on the block.'

Reginald sighed. 'Then there's only one answer – we've got to get it turned down at the Planning meeting, that's all there is to it.'

The other man nodded. 'That's what I thought you'd say, although it's not what you intended.'

Reginald gave a dry laugh. 'Adaptability, that's the name of the game. So long as the right decision's made it doesn't matter how or why. Stop the Swan Lane plan and Metcalf's done out of his golden handshake, and that's all that matters.'

'Aye, you're right,' said the other man, rising and picking up his coat. 'After all, the flats is nowt. We've got the big tender for the Tech building next.'

'That's the one I'm banking on,' agreed Reginald. 'Just so long as we get our tender through.'

* * *

Rosa folded the ironing-board, then looked up as Dan came in, and her brow furrowed in concern. His eyes were hollow and weary and he looked as pale as death.

'What is it, love? You look bad.'

He shook his head as he sank onto a chair. 'I been sick, that's all. I'll be OK now.'

She tried not to show too much undue concern; if there was one thing Dan hated, it was fuss. 'Where've you been?' she asked.

'Down the Working Men's Club. Had a couple of games of snooker.'

'And a couple of pints.'

He groaned. 'I reckon that's what did it – beer must have been off.'

'Were any of the others sick?'

'Not as I know of, but that means nowt. They might well be suffering bellyache and all by now.'

Rosa folded the ironed shirts in silence. It wasn't the first time he'd had a bout like this. It couldn't be the dinner he ate before he went out; she'd eaten the same with no ill-effect. If he still felt bad in the morning it might be wise to try and persuade him to go to the doctor's, though she knew full well he'd resist.

'He'll only give me indigestion pills – I can buy them meself at the chemist's,' he always argued. 'It's nowt but a tummy upset. It'll soon be gone.'

'You've had these attacks before,' she said quietly. 'It's got nothing to do with the beer.'

He ran a hand across his forehead. 'Leave it be, lass. I'm all right,' he muttered. 'Now tell me about this idea of yours.'

She told him briefly about Mr Kadinski and the shop and her idea for the tearoom, but somehow the excitement had gone. Dan listened, but his eyes looked far away.

'What do you think?' she asked.

He shrugged. 'If you've got a mind to it, make some enquiries. It won't do any harm looking into it, I reckon.'

'You wouldn't mind?'

'Course not. You do what you want.'

There was no enthusiasm in his tone; he was merely humouring her. Rosa knelt before him.

'You'd help me, though – to strip and rebuild it, I mean?'

He gave a faint smile. 'Course I would. Now how about a nice hot toddy to settle my stomach? You've a drop of whisky left in the cupboard, haven't you?'

She rose, looking down at him with a teasing smile. 'On one condition,' she said firmly: 'you make an appointment tomorrow to see the doctor.'

'Oh Rosa,' he growled.

'I'm serious. No doctor, no whisky.'

He pulled her close. 'That's what comes of marrying an Irish bully,' he chuckled. 'OK, I give in.'

Dorothy Challis smoothed down the pink nylon nightdress over her hips and climbed into bed. Theo was reading one of those dreadful thrillers he'd brought from the library. She'd delay a moment or two before switching off the pink-shaded bedside lamp so that he would have time to admire the new nightie, then she'd return to the attack.

Theo carried on reading. He seemed unaware of the nightie. She cuddled up close to his side.

'You should see the Wallaces' house,' she murmured. 'They must have found a really good builder.'

'Hutchinson,' he murmured. 'He did all that road.'

'No, I mean for the extension,' Dorothy went on. 'It's wonderful. The kitchen's twice as big now, with a breakfast bar too. And the utility room – you should see it.'

183

He sighed as he closed the book, put it down and switched off his lamp. As he settled down she curled her body to fit against his.

'All the shoes get left out there, and the dog's basket.'

'We haven't got a dog.'

Undeterred, she ploughed on. 'There's room, not only for the washing-machine, but all the children's toys and all the clutter that makes the house a mess. And a clothes-line – just think, she can dry her clothes even when it's raining outside. Imagine!'

'Good.'

'Because it's got a glass roof like a conservatory so the sun shines through. Isn't that a wonderful idea?'

'Great.'

'So I was thinking, we could do that. We've got plenty of room to extend – all that paved area. You could do it in no time, I'm sure.'

'Dorothy,' he said in a weary tone, and she knew at once that her silky persuasions had got her nowhere, 'I've already told you. It'd take a lot longer than you think, and what with this new contract for the corporation coming up—'

'But it's already paved,' she persisted. 'It only needs covering in.'

'It's not that easy. It'd need digging out several feet deep to put the footings in, mud and mess everywhere for a week or two at least.'

Mud? Oh no, not that. Not only the children running in and out but muddy-booted workmen too, wanting cups of tea at regular intervals. It was unthinkable.

'Is that the only way?' she asked in a desperate last attempt.

''Fraid so.'

With a sigh she switched off the lamp. So much for the Marks and Spencer nightie.

* * *

Greta was almost asleep when she heard the car. Pulling on a dressing-gown she hurried downstairs. Reginald was just hanging up his coat.

'Reginald, about Swan Lane – Mafeking Street,' she began. He darted her a defensive look.

'What do you know about that?' he demanded.

She reddened. 'I heard you – on the phone ...'

'It's none of your business,' he said tersely. 'You just keep your mouth shut.'

'Of course. It's just that I think it would be a terrible shame to see it demolished. Tower blocks aren't the same.'

'That's why I'm going to oppose it,' he said quietly.

She stared at him, bewildered. 'Oppose it?' she echoed. 'I thought – well, I thought you wanted to pull it all down. I thought—'

He smiled. 'You know where thinking gets you. Well you were wrong. I'm going to fight it tooth and nail, but you mustn't breathe a word, remember?'

'Not a word,' she whispered. 'I'm so glad.' And then a sudden thought crossed her mind and before she knew it she'd spoken the words. 'Reginald – is it for me?'

He frowned. 'For you? How do you mean?'

'Because I was born there. You came courting me there.'

The perplexed look faded from his eyes and even before the laughter began she realized her mistake. By the time he was clutching his sides helplessly, tears forming in his eyes, she was blushing from head to toe in hurt embarrassment.

'You?' he gasped between breathless bouts of laughing, 'What on earth gave you that idea? I'm doing it to spite the Housing chairman, you idiot. Haven't I tried my best all these years to forget you came from the slums?'

Greta shrank back, her fingers to her face. It felt as though he'd slapped her across the cheek. He wiped his eyes.

'As if I'd let silly romantic notions like that get in the way of business,' he chuckled. 'Oh Lord, you'll be the death of me.'

Greta crept back upstairs to the privacy of her room, steaming with rage. How could she have been so stupid, opening herself up to such humiliation? Reginald Holyoak, solicitor or not, mayor-to-be or not, I hate you. You'll portray yourself as the defender of the weak and thereby earn yourself yet more prestige, but it's only to score a point over a political rival on the Council. In fact you don't give a toss for the people of Lockwood, any more than you do for me.

She sat upright in bed, her arms clenched tightly about her knees.

Then suddenly the idea came to her. Maybe she'd tell Reginald at breakfast. Or better still, maybe she wouldn't. This was one battle she'd make sure he won.

Chapter Sixteen

As soon as Reginald had left for the office Greta wasted no time. She dried her hands and picked up the telephone in the hall. It took a few moments before the receptionist put her through.

'Mr Smythe? Good morning,' Greta said confidently. 'I just wanted to let you know that I'm ready to go through with the purchase of seven Jubilee Terrace. Straight away.'

She heard the quiet sigh at the other end of the line. 'I thought I'd explained to you, Mrs Holyoak,' the solicitor said patiently, 'the search is not yet concluded. It won't be until the result is known about the planning application.'

'Never mind that,' she said firmly. 'I want you to go ahead – now.'

He paused before he answered. 'You do understand the risk you're taking?' he said slowly. 'If you're obliged to sell to the Council – as well you might be – the compensation won't approach anywhere near what you're proposing to pay.'

Greta could feel her fingers tremble, but was determined to remain adamant. 'I know that,' she said. 'Go ahead, Mr Smythe. I want to be the owner of Jubilee Terrace just as soon as it's humanly possible.'

The solicitor wasn't ready to desert his responsibility yet. 'It's my duty to warn you, you understand—'

'Mr Smythe,' she cut in gently, 'don't waste time arguing. I've made up my mind. Just go ahead and buy it.'

She smiled as she put the telephone down and went back into the kitchen. Maybe she was being a fool, but it was the first time in years she'd been so forceful, and she'd enjoyed it. Once she'd finished clearing up the kitchen and made the beds she'd put on her hat and coat and headed down to Mafeking Street. She couldn't wait to begin the next move.

Rosa stood on the corner of the street, waiting for Dan, her laden shopping bag at her feet. He'd still looked grey this morning and agreed to go down to the doctor's, but he'd drawn the line at her going into the surgery with him.

'I don't want to look like a big kid, having me mam take me to the doctor's,' he muttered. 'I'm going in on me own.'

'Then just make sure you tell him everything; how often you've had these attacks.'

'I will. I just hope there isn't a long queue.'

'You'll wait even if there is. I'll be at the Co op.'

But she'd finished the shopping and he still hadn't come. Rosa hung around outside the doctor's tall house with its big bay windows, wondering if Dan had changed his mind and fled. She was just about to go inside and enquire when his broad figure appeared on the doorstep. She picked up the shopping bag and hurried to meet him.

'Well? What did he say?' she asked, falling into step beside him.

Dan shook his head. 'Nowt to worry about. He's given me a prescription.'

'But did he say what it was?'

'Ulcer, he said. That's nowt. Fred Sykes has had one for years.'

An ulcer. Rosa thought it over for a moment. She knew nothing about ulcers. She studied Dan's profile. Under that weathered tan from years of outdoor work it was hard to tell if he was still pale or not.

'How are you feeling now?' she asked.

'Fit as a fiddle. I'm off back to work.'

'Oh. You're not coming with me to look at this shop then?' She hadn't meant to sound reproachful.

'Not today. Another time. You go.'

She felt a prick of disappointment. 'Did the doctor say anything about eating?' she asked. 'Any special kind of food?'

Dan looked down at her with a smile. 'He told me to keep off the pickled eggs from now on. They're too acid.'

'Nothing about the ale then?'

Dan threw back his head and laughed. 'He'd know better than to try and stop that,' he rumbled. 'Anyway, Guinness is good for you.'

He seemed far brighter when they parted in town, much more like his old cheerful self. Rosa felt distinctly reassured as she headed towards the arcade.

As she entered the shop she was almost carried away by the heavenly aroma. Mr Kadinski was grinding coffee for a very elegant middle-aged lady, the kind who sat in Field's drinking coffee with a plate of French fancies. She smiled at Rosa as she tucked her change away in a leather purse and replaced it in her handbag.

'Lovely weather for the time of year,' she commented. Rosa watched her place the packet of coffee in her shopping basket between a bag of sugar and a cardboard box which looked as if it held French fancies.

'Indeed it is,' she replied, then, on an impulse, she added, 'Do you drink a lot of coffee?'

The lady looked surprised. 'Quite a bit, I suppose. Why do you ask?'

'I just wondered – what's the best way to make it?'

The lady set the basket down again on the counter. 'For me it's just a warm jug and boiling water, then leave it for a few minutes to draw. You need a strainer, of course, but I can't be doing with those percolator things. I like my coffee hot and strong.'

'Thanks,' said Rosa. 'I'll take your advice.'

'With a dash of cream for me, though my hubby prefers milk. And always brown sugar, of course.'

'I'll bear it in mind.'

The creases around Mr Kadinski's eyes indicated he was near to smiling as the lady left.

'You got on well with Mrs Harvey,' he remarked. 'She's a nice lady.'

'She's the kind of customer I want,' said Rosa.

His eyebrows rose. 'Don't tell me you're still thinking of setting up that tearoom,' he teased.

'Why not?' retorted Rosa. 'You said you had a spare room.'

'It's a tip up there – filthy.'

'So what? If you're not using it, it would be a bonus to have it all cleaned up – keep the mice away. Can I see it?'

He shrugged. 'OK, I'll show you just how bad it is. Then if you're still interested …'

'Right,' she said, and dumping her shopping bag under the counter she followed him to the stairs.

She had to push her way past the piles of boxes heaped on every step but at least, she noted, the staircase was wide, with a handsome mahogany banister. At the top Mr Kadinski stood back to let her see.

He hadn't exaggerated. It was filthy all right. Even in the gloomy light which managed to force its way through the dirt-encrusted windows she could see the cobwebs hanging from the beams and the thick layer of dust covering the floor clearly betraying their footsteps. But in one corner she could see a small sectioned-off area which would do perfectly as a little kitchen.

Mr Kadinski waved an airy arm. 'See what I mean?' he said.

Rosa ran a finger along a ledge and surveyed the blackened tip. 'Never mind,' she muttered, 'there's nothing that soap and water and a bit of elbow grease won't shift.'

'I'm sorry about the mess,' he apologized. 'It hasn't been used in years.' He pointed to the far wall. 'As you can see, it's been partitioned at some time – it used to be a large area covering my shop and the one next door. They did that when the sweetshop opened.'

He walked over to the little room in the corner and threw open the door. 'There is running water, but only a couple of power points.'

'My Dan could sort that out.'

'It needs a heck of a lot of work to get it right.'

Rosa stood by the floor-deep windows, looking down through the murk into the arcade below. 'I could make something of this place,' she murmured. 'It could be lovely – a place Mrs Harvey would be glad to come to.'

'And then you'd need capital to get started,' Mr Kadinski went on. 'Furniture, tablecloths, cutlery.'

'I've got a bit put by. And I could make my own tablecloths.'

He grinned down at her. 'You've got an answer for everything, haven't you?'

'Why not?' said Rosa. 'I'm not going to be put off easily.'

'I can see that. Well, what next?'

Rosa faced him squarely. 'I need to do some sums. First I need to know what rent you'd want, Mr Kadinski.'

191

'Alex, please. No-one calls me Mr Kadinski. But first things first. You need to apply to the Council for permission before you go any further.'

'Permission?' she frowned. 'What for?'

'Change of use of the premises. I suggest you go down to the council offices if you really mean this.'

Rosa headed for the stairs. 'I mean it all right, Mr – I mean, Alex. I've never been more serious in my life.'

Greta's step was buoyant as she walked along the sunlit cobbles of Mafeking Street and inside she felt a tremor of excitement. She had a proposition to put to Betty Tasker. The woman looked formidable, but if she could be convinced that Greta had her interests at heart . . .

But as Greta neared the house she could see that, despite the sunshine, the lady was not sitting outside her front door today. Greta rapped the knocker and waited. No answer. She rapped again.

Still no answer. Disappointment filled her. She'd been so eager to tell the woman of her plan. She'd come back later.

She was turning to go when an upstairs window next door shot up and a woman's head appeared.

'You looking for Mrs Tasker?'

Greta squinted up against the sun's glare. 'That's right. Do you know where I can find her?'

'Try round the back. She'll no doubt be gossiping with Mrs Taylor.'

'Thank you.'

Half a dozen houses further on Greta turned into the narrow passage leading to a back alley where she used to hide as a child. She made her way back to the Tasker house and heard women's voices over the wall. She tapped at the back gate, then opened it.

On a short washing line a row of newly washed antimacassars flapped in the breeze. Beneath them Betty Tasker and her neighbour, both in print aprons and their hair in metal curlers, stood facing each other over the low wall. They turned to stare at the intruder with barely concealed annoyance.

'What do you want?' demanded Betty Tasker. 'Barging in on a private conversation?'

Two hostile faces stared at her, both women's arms folded across their chests. Greta bit her lip.

'I'm sorry, I didn't mean to intrude,' she said awkwardly. 'I wanted a word with you, Mrs Tasker.'

'What about?'

'What we were talking about the other day – the plans for redeveloping the area.'

'What's it to you?' demanded the other woman. 'You don't live hereabouts.'

Greta felt on firmer ground now. 'No, but I shall do shortly,' she said. 'I'm moving into Jubilee Terrace.'

She saw the neighbour's jaw drop. Betty Tasker clearly wasn't satisfied yet.

'You – Jubilee Terrace?' she repeated. 'Whereabouts?'

'Number seven. It used to belong to Mrs Clancy.'

'Aye, it did and all,' said the neighbour. 'Poor old soul.'

'So you see,' said Greta, 'the plan affects me too. I'd like to do something about it.'

The neighbour was shaking her head in disbelief. 'We don't usually get your sort in this neighbourhood,' she murmured. 'Specially not now.'

'Hang on a minute,' said Betty, unfolding her arms and coming a step closer. 'Do what? What can anybody do?'

Greta could see the gleam of interest in her eyes and leapt in. 'We could organize a petition,' she said. 'We could get everybody who objects to the plan to sign their name. If we get enough, the Council will have to listen.'

The neighbour snorted. 'Who are you kidding?' she said scornfully. 'When do they ever listen to the likes of us?'

'They'd have no choice,' said Greta. 'Have you got a Labour councillor?'

'Aye,' replied the neighbour slowly. 'Moxon.'

'And how would we go about it?' asked Betty.

'You must know everybody round here – get them to sign.'

'You mean go round knocking at doors and asking folk?'

Greta dipped into her bag and pulled out a clipboard. 'It's all ready here,' she said, rippling the pages of foolscap clipped to the plastic board. 'It says "We, the undersigned, wish to let it be known that we deplore—"'

'Hang on,' said Betty, ducking under the row of antimacassars and crossing behind Greta to close the gate, 'this is going to need some thinking about. We'd best talk about it over a cup of tea. Come on inside.'

Theo had time to reflect as he drove over to Dewsbury to see the architect, and more time again as he made his way back to Leeds.

Maybe he'd been a bit unreasonable with Dorothy about that utility room idea of hers. Like she said, it needn't prove so expensive with all the materials at cost, and it would add to the value of the house. It was a justifiable enough request after all, and she'd given good reasons. He couldn't help feeling a twinge of guilt at his cavalier lack of response.

The truth of the matter was that he just didn't want to be bothered. He felt so tired these days; he needed his weekends free. He wanted to have time with the children, time to go to the match if he felt like it. The last thing he wanted was

194

to have to spend all his free time supervising the building work – as he'd have to, otherwise Dorothy would, and he could think of no quicker way to alienate his workforce.

Still, if she had her heart set on it she wasn't going to give up easily. The threat of mud and mess had only daunted her momentarily. He knew her of old. She'd keep up the campaign, not by overt nagging and reproach, but far more subtly than that. He'd been well aware of the pink nightie.

So, maybe it would be more wearing in the long run to have to cope with her skilful manoeuvrings. Maybe he should give in gracefully now. After all, she was a good housewife; she deserved the best.

The trouble with sunshine was that it showed up every speck of dust. Rosa washed down the woodwork and turned out every cupboard in the house. After all, she'd filled in and sent the forms to the Council so with luck she'd soon be too busy elsewhere to worry about housework.

There was an eager feeling of hope rippling inside her. Dan was looking so much better now, back to his old laughing, teasing self, and with it had come an obvious eagerness to help her.

'No worry, Rosa lass,' he said cheerfully. 'I'm a dab hand at the electrics though I say it meself. And did I tell you, I called in The Bull and Bear the other day—'

'No, you didn't.'

''Cos I heard they had a couple of old pub tables to get rid of. I had a look at 'em. Nice little square ones, not too bad. I could fix 'em up fine for you.'

'How much?'

'That's the best bit – nowt.'

'We'll have them.'

Rosa squeezed herself. The next step now was getting the Council's permission.

Lucy sat down on the garden seat. She was becoming exasperated with her little brother. If only Mother would come back from the neighbour's house quickly, but if they'd got settled down over a cup of tea it could be ages yet.

'I want to climb the tree,' said Graham petulantly. 'You can't stop me.'

He put one small foot against the bark and tried to climb. Lucy rose and went over to him.

'You can't, it's too big for you.'

'Not if you give me a leg-up, then I can reach the branch.'

'Graham, you know you mustn't. You'll get into trouble.'

'Shut up, bossy-boots. Just 'cos you're older than me.'

'Mummy will be cross. Just look at your shoes.'

With a growl he gave up and wandered over to the swing. 'Push me,' he ordered. 'I want to go high.'

'No,' she said. 'I won't.'

'Why? 'Cos you think it's your swing?'

She sighed. 'You're not supposed to go on it except when Mummy's here.'

He took no notice. Pushing the swing back as far as he could with his little bottom, he let the swing carry him forward and he grinned in triumph. She watched him working hard with his short legs to make the seat swing higher and higher.

'You'd better stop now.'

'Shan't.'

Lucy was growing anxious. The swing was soaring far too high for him. 'She'll be back in a minute,' she warned.

'Don't care.'

She strode purposefully across to stand beside him.

'Graham, you heard me. Stop it, now. Slow down and I'll catch you.'

'Whee-hee,' he cried, flailing his legs in the air, 'I can see right over the hedge into next door.'

'She'll see you,' Lucy cried. 'You're going to cop it.'

She stretched out an arm to try to catch the chain as the swing flew past. Graham saw and kicked out at her hand.

'Get off!' he yelled. 'I'll tell!'

He lashed out again with his foot and Lucy ducked. Then, to her dismay, she saw his foot strike the metal upright, the seat swing round, the chains twist up at a crazy angle, and suddenly Graham's small figure crashed down on the concrete beneath. She saw his white startled face, and then he let out a hideous howl.

'Oh Graham!' she cried, bending over him. 'What have you done? Where does it hurt?'

She saw the trickle of red in his hair just as Mother came running round the corner of the house. Graham was crying loudly.

'Oh my God!' she exclaimed. 'What have you done?'

Lucy stood back to let her stoop down by Graham. She tried to help him to his feet but he shrieked in pain. Blood was trickling down his forehead.

'Is it your leg, love? I'll carry you indoors then.'

Mother looked pale as she carried him in, still whimpering. Frightened by the atmosphere of crisis, Lucy followed. She watched her mother fetch Dettol and cotton wool from the cabinet, then suddenly remembered her nurse's uniform.

'Can I help?' she offered. Mother shot her a baleful look.

'You can get out from under my feet. But for you this would never have happened.'

Lucy felt stung. 'It wasn't my fault. He wouldn't listen.'

'And it doesn't help pushing the blame on your little

brother,' Mother snapped as she dipped the cotton wool in the antiseptic. 'You were supposed to be looking after him.'

'I told him not to swing high.'

Graham snivelled through his tears. 'She pushed me higher and higher. She wouldn't stop.'

'That's not true,' cried Lucy; 'you know it isn't.'

Mother's voice was icy. 'Shut up, madam. I'll deal with you later. Right now I've got to call the doctor.'

It was almost as though they'd forgotten about her, thought Lucy as she sat in the bath that night. There'd been a flurry of activity all evening, rushing Graham up to the hospital then bringing him home again; Mother feeding him his favourite egg and chips for tea and then bathing him and putting him to bed. She'd left Lucy to bath herself.

She could hear Mother now, in the bedroom next door telling Daddy all about it. Lucy lifted a pile of foam to her lips and blew a wisp of froth off the top, watching it float down to settle on the tap.

'An impacted knee, they said,' Mother murmured. 'He must have fallen heavily on it.'

'I suppose we should be glad it wasn't broken,' said Daddy.

'I was sure he had concussion too,' Mother went on. 'At least he escaped that. I suppose it's my own fault. I was only gone five minutes, but I should have known better than to trust her.'

'She's only nine, Dorothy. A child still,' Daddy murmured.

'It's just a mercy I came back when I did. Fussing around under my feet, she was, trying to play nurses at a time like that. I'll give her nurses indeed! After nearly killing her little brother!'

'Now, now,' Daddy soothed. 'There's no malice in the child. It was an accident.'

198

'It was her fault. Graham told me she was pushing him far too high.'

'You can't always believe what children tell you, especially when they're upset. You're upset too, naturally, but I don't want you taking it out on Lucy.'

'Lucy, Lucy – that's all I ever hear from you!' Mother's voice was shrill now, and apprehension filled the child. 'How could you possibly believe what she says rather than your own son?' Mother cried. 'Graham's always been a truthful child.'

'And hasn't Lucy?' Daddy sounded stern now.

'How do we know what's in her genes?' Mother demanded. 'The mother an illiterate Irish woman no better than she ought to be.'

'That's enough!' Daddy cut in. 'You're getting hysterical. Now look, you've had a trying time today. Why don't you take a bath and have an early night?'

Lucy shrank back into a corner of the cooling water. What were they saying? It sounded as if Mother wasn't her mother, but how could that be?

'I know one thing,' she heard Mother mutter. 'I've had enough of this stupid nurse talk. I'm throwing that uniform outfit away first thing tomorrow.'

'No!' shouted Lucy, and the tears ran down her face. 'I hate you! You're not throwing it away!'

From the bedroom came only the sound of silence.

Chapter Seventeen

Greta found it hard to control Betty Tasker's enthusiasm which seemed to be spilling over on to her talkative neighbour Winnie Taylor.

'I've got ninety-seven names already,' Betty declared, 'and that's only in Horner Street. Just wait till I get cracking on the rest.'

She held out the clipboard for Greta to inspect. 'I've been invited into that many homes for a cup of tea you wouldn't believe. They even offered me a glass of sherry at number nine.'

Winnie came close, jabbing a finger on the board. 'I could do some if I had one of them boards,' she said.

Greta looked down dubiously at the scrawled signatures. 'You did remember that they had to be of voting age?' she asked.

'Course I did,' retorted Betty. 'What do you take me for? And soon as I've given me husband his tea I'm off to do Silver Street.'

Winnie wasn't going to be left out. 'I could be doing the top end while you're doing down here,' she persisted. 'I know a lot of folk up there.'

'The more hands the better,' smiled Greta. 'I'll bring you a clipboard tomorrow.'

Winnie's small chest swelled with pride. 'And I know

200

where Councillor Moxon lives and all,' she announced. 'Have I to take it to him when I've done?'

'No, to me,' replied Greta. 'I'll tell you when the time is right.'

Theo felt concerned about Lucy. The child had been even more subdued than usual ever since her outburst that night in the bath. Dorothy hadn't spoken of it since, but she hadn't thrown the nurse's outfit away either.

He knew for a fact she'd tucked it away on the top shelf of the airing cupboard.

She was downstairs now, fingers still busily knitting while she chuckled over some late-night comedy show on the radio. He paused on the landing for a moment, then turned the handle of Lucy's door quietly.

She was sitting up in bed, her face a pale oval in the light streaming in from the landing. He switched on the bedside lamp and she rubbed her eyes, blinking.

'Hello, sweetheart,' he said. 'Hasn't the sandman come yet? It's very late.'

'I can't sleep,' she said.

'Why ever not? You've to be up early for school in the morning.'

She draped her arms about her hunched knees. 'Daddy—'

'What is it, lovey?'

She didn't look up at him. 'Whose little girl am I?'

He felt his heart contract. So she had heard and understood Dorothy's words. 'Why, you're ours,' he said in tones of mock surprise. 'Mummy's and mine.'

'She doesn't want me any more. I wish I could run away.'

The little voice, bleak with sadness, tore at his guts. He sat on the edge of the bed and took hold of her arms. 'You

201

mustn't say that!' he croaked. 'It's not true. You're the most loved little girl in the world.'

She turned large eyes up to meet his. 'She doesn't. She loves Graham, but not me. Am I an Irish lady's baby?'

Theo closed his eyes. They'd always known that one day she'd have to be told, but not like this. Still, she'd asked, and he couldn't lie to the child. He pulled her close.

'Yes,' he said softly. 'The Irish lady loved you very much, but she couldn't afford to keep you. She let us have you because we wanted you so much.'

The big eyes were still fixed on his face. 'Where is she now?' Lucy asked. 'Where did she go, my real mummy?'

He shook his head sadly. 'I've no idea, sweetheart.'

'Will she come back for me?'

He swallowed hard. 'She wouldn't want to upset you like that, knowing you're happy with us. She's too kind to do that to you.'

The small face looked away and the small voice sounded as if it was about to choke. 'She didn't want me, so you had to take me instead. That's why Mummy doesn't like me.'

'No, it wasn't like that!' Theo exclaimed, snatching the little body to him. 'Out of all the millions of little girls in the world we chose you – you're very special, sweetheart. You're my princess; the dearest thing in the world to me. I love you very much and I always will.'

The small head burrowed into his chest, but he heard her muffled words between the tears.

'I love you too, Daddy, so hard I could burst.'

Greta peered out of the window into the darkness of the front garden. Still no sign of Reginald's car, and it looked like it was becoming misty out there. He was late, and he hadn't rung to say not to keep the dinner hot.

Never mind, she had plenty to occupy her, what with the

reams of signatures her two able lieutenants had come up with already. And she also needed to plan a list of things she'd take down to Jubilee Terrace just as soon as the purchase went through. Things which would never be missed here, but would help put her stamp on the place and make it feel like home.

Not that she was going to live there, of course. The thrill lay in having her own secret hidey-hole, something of her own which Reginald knew nothing about. It gave her the same furtive excitement she'd felt as a child when she built that secret house in the undergrowth up there on the railway embankment alongside Mafeking Street. She'd let her best friend Alma in on the secret, entertaining her there with the doll's teacups and saucers. Hilda had been furious when she found out.

'You ought to let me share it,' she fumed. 'I'm your sister, and I'm older than you.'

But by then bully-boy Denton's gang had discovered the hideaway and claimed it as their own. But this time, she vowed, would be different. No bully-boy was going to rob her of Jubilee Terrace.

The sound of the car in the drive made her jump. She gathered up the petition papers hastily and pushed them into her bag.

'Sorry I'm late,' Reginald muttered as he came in. 'Fog was bad on the Leeds road, traffic nearly at a standstill.'

'Leeds?' she repeated. 'I didn't know you were going over there.'

'No choice, had to see some clients after the Planning meeting,' he said, slumping into the easy chair and picking up the *Examiner*. 'Went on a bit longer than I thought.'

Greta could see only the newspaper, raised like a barricade between them. 'Do you want dinner?' she asked. 'It'll be a bit dried by now.'

'Don't bother,' she heard him murmur, 'I had something to eat with my clients. I needed to relax.'

'Busy day?'

'Same as always.'

Greta paused before posing the question burning in her mind, then tried hard to make her voice sound casual. 'Anything interesting in the Planning meeting?'

He yawned. 'Only bits and pieces. Applications for a hairdressing salon in Byram Street and a tearoom in one of the old arcades.'

She sank back in the chair. It was all right, there was still time.

'But there was one interesting thing today,' Reginald murmured.

'Really?' said Greta. 'What was that?'

'The mayoralty.' Reginald lowered the newspaper, just far enough to beam at her over the top. 'You're looking at the town's new mayor, my dear. As from May I'll be the first citizen of Hawksmoor.'

'Congratulations!' she enthused. 'I'm so glad. It's what you've wanted for so long.'

'And deserved,' he grunted. 'No-one's worked harder for the town than I have.'

'True,' she agreed. 'I'm sure no other councillor has put in all the hours you have.'

He nodded and disappeared again behind the *Examiner*. 'And even more hours next year,' she heard him mutter. 'All those functions I'll have to attend. Still, it's my duty and I won't shirk it.'

'I know you won't. Goodness, I shall have to look through my wardrobe. I know for a fact I haven't a single evening dress to do credit to the mayoress. Still, with the allowance you give me ...'

'Actually,' he cut in, 'I've been thinking about that.

204

Knowing how much you dislike the limelight, my dear, and with your various other obligations, I thought I might perhaps relieve you of the responsibility of that job. I could always have someone else for my mayoress.'

Greta sat thunderstruck. 'Someone else?' she repeated. 'Who?'

Reginald laid the paper aside and went across to the cabinet. 'Well,' he said, opening the whisky bottle, 'I thought I might ask Mrs Thewlis – you know her, don't you?'

Greta sat aghast. She could see the woman now, confidently queening it in the mayor's parlour, her junoesque body spirella'd into a svelte hourglass shape and jewels glittering on the overspill bosom. Tasteless creature. Only a woman with no taste and a name like Phyllis would marry a surname like Thewlis. Phyllis Thewlis, indeed! It sounded like a hissing cat.

But the woman could be charming all right, gracious with the ladies and flirtatious with the men. She'd be in her element flaunting the mayoress's golden chain of office.

Reginald cut in on her caustic thoughts. 'Only it seemed to me,' he said, holding up his glass to see whether it was sufficiently filled, 'that what with her being a widow she has no family commitments to get in the way. She'd be available at any time and she does enjoy socializing – she's good at it.'

And I'm not, thought Greta. A woman from the slums isn't good enough. So be it. I won't let you see the hurt.

'And to be fair to you,' she heard Reginald's complacent voice go on, 'I thought it only right not to rob you of your time, you being so involved with your maternity home and things.'

'Very thoughtful of you, Reginald.'

He did not notice the irony in her tone. 'Not at all. One has to think of others,' he said. 'I'll simply let it be known that you were unable to accept because of pressure of other commitments. OK?'

He sat down again, sipping the whisky, rolling it round his tongue in satisfaction, completely unaware of his wife's baleful glare.

Dan was standing at the kitchen sink, bare-chested, stroking his cheek gently with a razor. Rosa was brewing the breakfast pot of tea when she heard the letter-box rattle and letters plop on the doormat. She picked them up and brought them in.

'Anything?' Dan asked, pulling a face in the mirror.

'The gas bill,' she groaned, and turned to the second letter. It was official-looking, addressed in typescript to Mrs R. Pearson. She tore it open and scanned the single sheet quickly, then punched the air and let out a whoop of delight. Dan paused in his shaving.

'They've agreed!' Rosa cried. 'They've given me permission for the tearoom!'

Dan turned back to the mirror. 'That's great,' he said. 'I'm really glad for you.'

She dropped the letter on the table and came up close behind him. 'Will you come with me – to talk to Mr Kadinski about rent?' she coaxed.

He smiled at his reflection. 'Best you go on your own, lass. A pretty face'll get a better deal without a husband in tow.'

'Not in tow,' she protested. 'You're my partner, aren't you?'

She watched him wipe away the last of the soapsuds from his face and then he turned to her. 'Listen, love,' he said quietly, 'this is your baby. I'll help you every way I can, do all the work necessary to get it ready, but the business is yours.'

'Oh.' The joy of the moment was leaking away. 'I wanted it to be ours, Dan,' she murmured. 'Our future.'

He took hold of her shoulders. 'Does it matter?' he said softly. 'Like I said, I'll back you all the way, do everything you want, but I don't want to be an owner. It's just not me.' He let go of her shoulders and reached for his shirt. 'Tell you what,' he said brightly, 'I'll ask Ted for a lend of one of his lorries, then happen I'll go down the pub this aft and fetch those tables for you – how's that?'

Dorothy felt a little subdued as she hoovered the lounge after Theo had left for work. He'd sounded very short when he told her about Lucy.

'I didn't mean for her to know yet,' Dorothy had muttered. 'She shouldn't have been listening.'

'She wasn't listening. She just overheard.'

'There you go, defending her again. Anyway,' she added defensively, 'you didn't have to spell it out to her.'

'What else could I do? She had to be told the truth when she asked,' he snapped. 'I wasn't going to lie to her.'

Dorothy thought it over. 'How did she take it?'

'How do you think? She feels unwanted, poor kid. Rejected by her own mother.'

Herself, did he mean? Dorothy bridled. 'I haven't rejected her,' she retorted. 'I've given her the best upbringing any mother could. She ought to be grateful.'

Theo scowled. 'Kids don't understand gratitude – they aren't meant to. It's loving she needs, and plenty of it. I'm off now.'

He hadn't even kissed her goodbye. Dorothy pushed back the easy chair and heaved a sigh. More of Theo's cream-cracker crumbs to hoover up. He could be as messy as the children at times. He was little more than a big kid himself, doting on Lucy the way Graham did on his battered old teddy bear. It really was infuriating the way he always stood up for Lucy and seemed to understand the girl's feelings more than hers.

A wave of sadness swept over her as she recalled the days he'd have done anything for her. In their courting days he'd thought nothing of walking four miles home after seeing her to her door. He'd wait an hour if need be just to catch a glimpse of her in the office, in the days when he used to spend his last sixpence on roses for her. But nowadays it was always Lucy on his mind, Lucy he talked about, Lucy whose feelings mattered more than her own.

Drat the child. She knew what she was doing; she wrapped Theo round her little finger. She was an angelic little scene-stealer all right with her glossy fair hair and those wide blue eyes. As Theo said, she'd break a few hearts when she grew up. She'd certainly been the prettiest baby by far in the nursery that day they first went to the home.

Dorothy switched off the hoover and straightened. She'd loved the child then, hadn't she? She still tried to, but it wasn't easy. It was as though Lucy deliberately kept at a distance from her, with the cool remoteness of an alien being from another planet.

With Graham it was very different, but then he was her own flesh, the result of hours of painful labour. It was only natural that a special bond existed between him and her. The mother-and-son relationship was as well-known as the father-and-daughter bond, but how on earth could Theo relate to this adopted child better than to his own son? It just wasn't right.

The telephone rang in the hallway. Dorothy dragged the hoover out behind her.

'Hello?' she said cautiously, and then her voice brightened. 'Oh, hello, Mrs Wallace ... No, I'm not doing anything special this morning ... Oh yes, thanks, I'd love to come round ...'

*   *   *

208

Rosa was flushed with success when she came out onto the doorstep of the grocer's shop with Alex Kadinski. The rent he asked was well within her calculations, and he'd been very helpful.

He looked handsomer out here than she'd realized, she thought, the sunlight streaming down into the arcade through the high glass dome shone on his glossy dark hair as he leaned nonchalantly against the door-frame. He dipped a hand into his trousers pocket and pulled out a key.

'Here,' he said, 'I see no reason why you shouldn't come in right away to get things rolling. We'll get the lease drawn up properly.'

'Oh thanks,' she replied. 'Just tell me when it's convenient – I don't want to get in your way, but the sooner the better.'

He shrugged broad shoulders. 'Any time, just let me know. And I'll get all that old furniture and rubbish out before you come.'

'No, leave it, there may be something Dan can use. He's a dab hand at finding a use for things you'd think were rubbish.'

Alex grinned. 'I look forward to meeting him. When do you think you might open up?'

'As soon as it's humanly possible,' she smiled, then held out a hand. 'Thanks for all your help.'

He gripped her hand tightly. 'Don't mention it,' he said earnestly. 'It's purely selfishness on my part – I'll have company and I get to supply you.'

'Oh Lord,' she said, pulling her hand away, 'that reminds me. Could I have a quarter of coffee, please? I need to practise what Mrs Harvey told me.'

He pushed the door open. 'What kind? Kenyan? Colombian?'

She followed him inside. 'Do you know,' she said, blushing as she laid her basket on the counter, 'I haven't a clue. I don't know one from another. There's an awful lot you're going to have to teach me.'

'Greta Holyoak here, Mr Smythe,' said Greta, clutching the receiver tightly. 'Is there any news about Jubilee Terrace?'

'Ah yes, hold on a minute.'

She heard him shuffling papers, then mutter to his secretary, and finally his voice came back on the line. 'Contracts on both sides have been signed ...'

'I know, they're due to be exchanged on Friday.'

'... and Mr Mellor's solicitor has written to say that his client has now removed all the contents he requires from the property.'

Greta's heart was thumping. 'So everything's going smoothly? The house will be mine on Friday?'

'Indeed,' he replied urbanely, 'provided contracts are exchanged and the balance of the money changes hands. But I should point out to you, Mrs Holyoak,' he went on quickly, 'that if you have thought better of it, it's still not too late to pull out. Contracts have not yet been exchanged. You'd lose your deposit, of course, but there's nothing binding.'

Greta held her head high. 'I shall be in your office tomorrow, Mr Smythe,' she said proudly, 'with my cheque for the balance. Nothing on earth would make me pull out now.'

Chapter Eighteen

Spring had slipped effortlessly into a balmy summer by the time the café was ready. Dan had laboured hard, gutting and restoring the room above Kadinski's shop, mending and repolishing the pub tables, building a counter, shelving and pelmets.

Rosa carried in a pile of pale-pink tablecloths and matching napkins she had laboriously sewn herself. White crockery would look attractive against the pink.

Dan stood on top of the ladder, fixing up the lights. Rosa looked around with pride. Alex said he could barely recognize his old storeroom now with its pale-ivory walls and deep-rose curtains falling from ceiling to floor. Now the high windows had been freed of their encrusted dirt, the light streamed in across the tables, making the room look twice as large. Only the last touches remained to be done. That pair of white vases she'd picked up in the Monday market, filled with pink and white plastic flowers, would go perfectly in those two recesses in the far wall. Quiet, dignified, an atmosphere she hoped her customers would appreciate.

'It was worthwhile spending time in Field's, taking everything in,' she said to Dan. 'This place is going to be just as posh, even better.'

'Why posh?' Dan wanted to know. 'Young folk these days want somewhere cheap and cheerful, all modern and plastic.'

Rosa shook her head. 'It's not the love-beads and flowers-in-their-hair brigade I'm after, it's the likes of Mrs Harvey who've got money to spend.'

Dan clambered down the ladder. 'Who's she, when she's at home?'

Rosa smiled. 'God willing, you'll see. I'm going to send out invitations to all the important people in Hawksmoor. I must ask Alex's advice.'

Dan sighed. 'Give it a rest, love. You've thought and talked of nowt else but the café for months. Let's have a day off Saturday – let me take you to Manchester. You've never been to Belle Vue, have you?'

'Manchester – great,' she replied. 'I can buy something smart to wear for when I open.'

Alex was a fount of useful advice. 'Influential people?' he repeated. 'Well, if you mean the ladies, there's Mrs Jardine who runs the Business and Professional Women's Club – she might invite you to join.'

Rosa added the name to her list. 'Anyone else?'

He rubbed his chin. 'There's Alderman Mrs Dickinson, but I don't know that I'd bother about her.'

'Why not?'

'She's from Marsden. They're funny folk up in Marsden – see themselves as a town apart.' Alex's face lit up. 'But there's Mrs Thewlis – she's president of the Hawksmoor Thespians, very colourful lady. Love her or hate her, she's influential all the same. She's mayoress now.'

'Right,' said Rosa. 'I'll certainly add her to my list.'

Rosa leaned her head back against the rough texture of the upholstery as the train rattled homewards towards Hawksmoor. It had been a wonderfully relaxing day, first at the fair and then touring the big shops in the city.

She'd found just what she wanted – a navy jacket, skirt and white blouse – and they lay now in the bag up there on the luggage rack.

'Waitresses wear a cap and apron,' Dan had teased her, 'over a cute little miniskirt. Where's your apron?'

'I'm the proprietress,' she'd retorted. 'I won't be wearing a mini.'

'Pity. You've got good legs.'

'I'll only be waiting on till I see if I can afford to take on a girl.'

'You won't get tips in that outfit.'

'Maybe not, but everyone will know I'm the boss.'

The boss. The thought gave her a warm glow of pride. Dan had been wonderful. She must have dragged him into dozens of cafés over the last few weeks to spy out the land – 'reconnoitring', he called it – until he'd complained at last that he was awash with coffee and couldn't face another cup. But at least she knew now she was on the right lines; she had the right equipment and she knew how to make good coffee.

She looked across at Dan in the corner seat gazing out of the window into the darkness. He too seemed lost in thought. Rosa let her mind drift.

By Monday, when the café opened, the lingering smell of fresh paint should have gone. She'd be opening her doors for the first time, the climax of all the hard work and plans. How different life was now from the day she'd first arrived in Hawksmoor – on this train, destitute and anxious – what was it? More than nine years ago now.

So much had happened since then, losing poor Maggie and then the baby. Little Angela. No, I mustn't think about her. She has her own life now. Think about the nice things, like the kindness of Kitty and Ted. And Mrs Clancy. After the birth she'd only ever seen the old lady once more, by chance, in town.

'Eeh love,' she'd said, her old face wrinkling in concern, 'you don't look well at all, you've lost that much weight. Looking after sick folk has fair taken it out of you.'

Rosa had held her tongue. Not long after that she'd heard from Clondarra about Daddy Kerrigan's death, and about Mammy moving up to Dublin to live with Dominic. Grandma Sheridan, if she was still alive, was probably singing her old Irish songs in a home somewhere.

And then Dan came along, bringing a glow into her life. If only they had that child ... She looked across to where he sat, seeing his rugged profile as he stared out into the night.

He became aware of her gaze and smiled sheepishly. 'We're coming into Hawksmoor, just going over the viaduct,' he said, rising to take the bag down off the rack. 'Funny how you can be fond of a mucky old town like this, but I am. I wouldn't live anywhere else for the world.'

Greta hurried through the darkness under the viaduct as the train clattered overhead. She was nervous there at the best of times, but at night and when the thundering noise above would more than drown out a woman's cries for help ...

Once out into the lighted street she felt the eagerness return. She was going home, to her own house: Jubilee Terrace. The very name had the right ring of triumph. It had been hers for weeks now, but she never lost the feeling of exultation every time she came here.

She let herself into number seven, put down her bag and poured herself a glass of sherry. She'd celebrated her freedom that very first day by buying a bottle of sherry and a packet of those new tipped cigarettes they said were safer for you. She'd lain back in Mrs Clancy's fireside chair, blowing smoke into the air, savouring the warmth of the sherry on her tongue and listening on her transistor radio to those boys from Liverpool playing their brash music. Not that it was her style, but because it was the kind of modern tripe Reginald would have banned.

She refilled the sherry glass. Nowadays she'd given up the cigarettes – she hadn't really enjoyed them anyway. But the occasional glass of sherry did no harm, if she remembered to take care to suck a few mints on the way home.

Not that she needed to bother. Reginald was hardly ever there. Ever since that ghastly mayor-making ceremony when the Thewlis woman could hardly contain herself for glee, function after function meant he hardly ever had a free . night. It was wonderful.

Tonight, for instance, he was receiving a cheque for charity at some club or something and then on to the Chamber of Trade dinner. So she could take her time. She set the glass down and stood up. She could make a start on clearing out those drawers in Mrs Clancy's old bureau.

Reginald Holyoak, Mayor of Hawksmoor, had enjoyed being fêted as the guest of honour at the Chamber of Trade dinner. He'd imbibed rather more whiskies than was his wont, but then when the company was good and the alcohol free ...

He sank back beside the mayoress against the leather of the mayoral Rolls and fingered the gold chain about his neck in satisfaction. He was the latest in the long line of redoubtable Hawksmoor men to wear this chain, and the thought filled him with pride.

'Penny for 'em. You're not planning to squeeze my knee again, are you?'

The teasing voice startled him. He'd almost forgotten the mayoress. Phyllis's plump face dimpled as she smiled at him.

215

'No, no,' he said. 'Sorry. I was miles away.'

'You're a very naughty boy,' she went on, 'doing that under the table where no-one could see.' She tapped his nose playfully with the dinner menu. 'You a happily married man and all – you ought to be punished.'

Punished. The word caught his attention. He glanced at Phyllis speculatively. Even with her bantering tone and that curvy body encased in tight black satin she didn't come anywhere close to Madame Zara's leather-clad, tantalizing cruelty. Madame Zara. He hadn't been there in ages. Whisky fumes and memory combined to stir an old familiar feeling in his guts.

He leaned forward and slid back the glass partition. 'Go to my place first,' he ordered the chauffeur. 'I've got to go out.'

Phyllis sat up with an impatient click of the tongue. 'At this time of night? I thought you were going to see me home. Whatever's wrong, Reginald?'

'Nothing. There's something I have to see to.'

The car drew up at the pavement edge. Phyllis sank back with a sigh. 'Politics again,' she muttered. 'It's that file of John Moxon's, isn't it, that petition or whatever? You've been odd ever since he gave it to you.'

Reginald took her hand. 'That's got nothing to do with it,' he said. 'Thanks for your company – it was a good night.'

'I can't fathom you out,' she sighed. 'I thought it was what you wanted, stopping that development.'

'For the time being,' he retorted, 'to spite a certain grasping individual. I've got other plans, but look, I must be off. Arrange with Fred about picking you up for the lunch tomorrow.'

As the Rolls drew away she saw him walk up the drive to where his car was parked. Pity, she thought, just as things seemed to be warming up nicely. She could have sworn she'd spotted that gleam in his eyes and she hadn't imagined the knee-squeezing. Now why on earth had he suddenly lost interest?

Well, one thing was sure, it wasn't that wife of his who'd suddenly taken his fancy. She was too colourless a woman – he hadn't even wanted her to be his mayoress. That dull Greta Holyoak would never amount to a row of beans.

Gas bills, electricity bills, the rates demands – Mrs Clancy seemed to have stuffed every bit of paper into this drawer as soon as she'd dealt with it, thought Greta as she surveyed the pile of paper she'd tipped out of the bureau drawer. No wonder the nephew had left this lot untouched.

One by one she dropped the pieces of paper in the coal bucket by the hearth. A small notebook – details of the old lady's accounts. 'Milkman, four shillings. Window cleaner, two-and-six.'

Greta dropped it in the bin and picked up another notebook.

'... thinking of getting another lodger to help out with the bills ...'

It was a diary. The old lady was thorough, keeping account of her affairs. She ought not to pry, but ... Greta flicked over the pages.

'That nice Mrs Holyoak came today. Lovely perfume she wears ...'

Greta smiled and flicked on.

'... the new lodger, Rosa ...'

Rosa? Greta frowned; the name rang a bell. She read on.

'... such a look of pain in her eyes. Solemn little lass, but lovely with it. I wonder what it is causing her grief ...'

Of course, thought Greta, the young Irish girl who was

pregnant, who came to Wood Lea to have her child. Heavens, that was years ago. She flicked over more pages to the end of the book.

'... I've missed Rosa. It's not like her to leave without a word. I never did believe that tale about nursing a sick cousin. I bet she was in the family way and daren't tell her folk. Haven't set eyes on her since that day in town. Such a nice girl. Hope she does well.'

Well, well, thought Greta as she dropped the notebook on the table, you didn't miss much, Mrs Clancy. You were a deep one all right. There was far more to you than we thought. We never really know anybody inside out. She smiled to herself. Just as Reginald doesn't know the real me.

She stood up to survey her reflection in the mirror over the fireplace. That's Greta Kaye there, not Greta Holyoak. She'd made sure to have all the bills sent to Mrs Kaye so that no-one would connect her with Reginald. Greta Kaye. A woman who, in her own small world, could do exactly as she liked.

A ripple of pleasure ran through her. Here she could become the Greta she might have been if only she hadn't been sidetracked into a cul-de-sac. She could wear trousers if she liked, smoke cigars, walk about naked if she chose. She could lock the door against the outside world, or open it up to people of her choice. She could take a lodger – a lover even! The world, bordered by these four walls, was her domain, to rule as she wished.

Turning to the table she picked up Mrs Clancy's diary once more. She hadn't the heart to throw out the one last vestige of the old lady's thoughts. Carefully she replaced it in the drawer.

Rosa. Rosa Sheridan, that was it. I'd all but forgotten her. Pretty girl, in an elfin sort of way, with her pale skin and jet-black hair, and her softly spoken Irish brogue. I remember

218

her now, but I can't for the life of me remember who adopted the baby. But Rosa was a good girl, strong-minded and capable. She'd make something of her life. I wonder where she is now? I wonder what she's doing?

Madame Zara was ready for him. Reginald closed his eyes and let himself sink into his favourite fantasy: the spider. The great fat she-spider squatting in the centre of her silken web, waiting for her puny mate.

'Are you there, spider?' Madame Zara's tone was husky.

'Yes, mistress.' He could hear the squeak in his own voice.

'Then take care how you approach,' the she-spider warned, 'or I must punish you.'

Gingerly he touched the web of his desire. If he made the right vibrations she would let him move closer, but if he got it wrong she would pounce. No sound. He moved again, and felt a crack across his bare shoulders.

'Clumsy!' she hissed. 'You must try harder.'

Fearful, yet forced to yield to the fever mounting inside him, he moved again, climbing cautiously towards the centre of the web. She lay there, waiting, smiling, spreading her possessive black body.

'Do you want to please me, spider?'

'Yes, oh yes, mistress.'

'Then come.'

It was an invitation to death, but he didn't care. His whole body was pulsating, heaving, with the overpoweringly irresistible urge to mate. Even though he knew the outcome, he had no will to resist a seductive instinct as old as time.

Trembling, swaying, he reached the black body, but she did not bite. Shivering with delight, he lunged, plunging into a whirlpool of eddying nirvana. Senses aching with ecstasy he clung to her, feeling her body's relentless suck, knowing her mouth was opening, ready for the fatal bite. Then, suddenly, in the orgasmic moment when the world exploded, she snapped off his head ...

He lay flaccid, lifeless, in the black void, not opening his eyes. He knew she sat there smiling, sated, her body bloated with his vital juices. Now she had no more use for him but to hang out his drained carcass on the edge of her web as a trophy. He was content.

A sharp tap on his shoulder made him open his eyes and a crisp voice spoke. 'Come on now, Reggie, time's up. Leave the money on the hall table on your way out.'

Lucy kept her eyes closed when Daddy came into the bedroom. She felt him gently brush away the tears on her cheek before he crept out again.

Mummy was hateful, making her go to bed early just because she was going out. She wouldn't even let her read the next bit of *Swallows and Amazons*.

'Why can't I?'

'Don't ask questions – just do as I say.'

'My real mummy wouldn't say that. She'd let me read.'

She'd seen the face turn pale and the lips tighten into a hard line before Mummy marched out, but she felt no regret. She was right. Her real mother would sit and read the story to her, the way Daddy did.

Funny, but she'd always known that Mummy wasn't really her mother. When she was little she used to think she was really a princess, stolen away by a wicked fairy and switched with Mummy's child. Daddy was real though – he loved her. If only Mummy wasn't there any more they could be so happy.

Or if she fell asleep for a long time, like Rip Van Winkle. She had tablets in her bedroom to make her sleep. Sometimes when she got very cross she complained that she had a

220

headache and Daddy would give her some of the pink pills with a glass of water. Then she'd go to sleep.

'Mummy, I've made you a cup of tea.'

Dorothy looked up from the *Woman's Journal* in surprise. Lucy was standing by her side, holding out one of her best china cups.

'Good gracious!' she exclaimed, taking the tea from her. 'How on earth did you manage that without scalding yourself?'

The child's gaze was earnest. 'I wanted to give you a surprise.'

Dorothy took a sip, then pulled a face. 'Ugh! What on earth have you put in it?'

The child looked up, wide-eyed. 'Two spoons of sugar – that's right, isn't it?'

'Salt, more like,' snapped Dorothy. 'Stupid girl, it tastes disgusting. Take it back to the kitchen and throw it out.'

She watched the small figure walk slowly away, carrying the cup with care, and felt a twinge. Maybe she shouldn't have been so sharp with the child. After all, she was trying.

PART THREE
1979

Chapter Nineteen

Humming to himself Reginald Holyoak locked up the garage and headed for the front door. He had good reason to feel pleased with himself. Ever since that time he'd been mayor he'd wanted so much to oust that sleazy Metcalf from the chairmanship of the Housing Committee and secure it for himself. It had taken time, but now at last he'd done it. And he had a shrewd idea how he was going to put it to good use.

Nothing illegal, of course, he thought as he unlocked the door – Heaven forbid, him a well-respected solicitor and all. As the senior partner of Holyoak, Brett and Fenton he could not afford to risk his hard-won reputation. But it was accepted that discreet little backhanders oiled the wheels in local government, everyone knew that, none better than that old creep Metcalf. He'd lined his nest well over the years, but never anything you could put your finger on. Nevertheless, millions had been spent on the building programme over that time, and who was to say if a thousand or two hadn't landed up where it shouldn't?

And the building budget looked like being even bigger next year, Reginald thought as he hung up his coat, and perhaps even bigger the year after if the sports centre and college campus votes went through.

'That you, Reginald?'

'Yes, dear.' He walked through into the sitting-room. Greta

was painting her nails by the fire. He stood on the hearth, warming his backside.

'Any supper?' he asked.

She held out her little finger and inspected it carefully. 'I didn't bother keeping anything hot when you weren't here,' she said without looking up. 'There's cold meat and salad if you fancy it.'

She didn't offer to go and fetch it. Reginald wandered out into the kitchen and opened the fridge. It was curious how off-hand she was these days, not unfriendly, but with a kind of amiable reserve, as if her mind was elsewhere. Now and again, however, it would snap into sharp focus.

'Did you remember to fetch your blue suit from the cleaner's?'

'Heck no – I forgot.'

Time was she'd have fetched it for him. Now all he got was a faint smile. 'Then you'll have to wear the grey one again tomorrow.'

He abandoned the idea of eating and went back to pour himself a whisky. As he did so Greta screwed the top back on the nail-varnish bottle.

'Pour one for me, please, Reginald,' she said as she stood up. 'I rather fancy having a drink in the bath.'

He stopped pouring and looked at her in surprise. 'Sherry?' he asked. 'Or dry Martini?'

'No, whisky – make it a double.'

As she left the room he shrugged and reached for another glass. She wasn't bad as wives went. At least she never asked awkward questions about where he'd been.

Dorothy Challis cocked her head to one side as she stood in the centre of the utility room, sizing up where she could put a new chest freezer. Not under the counter – she wouldn't be able to lift the lid. Now, if the washing-machine and the drier could be butted up against each other in the corner, it would just about leave enough space ...

This tiled room had been an enormous boon, ever since she'd finally got Theo to agree. It had taken him enough time to get round to it, and even then the work had dragged out over months and caused a terrible upset, but it had been worth it in the end. Nobody else in the avenue, she thought with pride, had a room like this, not yet anyway.

It had been worth its weight in gold when the children were younger, what with their bicycles and muddy hockey and football boots. Thank goodness Graham had reached a more sensible age; at sixteen he finally seemed to have outgrown his childish passion for football. It hadn't been good for him anyway with his knee. It was Theo who kept encouraging him, taking him down to Elland Road in all weathers. God knows what he was thinking about, knowing how bad the boy's chest always was in the winter.

Dorothy leaned across the counter to peer through the window to where Lucy was pegging out the washing. She clicked her tongue. The silly girl was hanging Theo's shirts by the shoulders again instead of by the tail. And Theo thought she should have been university material!

'You could easily get a degree,' she'd heard him tell the girl. 'You really ought to consider it.'

'I don't want a degree,' Lucy had replied.

'No point in forcing her,' Dorothy had cut in. 'Not if she doesn't want to.' It would have meant a deal of expense, and there was still Graham to send to college.

'Then what do you want to do?' Theo had asked.

'I want to do a nursing course,' Lucy had said. 'You know that's what I've always wanted to do.'

Dorothy sighed. Here she was, nineteen years old and still going on about that same silly notion. She'd tried in vain to make the girl see sense.

'You'd bring all kinds of germs into the house,' she'd pointed out.

'No I wouldn't.'

'Just think, having to touch people all day with TB, awful skin diseases, anything. It makes me feel ill to think of it.'

'It's not like that, not nowadays.'

Dorothy shook her head. 'Hospitals are known breeding grounds for infection. I've heard of people going in with one illness and coming out with another. No, it doesn't bear thinking of.'

She watched as Lucy came back up the garden path. She walked gracefully enough, even if she hadn't had deportment lessons. And she was becoming quite a pretty girl too. She'd probably marry quite young.

Lucy came in and closed the door, wiping her feet on the coir mat.

'It's getting cold already,' Dorothy remarked. 'I haven't seen those liberty bodices in the wash.'

'I'm not wearing them, that's why,' Lucy answered.

'What's wrong with them? They're very good quality, they are, good and fleecy, and they weren't cheap.'

'Kids wear liberty bodices,' Lucy said quietly. 'Not adults.'

'They're fine for the winter,' Dorothy protested. 'I don't know, after me traipsing all the way along to the Co-op, and me with my bad back. No gratitude, that's your problem.'

Lucy said nothing. She went on through to the kitchen and turned on the tap to fill the kettle. Do you realize, Mother, she fumed inwardly, how much you get on my nerves with your obtuse ways? I can remember times as a child when I could have killed you. Thank God that on the one occasion I tried, I failed. Nobody ever knew, not even Daddy. Even so, there are still times when I fantasize about beating some sense into your thick head with a broom handle.

228

As she plugged in the kettle, Graham arrived home and flung his school bag down on the table. 'Making coffee?' he asked. 'Good, I'll have one.'

His mother overheard and called out. 'It'll have to be instant, dear – there's no ground coffee till I get to the shops. All right?'

She appeared in the doorway, all smiles. Graham grunted as he pulled out a stool and sat down. His mother ruffled his hair as she passed.

'And then we'd better make a start on the vegetables,' she said, turning to Lucy. 'Your father will be home in no time.'

Lucy handed Graham a mug. 'I'll take my coffee up to my room,' he said, taking it from her and picking up his bag. Dorothy sighed as she watched the slight sway of his body as he transferred his weight to the weak knee.

'I don't know,' she murmured when he was out of sight, 'I wish I'd never let your father put up that wretched swing.'

Once again Lucy held her tongue. She was well aware of the accusation implicit in the words, that it was her fault Graham would always have a limp, but there was no point in arguing over it again. It was true his knee was fused and he'd never get in the school football team, but he suffered no pain and he'd long ago dismissed the slight limp as a mere trifle. Even if he didn't remember exactly how the accident happened, he certainly didn't blame Lucy. But Mother would never forgive her. She glanced at her set face as she dried leeks and lay them on the chopping board.

'Have you done anything about filling in those forms for the secretarial course?' she asked crisply.

'No,' said Lucy.

'Why not?' The knife attacked the leeks with energy. 'You'll miss the closing date if you're not careful.'

229

Lucy laid the scraped carrots alongside the unchopped leeks. 'You know why not,' she replied patiently. 'Because I'm not going to do it.'

The knife slammed down so hard half a leek shot off across the table, fell, and scudded across the floor. Mother ignored it. 'Then what are you planning to do?' she asked icily. 'You can't just loaf about doing nothing.'

'I'm going to be a nurse,' said Lucy, bending to pick up the leek. 'I've enrolled. I start a week on Monday.'

The knife paused in mid-air and her mother's startled face turned to her. 'Enrolled?' she echoed. 'When?'

'Yesterday.'

Mother reddened. 'You kept very quiet about that.'

'Because I knew how you'd react.' Lucy was surprised at her own calmness. 'I didn't want a scene.'

Mother laid down the knife. 'I only want what's best for you; you and Graham. That's all I've ever wanted. But nursing – really. That's little better than being a waitress.'

'You wouldn't say that if you were ill in hospital.'

Her mother turned back to the chopping board and picked up a carrot. 'Nursing,' she muttered, decapitating the defenceless carrot with venom, 'you'll have to do as you're told then, like it or not.' She waved the knife in Lucy's direction. 'That hair, for a start. They'll make you get it cut even if you wouldn't listen to me. I'll never forget how you got nits once, and then gave them to Graham.'

Lucy ran a hand down her long blond hair. 'We've talked about that. I only have to keep it out of sight under my cap.'

Her mother's lips were set. 'I can't get over you going to see them without telling us. Really, Lucy, you're too secretive for your own good. I'm very disappointed in you.'

She piled the chopped vegetables into the casserole and

turned away to open the oven. Lucy could feel her mother's air of frustrated anger as she left the room. Well, at least I got that over with, she thought. Mother just has to learn that she can't dominate everybody.

'I don't know why you're making so much fuss,' Theo said patiently without lowering his newspaper. 'You and she have never really got on. I'd have thought you'd be glad to see her go.'

'Go?' Dorothy said sharply. 'She'll still be living here, won't she?'

'Not if she's going to train at the infirmary in Hawksmoor. Didn't she tell you?'

Dorothy's lips tightened. There was a lot Lucy didn't tell her, but Theo always seemed to be taken into the girl's confidence, and she felt a gnawing pain somewhere near her stomach. If she didn't know better she could believe it was jealousy.

For a time there was silence except for the sound of voices on the television. 'She'll be taking her things then?' Dorothy said quietly.

'I expect so.'

'Will you drive her over to Hawksmoor?'

'Mm-hmm.'

So that had already been arranged. Dorothy picked up a wooden mushroom from her mending basket and pushed it into a sock. 'Right,' she said, 'then I'll come with you. I can see she's properly settled and has got all she needs.'

Theo lowered the newspaper. 'For heaven's sake, Dorothy, she's nineteen, not a child any more. She won't welcome you shoving your nose in. Let her manage on her own, for God's sake.'

Dorothy said no more. She bent her head, pretending to busy herself with darning Graham's sock. Theo would be

231

permitted to enter the girl's new life, but not her. She felt shut out of their world.

Her stomach knotted a little tighter. Envy and irritation were now somehow mingled with a tinge of loneliness.

The new girl had gone home and Rosa was counting the day's takings when she heard Alex shoot the bolt on the shop door. A few minutes later she heard his step on the stairs.

'Well,' he said, leaning his tall frame against the doorpost, 'need any help?'

She shook her head as she flipped the last of the notes and secured them with a rubber band. 'No thanks. I'll just take this lot to the night safe and then I'm off home.'

'Can I give you a lift then?'

'No thanks, I'm fine.'

As she swept the money into a canvas bag Alex straightened and took a step closer. 'You're a very independent lady, Mrs Pearson,' he said with a teasing smile. 'I'll give you that.'

She looked up at him quizzically.

'I don't want to push my nose in,' he went on quietly. 'I only want us to be good friends. We've known each other long enough now.'

'And we are,' she replied. 'I'm very grateful for all you've done for me, staying late to sort out my accounts and all that—'

'It works two ways,' he cut in. 'Your customers have brought me a lot more trade, so it's me who should be saying thank you.'

She went on, ignoring him. 'You've taught me a lot but—' She hesitated.

'But what?' he urged. 'What's bothering you? That there could be more to it than that? That I might have some other motive?'

She looked away, unwilling to meet his gaze. He disturbed her, those magnetic eyes always on her, following her everywhere. And what was more disturbing, she quite liked it.

'I only want to support you, Rosa,' he said softly, 'help you every way I can. Nothing more.'

She rose quickly and picked up the canvas bag. 'I know that. Goodnight, Alex,' she said, pushing past him towards the stairs. 'I'll see you in the morning.'

Dan Pearson watched his wife as she bustled about the kitchen sink, drying the supper dishes. She was so happy nowadays, he thought. It would be a pity to spoil her contentment, just when her café was doing so well.

She dried her hands and pulled off her apron. 'I've been thinking, Dan,' she said as she pulled out a chair and sat down. 'I've been going through my accounts and with things going the way they are we could afford now to think about a mortgage. There's some nice new houses being built—'

'No,' he said shortly. She looked at him in surprise.

'Why not?' she asked. 'We always said we'd like a place of our own. We've paid out enough in rent.'

'I know, but I can't,' he replied.

'We can, now I'm well in profit, and with your wage as well—'

'That's just it,' he cut in 'We can't count on my pay any more. I saw the doctor again today. I've been meaning to tell you.'

For a moment Rosa sat silent and then she reached a hand across to touch his. 'Stomach been playing you up again?' she asked.

He nodded. 'I didn't say owt – didn't want to worry you, but when I saw blood—'

Rosa started. 'Blood?' she repeated. 'Where?'

233

'When I was sick.'

He heard her quick indrawn breath and clasped her hand. 'I didn't want to worry you,' he muttered. 'I wouldn't now only the quack says I'm not to go to work. I'm on the sick list – for the time being, that is.'

She patted his hand with a smile. 'Only for the time being – you'll soon be right. We'll forget about the house till you're better.'

She got up and turned away to stack the dishes in the cupboard. He couldn't see her face, but he knew she'd be biting her lip. Not with disappointment but with worry about him, and that was the last thing he wanted. She was a good woman. She took disappointments on the chin. Like the fact that he'd never given her a child in all these years. She'd even tried to take the blame herself, but he knew. Dan Pearson accounted himself a very lucky man to have found a wife like Rosa.

Chapter Twenty

After leaving Lucy at Hawksmoor's impressive new infirmary Theo drove home to Leeds. He had no worries about how his daughter would get on; almost at once she'd befriended a couple of the other young student nurses who'd arrived to take up the course. He'd left the three of them – Lucy, a redhead from Wales and a lovely Indian girl – chattering away together as if they'd known one another for years. One copper head, one blonde and the other as black as coal.

He'd seen the glow of anticipation in her eyes as she kissed him goodbye, and he wished with all his heart that her new life was all she hoped for. It had been her dream for so long.

Dorothy would soon come to terms with it. Give her her due, she liked her own way, yet she had a knack of accommodating quite quickly to circumstances. Before long she would forget she'd been outmanoeuvred and begin to see the advantages; she'd be talking of Lucy's chance to meet doctors, 'people of the right sort'.

A sudden pain shot through his chest and he winced and braked. He must have jerked the steering-wheel because the driver behind flashed his lights angrily and then scowled as he overtook. Theo slowed the car to a halt and sat still, waiting to see if the pain returned. Sometimes it gave two or three painful jabs, sometimes down his arm as well, before it left him in peace.

For long minutes he sat tense, waiting, but nothing happened. Weariness swamped him, as though someone had drained the lifeblood out of him. Hands on the wheel, he stared dully ahead through the windscreen. A woman paused on the pavement edge, then ushered a crocodile of small children across the road. They skipped and giggled into line on the far side, then set off hand in hand towards the park.

He felt sick. A chilling sensation of finality came over him, a sense of impending doom. He sat upright cautiously, reaching for the ignition. Snap out of it, Theo, he told himself sharply. You're not ill; it's only because you've said goodbye to Lucy. There's no need to start feeling maudlin. Get a move on. There's still a dozen miles or more to go before you reach home.

'Coming to bed, Rosa?'

She didn't look up. 'Not yet, love, I want to finish these. You go on up – I'll try not to wake you.'

Dan stood in his pyjamas in the living-room doorway. From here he could see only the back of Rosa's dark head, haloed in golden light from the lamp, and the clutter of papers scattered around her on the table. He turned to the stairs sadly.

She hadn't even lifted her head. These days the paperwork seemed more important to her. Not that he resented it; on the contrary, he'd desperately wanted her to realize her dream, but somehow he seemed to be slipping out of sight.

Especially now, when he was no longer working. He hated the feeling; being a sick man kept by a woman would have been unthinkable not so long ago. He was less than a man – he was nothing. She couldn't even turn round to say good night.

He fetched the plastic bucket from the bathroom and

placed it by his side of the bed, just in case, then crawled between the sheets. Please God the gnawing pain wouldn't turn into another of those bilious attacks again tonight. He couldn't bear the retching, the foul smell, the shame of being mopped up like a child, and her soothing words.

She must have crept up quietly because he didn't hear her until she came into the room. 'Awake, love?' she whispered.

He grunted.

'How are you feeling?'

'OK, I suppose.'

She slithered in beside him and snuggled up close. He could feel the silky texture of her nightdress against his skin. A slim arm reached around him.

'How OK?' she murmured against his ear.

He groaned and removed her arm. 'Not that good,' he muttered. 'Sorry.'

'No matter,' she said. 'Sleep well, Dan. God bless.'

She rolled over and pulled the sheets around her. For a long time he lay staring miserably into the darkness of the room. He was right. For her he was less than a man.

Maybe the time had come, Greta Holyoak decided, to take a lodger. For some years now she'd enjoyed her privacy in the little Jubilee Terrace house but it seemed unfair to hog it to herself when so many people were in need of accommodation. The tenant could have the run of the place, except for her locked room.

A student, perhaps – but then again, perhaps not. Mrs Clancy said she'd never found them to be reliable. A woman, preferably, who'd keep the house warm and tidy. Maybe she should put an advertisement in the *Examiner*.

Or better still, Betty Tasker might know of someone she

could recommend. That was it. She'd go round to Mafeking Street and have a word with her.

Betty Tasker wasn't in, but her husband was.

'Come on in,' he said, stepping back to let Greta enter. 'She'll not be long – she's nobbut taken some fresh-baked scones round to Mrs Kadinski.'

Greta lifted her nose as she went inside. The delicious scent of freshly baked pastry filled the air. Fred Tasker stood uncomfortably on the hearth for a moment, then jerked his head in the direction of the back door.

'I were just off out to feed me pigeons,' he said gruffly. 'Want to come and have a look?'

'I'd love to.'

Greta followed him out into the yard and watched him as he unlocked the door of the pigeon loft. He lifted out one of the birds and, cradling it gently between his leathery hands, held it out to her.

'She's a bonny 'un, isn't she?' he murmured. 'I'm putting her in the show next week. She'll do all right, she will.'

He lifted the bird to his mouth, pursed his lips and blew gently into its beak. Greta watched as the bird's feathers seemed to swell before her eyes.

'That's what you have to do to display a pouter's plumage better,' Fred told her, 'but you mustn't blow too hard. There's a knack to it, do you see?'

Greta was fascinated. There was so much going on around her that she didn't know about. 'Do you race your pigeons, Mr Tasker?' she asked.

'Oh aye,' he replied. 'Taken many a prize, my birds have, but my lead pigeon's missing at the moment. He'll be back tomorrow.'

'Will he? Can you be sure?'

Fred replaced the bird in the loft. 'Oh aye,' he said.

'There's always a rogue pigeon, one that won't come home nights with the rest. It'll roam free for a bit till the others fly out again, then it'll join in with them. Just needs a bit of space, do you see?'

Greta smiled to herself. A rogue pigeon, she thought, rejoining the crowd when it feels like it. Just like me. Behind her there was a rap at the kitchen window and Betty Tasker's voice called out.

'Fred! What are you keeping Mrs Holyoak out there in the cold for? Bring her indoors this minute.'

Betty saw her visitor settled with a cup of tea and a buttered scone and then put her feet up on the pouffe.

'Me legs, you know,' she explained. 'They keep swelling up. Now then, I been meaning to ask you summat.'

'What's that?' said Greta.

'I pass your house in Jubilee Terrace many a time and there's never a sign of life, no smoke coming from the chimney or owt.'

'No,' admitted Greta. 'I'm not there a lot. That's why—'

'And many a time and oft I've wondered why, you having a nice place up in Edgerton and all.'

'That's what I've come to see you about,' said Greta. 'I only use the place as – as a kind of office, you see. I thought it might not be a bad idea to have a tenant, and I wondered if you knew of anyone.'

Betty rubbed her aching thigh thoughtfully. 'Not off-hand, I don't, but I'll keep me eyes and ears open. There's always folk wanting to get out of them flats they built up Swan Lane.'

'Really? The new tower blocks?'

'Horrible places they are, running with damp. Mrs Fletcher were showing me only the other day how damp her wardrobe was, and, if it's not in the fridge, her bacon goes reesty overnight. It fair sickens me to see such waste.'

Greta laid down the cup and stood up. 'I'd better be off now,' she said. 'It looks like it's coming on to rain. So if you do hear of anybody—'

'I'll let you know,' said Betty, levering herself out of the chair. 'And here, take a couple of my scones with you – I'll put 'em in a paper bag.'

Greta was nearing the viaduct, her umbrella lowered against the driving rain, when she fancied she heard a distant cry. She peered under the umbrella, but could see nothing in the rapidly darkening street.

Silly, she told herself, it was only her imagination. Trudging under the eerie archway in the gloom always made her fearful of attack. She should have noticed the sky turning to lead-grey and set off for home sooner.

The hiss of the rain ceased and in the silence under the vaulted arch she could hear the echo of her own footsteps ringing out. As she emerged again a dark shape suddenly leaped round the corner of Victoria Street and collided with her so sharply that for a second she felt as if the breath had been driven out of her lungs. She clutched the umbrella, ready to do battle.

'For Christ's sake, don't let him get me!'

A white-faced girl, her cheeks tear-stained and her long hair plastered to her forehead, stared up at her, clutching her arm. 'Please,' she gasped, 'he'll hit me again!'

Greta grabbed her and turned her about. This was no time to ask questions. The girl was clearly in distress. 'Come on,' she said, and broke into a run, back through the arch into Mafeking Street. At the first entry she pushed the girl into the passage.

'Get round the back,' she ordered. 'Stay out of sight till I come.'

The girl fled into the darkness. Greta retraced her steps towards the viaduct. She could see him now in the shadows, a short, thick-set man, looking this way and that, wavering.

'You seen a lass?' he demanded as Greta came near. 'Little and dark?'

'Why?' Greta was surprised at her own coolness.

He scowled. He had an unpleasant swarthy face. 'What do you mean, why?' he snapped. 'She's my lass, that's why. She's in for a right hiding when I get hold of her. Are you sure you haven't seen her?'

'I don't know that I'd tell you if I had,' said Greta, 'the mood you're in. But I did see a girl running down Victoria Street.'

'Did you now?' He wheeled about, back into the street, and hurried away in the direction the girl had been running. Greta waited until he was safely out of sight and then turned and retraced her steps.

The girl was cowering behind the gate of somebody's backyard. Seeing Greta alone she sidled out.

'Has he gone?' she asked, fear rounding her eyes.

Greta took her arm. 'Yes, you're safe now. Let me take you home and get you dried out.'

The girl stared, resisting her tug. 'Come on,' Greta urged, 'you're drenched to the skin. You needn't worry, he won't see you, my place is up the other way in Jubilee Terrace.'

She drew the girl under the shelter of the umbrella and led her out into the street.

The fire was low but at least it was still burning. Greta coaxed the embers into a comforting blaze, swathed the girl in a blanket and gave her a hot cup of tea.

She was only a slip of a thing, she thought, barely more than a teenager, wearing one of those cheap Indian cotton frocks that were so fashionable these days. And, she noted sadly, there were dark bruises on her thin wrists.

The girl seemed to become aware of her scrutiny. Her hands still curled tightly around the teacup as she looked up at Greta with huge liquid eyes.

'He'd have killed me, you know,' she whispered. 'He's a bad 'un.'

Greta felt anger ripple. Some people didn't deserve to have children. 'Your father?' she asked.

'Is he heck!' the girl snorted. 'Me mam married him last year. Jack's me stepdad. He's no right to beat me.'

'Indeed no, we're not having that,' Greta said sharply. 'Now tell me, what's your name?'

The girl looked down at the teacup. 'Dodd,' she muttered.

Greta smiled. 'I can't call you Dodd,' she said gently. 'Look, my name's Greta Kaye. What's yours?'

The girl jutted her chin. 'Linda Mason, that's me name,' she said stoutly. 'I'm damned if I'll be called Dodd just 'cos me mam married him. He'd like it and all, but he's nowt to me, he isn't. He'll never take me dad's place, not to me.'

Greta could hear the quiver in her voice. 'Now, now,' she said, patting the girl's hand, 'there's no need to take on. Of course you can't think of him as your own father; no-one would expect you to.'

'I hate him,' Linda muttered savagely. 'If me mam knew what he does ...'

Greta looked down at the bruises. 'One day,' she soothed, 'when you're old enough to work—'

Linda gave a dry laugh. 'I am working – at Chadwick's – and much good it does me. Jack takes me money off me.'

Greta's eyebrows rose. 'How long have you been working?'

'About two years – I'm seventeen.'

Greta thought for a moment. 'Maybe the time has come to think about leaving home,' she murmured, 'but let's not talk about that tonight.'

A flicker of a smile touched the girl's lips. 'Nice place you got here,' she said. 'Ours used to be like this before we moved. I liked it there.'

'Where do you live now?' asked Greta.

'Up Swan Lane, in one of them two-bed flats. It's not the same, specially since he came.'

Greta noted the venom with which she emphasized the pronoun. 'Is he always bad-tempered?' she asked, then touching the thin arm she added, 'Does he often hit you?'

The girl shrugged. 'Sometimes. It's worst when me mam's away, like now – she's at me auntie's in Bridlington.'

'So she can't stop him hitting you.'

'Hitting me?' Linda looked up with forlorn eyes. 'She'd stick the carving knife in him if she knew what he got up to behind her back. The minute she's gone he's in, and the bugger knows I'm not strong enough to fight him off.'

She pushed the blanket back to reveal her arms, covered in black bruising. Greta sat stunned, horrified by the image the girl's words conjured up.

'That settles it,' she pronounced firmly, 'you're staying here tonight.'

Linda shook her head. 'I can't upset you like that – you were going out.'

'No matter,' said Greta. 'No hurry. Can you get any of your things in the morning? So you can go to work?'

'Oh aye, once he's gone to work.'

'Right,' said Greta. 'I'll see you settled and give you a

243

key. Tomorrow you go to work as usual, then meet me here at teatime.'

Poor little thing, thought Greta as she hurried for the bus. Abused by a foul creature like that! If her mother knew nothing about it then the best thing Linda could do was to get out. If she was telling the truth, at seventeen she was legally entitled to leave without her parents' consent. No-one, least of all that disgusting Dodd, could demand her return.

At least Reginald was at that dinner in Leeds so he wouldn't be there to ask questions when she arrived home.

Chapter Twenty-one

The group of men around Reginald's table broke up and headed for the bar. He pushed back his chair and rose to follow them.

It had been quite a decent meal, as these business dos went, and even the speeches hadn't proved as boring as he'd feared. The trouble was though, they'd interfered with the conversation just as he'd discovered that Challis, the rather reserved man opposite with the quietly confident manner, was a flourishing builder. With luck Reginald could catch up with him in the bar, then he could probe a little while he savoured a cigar.

Theo didn't wait for the others. He headed straight to the bar and ordered a peppermint cordial. That bloody pain in his chest – it must be indigestion from that rubbery Yorkshire pudding; it bore no resemblance to the fluffy confection Dorothy always served up for Sunday lunch alongside the sliced roast beef.

He took his drink to a corner where he could watch the others come in, laughing and joking as they approached the bar. He felt in no mood to join in tonight.

He took a sip of the peppermint. Over there was that fellow who'd sat opposite him at dinner, the rather self-assured chap with the receding hairline. Someone said he was a lawyer. Theo could just imagine him holding forth in the courtroom.

Ouch! Another stab of pain. He closed his eyes and took a long swig of the cordial. As he set the glass down and licked his lips he became aware of a shadow falling across the table. He looked up.

'It's rather crowded over there,' a cheery voice said. 'Mind if I join you?'

It was the lawyer fellow. Without waiting for a reply he pulled out a chair and sat down. For a few moments he sat looking around him, taking out a cigar and inspecting the tip before lighting it. He threw back his head, watching the smoke rise to the panelled ceiling.

'You're a builder, I understand?'

Theo nodded. 'For my sins.'

Holyoak smiled. 'So am I, in a manner of speaking. It's my business to see the best tenders are accepted. Value for money and all that.'

He lay his cigar down in the ashtray. 'Hawksmoor Council. You handle big contracts yourself?' he asked.

'Hospitals, schools – you name it. Do you have anything particular in mind?' asked Theo.

The other man ignored the question and picked up his cigar again. 'Tell me, what do you think about prefabricated buildings?' he asked smoothly.

Theo took a deep breath 'System-built prefabs? Depends on the material. Some are far better than others.'

'But a fast cheap way of providing people with comfortable homes quickly, wouldn't you say?'

Theo had the measure of him now. With those crafty-looking eyes, he was up to something.

'Like I said, it all depends,' he replied wearily. That feeling of lassitude was coming over him again.

Holyoak blew a perfect smoke ring. 'We're about to spend a small fortune on housing. We've got people falling over themselves to get contracts.'

So that was it, thought Theo. He'd come across his sort before. Grease my palm and I'll see you're all right.

'Maybe so,' he sighed, 'but not me. I've got as much as I can handle.'

He'd had enough of this fellow. He wanted to get home to his bed. Tossing back the last of the peppermint cordial he stood up.

Holyoak smiled up at him. 'Sure you're not interested?'

Theo was in no mood to juggle with words. 'Now look here,' he said wearily, 'if I understand you aright, Mr Holyoak, just let me put you straight. You're wasting your time with me. My name's not Frank Crawshaw. Good night to you.'

Holyoak's jaw dropped open in an expression of bewildered innocence. 'I was suggesting nothing – what did you think I meant?'

But Theo was already making for the door.

Reginald watched the builder as he pushed his way through the group around the bar and headed for the exit, and a smile curved his lips. So Challis was one of those boring sea-green incorruptibles; they were a rare enough breed these days.

He rose to his feet. Time to join the others at the bar. What was that name again? Crawshaw, that was it.

Reginald pulled his car out of the hotel car park. It hadn't exactly been a waste of time, but his fellow drinkers hadn't been too eager to talk much about Crawshaw. The name had cropped up briefly, but whenever he'd tried to pursue the subject they'd seemed to clam up. He'd learned that the man was in quite a big way and that his yard was in Sheffield, and that was it. It was as if, to a man, they wanted to disclaim all knowledge of him.

Reginald had left it at that. Never mind, he thought as he

headed towards home, there was no hurry. It was another step in the right direction.

Greta already had the kettle on to boil when Linda arrived the next day. It had been a pleasure to come in and find the place tidy and the bed made. Clearly the girl was not the irresponsible sort.

She was different again today from the frightened child of last night. She sat now at Greta's table, sipping tea and chattering excitedly.

'He wasn't there, and me mam's away, of course, so I got all me stuff together and packed it up in a bag. I kept shaking, thinking he might come in any minute – he didn't, but I couldn't help shaking.'

'Well that's all over now,' said Greta. 'You won't need to see him any more.'

'I'll have to find a place,' Linda said dubiously. 'Round here, 'cos me mates are here, but I daren't put a card in the shop window for fear he sees it.'

Greta poured more tea. 'As I told you, Linda, I don't spend much time here. How would you like to be my tenant?'

The girl's face lit up. 'You mean it? Stay here? Oh, I'd love it! I've got money – I can pay.'

'We'll talk about that later. I'd want you to do a bit of cleaning and keep the house warm—'

'My own place,' Linda breathed. 'I can't believe it. Oh, don't you worry, I'll keep it clean as a new pin. I like things to be nice.'

'Thank you, Mrs Kadinski, that was lovely.'

Rosa stared after the departing customer in amazement, then chuckled to herself. When she packed up for the evening she couldn't help telling Alex.

248

He smiled. 'I know, it's not the first time. Customers often tell me that my wife's got a lovely place up there.'

'And you don't say anything?'

'No, I quite like the idea. It's your fault.' He pointed to the sign on the wall at the foot of the stairs. 'You shouldn't have called it The Coffee Shop. People think it's mine.'

Rosa shrugged. 'Well, I'm not bothered. Just so long as the money keeps coming in.'

'Judging by the number of people going up those stairs,' he replied, 'you're doing that all right. You're doing really well.'

She smiled. 'I'm not grumbling. Well, I'm off now. Good night Alex. See you in the morning.'

He came round the counter to open the door for her. As she passed he touched her shoulder. 'Mind how you go now.'

She smiled and went out, and as she walked along the deserted arcade towards the sodium-lit street she heard his voice call out softly.

'Good night, Mrs Kadinski.'

Dorothy clicked her tongue in irritation. 'That's the second time this week you've not finished your dinner, Theo. Whatever is the matter with you?'

'Nothing, dear. It's delicious but I'm just not hungry.'

She surveyed him thoughtfully. He looked pale and drawn. 'You're not worrying about Lucy, are you?' she challenged, 'because she'll be home at the weekend.'

'No, love. I'm fine, honestly.'

'Well I don't like the look of you at all. It's high time you saw the doctor.'

He sighed and laid his napkin aside. 'Doctors don't want to know about indigestion, my dear. Too many business lunches, that's all it is.'

'It's more than that,' she retorted. 'You've eaten enough of those Rennie things to sink a battleship and it still hasn't gone.' She threw down her napkin and stood up to stack the pudding dishes. 'But I tell you this, Theo,' she went on, 'next time you leave so much as a brussels sprout I'm ringing the surgery and making an appointment for you whether you like it or not. So there.'

For a week Greta stayed away from Jubilee Terrace. She wanted the girl to have time to settle into her new home; she wouldn't want to have her new landlady hanging about.

It had been agreed that Greta should come and go as she wished, mostly during the daytime, but generally speaking, in the evenings, Linda would have the house to herself, free to use all of it apart from the locked room upstairs. After a week of abstinence Greta was looking forward to spending a little time in her retreat once more.

The moment she opened the front door she noticed something different. She sniffed. There was a strange scent in the air, heady and sweet. She opened the door to the living-room and gave a start of surprise. The room was immaculate, not a speck of dust to be seen on the gleaming woodwork, and even the fire in the grate laid ready to light. The perfume in the air must be from the polish the girl had used, but it was certainly not a brand Greta had ever come across before.

She made herself a pot of tea and took it into the living-room for a time. She must have dozed off, for the next thing she knew a key was grating in the lock and Linda came in, her pretty face flushed.

'Hello,' she said brightly, then added shyly, 'I do hope it's to your liking. I spent ages on it.'

'It looks lovely, a real credit to you,' Greta replied. 'What's that perfume I can smell?'

Linda blushed. 'It's me joss-sticks, I reckon. I like burning them – I meditate, you know.'

Greta couldn't help the look of surprise on her face. 'Do you? How interesting. You must tell me about it.'

'Sandalwood's me favourite,' Linda went on, turning away to hang her coat in the hallway. She picked up the teapot. 'Though sometimes I get jasmine. Fancy another cup of tea?'

She bustled out into the little scullery and Greta could hear her humming as she filled the kettle. There was more to this girl than she'd given her credit for.

Reginald could hear Greta on the telephone in the hall.

'I'll see if he's free. Hold on a minute.'

He looked up from his newspaper as she came back into the room. 'Man on the phone for you,' she said as she picked up her book. 'He didn't give his name.'

'No name? Why not?'

'He said it wouldn't mean anything to you. You'd better go and see what he wants.'

With a sigh Reginald heaved himself out of the armchair. It clearly wasn't a friend, and a client had no damn right to be ringing him at home.

'Yes?' he said testily. 'Holyoak here.'

'Good evening,' a voice said smoothly. 'I understand you've been asking after me. My name's Crawshaw.'

Reginald's brow furrowed. The name rang a bell. It wasn't one of his current clients. Then in a flash it came to him: that dinner in Leeds, weeks ago ...

'Really? Who told you that?' he asked mildly. It paid to be cautious.

The voice sounded amused. 'I get to know everything sooner or later.'

'I see,' said Reginald, 'and what can I do for you?'

251

'Let's have a meal together and maybe we can find out. Lunch on Tuesday?'

'I'm in court on Tuesday.'

'Thursday then. I'm in Leeds that day. How about the Queen's, say about half-past twelve.'

Reginald tried to look nonchalant as he returned to the lounge and picked up the newspaper once more. Greta looked up from her book.

'Who was it?'

'No-one – just a builder after a contract.'

She snorted. 'Cheek of it, bothering you at home.'

'Well,' he said, patting his stomach in satisfaction, 'they're like bloodhounds, sniffing out who's in control of the big money. You can't blame them for trying.'

Reginald felt just the tiniest bit uneasy as he walked in through the imposing doors of the Queen's Hotel. It lay just a little too close for comfort to the Dark Arches, the area where Madame Zara lived.

Not that she'd embarrass him even if they came across one another – she wasn't the sort to tout for business in the street. Hers was a very exclusive clientele who visited by appointment only.

He forgot about her the moment he spotted the solitary diner over in a corner of the restaurant.

He was an insignificant-looking individual, he thought, with thinning sandy hair and lean features. His face was florid, as though the normally fair skin of the redhead had been too long in the sun.

'Crawshaw?'

The weaselly face smiled up at him. 'Holyoak, do sit down.' He waved towards the empty chair opposite. 'I've taken the liberty of ordering a bottle of wine – I do hope it's to your taste.'

Reginald sat down as Crawshaw beckoned to the waiter to bring the menu. The little man gave Reginald the distinct impression that he was accustomed to being in charge. Reginald ignored the menu and leaned forward.

'Now then, what's this all about?'

Crawshaw put down his menu. 'I see you're not going to waste my time – that's good.'

'Or my own,' snapped Reginald. 'I have clients to see today.'

'Right, to business.' The little man poured two glasses of wine, then leaned back in his chair, arching his fingertips together. 'Your Council has a number of big building contracts which you'll be putting out to tender in the near future.'

Reginald took a sip of the wine. It wasn't bad at all. 'We've been forced to make cut-backs in our housing programme,' he said. 'Not so much spending power as you might think.'

'I know the figure,' said Crawshaw. 'I make it my business to know these things.'

'So you know what we're after?'

'System-built prefabricated tower blocks.'

'That's right. For decent homes and for the college.'

'And I've got exactly what you want. Good spacious homes, well-built and cheap.'

Reginald sat back, twisting the wineglass between his fingertips. 'Mr Crawshaw, there must be at least a dozen other builders who could say just the same. Why don't you just put in your tender with the rest?'

'They can't offer what I'm offering: quality and economy. You don't get Brownie points for squandering tax-payers' money.'

'True,' admitted Reginald, 'but cheapness isn't everything.'

Crawshaw leaned forward and set his glass down, a

253

gleam in his small eyes. 'I'm glad to hear you say that,' he said. Reginald tried not to appear too concerned, but the hair was prickling on the back of his neck.

The builder smiled and picked up the menu again. 'We could do each other a favour, Holyoak, and it could be to our mutual advantage,' he said quietly. 'You'd like to have a look at some of my work, I'm sure.'

Here it comes, thought Reginald, an offer of a free weekend in some country hotel.

Crawshaw was scanning the menu. 'Or better still,' he murmured, 'why don't you come and meet some of the others I've worked with? We're having a bit of a get-together, my fellow directors, and you'd be very welcome to join us – you and your wife.'

Reginald tried his best to sound casual. 'Really? Where?'

'In Spain,' replied Crawshaw, 'a new luxury hotel complex we've just completed. You could spend a few days, looking it over and talking to the others. They'll tell you how I operate. Then you can decide.'

'Spain? Ah, well,' Reginald murmured, glancing down the menu, 'give me some time to think it over.'

'First-class flight, of course,' added Crawshaw. 'Waiter, we're ready now.'

'Spain?' Greta echoed in surprise. 'Good gracious!'

'I really think I should go,' Reginald said mildly, reaching for the salt. 'It's best to check these things out thoroughly.'

'Of course,' replied Greta, her imagination conjuring up visions of cool drinks on colourful, sun-washed beaches. 'Thinking of taking Phyllis Thewlis with you?' she added mischievously.

'Good grief no!' he exclaimed. 'Heaven forbid! Anyway this is a business trip. And it's just between the two of us, remember.'

She pushed her plate away. She wouldn't have minded a spot of sunshine, but not with Reginald. Anyway, she had other things here to occupy her mind and, quite frankly, she didn't give a damn if he took the Thewlis woman or anyone else for that matter.

Chapter Twenty-two

Theo watched the doctor's face anxiously as he removed the stethoscope from his ears and laid it aside. He looked serious, too serious.

'Well?' Theo asked.

The doctor turned to his desk and pulled forward a notepad. 'I'd like you to go for an ECG,' he said quietly. 'I'll arrange an appointment for you.'

'It is my heart, isn't it?' Theo persisted. The doctor scribbled away intently. 'Well, there does seem to be a murmur,' he agreed, 'but I'd prefer to have confirmation.'

'So what do I do?' asked Theo. 'Apart from the ECG, that is?'

'Take it easy, no excitement. Maybe lose a little weight. But let's not jump the gun – let's leave all that till we have the results of the test, shall we?'

He'd said the right soothing words to try and allay his fears, thought Theo as he drove away from the surgery, but that look on his face spoke volumes. Dorothy mustn't know, not yet. No point in alarming her until he knew for sure and the truth was unavoidable.

But even so, his mind would not be diverted from facing the possible outcome. He had to make sure everything was in order, just in case, so there would be as little upset as possible for the family. At least Lucy had started on her career and was clearly enjoying it, the house and car were paid for, and the business was doing all right. If only Graham was a little older and able to take over.

He had to hang on, for their sake.

Greta found more to delight her each time she went down to Jubilee Terrace. First it was the fresh flowers in the vase on the window-sill, then the new scalloped net curtains in place of the old lace ones.

'I hope you don't think me cheeky,' Linda explained, 'only I did wash them lace ones and put 'em away in the drawer.'

'Not at all,' said Greta. 'It looks lovely.'

'And I seen me mam – she's real pleased I've got me own place and she gave me a lovely quilt for me bed.'

'I'm so glad she's happy about it,' said Greta.

'And I was wondering if you'd mind if I got some new wallpaper for me bedroom to go with the quilt,' Linda went on. 'Only it clashes with that paper up there.'

'Which has probably been up for years,' said Greta. 'You're welcome to decorate it as you wish.'

It afforded her genuine pleasure to see the girl's face aglow with eager enthusiasm. Reginald, on the other hand, though his face glowed equally redly when he returned from Spain, was far less buoyant.

'It was a damned disaster from start to finish,' he fumed. 'First the plane was delayed because of some air-traffic-control problem or other, then the Spanish customs were searching every twentieth passenger. Guess who was the twentieth? I ask you, do I look like the sort to be smuggling drugs?'

'Or pornographic material,' said Greta mildly. 'Whatever were they thinking of?'

'Then I lost my ring – my father's signet ring,' he rumbled, 'and to cap it all, the damned hire-car broke down right up in the mountains. I had to wait an hour and a half for someone to give me a lift back into town.'

Greta surveyed his ruddy face. 'At least it looks like you had decent weather,' she remarked. 'Better than we had here.'

'It wasn't too hot at this time of year, out of season, but it's deceptive. It was the wind up in the mountains that did this.'

Greta couldn't help a secret smile. Reginald wasn't amused.

'Sunburn's no joke,' he muttered. 'I'll be stuck with a peeling face for days yet.'

Greta composed her face. 'But otherwise it was all right, was it? What about the hotel you went to see?'

Reginald's expression brightened. 'Couldn't be better,' he said. 'Fine building, well-equipped, and I couldn't have had better service if I'd been the Queen herself.'

'Good,' said Greta, 'so the builder's in with a chance?'

'He might be,' replied Reginald. 'He might well be.'

Theo didn't really take in the doctor's careful explanation, something about a leaky aortic valve and not enough blood and oxygen reaching the heart. All he registered was that he had a dicky heart and on no account was he to exert himself or become excited or the result could be fatal.

'A quiet way of life from now on,' the doctor had said. 'Maybe you should think about retiring.'

But Theo couldn't face the prospect of staying at home all day under Dorothy's shrewd scrutiny. Anyway he wasn't going to tell her. After all, the doctor had clapped him on the shoulder as he left and said with a smile that, with care, he could live to be a hundred.

Maybe that was a little optimistic, thought Theo, but he would like to see the children grow up and marry, to see a grandchild or two frolicking under the trees in the garden. He smiled to himself, thinking how Dorothy would be in her element, once again marshalling little ones into paper hats and party games.

As he turned the car into the avenue he caught sight of Lucy's slim figure striding ahead towards the house. He pipped the horn as he passed her and pulled into the drive, then sat waiting. She arrived, a smile spreading across her pretty face. He wound down the window.

'How's it going, sweetheart?'

She leaned her elbows on the window-frame. 'Oh, it's great, Dad. I love it. There's some terrific people on my course – you've got to meet Neela. She's so funny.'

It gave him pleasure to see the happiness in her eyes as she chattered on. 'Let's go in,' he said at last. 'Your mother will want to hear it all too.'

Dorothy sat on the sofa surrounded by a heap of colour brochures.

'What's all this?' said Theo in surprise. It wasn't like her to permit such a litter of magazines in her immaculate show-house lounge.

'Cruises,' she answered brightly. 'We're going on holiday. I've decided and I'm not going to have any argument.'

'That's not a bad idea,' said Lucy. 'Dad could do with a break.'

Dorothy's eyebrows rose, then she nodded. 'You can arrange a couple of weeks off work,' she said to her husband. 'The minute Graham's exams are over. He'll deserve a holiday.'

Theo sank into a chair. The idea had its appeal – lazing all day on deck in the sun, watching the world go by, no obligation to do anything beyond the occasional game of deck quoits.

'Fine,' he said. 'Where to?'

'The Mediterranean,' Dorothy pronounced. 'Stopping off in some lovely cities. Just think – sight-seeing, lots of shopping. It'll be a wonderful change.'

Over her head Theo caught sight of Lucy's smile.

He could hear Lucy running the shower in the bathroom as he undressed for bed. Dorothy, already in her nightdress, sat at the dressing-table, smothering her face with cream.

'Well, Lucy seems happy enough,' he remarked. 'I'm so glad.'

Dorothy snorted. 'If she isn't now she's got her own way, she never will be. Always had a mind of her own, that one.'

Theo climbed into bed. 'Aren't you happy for her?' he asked as he settled down. 'We all need to do something we care about.'

His wife shrugged satin-clad shoulders. 'If it's what she wants, well and good, but I'd much rather she'd study to be a doctor. Still,' she murmured thoughtfully, rubbing the last of the cream into her hands, 'I suppose she's meeting doctors every day ...'

Under the cover of the sheets Theo smiled to himself.

Rosa watched the old lady puffing her way to the top of the stairs where she paused, leaning on the balustrade, then placed her dripping umbrella carefully in the brass umbrella stand. That old stand from the junk shop had proved a boon.

The old lady looked like a small pyramid, thought Rosa as she went across to greet her. Short and squat, with huge hips blossoming out under her tweed coat, on second thoughts she reminded Rosa of a jelly which hadn't had time to set before someone tipped it out on a plate.

'Good morning,' said Rosa. 'Would you like a table in the window?'

The old lady transferred her handbag so as to hold out her right hand. 'Mrs Kadinski,' she said, and Rosa noted the strange, guttural sound in her voice.

She shook the proffered hand. 'No,' she said quietly. 'My name is Mrs Pearson.'

'No, no,' replied the lady, an apologetic smile creasing her plump face. 'I am Mrs Kadinski. I come for coffee with you because my son tells me I should meet you.'

'You're Alex's mother?' Rosa exclaimed, folding the pudgy hand between her own, 'I'm so glad to meet you. Come and sit down.'

Layers of flesh settled over the edges of the chair as Mrs Kadinski seated herself. She glanced around the room. 'You have done well,' she commented. 'This place was a right tip before you came.'

It was curious to hear the foreign voice using the local vernacular, but then the old lady must have been in this country for many years. 'Thank you,' she answered. 'Alex gave me a lot of help.'

Mrs Kadinski nodded. 'He's a good boy, so like his father. He tells me your husband did a lot of the work.'

'That's right,' said Rosa. 'He's a genius with his hands. Or at least . . .' Her voice tailed away. 'But now I'm thinking of expanding,' she went on. 'If I could knock that wall down over there—'

Mrs Kadinski wasn't listening. 'He's a sick man now, your husband,' she said. 'It must be very difficult for you.'

Rosa bit her lip. 'He's not very well,' she admitted, 'but we have a good doctor. He'll keep an eye on him.'

'So you are the one who has to work?' The old lady surveyed her speculatively. 'You're a good woman, Mrs Pearson.'

261

With an embarrassed smile Rosa changed the subject. 'Let me fetch you a nice pot of coffee,' she suggested, 'freshly ground by your son. Which sort do you like best? French?'

'I'll have the Kenyan,' Mrs Kadinski replied. 'With a big jug of cream.' Mrs Kadinski watched the girl hurry away into the kitchen. Alex should be so lucky, to capture a wife like this one. All these years she had waited, ever since he became a man, and still he brought no woman to the house. Feodor would have loved grandchildren, God rest his soul.

'Ivana,' he used to say to her, 'we were never blessed with a daughter, but one day Alex will bring a woman to us. She will be the delight of our old age and surround us with grandsons.'

Dear Feodor. He had never seen his dream fulfilled, and as each day passed it seemed as though she too would go to her Maker without seeing a grandchild. But it was more important to see Alex settle down with a woman who would love him as she did.

Rosa came back, carrying a tray with the coffee smelling like heaven in pretty flowered china. She set the tray down with a smile. Mrs Kadinski looked up at the oval face framed in dark hair. She was beautiful, this girl, hard-working and affectionate. Her husband was a very lucky man.

God grant that maybe one day Alex should be so fortunate ...

Greta didn't stay long the next time she called at the cottage in Jubilee Terrace. Dust-sheets and tins and brushes everywhere and the pervasive odour of fresh paint – it was clear that Linda was making a real blitz on the place. She evidently meant to carry on just as soon as she arrived home that evening.

Greta picked her way out again carefully and closed the front door. As she turned to go she became aware of a pair of brown eyes watching her hopefully. A small mongrel dog sat gazing up at her, one tattered ear flopping while the other stood erect.

'Hello,' she said. 'Where are you from?'

She bent to pat his scruffy head and he twisted it away, turning to nuzzle her hand. 'I've nothing for you, I'm afraid,' she said. 'Go on home.'

At the end of the street she looked back. He was there, trotting along not five paces behind. 'Go on now,' she urged, 'I'm going home. You go back to where you belong.'

He wagged his stumpy tail and came close, looking up with soft eloquent eyes. Greta tried to ignore him as she walked away.

At the next corner she refused to look back. To smile or speak to him again would only encourage him. If he came too far he'd get lost. Poor little thing – he seemed scrawny and underfed so he couldn't afford to miss his supper.

Her shopping bag seemed to be growing heavier with every step. When she reached the bench outside the railings of Greenhead Park she'd sit down and rest a while. From there it was only a short walk home.

She sank gratefully onto the wooden bench under the trees. The cherry blossom was just coming out, gentle sprays of pink mingling with the translucent pale green of the leaves. It was beautiful here, even with the traffic rushing by. Who needed to go to Spain when even a smoky old town like Hawksmoor could hold such loveliness?

Something cold and wet prodded the back of her calf. Greta looked down into a pair of melting brown eyes.

'I thought I told you to go home,' she said sternly, rising to her feet. The little dog skipped hopefully around her, his tail wagging eagerly. Greta picked up the shopping bag.

'Come on then,' she grumbled, 'but you're not stopping. Just a plate of cold bits left from last night and then you're on your way. Understand?'

Reginald felt supercharged with adrenalin. Energy was bursting out of him, and it wasn't all due to Crawshaw's proposition in Spain.

One per cent of the total contract price, he'd offered, and the resulting figure was enough to tempt Saint Peter himself. Not that it would be handed over just like that – oh no, Crawshaw was far too shrewd a character. Like the other fellows Reginald had met out there, he'd become another non-executive director of one of Crawshaw's companies, drawing a 'consultancy fee' in another year or so. And then again the year after that.

Reginald hugged himself. All he had to do was to steer a certain tender safely through the Housing Committee and it meant a reasonable pension for life. In the days ahead there could be more such tenders.

The fire inside him began to focus in his guts and he felt once again the old familiar hunger. He looked around. Dusk was falling but Greta was still outside in the garden, doing something with her spring bulbs. He slipped out into the hall and dialled a Leeds number.

'It's me,' he whispered into the mouthpiece. 'Tonight? ... Nine-thirty? ... Fine.'

Greta sat nibbling the tip of a pencil as she struggled with *The Times* crossword. Reginald yawned and laid his book aside.

'Mind if I pop down to the club for a drink?' he enquired. 'I think it might help me sleep.'

'Not in the least,' she replied absently. 'Off you go. Seven letters, starting with m ...'

He was just rising from his chair when he heard it, a strange scuffling sound in the hallway, followed by a yelp. 'What the devil's that?' he exclaimed, and crossed to open the door.

A ragged little face gazed up at him for a moment, pink tongue dangling, then the eyes swivelled and focused on Greta. Reginald stared as a dirty little mongrel raced across to the sofa and leaped up, planted its front paws in her lap and then tried to lick her face.

'What the hell's that?' he demanded. 'Get that filthy beast out of here!'

'He's a stray,' Greta said calmly. 'He followed me home.'

'We don't have to have a mangy mongrel in just because he's a stray!' Reginald fumed. 'Get rid of him quick, for God's sake, before he fills the place with fleas.'

Greta stroked the dog's head. 'He's quite nice, really. If he hasn't got a home—'

'He's not finding one here, and there's an end to it! Whatever are you thinking of?'

'Somebody needs to care for him.' Greta's voice sounded more tender than he'd heard for years. 'We all need to be cared for.'

Reginald had had enough. 'He's going out, right now,' he said firmly, and he strode purposefully across to the sofa. As he drew near the little dog turned its head and growled.

Greta smiled. 'I think he has other ideas,' she said softly. 'And come to think of it, so do I. He'll be my dog.'

Reginald stood unmoving. The dog might be small but he didn't like the look in its eyes. 'Dog?' he muttered. 'That's not a dog, not like Rex – now there was a real dog.'

'A guard dog,' corrected Greta, 'a ferocious thing to keep prowlers away. You couldn't even stroke him.'

'He was a pure-bred bull mastiff, not a mangy little runt.

That thing's neither use nor ornament and I want it out of here – now.'

Greta scooped the scruffy little beast up in her arms. 'You could be right,' she agreed, 'but he's mine now and I'm keeping him.'

Reginald hesitated. Madame Zara would be waiting for him. 'We'll see about that,' he muttered, but as he turned to go he could swear the creature was grinning at him in triumph.

Greta heard the car pull out of the drive and she cradled the dog close. He flopped his head down on her shoulder, staring at his own reflection in the mirror. He felt disgustingly tacky and his matted fur was full of grit. But then so was he, she thought. True grit. She turned the little face round and looked deep into the trusting brown eyes.

'That was very brave of you, standing up to Reginald like that,' she murmured. 'He's been known to make even hardened criminals quail in the dock. You're a little hero, you are.'

The rasping pink tongue slapped sticky marks of affection on her hand, and Greta felt a glow of tenderness. Under the skinny ribs of this warm little body beat a heart eager for love and life.

She set him down on the floor. 'You know what, Hero?' she said with a sigh, 'Reginald's right, you do stink. You'll have to sleep in the porch tonight.'

The dog lowered its ears and stretched out full-length on the carpet. 'And tomorrow,' Greta went on, 'I'm going to give you a good bath and then go and buy some flea powder.'

Hero sank his head and buried his nose beneath his paws.

Chapter Twenty-three

Reginald groaned as he got out of bed. He was aching from head to toe. Today, of all days, when he had that important Housing Committee meeting. In place of his usual morning shower he'd take a bath, he decided, and maybe that would make him feel easier.

It was too early for Greta to be awake yet so she wouldn't question the change from his customary routine. He tiptoed past her bedroom door to the bathroom and turned on the taps.

While he waited for the bath to fill he might as well clean his teeth. Groaning, he wriggled out of his pyjama jacket and stepped out of the trousers. God, but Madame Zara had been vigorous last night, maybe even a little overzealous. He'd begged for punishment and her coolly efficient treatment had borne him aloft in a frenzy of passion. It had been fantastic, but he was paying for it now. He turned about, twisting his neck to survey his rear view in the mirror.

Hell's bells! His backside was latticed with red weals! No wonder it was so painful to move. Thank heavens no-one would see the damage. He pushed the bathroom door to, then reached for the bottle of green herbal liquid to pour in the water, the stuff Greta said was incredibly soothing and relaxing. With luck that might ease the sting.

Cautiously he lifted one leg over the side of the bath, dipped his toe in the water, then stepped in. Inch by inch he lowered himself into the murky green, wincing at the sheer agony of it. At last he lay full-length, moaning. It was so bloody painful it was almost gratifying.

To his surprise Greta was already in the kitchen when he came downstairs. Still in her dressing-gown, she stood at the counter waiting for the toast to pop up from the toaster. She glanced back as he came in.

'Reginald—'

He lowered himself gingerly onto the chair. 'You're up early,' he remarked. 'You're usually still asleep at this time.'

'It's this lovely sunshine. It woke me up. Reginald—'

'What?'

'I didn't mean to spy but I couldn't help noticing as I passed the bathroom this morning ...'

Oh Lord. He hadn't closed the door in time. He cast around quickly for an excuse.

'... that you had some nasty bruises,' she said. 'What happened?'

If she'd seen the pattern of marks on his backside it was no use pretending he'd had a fall. He shook out the morning paper. 'I wasn't going to tell you,' he said casually. 'I didn't want you to worry.'

'Worry about what?' she asked, smoothing butter over the slices of toast.

'I was attacked on the way home last night – somebody jumped me in the dark.'

'Good heavens!' She brought the toast to the table. 'Were you hurt anywhere else?'

'I'm fine, don't worry.'

He dolloped marmalade onto a slice of toast while she poured the coffee. 'Where was this?' she asked.

'Does it matter? They didn't get anything.'

Greta sipped her coffee. 'Did you report it to the police?'

'No point,' he replied, 'I never saw them.'

'It's odd, though, isn't it?' Greta murmured.

He searched her face. 'What is?'

She shrugged and set the coffee mug down. 'Why did they attack you if they didn't mean to rob you?'

He folded the newspaper into a convenient square. 'Could be somebody I sent down – who knows?'

'And what on earth made them wallop your bottom like that?'

'I fell,' he said irritably. 'I was sort of curled up – they must have had a stick or something. I don't know, as I said, I never saw them. Anyway, my pride was hurt more than anything and I don't want the story spread all over the place.'

'No,' she said thoughtfully, 'I don't suppose it would look too good on the front page of the *Examiner*. Are you sure you are feeling all right, why don't you take the day off?'

'No,' he said firmly. 'Not today. I've got an important council meeting and I can't miss that.'

Greta could understand why he didn't want to report it to the police and have it broadcast throughout the town. After all, it didn't look very dignified, a well-respected solicitor getting his backside tanned. As he said it could have been anybody who held a grudge against him. Even if they did seem to have beaten him in a rather curious place, she might have dismissed it entirely from her mind, but for Linda Mason.

A couple of weeks passed before she returned to Jubilee Terrace. She left Hero at home. He would be bored she had told herself, but to tell the truth she couldn't bear the thought that his real owner might spot him and claim him back.

269

By now, she thought, Linda should have completed her decorating and the messy clutter of dust-sheets and paint tins would be cleared away. And now, at ten in the morning, Linda would be at work.

But even as she opened the front door Greta realized she was wrong. From the scullery came the sound of clattering pans and in the living-room the radio was playing a pop song, the one about Eleanor Rigby who kept her face in a jar by the door.

Linda had evidently heard the key in the lock for she appeared in the scullery doorway, a milk pan in her hand. She was still in a dressing-gown, her fair hair tousled and a dark blur around one eye.

'Oh, hello,' she said, smiling shyly. 'I'm late, I'm afraid. You didn't expect me here, but I had a bit of an accident.'

Greta set down her bag on the table and came close, touching a finger to the girl's face. 'Oh, my dear, whatever have you done?'

'Not me,' said Linda. 'Some bloke hit me. Must have been after me wages but he didn't get 'em.'

'You mean – you fought back?'

'Didn't need to. He ran off when he heard somebody coming.'

Greta drew the girl to the fireside chair. 'Oh you poor thing! Sit yourself down and I'll make a pot of tea. And have you got some witch-hazel for that bruise? You're going to have a real shiner if we don't see to it.'

'Funny thing,' Greta said later as they sat together by the hearth, 'but the same thing happened to my husband a couple of weeks ago.'

Linda picked up the mug of tea. 'What? A black eye?'

'No, being mugged in the dark. They had a stick or

something, and they beat him with it. You should have seen the marks.'

Linda tossed back her long hair. 'Gets your arms, doesn't it, fending 'em off?'

Greta smiled. 'He got hit in a place he'd rather not show anyone. You'd think he'd had a good caning from his headmaster.'

Linda spluttered into her tea. Greta looked up in surprise. 'You think that's funny? He didn't.'

Still smiling, Linda shook her head. 'There's folks who enjoy having that done to them. It turns them on – they'll pay good money for it.'

'Pay?' echoed Greta. 'Who do?'

Linda wriggled slender shoulders. 'Sometimes fellers who don't get it at home, or who can't do it otherwise,' she said, then she added hurriedly, 'not as I'm suggesting owt, you know.'

'Of course not,' said Greta, setting her mug down on the table. 'Now I'll just pop down to the chemist's and get you that witch-hazel.'

Linda's words still echoed in Greta's head as she hurried along the cobbled street. The young grew up so fast these days; they were far more worldly-wise than we were in our youth.

'*They can't do it otherwise* ...' Could that possibly apply to Reginald? Surely not. He hadn't been interested in sex for years. Whatever else he was, he didn't have a high sex drive, and he certainly wasn't given to kinky behaviour – was he? But then again, if he hadn't shown interest in all this time, it might only be with her. It didn't necessarily mean he had no interest at all. And if someone else had taken his fancy – who could it be? Not Phyllis Thewlis? Surely not.

'They'll pay good money for it.' But who, in their right minds, would pay to be humiliated and hurt? Even as she thought it, a sudden memory sprang back into Greta's mind. Years ago, when they were first married, one night after they'd come home from a dinner party with friends, when she peeled off the silk stockings he'd given her.

'Just for fun, Greta – tie them tight to the bedpost.'

'Why? You won't be able to move or do anything.'

'Go on, just to please me. Afterwards I'll please you. Pretend I've done something really bad. Go on – harder than that.'

What followed left her with an unsavoury feeling of distaste. Reginald must have been aware of it for it never happened again. She'd dismissed it at the time as a mere caprice born of too much to drink and a fleeting fancy to experiment with something different. But maybe she'd been wrong. Maybe Reginald still wanted – or needed – such things. Maybe after all she didn't know her husband as well as she thought she did.

'Can I help you, madam?'

The chemist was waiting, a polite smile on his face. Greta had to struggle to come back to reality.

'A bottle of witch-hazel, please.'

'Let me help you, Dan. If you won't use the chamber-pot, lean on me and I'll help you to the bathroom.'

Rosa stood anxiously by the bed, watching him struggle to rise. He'd had another of his bad bouts, sick half the night, and it had drained all the strength out of him. But he was a proud man and he only shook his head irritably.

'Leave me alone,' he grumbled. 'If the day ever comes when you have to unzip me flies for me you can have me put down.'

She watched, helpless, as he levered himself slowly off the bed and reached for the dressing-table to support his

272

weight. He'd be bad for the whole day now, she knew. It always left him as weak as a kitten when he'd had one of these dreadful dos.

He paused to lean against the door-frame. 'Go on,' he said with a thin smile, 'get off to work. I'll be OK.'

His eyes burned bright in his hollow cheeks and the hard muscle of his arms was turning to slack flesh. She felt a lunge of pity for him. Dan was far weaker than he'd ever admit. He was never going to get back to work again, not after all this time. Whatever it was that plagued him, it always came back.

'Go on,' he said. 'What are you waiting for?'

She hesitated. More than ever these days she was eager to get to the café. She loved just being there, touching the china and fingering the texture of the curtains, watching the way the sunlight fell through the tall windows across the floor, savouring the joy of knowing it was all hers. And there was this idea simmering in her mind, the plan to extend over next door. She'd been going to talk to the sweetshop owner today, but now ...

She must stay with Dan. Not because of a sense of duty, but because she loved him as deeply as she'd always loved him. So what, maybe he could be fractious and difficult when he felt queasy, but she had to remember that underneath all that he was still the same old Dan; kindly, loving and generous to a fault.

She could hear him now, running the taps in the bathroom. 'Stop hanging about,' he called out. 'The girl will be waiting for you.'

True enough. Mandy was a willing and amiable enough waitress but she was hopeless on her own. 'Sure you'll be all right?' Rosa called back.

Dan poked his head round the bathroom door. A smile sat awkwardly on his thin face. 'Be off with you, woman,' he ordered. 'If you hang about here any longer losing money you'll never be able to afford my car.'

Rosa sat on the top deck of the bus, watching the grey slate roofs slide past. He joked about the car, but it would help him to get about more easily. The local shops were the best he could manage nowadays. The steep climb into town was too much for his legs.

A car. She chewed her lip thoughtfully. Maybe she should forget the notion of expanding – for the time being, at least – and buy a little car instead. Dan could teach her to drive – now that was an intriguing idea. No more queuing for buses in the rain, able to give Mandy a lift home and to go anywhere, any time. It was an idea. She'd have a word with Alex about it, see what he thought.

'I don't see why you need to give up on the other idea just because you want a car,' Alex said.

'I can't afford both, not at the same time, that's why.'

'You're talking of paying cash for the car – why not buy on hire purchase? That way you'll be able to afford the instalments out of your takings.'

'Buy on credit?' she mused. 'I've never done that before. I like to pay cash and then I know where I am.'

Alex smiled. 'You'll never make a good businesswoman unless you learn to use other people's money – so long as you plan for it. Of course it costs more in the long·run because the bank wants its interest on the loan, but it means you can get what you want, when you need it. Considering Dan's health ...'

He was right, she thought as she climbed the stairs to the café. She'd talk to the sweetshop owner and to the bank and see just what she could afford. If some way could be found to get both the extension and the car ...

There were only two customers in the place. Mandy was standing idly by the kitchen door, picking at a flaking fingernail.

'Hold the fort a minute, Mandy,' Rosa said. 'I'm just popping round next door.'

Theo Challis drove slowly back into Leeds, his hands limp on the wheel. He hadn't been feeling too well all day, and trying to conduct consultations with the Harrogate architects had been hard to continue in the face of a rising sensation of queasy weariness.

It had been a welcome relief to escape at last from the claustrophobic closeness of the office suite, out into the cool breeze blowing along The Stray, but it had only been a brief respite before he'd had to drive on to the next appointment. Now his head was aching, his body felt limp and all he wanted was to lock the car, sink into a chair and sleep.

Ouch! The car jerked as a stab of pain shot across his chest and travelled down his left arm as well. He curled the arm across his body, steering the car towards the kerb where he pulled up. God, he felt bad. A weight seemed to be pressing on his chest, making it hard to inhale. A breath of fresh air, that's what he needed. He pushed the door open and clambered out slowly.

That tightness was still there. He walked slowly under the trees until he reached a gate. A park. If he was going to be sick he'd rather passers-by didn't see. He turned into the park, into the privacy of the shadows under the trees.

But the tight feeling in his chest would not go away. Instead, as he walked painfully around a children's paddling pool, its waters rippling softly under the lamplight, the feeling seemed to grow stronger, fiercer. Theo gasped for breath. He couldn't go any further. He had to sit down. Alongside the pool, in a sheer rock-face, an arched recess held a rough-hewn seat. He stumbled towards it and sank down on the cold stone surface.

Another pain streaked through him and he cried out. The weight on his chest was crushing him, driving the breath out of him, and the feeling of cold inevitable finality sent waves of panic through his brain.

He needed help, but he couldn't move. Under this arch, so far from the street, no-one would hear even if he could cry out. Terrified, he slumped on the seat, the overpowering weight bearing down on him, oppressive, crushing the life out of him. He was done for.

For a moment blank, fear-filled eyes stared out across the rippling silent water, then darkness closed in around him and he toppled to the ground.

Chapter Twenty-four

Dorothy was stunned by the news. When Lucy was summoned home she found her sitting on the sofa, her eyes staring, her usually immaculate hairdo awry. The two women sat together in the drawing-room, one in widow's black at the window end of the sofa, the other still in uniform at the far end. Neither woman spoke, neither wept. For long minutes the only sound in the room was the slow tick of the clock.

Dorothy broke the silence. 'Under an arch, in the park,' she repeated over and over again, her fingers knotting in the handkerchief on her lap and her bewildered face betraying her total incomprehension. When at last she did shed tears it seemed to come more from anger than sorrow.

'It was his heart, they said,' she raged to Lucy. 'He never told me. Fancy keeping a thing like that from his own wife!'

'Maybe he didn't know himself,' Lucy tried to console her. 'He always thought he had dyspepsia.'

'He must have known,' her mother wailed. 'I made him see the doctor. But even if he didn't, I'd have thought you might have recognized the symptoms, you being a nurse and all.'

'Mother, I'm only a student,' Lucy sighed. 'Yes, I've seen patients on the ward with heart disease, but that's different. It was heart failure with Dad. It just happens – you can't spot it coming.'

Dorothy dabbed her eyes. 'Even so, he didn't have to die like that,' she complained, 'on his own, on a bench in a park shelter. It's no way for a man of his reputation to go.'

Lucy edged closer to her mother. 'At least he probably didn't suffer, Mother. It would all have been over very quickly.'

Dorothy was not to be consoled. 'He missed his holiday,' she moaned. 'I suppose we'll have to cancel the cruise now.'

'I'm afraid so.'

'And I've already paid the deposit.'

'Never mind,' said Lucy, 'I'll speak to the travel agent, don't worry. They've given me a few days' compassionate leave to see to things.'

Her mother shook her head sadly. 'Poor Graham. He was so looking forward to the trip.'

'Where is he?' Lucy looked around.

'I made him go to school,' sniffed Dorothy. 'Exams coming up you know, and I didn't want him bothered with all the arrangements. There's the funeral director coming this afternoon.' She glanced up at the clock on the mantelpiece. 'What time did he say he'd be here?'

'Very soon now, but don't worry, I'll talk to him for you.'

'Oak, be sure to tell him, and brass handles. I want the best for him even if it's going up in flames.'

'I know.'

'And what about the flowers, do you think?'

Lucy shrugged. 'You could give people a choice – flowers or a donation to heart research, if you like.'

'Oh no,' Dorothy exclaimed in alarm, 'I want the coffin to have plenty of flowers on it in the hearse. He's got to look good on his last journey. He deserves the best.'

Lucy slid an arm about her mother's shoulders. 'Leave

278

it to me,' she said softly. 'I'll tell Mr Greaves what you want.'

Her mother gave a watery smile. 'You're a good girl, Lucy. I don't know what I'd do without you.'

Lucy bent her head, her forehead touching her mother's shoulder.

At this moment she felt closer to her than she'd ever done before, and felt a wave of tenderness for her in her sorrow. She'd never been more insecure, more vulnerable than now. Lucy could barely speak for the lump in her throat.

'We'll miss him badly,' she croaked.

She heard the long-drawn sigh. 'Yes,' agreed Dorothy, 'but maybe it's better he's gone first. He'd never have coped on his own without me. He always left the decisions to me.'

Lucy made no answer. This was no time to argue, to point out that the truth was they had all depended on his quiet strength. Dad had just got on with life, running his business and ironing out their problems with the minimum of fuss. Whatever problems he'd encountered he'd solved them on his own, leaving to his wife only the minor domestic decisions, like where to place a new freezer.

'There's lots of other things we'll have to sort out,' she murmured. 'If I can help—'

'You mean the will and insurance and things?' said Dorothy. 'He'll have seen to all that – I told him to.'

'There's the business,' said Lucy.

'Oh, that.' Dorothy disentangled herself from Lucy's arms and stood up wearily. 'No need to bother our heads about that just yet,' she sighed. 'We'll leave that to Graham. He's the man of the house now.'

Lucy couldn't bring herself to watch the coffin slide away through the crimson velvet curtains. She closed her eyes, fighting back the tears while Mother's choice of music filled the little auditorium.

'Rock of ages ...'

She watched the others stand waiting while her mother shuffled out, sobbing and clinging to Graham's arm. Lucy followed and stood alone under the shade of a tree. She couldn't bear to watch her mother standing beside Graham by the porch in the sunlight, dabbing her eyes and bowing her head in acknowledgement as mourners paid their tributes.

The mayor was among them, Lucy noted. It would be a source of disappointment to her mother that he was not wearing his gold chain of office. She felt desperately alone and shut out, and it angered her to think that her mother was playing the part of the bereaved widow to perfection, helpless, inconsolable. She'd be very conscious of how she looked, how she behaved.

'Should I have my son at my side, Lucy, or my brother-in-law? I'd much rather be with Graham ... I shall have to wear black, of course, but it doesn't suit my colouring at all.'

Poor Daddy. I wonder if for one moment this afternoon she's given a loving thought to you. I miss you so much, so very much.

Only a few of the mourners came back to the house afterwards. When the final condolences had been spoken and the door closed again, a gloomy silence fell over the house. Graham muttered something about changing his clothes and revision and disappeared upstairs to his room.

Lucy felt she could choke. She stood by the window, watching the dusk creeping across the garden. He'd loved his garden, disbudding the chrysanthemums, mowing the lawn, tending his roses ...

'Come away from the window for goodness' sake, Lucy,' her mother snapped. 'The Whiteleys'll think it odd when we've just had a funeral.'

Lucy stood unmoving. Behind her in the dusk she could hear the knitting-needles start to click. Mother was a firm believer in making good use of every minute. Today was no exception.

'The devil finds work for idle hands,' she used to recite in a singsong tone, 'so best not give him chance.'

'It's all right, Mother,' Lucy murmured, 'there's not a soul about. The Whiteleys are all indoors having their tea.'

'What are you doing then?' The voice held a trace of irritation. 'What's there to see?'

Nothing new, thought Lucy, only the same view of the landscaped gardens as always, the rose-covered archway leading down to the boundary wall and, beyond that, the descending rows of terraced stone houses, every one identical to its neighbour. If she strained her neck she could just glimpse, there in the gap between grey slate roofs, the shimmer of lamplight in the town below.

'The lights down in town,' she murmured, 'they've just come on.'

There'd be people down there under those lampposts now, waiting for buses to take them home from work or on their way to the cinema. Eager giggling girls, excited about going out on a date, maybe. All humanity was buzzing about its business, unaware of the death of a wonderful man. It was wrong; it was unfair.

Behind her the clicking stopped. 'You haven't said a word since we came home,' her mother muttered. 'What were you thinking about?'

'Nothing, Mother. Just looking at the lights.'

She heard her mother snort. 'I don't know, I've never been able to fathom you out, Lucy,' she complained. 'Not

281

like our Graham – I can read him like a book. Just what goes on in the dark corners of your mind, I wonder? Go on, tell me, what were you thinking about just then?'

Lucy concealed a sigh. I'm not telling you. If I said I was thinking of Daddy you'd only see it as an accusation. You want to own me, Mother, but I won't let you take my thoughts. They're mine.

She turned to look down at the figure in the fireside chair, her face a pale oval in the half-light, slippered feet propped on a footstool, and felt ashamed. The figure looked so small, so vulnerable. 'Nothing special,' she said. 'Shall I put the television on for you?'

Her mother peered up at the clock and laid her knitting aside. 'Is it news time already? Ah well, I suppose we ought to know what's going on in the rest of the world. We can't think only of ourselves.'

Lucy switched on the television and turned away. 'I'm going out for a while,' she said quietly. 'I need a breath of air.'

Dusk had deepened into darkness by the time Lucy turned into the park gates, leaving the roar of traffic behind her as she walked slowly down the main avenue.

She hadn't intended to come here. As she walked, deep in memories of her father, she'd found herself inadvertently following his last steps.

She headed down a side path towards the paddling pool. 'I want to be close to you, Daddy,' she murmured to the overhanging bushes. 'Without you I feel lost. Mother and Graham aren't my family, not the way you were. In you I could confide all my childish hopes and secrets, safe from the fear of being mocked. You understood, you stood by me.'

She rounded the bend in the path and came to the edge of the pool, tiny shimmers of light playing on the surface. Over there was the arch cut in the rock. She made her way resolutely towards it. She would sit where they found him.

'I want to see with my own eyes what you last saw, before you closed your eyes for the last time.'

The stone seat struck cold through her skirt as she sat. She closed her eyes. The only sounds were the distant hum of traffic and the gentle rustling of leaves in the breeze. It was lonely here, hopelessly, desperately lonely. He must have felt so forlorn.

'So do I, Daddy, without you. It's selfish of me, I know, but I needed you. You were the only family I ever had – not my blood-father, but as good as. I have no mother to turn to now. I've spent my life trying to please your wife, trying to ingratiate myself with her, but all to no avail. She'll never acknowledge me as her child, not like Graham. I'll take care of her, for your sake, but I can't allow my life to be hostage to her demands any longer. Now you've gone we've nothing in common any more.'

The breeze fanned Lucy's face. 'Why did you come here that night, Daddy? Was it a whim? Were you feeling bad, or did you have a premonition of death? Oh God, you must have felt so frightened, and I wasn't here to help!'

Tears trickled from under her closed eyelids as she tried to imagine his last moments, when he opened his eyes for the last time. She could feel the cold strike up from the rough stone and spread through her body. This is how death must feel. She raised her eyelids slowly, seeing through the blur of tears the ripple of light on the water. This was the last thing he saw.

'Oh Daddy,' she sobbed, 'forgive me! I loved you so much!'

*   *   *

283

Reginald Holyoak felt very pleased with himself as he stuffed the putter back into the golf trolley. He'd won the round by two strokes – it served old Metcalf right for challenging him.

The two men strolled back to the club-house bar. 'What'll you have?' asked Metcalf.

They took their glasses to a window table. Metcalf seated himself and stretched his arms behind his head.

'I see they've got cracking on those new tower blocks on the ring road,' he remarked. 'They're going up fast.'

Reginald nodded and set down his glass. 'That's the advantage of system-building. Crawshaw obviously doesn't believe in wasting time.'

'You didn't get a bid from Challis then?' murmured Metcalf.

'Challis?' Reginald repeated with a frown. 'Don't think I know the firm.'

'Really?' Metcalf leaned forward, picked up his glass and took a sip. 'I heard you were talking to him in the bar at that do in Leeds. I thought maybe he was touting for business.'

'In Leeds?' Reginald let the frown slip away. 'Oh, him – no, I just went to join him in the bar because he sat near me during the meal, that's all. He never mentioned the contract.'

Metcalf nodded. 'Just as well he didn't put in a tender, as it turns out.'

'Why's that?'

'Poor chap – he snuffed it last week. Heart, I heard.'

Reginald swivelled away to signal to the barman, then turned back. 'Sorry to hear that,' he murmured. 'Just let's hope the same fate doesn't befall Crawshaw before he finishes our job.'

*   *   *

It must be half-term, thought Greta as she came out from under the gloomy viaduct into the sunlight in Mafeking Street. There were children everywhere, playing hopscotch on the pavement and four-a-side football on the cobbles, squealing as they chased one another round the lampposts and up the entries. At the far end of the street she could see Betty Tasker, sitting outside on her chair again, sunning herself and watching the activity with folded arms. A corpulent little pear-drop of a woman nodded to her as she passed and went into the house next door.

That's my old home, thought Greta. That must have been the Polish lady Betty had mentioned. I wonder if I'd recognize the place inside now.

Betty looked up as she approached. 'Kids these days,' she growled. 'Don't know they're born.'

Greta smiled. 'Oh, I don't know. They don't seem to change much. I remember we used to play the same games.'

'Get away with murder, they do, making all this racket,' muttered Betty. 'I wonder old Mrs Kadinski can get her nap with this lot going on.'

Greta looked around at the small flying bodies. 'They're doing no harm,' she said, 'not breaking things and vandalizing.'

'In my day they'd have had jobs to do, blackleading the grate and errands and such. No sense of responsibility, they haven't – all the parents' fault. And that young lass who's in your house is no better.'

'Linda?' Greta was startled. 'Why? What's she done?'

Betty shrugged plump shoulders. 'Nowt, so far as I know, but she makes a hell of a racket with that tranny of hers. Blaring out when I go past the door, it is.'

Greta smiled. 'Ah well, that's young folk for you. They like their music loud.'

'At half-past ten at night when folks are off to bed?'

Betty snorted. 'Sounded like a party going on, such a rumpus. No consideration for the neighbours at all. You should speak to her.'

'I'm sorry,' murmured Greta. 'I'll certainly have a word.'

She could see the blue-uniformed figure on the doorstep long before she reached number seven, and she frowned. A policeman, calling at her house? And then a sudden anxious thought occurred – nothing had happened to Linda, had it?

'Can I help you?' she said as she neared him, taking the key from her bag. 'Is anything wrong?'

'You live here?' he asked.

'I do. I'm the owner. What's the problem, Officer?'

He took a notebook from his breast pocket and consulted it. 'I'm making enquiries about a missing girl,' he said. 'Last seen in this neighbourhood. Name of Dodd, Linda Dodd.'

'Really?' Greta's mind raced. If that lout Dodd laid hands on Linda again ... 'I'm sorry,' she said calmly, 'I know nobody of that name.'

It wasn't really lying. Linda's name was Mason. 'What has the girl done?' she asked. 'Something criminal?'

'No, no,' the police officer replied, tucking his notebook back into his pocket. 'She's run off, that's all. Family dispute. Been gone a few weeks now and her father's worried for her.'

'I see.' Lying brute, thought Greta. Worried she might tell.

'So if you do happen to hear anything,' the policeman said.

'Of course. Good afternoon, Officer.'

She watched him stride away. You won't hear a word from me, she thought. Linda is happy here and getting on well. The last thing in the world I'd do is send Linda back to that animal.

Chapter Twenty-five

'So it's all sorted out,' Rosa told Dan with an air of triumph. 'The bank's happy, I'm happy, and tomorrow we'll go and have a look at these cars I've seen.'

Dan reached across the table and covered her hand with his. 'I don't deserve you Rosa,' he murmured with a smile. 'You didn't bargain for an invalid husband when you married me.'

She patted his hand. 'I got what I wanted, Dan. I know how lucky I am. Now then, you did say you fancied an Escort, didn't you? Because that's what I've been looking at.'

'Aye,' he admitted, 'I've always had a hankering for one of them, but the price—'

'Second-hand, low mileage,' she cut in. 'I've seen three within my budget and I think they're right up your street. So first thing tomorrow I'll order a taxi to take us down.'

'Tomorrow? What about the café?'

Rosa stood up and touched his shoulder. 'Just for once Mandy will have to cope on her own – it'll do the girl good.'

Dorothy watched as Lucy unpacked the shopping on the kitchen table.

'Well?' she said.

'Well what?' asked Lucy.

Dorothy clicked her tongue in irritation. 'For heaven's

sake, girl, I can't get a word out of you these days. What's the matter, cat got your tongue?'

'There's nothing to say,' Lucy replied quietly. 'Look, it's time I got back to the hospital. Everything's been dealt with now, and they've been very patient with me.'

Dorothy looked stricken. 'You can't just go and leave me to cope,' she exclaimed, 'not till Graham's finished his exams. Oh Lucy, you can't do that!' She reached into the cupboard for her nerve pills.

Lucy turned to face her. 'You don't need me any more. The solicitor's handling the bank accounts and the will. You'll be all right now.'

Dorothy swallowed the pills then shook her head. 'What about the business?' she complained, spreading her hands. 'Someone has to see to that.'

Lucy sighed. 'The construction director said he could carry on for the time being, and as you said, Graham will soon be free to see to things.'

Dorothy pouted her lower lip. 'He doesn't want to know about the yard,' she muttered. 'He says he's still going to college.'

Lucy's eyebrows rose. 'Does he now? How very selfish.'

Her mother glared, and slapped a bag of sugar into the cupboard. 'Don't be silly – he's not cut out for the yard, not with his disability. You ought to know that.'

Lucy faced her squarely. 'You still blame me for his limp, don't you? But he's not disabled, not in the least. He does whatever he wants to do and you encourage him.'

Her mother's eyes widened. 'Are you suggesting I spoil him?' she demanded.

'You tell me – but that limp is nothing to what he might have had.'

'Might have had? What are you getting at?'

'You and your pills, Mother. There isn't one going you

haven't tried. I wonder you didn't take Distavel when you were expecting him – you might very well have had a thalidomide baby – no arms, no legs at all. Maybe even blind.'

Without warning Dorothy's arm rose and swung, and Lucy felt a searing blow across her cheek. She stared in astonishment.

'How dare you try to visit your sins on me,' Dorothy hissed. 'How dare you accuse me of spoiling my son! Just who do you think you are?'

Lucy pressed a hand to her stinging face. 'I don't know,' she growled, and then came the words she hadn't planned to speak. 'I only know I'm not your daughter, and I'm glad.'

She heard the disbelieving gasp and half expected another blow, but it didn't come. 'Get out of here,' Dorothy muttered. 'After all I've done for you, you dare to speak to me like that? Get out.'

'I'm going,' said Lucy. 'I've got to get back to Hawksmoor.'

She turned to leave the kitchen. As she opened the door she heard the rasping words behind her.

'I should have known better than to take a child from the gutter.'

Alex leaned one elbow on the top of the till.

'So you got it?' he said. 'Is it an Escort? What colour?'

Rosa's face glowed with happiness. 'Sort of milky brown, like a bar of chocolate. Dan's thrilled to bits with it. He could hardly wait to drive it. In fact,' she added with a mischievous smile, 'he took me up to Grimscar Woods straight away, even before it was insured.'

Alex smiled. 'I'm glad. It'll make all the difference.'

'He won't be so miserable now he'll be able to get out and about on his own. Oh Alex, I'm so glad you put me right.'

He looked mystified. 'How do you mean?'

'You know. Now I can extend my place as well. Just so long as I can get permission.' Rosa twirled about in happiness. 'Oh Alex! I feel the world is opening up again.'

He grinned as he crossed to turn round the sign to read 'Open'. As he did so a fair-haired girl appeared on the doorstep and he opened the door to let her in.

'Morning, Mandy,' he said with a smile, then, turning to Rosa he added, 'You should get Dan to teach you to drive,' he suggested. 'You'll find the world's an even bigger place than you think.'

'That's what I keep telling her,' Mandy commented as she headed for the stairs. 'There's more to life than just sleeping and working.'

There was a note on the table when Greta let herself into the Jubilee Terrace house. She saw it at once, the square of white propped against the vase of fresh freesias.

'Please can I have a word with you?' it read. 'There's a couple of favours I want to ask you.'

Greta smiled to herself. The delicate scent of the freesias hung in the air, accentuating the gleaming cleanliness of the place. The girl was welcome to anything within reason, the way she kept the house. What could it be this time? Permission to decorate the bathroom perhaps?

Whatever it was, she'd hang on until the girl came home. Linda could be sure of an attentive ear. And she needed to talk to her about the noise.

'A telephone?' Greta repeated in surprise. 'Goodness me! I guessed at a number of things, but I never thought of having a phone put in.'

'It would be ever so useful,' Linda said with a shy smile. 'I could talk to me mam without having to go round there.'

'Yes, I can see that,' said Greta slowly.

'I'd feel that much safer if I had me own phone.'

'Safer?'

'I could ring for a taxi without going to the main road. It's not safe on your own in the dark.'

'Linda,' said Greta patiently, 'Your stepfather's not going to get you now. You're safe here.'

'Not him – the Ripper. Don't you read the papers? That maniac who's been killing girls left, right and centre. I daren't go out till they catch him.'

Greta had a vague recollection of reading about a number of girls attacked and even murdered in the North recently and the police's belief that the same man might be responsible. She frowned.

'And I wouldn't ask you to pay for putting it in – I'll do that,' the girl urged.

Greta smiled and nodded. 'Very well. If it makes you feel better I'll get it put in right away, then you can pay your own quarterly bills afterwards. How's that?'

Linda clasped her hands, her eyes shining. 'Oh, thanks, that's great! And can I ask you summat else?'

'Fire away.'

'Well,' said Linda, leaning forward, elbows on knees, 'I've got this friend, Mandy. She's working – got a job as a waitress in a café in town, but she's getting kicked out of her digs this weekend so she needs somewhere to live.'

'Kicked out? Why?'

Linda shrugged. 'Summat about the landlord needing vacant possession to sell the house. She likes it here, so I wondered if you'd let her come and stay with me? Just for the time being, till she finds another place.'

Greta's eyes twinkled. 'She's been here? Was that why there was so much noise?'

Linda blushed. 'You heard. I'm sorry. We was only playing our new records. It won't happen again.'

291

Greta searched her face. Chances were, if this girl was Linda's friend, she'd be just as clean and reliable a tenant. 'Of course,' she replied, 'just remember to keep the music down. I leave it to you to sort out the sleeping arrangements.'

'That's easy,' smiled Linda. 'There's that back bedroom going begging. We'll make it right nice between us, Mandy and me.'

Rosa was alone in the café, cashing up the day's takings, when Alex appeared at the top of the stairs.

'Mandy gone home?' he enquired.

Rosa swept the last pile of coins into the cash-bag and pencilled a note of the total. 'On the dot at six,' she answered. 'She's a pain in the neck, that one. Do you know, I keep finding her hiding in the toilet, plucking her eyebrows or backcombing her hair, anything but serve coffee. You should see the lip when I tell her to get moving.'

'You surprise me,' said Alex. 'She always seems pleasant enough to me.'

Rosa began doodling on the notepad. 'You're a man,' she snorted. 'Funny how the minute a male customer appears the sulky lip always vanishes. Suddenly it's all Marilyn Monroe, right down to the giggle and the wiggling hips. Man-mad, she is.'

'In that case,' said Alex, coming up behind her chair, 'maybe you should think of letting her go.'

'Maybe I will, when I re-staff the place. I'll need more help if and when the extension goes through.'

Alex looked down over her shoulder, following the lines she was scribbling on the notepad. Several times she'd repeated the same design, a half circle with a firm line sealing off the straight edge. She was still scratching the last line, over and over, with determined fierceness.

'What's that?' he asked. 'A rising sun?'

She stopped scratching and looked down at the doodle. 'I don't know – I wasn't thinking of anything in particular,' she replied.

Alex cocked his head to one side. 'Not a sun, there's no rays round it,' he murmured. 'Even children put the spokes in. I wonder ...'

She put the pencil down and looked up at him, her face cupped in her hands. 'Go on,' she teased, 'psychoanalyse me, if you can.'

He swung a chair round and sat down, then drew the piece of paper towards him. For a moment he studied it. 'I'm no psychologist,' he said slowly, 'but it seems odd to me.'

Rosa frowned. 'Odd? How?'

'The way you've filled in the circle, all black and solid.'

'Well?' said Rosa defensively. 'What's odd about that?'

'And the way you've drawn such vicious hard lines under the circle – as though you want very much to shut it off and have done with it.'

'Shut what out? You're talking tripe, Alex.'

He pushed the paper away and looked deep into her eyes. 'I've always thought of you as a woman of mystery anyway, Rosa,' he murmured, 'with something hanging over from the past, but I wouldn't dream of prying.'

She felt distinctly uncomfortable under his scrutiny. 'Go on with you,' she gibed, 'just because I draw archways.'

'Is that what it is?' Alex looked down at the scribbles again, rubbing his chin thoughtfully. 'They seem to mean something bad for you,' he said, 'but for Orthodox Jews they're good. There's the shelter we build to celebrate succoth.'

'The what?'

'What you call harvest festival. It's a shelter with no roof, covered over with fruit and vegetables – well, nearly. You have to be able to see the sky.'

She said nothing. He gave an apologetic laugh. 'My family's drifted a bit, of course, but we still get married under an arch of flowers. It's a symbol of union and happiness.'

'That's what marriage ought to be,' said Rosa, snatching up the paper and screwing it into a ball. 'That's what my marriage is.'

Alex smiled as he pushed back his chair and stood up. 'You're a lucky woman then, Rosa.' He moved to the top of the stairs, then turned and added, 'Whatever your dark secret.'

Reginald was away on a trip to London for a couple of days. Greta and Hero revelled in having the house to themselves.

The little dog had been baffled at first by his new sweet-smelling coat and the leather collar about his neck, but he'd soon grown accustomed to his new image of bourgeois cleanliness. It was all right if it meant being accepted on Greta's bed. In return he was happy to be her champion, protecting her against the world.

He'd thoroughly sniffed out the milkman and the postman; they were OK. The cleaning lady was still a doubtful quantity since she seemed a bit careless about where she shoved the hoover, but she had dropped him a titbit of roast beef a couple of times so maybe she was trainable.

The only real enemy he'd come across so far in this new patch was the pompous striding creature who slept in another room, thank goodness, but who clearly had no understanding at all of canine requirements. There was no sense of fun, no affection, no loyalty in that tweedy creature. The mistress didn't seem to like him much either. At all costs he had to be kept away from her.

*　　*　　*

'What the devil's wrong with that animal? And what the hell is he doing in here anyway?'

Reginald, newly arrived home, stood in the living-room doorway, pointing down at the crouching dog with bared teeth growling and yapping at him. Greta simply looked up and smiled.

'Call him off, for God's sake,' he cried. 'He'll have my trousers if I move.'

'You'll be lucky if that's all he gets,' she said smoothly. 'Hero, come here and sit.'

The little dog gave one last menacing growl in warning, then slunk back to squat by his mistress. Reginald moved cautiously to his chair and sat down.

'I thought we said he should stay out in the porch,' he muttered.

'You said, not me,' replied Greta, reaching down to fondle the dog's tattered ear. 'I keep him with me. He's a marvellous guard dog. I feel completely safe with Hero.'

Reginald grunted and unfolded the *Yorkshire Post*. For a few moments he read in silence. Greta could swear the little dog was looking up at her with a grin of triumph.

'Good trip?' she enquired.

Reginald grunted. 'So so. Just took a client to meet the barrister in Lincoln's Inn.'

'No fun, then? No shows or nightclubs?'

'I don't call nightclubs fun. Waste of good money.' ·

'Of course.' Silly question, she thought. Reginald and fun were two words that didn't easily fit together.

'Actually, someone recognized me coming out of the hotel,' he said casually from behind the newspaper. 'Funny, isn't it, going all that way and being spotted by someone from Hawksmoor.'

Greta shrugged. 'It's not really surprising. Someone of

your standing who's been mayor and all is bound to be noticed.'

Reginald snorted. 'Yes, and but for that damned reorganization into a metropolitan borough I'd have been an alderman now.' He glanced down at the page. 'Hey, look at this,' he exclaimed, 'there's been another one of those murders.'

Greta looked up. 'The serial killer? The one they call The Ripper?'

Reginald read on, muttering to himself. '*Six victims now, some of them known prostitutes ... all of them in the area now being called the Terror Triangle, between Manchester, Leeds and Bradford ...*'

'Ghastly business,' said Greta. 'It's certainly not safe to be walking the streets alone at night.'

Curtains twitched in Jubilee Terrace as two couples climbed out of a battered blue car and stood laughing and joking outside number seven.

'Hurry up and find the key, Linda. We can't keep the lads waiting out here. Folks are watching.'

'Sod 'em,' said Linda. 'They're only jealous.'

'Hey, I've forgot the bottle,' said one of the men. 'Hang on while I get it out of the boot.'

He detached his arm from Mandy's waist and pulled up the boot lid. The other man nuzzled the back of Linda's neck with his nose as she fumbled to fit the key in the lock.

'Gerroff,' she simpered. 'Be patient, can't you?'

He reached round and took the key from her. 'Here, let me get it in for you,' he chuckled. Mandy dissolved in shrieks of laughter.

'Shut up.' warned Linda. 'You'll get us thrown out, making all that racket. You know what tell-tales they are round here.'

Her escort drew her close, whispering in her ear. Mandy swayed a little as she stumbled towards the step. The man with the bottle grabbed her arm.

'You need another little drink to steady you up,' he teased. 'Come on, Tom, don't clutter up the doorway.'

Linda went inside and Mandy followed. Tom glanced back as he steadied himself against the door-frame. 'Just negotiating terms,' he muttered. 'All settled.'

Chapter Twenty-six

.

Mrs Kadinski waddled down the backyard wielding her broom. Over the wall she could hear her neighbour, panting as she beat the living daylights out of a rug or something.

'That you, Mrs Kadinski?'

Betty Tasker's head appeared over the top of the stone wall. 'What you doing?' she asked.

'What am I doing?' exclaimed Mrs Kadinski. 'I am sweeping all these feathers, that's what I'm doing. Just look at them – I have enough pigeon feathers here to fill a pair of pillows.'

'I'll not charge you for them,' said Betty. 'Is your Alex at home? Only I need my sideboard shifted so I can clean underneath and Fred's off in Blackpool for the day.'

'With the pigeons?' asked Mrs Kadinski.

'Aye, he's racing 'em.'

'Good.' Mrs Kadinski swept all the harder.

'Well?' said Betty. 'Is your Alex in?'

Mrs Kadinski paused to lean on her broom, wiping a pudgy fist across her forehead. 'Why should he be home on a working day, I ask you?' she demanded. 'He works hard, like his father. He is doing well now, with the café upstairs. Every day Alex talks of moving to a new house.'

'Move?' said Betty. 'You never told me owt about moving.'

Mrs Kadinski shrugged her shoulders. 'I like to stay here where I always been – but for those pigeons. Any road,' she added, 'tonight Alex will come round to help you.'

'No matter,' said Betty. 'Fred'll be back tonight.' She paused for a moment's thought. 'No sign of your Alex bringing a young lady home yet?' she asked. 'I can't understand it, good-looking fellow like him.'

Mrs Kadinski chased the last of the feathers into a small heap in the corner where they couldn't escape, then straightened. 'It seems I shall have no grandchildren in my old age,' she sighed. 'He does not find a girl good enough for him.'

Betty was shocked. 'Is that what he says? Well, of all the—'

'No, no, I say it, not Alex. But still I pray one day she will come. Jew or gentile, it's all the same to me.'

'That's right,' agreed Betty. 'Never give up hope.'

Mrs Kadinski opened the back gate. 'Now I bring your feathers round to you,' she said 'You shall have the pair of pillows.'

Rosa lay in bed, watching the early sun beginning to seep through the gap in the bedroom curtains. Beside her Dan still lay sleeping.

Today there was no hurry to get up and out to work. Sunday was the one day she could afford to laze and fit in with Dan. She looked down at his sleeping profile, the gentle curve of his lips, and felt a rush of tenderness for him.

He asked so little of life. Sick as he was, his eyes still shone with excitement over his car like a child's on Christmas morning. The minute he awoke he'd be thinking of it, suggesting where he should take her today.

'We can't waste a glorious summer's day like this,' he'd say. 'Where's it to be?'

She touched a finger to his bare shoulder. It was cold as ice. 'Dan,' she said, then more urgently, 'Dan!'

With relief she heard him groan as he started to come to terms with the day. Stupid, she told herself; you're as bad as those silly, over-anxious mothers who wake their baby up to make sure it's breathing.

He rolled over onto his back. 'Sunday,' he breathed. 'Where are we off to today, lass?'

'How about a picnic up on the moors?' she replied, leaning her body over his and stroking his forehead. 'You like the moors.'

'Aye, I do,' he agreed. 'I can breathe up there.'

'You're very cold at the moment, Dan. Are you all right?'

'Right as rain. I just can't seem to get warm these days.'

She ran her fingers down his neck and over his chest. There was no flesh on him now, that was the problem. He'd lost so much weight he looked nothing like the Dan who used to swing a pickaxe on the motorways, muscles rippling under his tanned skin. This was a shrunken misshapen Dan, like those reflections she remembered seeing in the distorting mirrors, back in the old days in Clondarra when the funfair came to town.

Dan threw back the covers and sat up on the edge of the bed, then turned to take her hand. 'You've given me such freedom, lass,' he murmured, then, embarrassed, he smacked the back of her hand. 'Come on, let's get moving. If you behave yourself I might let you have a go behind the wheel.'

Lucy left the infirmary and hurried back to the nurses' home. She'd promised Neela she'd go shopping in town with her this afternoon and she was already late.

Neela was sitting at the dressing-table in the room they shared, brushing her silky black hair. 'What kept you?' she asked. 'Not that handsome Doctor Williams, was it?'

'No such luck,' smiled Lucy. 'I was just phoning home to see if everything was OK.'

'How's she doing?'

Lucy shrugged. 'All right, I suppose. I got a lecture about not ringing before now.'

Neela swung round on the stool to face her. 'Are you going home this weekend? You haven't been back since the funeral.'

'I know. No, I think it's better to leave her alone. We don't get on. We never have. I don't want to be emotionally hijacked by her any more.'

Neela stood up, buttoning her blouse. 'Will she be able to cope on her own, do you think? Your brother doesn't sound much use.'

Lucy smiled. 'He's off to university soon anyway, but yes, she'll cope, in her own way. She always has her own way. Ready?'

Neela shrugged on her coat and picked up her handbag. 'Maybe,' said Lucy thoughtfully, 'maybe I'll go on my next weekend off.'

Tight-lipped, Dorothy Challis sat at the head of the table in her late husband's office. She didn't much like the look of either of them: Carter, the construction director, spoke with a very common accent and wore a shapeless suit which looked as if he'd got it from Oxfam; and Overmeer, the Savile-Row-suited financial director, was a Dutchman and she'd never really trusted foreigners.

'He's a sound fellow,' Theo used to say. 'Keeps us on the straight and narrow. We've had no cash-flow problems since he came.'

301

Well, maybe Theo trusted him – Theo always believed the best of people – but she didn't like his close-set steely blue eyes. He was one to be watched, that Overmeer. Especially if he controlled the money.

She turned to Carter. 'You've been with us a long time, I understand?' she said sweetly.

He nodded. 'Aye, I been here man and boy nigh on thirty year,' he said. 'Started as apprentice right after me national service.'

'That's very good,' said Dorothy. 'We value loyalty in the firm.' She knew for a fact Overmeer had come only two years ago.

Overmeer cleared his throat. 'It's early days yet, Mrs Challis, and I'm sure you need time to get to know the workings of the firm, so I suggest we leave matters as they are for the time being.'

'Do you agree?' Dorothy cut in, smiling at Carter.

'Aye, well,' Carter grunted, 'we've work enough to be getting on with for now.'

'It would be as well to make no changes yet,' Overmeer went on, gathering his papers together. 'When you feel up to it we can go over the figures and projections in more detail.'

'I think now would be as good a time as any,' said Dorothy smoothly. 'I'd like to know just where we stand.'

The Dutchman inclined his head. 'Very well. I can assure you we are perfectly solvent and in a healthy state. There's no rush to change anything.'

Dorothy wagged a finger. 'Now there you're wrong, Mr Overmeer. It doesn't pay to be too complacent. I've seen things already which, as owner and managing director, I intend to change.'

It gave her pleasure to see the financial director's eyebrows rise. Carter too looked up sharply from under his shaggy brows.

'For a start that reception area,' she went on, with a sad shake of the head, 'it's a disgrace. Too stark, too clinical. Nobody could feel welcome there.'

'I'm sorry,' stammered Overmeer. 'It's as Mr Challis wanted.'

Another sad shake of the head. 'Poor Theo,' she mused, 'he never had any artistic sense. A few potted plants and some nice pictures, that's what it needs. I'll see to it right away.'

The two men watched her sweep up her handbag and sail graciously out of the room, then Overmeer glanced uncomfortably across to his colleague.

'Not so good, eh, Carter?' he murmured. 'I expected a grieving widow, but it seems we have a rather autocratic and ignorant woman for our managing director now. We could be in for trouble. She charges in like a bull in a china shop.'

Carter was smirking to himself as he pushed back his chair and stood up. 'Seems more like a mad cow to me,' he muttered.

Greta felt good this morning. The sun was shining brilliantly, the mirror told her she looked slim in the new pale-blue summer dress, and her skin felt like a young girl's. She was positively glowing when she came down to start the breakfast.

It was all Linda's doing, telling her that a woman ought always to put moisturizing cream on her face, no matter what her age, and always use a touch of lipstick and eyeliner. Her words had lingered in Greta's mind until she found herself at last in Boots, asking advice of the pretty young woman behind the cosmetics counter.

She'd spent ages last night at her dressing-table experimenting with the range of things she'd been persuaded to buy, trying not to apply so much eyeliner she looked like a black-eyed camel, and now she'd just about got it right. It surprised her how her faded blue eyes seemed to come to life. Even the silvering on her temples amid the light brown hair had somehow lost its ageing effect. And in the process of experimenting she herself had lost her lifelong attitude to make-up, born of Mother's insistence that only tarts wore paint.

'Get that muck off your face,' she'd once heard Mother scold big sister, Hilda. 'You look a right trollop.'

Hilda had gone on wearing it in secret but then, as it turned out, Hilda was a trollop. She must be turned sixty now; was she still at it, far away on the other side of the world?

A footstep behind her cut short Greta's musings. Reginald sat down at the kitchen table. He glanced around warily.

'Where is it?' he asked.

'It's all right,' said Greta. 'He's got a bone in the porch.'

Reginald relaxed and reached for his newspaper, then lifted his nose.

'Nice smell,' he commented. 'Perfume? What is it?'

Greta smiled. 'It's French and expensive. I'm going out.'

For the first time he looked up and his gaze met hers. She saw the startled expression leap to his eyes. 'You look different,' he said. 'What have you done?'

She twirled about, fanning her skirt. 'You're the perceptive lawyer whose keen eyes miss nothing,' she chuckled. 'You tell me.'

He surveyed her thoughtfully. 'New hairdo?' he ventured, then shook his head. 'I don't know what it is. You look somehow, younger, that's it. No-one would guess you'll be coming up for your bus pass before long.'

Reginald's unintentional compliment was still on her mind as Greta sauntered along the high street, looking in shop windows. Somehow she felt younger too. She might treat herself to some new nylons and a pair of those pretty high-heeled sandals which were in fashion this year. No more frumpish matronly clothes, she thought, though nothing too frivolous either. There was nothing worse than mutton dressed as lamb.

She found just the right sandals in the high-class shoe shop near the new supermarket. She almost chose the blue ones which went perfectly with her new frock, but settled in the end for a pair of elegant beige ones which would go with everything.

The heat was tiring, bouncing up off the pavement. Maybe it was a mistake to wear the new sandals straight away. They needed breaking in. They didn't feel as comfy as the old ones in this heat. A cup of coffee and a rest, that's what she needed.

What was the name of that place where Mandy worked? A foreign name, somewhere in the arcade in Westgate, wasn't it? That was only just around the corner.

The waitress who came to take her order had to be Mandy for she was the only waitress in the place. The girl had one of those smoothly pretty faces totally devoid of expression, like a china doll. She looked either tired or bored. Either way she didn't really fit in with the surroundings which someone with taste had fitted out with care.

When the girl brought the order of coffee and a cream cake she was yawning. Greta couldn't help remarking, 'You could do with going home to bed, it seems to me.'

'You can say that again,' the girl snorted. 'Hardly got a wink last night.'

'Sorry to hear that,' said Greta. 'I'm Linda's landlady.'

'Oh aye?' replied the girl. 'Do you want your bill now?'

Not a flicker of understanding or recognition marred

305

the bland surface of her face. Mandy certainly didn't have Linda's personality.

'Not yet,' said Greta. 'I might decide to have another cake.'

'Suit yourself,' said Mandy, and turned away.

The cake was delicious, melting in the mouth like candyfloss, and the coffee fragrant and fresh. As she lifted the jug to pour a second cup Mandy came back.

'Do you want another cake then?'

Greta smiled. 'I'd better not, though it's very tempting. I'll have my bill now, please.'

With a flourish the girl whipped out a pen and scribbled on her pad. 'Please tell the manager I think the coffee is delicious,' said Greta.

'Manageress,' said Mandy, then added with a toss of the head, 'that's her over there, just going down the stairs. She owns the place.'

Greta caught sight of the slim young woman with glossy dark hair wearing a well-cut suit, just a glimpse before her head sank out of sight. But in those brief seconds she felt a sudden leap of half recognition. She'd seen that face before, but where?

'What's the owner's name?' she asked Mandy.

The girl tore off a sheet from her pad and slapped it down on the table. 'I call her Bossy-Britches,' she said laconically, 'but her name's really Mrs Pearson.'

Pearson ... Pearson ... No, it rang no bells. Maybe if she were to have another look she might remember, but when Greta came down into the shop the café proprietress was nowhere in sight.

'You mean she were in Kadinski's?' said Linda in surprise. 'Maybe she wanted to have a look at you.'

Mandy kicked off her shoes and curled up on the settee

beside Linda. 'Well she looked a right mess, so she did,' she said, 'all tarted up like a teenager. Somebody ought to tell her.'

Linda giggled. 'Just so long as nobody tells her what we don't want her to know. She thinks I'm a nice girl.'

'Huh! She ought to see you in action. Does she know about your stepdad?'

'She does not. If she knew why he was giving me a good hiding she'd throw me out. So you just watch what you say.'

Mandy pouted. 'I said nowt. I hardly spoke to her. Hey – that's the phone.'

Linda reached across and picked up the receiver. 'Hello? ... Yes, that's me,' she said in a sultry tone. 'Well, that depends what you have in mind ...'

She covered the mouthpiece and grinned, wrinkling her nose, to Mandy, then uncovered the mouthpiece again. 'Oh, that'd be an extra,' she went on in a sexy tone. 'Is that OK?'

'Who's that?' asked Mandy as she replaced the receiver.

'Remember that chap in the cocktail bar in The George, the one I gave me number to? Him. He'll be here in fifteen minutes.'

Mandy uncurled herself from the settee with a sigh. 'In that case I'd better make meself scarce, I suppose.'

'That's right,' agreed Linda. 'Go down The Black Bull. I'll meet you there in an hour.'

Greta lay in bed thinking over her day. She'd enjoyed it enormously, indulging herself with shopping and sauntering round the town. Tomorrow, however, it was back to work.

First there would be the charity coffee-morning at Mrs Blackstock's in aid of the new hospice which she'd promised to attend and judge the jam-making competition.

That had been a foolish thing to do. The winner might become a friend for life, but the fifteen losers would never have a good word to say about her again.

And then in the afternoon she was going up to Wood Lea for the managers' meeting. They needed to sort out the details of the proposed new wing. If it was left to that new woman who'd joined the board of management only recently the extension would include everything from a sauna to a swimming pool and the funds would only run to a further six-bed ward with bath and toilets.

They needed those six beds, not for private fee-paying clients but for those less fortunate girls who, despite these days of easy contraception, still managed to fall pregnant with no-one to help them.

Time hadn't changed things. It was happening twenty years ago, when she first began to work at Wood Lea. In those days, of course, it had carried far more stigma than it did nowadays, but it was still as terrifying an ordeal for a young girl. So many of them had come and gone, some poor little lost things, some cocky and defiant ...

That's it! Greta sat up suddenly as the memory leapt into her brain. That was where she'd seen that face before! The girl – the Irish girl – it must be all of twenty years ago. The girl who'd wanted so desperately to keep her child.

Greta lay back on the pillow, seeing the proud little face once more, ravaged with anger and tears. I made her give up that child, thought Greta. I can't even recall whether it was a boy or a girl, but I knew the little Irish girl would make something of her life.

And now here she was, owner of a prosperous little café in Hawksmoor. Now what on earth was her name?

Chapter Twenty-seven

Rosa was still having problems with her plans to extend the café, but she was happy to see how Dan suddenly seemed to come to life again. Whatever the weather he was eager to get out and about in the new car. He was able to call round to see Ted and Kitty once again, and Rosa was glad for him.

Today the sun was beating down and she felt exhilarated as they drove high on the moor with the car windows down, the breeze blowing in her hair. Dan looked so much better, the pleasure glowing in his eyes and the wind bringing a flush to his cheeks. They were happy; there was a lustre in the air; it was almost like the old days, when they first met.

Dan glanced across at her. 'Want another go at the wheel?' he asked. 'You're coming on quite nicely.'

Driving wasn't as difficult as she'd thought, except for hill starts on those steep slopes of the moor.

'Find me a place that's not so steep as last time,' she said. 'I nearly had us in the ditch.'

'Come on,' he urged, 'you just need to get the balance between the clutch and the accelerator. Listen to the engine – feel it, with your foot.'

Before long he took over again, skimming over the moorland roads amid the heather, humming happily as he drove.

If only this could last, and he'd be fully restored

to health again. Rosa closed her eyes and sent up a silent prayer.

The car pulled up. When she opened her eyes Dan had opened the door and was easing himself out of the driver's seat. She went round to join him. He stood on the cliff edge, gazing out over a vista of distant mill chimneys and clustered villages. The wind was chilly up here. She nestled close against his side.

He smiled softly to himself. 'When I were a young lad I used to come up here with my pal Eric. See that rock over there?'

He pointed to the rock jutting out of the rim of the escarpment, a huge black projection spattered with green clumps of lichen at the top of a sheer drop. 'We used to lie face-down on that, looking across into the valley. Everything's so tiny from there. We felt like gods.'

She smiled. She could see him now, the young Dan eager to conquer the world. She snuggled her cheek against his arm.

'You know,' he murmured, 'I reckon there's been Pearsons hereabouts since the year dot. I know little about any of 'em beyond me grandma and grandad, but I feel I belong here.'

'Course you do,' she agreed. 'Yorkshire man through and through.'

'And I'm the last in the chain.'

The sadness in his tone wrung her heart. It wasn't an accusation; he wouldn't hurt her for the world. His eyes were misted and far away.

'You know what, lass?'

'What?'

He looked down, deep into her eyes. 'I'd like to lie here when I'm gone. If I go before you do, will you see to it for me, scatter me up here?'

310

She hesitated. He wasn't being morbid; it meant a lot to him, and that was all that mattered. 'If that's what you want,' she said quietly. 'Then I will.'

Together they turned back towards the car. Somehow despite the sunshine the sparkle had gone out of the afternoon. Rosa searched for words to lighten the moment.

'And what about me?' she said teasingly. 'Where would you scatter me if I go first?'

He shrugged as he opened the car door for her. 'All over the café floor, I reckon,' he smiled. 'Where else?'

'The café?' she laughed. 'Well that way at least I'll be immortal. Mandy would never get round to dusting me off.'

Greta stepped off the bus in Hawksmoor and strolled along the high street in the sun. She felt cheered by the morning's meeting.

For some years now they'd been raising funds to build a hospice for the terminally ill, and at last it began to look as if the dream was within reach.

It meant so much to have a place, not so much dedicated to death as a tranquil haven where people could end their days with grace and dignity. For years she'd been involved with Wood Lea and with homes for the aged – 'homes for the bewildered', Reginald called them. It was true there were old folk among them suffering from senile dementia who had somehow lost track of their lives, but often they were gentle souls struggling with their lostness. Like the old lady they called Aunt Josephine at Bracken Lodge with whom she'd had a long conversation only yesterday.

'I'm sure I can feel the ley lines running under here, can't you?' the old lady asked. 'Such power, so much energy ...'

Josephine had clearly had some education, and her bearing

and speech were those of a woman brought up in good circumstances, but from time to time she went out on an afternoon jaunt and was often brought back to the home by the police.

'Shoplifting in Boots again,' they said. 'Lipstick this time.'

Aunt Josephine seemed completely unaware of her misdemeanours. She was always naïvely excited about life and her discoveries.

'Wednesdays are blue, I've found out. And Fridays green. Every day has its own colour, just like numbers. Did you know that?'

Greta shook her head. 'Oh yes,' said Josephine, 'and if a green Friday falls on a green seventh of the month, it's going to be a really good day. Just you bear that in mind.'

'I will,' said Greta. 'Thank you.'

Josephine held up a finger. 'What's today?'

'Tuesday the tenth.'

'Hmm,' she frowned, 'brown and red. Drab. Never mind. Tomorrow will be better.'

Greta smiled to herself as she recalled the encounter, so deep in thought as she turned the corner into King Street that she was not at first aware of the bosomy woman barring her way.

'Hello there,' said a voice. 'Just the person I wanted to see.'

Greta looked up. Betty Tasker clutched a laden shopping basket between plump hands.

'Hello,' said Greta. 'What is it?'

'Well,' said Betty between tight lips, 'as a rule I'm not one for telling tales out of school, but them lasses in your house ...'

Greta felt a leap of concern. 'What about them?'

Betty's three chins settled into a triple fold. 'I hear tell

312

they've been seen with men going in there. Late at night and all.'

'I see,' said Greta. 'Well, it's probably perfectly innocent.'

'It's not nice, you know,' said Betty, shaking her head, 'even if there's nowt to it.'

'I wouldn't jump to conclusions all the same,' said Greta. 'I'll have a word with them about it.'

Lucy sat in the living-room, half wishing she hadn't come home. For the past hour her mother had done nothing but carp and criticize, but this time it was not directed against her but the Dutchman who seemed to be in charge of the business.

'I don't know who he thinks he is, just because he's got a fancy title,' Dorothy snorted. 'Financial director, indeed! He seems to think that means he can control the purse strings, but he'll soon learn who's boss.'

'I'm sure he knows what he's doing, Mother, or Daddy wouldn't have trusted him.'

'They're being very stubborn, him and Carter,' Dorothy said bitterly, 'just because I'm a woman. But if they think I'm a total ignoramus they've got another think coming. I won't be taken for a ride, not by those two I won't.'

Lucy tried to change the subject. 'How's Graham going on? Have you heard from him?'

'Two short phone calls,' her mother answered sullenly. 'He's having a whale of a time, evidently. Not a thought to what I'm going through here.'

Lucy took the hint. 'Well I'm here now,' she said soothingly. 'Is there anything special you want me to do?'

Dorothy shrugged cashmere shoulders. 'I've seen to most things myself. There's still that old trunkful of papers your father kept in the loft – mostly building magazines, I think.

They could do with clearing out. I never knew such a man for hoarding junk.'

Lucy sat cross-legged on the dusty floor and lifted the lid of the old trunk. They weren't magazines at all in here, but an assortment of odd bits and pieces which had evidently meant something to him, tokens and mementos of events he clearly wanted to remember ...

There were cinema tickets priced one-and-nine in the old money. She smiled to think they might date from the days when he courted his lady-love, and she tried to visualize them cuddling on the back row. He'd buy her ice-cream and maybe chocolates; he'd have treated her with all the old-world charm of the gentleman he was. It was a pity the lady he chose never really appreciated his worth.

There were a few faded snapshots, one of herself as a toddler on his lap as he sat in a deck-chair on a beach somewhere. She slipped it in her pocket. In another photograph his arms encircled Graham on one side and herself on the other. Gentle pride glowed on his handsome face, and she felt an overwhelming sense of tenderness for him. She put the photograph down and turned to the next item, a folded piece of white linen.

As she shook it loose she recognized it, the scorched remains of the tiny apron belonging to her nurse's outfit. She remembered how Mother had taken it away and threatened to burn it. It seems she had carried out her threat, but Daddy must have salvaged this one piece. He'd known what it meant to her.

The tears were starting. Lucy stuffed it back in the trunk and reached for the small bundle of papers. The topmost document appeared to be a certificate of some kind. She peered at it closely in the dim light.

'Adopted Children's Register,' she read, 'maintained at the General Register Office, Somerset House, London.'

It was about her. Presumably in place of a birth certificate. 'Date and country of birth – England ... District – Hawksmoor ... Name and surname of child ... Boy or girl ... Name, address and occupation of adopter ...'

It was all there, Theodore Challis, builder, and Dorothy Challis adopting the baby girl, Lucy.

'Date of adoption order and description of certificate by which it was made ... Date of entry into the register ...

'Signed by officer of the Register General. Certificate issued pursuant to the Adoption Act 1958.'

Not a word about the woman who bore her; her real mother. Lucy felt angry on her behalf, cheated of her right. She lay the paper aside. Where was she now, this ghost-like woman who sidled into her dreams every now and again? The woman whose blood coursed through her own veins? Lucy felt a sudden surge of fervour.

I want to find her. I want to know her.

Dorothy wasn't interested in harking back to the past.

'Yes, it is a coincidence you being born in Hawksmoor,' she admitted, 'but we only went there because we couldn't find anywhere nearer to adopt.'

'Where was it, Mother? Not the infirmary?'

'Of course not, silly. A private nursing home, out of town somewhere. I forget now.'

There weren't many private maternity homes around the town, thought Lucy. That narrowed the field.

'Did you meet my mother – my real mother?'

'No.' Dorothy gave a testy sigh and reached for the small bottle on the table beside her. Lucy watched her pop two pills into her mouth and then tilt the cup to swig the remains of her coffee.

315

'Still taking pills?' she asked.

Her mother glared at her. 'On doctor's orders. They're mild sedatives, for my nerves. You don't know the half of what I'm going through, here, alone, with no-one to care.'

Lucy held her tongue. She was never going to change.

'I'm going to start going to church again,' Dorothy said quietly.

'Why not, if it gives you comfort.'

'Mrs Whiteley said it gave her a deal of support when she lost her husband.'

'That's good.'

'I don't suppose you'll approve. It's a spiritualist church.'

'As I said, whatever you find helpful.'

Dorothy shook her head fiercely. 'But I don't care what anyone thinks. I'm going to do what I want from now on.'

For the first time she could remember Dorothy was quite sorry to see the girl getting her things together to leave. At least she'd been a bit of company. Since Graham had gone off to university the house seemed desolate and empty. In fact, it made her feel quite nervous. The sound of her own footsteps ringing out on the parquet floor of the hall as she made her way to bed at night was quite eerie. No wonder her nerves were getting bad.

'Sure you've got everything?' she asked as Lucy stood ready in the hall.

Lucy smiled. 'Dinner money, hanky – yes, Mother. Now do take care of yourself – remember to eat properly.'

Dorothy gave a sad shrug. 'It hardly seems worthwhile cooking meals for one these days.'

'And have a word with the doctor about those pills – too many aren't good for you.'

'Don't fuss, Lucy.' Dorothy opened the front door and looked out at the drizzle of rain. 'You should get yourself a little car,' she remarked. 'Graham is planning to.' She shouldn't have said that. Graham's car would be wangled out of the business if she could win the Dutchman over to the idea.

Lucy smiled. 'One day, perhaps. Student nurses' pay doesn't amount to a row of beans.'

Dorothy sniffed. 'You should have gone in for medicine. You wouldn't listen.'

Lucy laughed aloud as she picked up her bag. 'Medical students are poor as church mice too. We have to keep subbing them for a pint.'

'A pint?' echoed Dorothy.

'Down the pub. After we come off shift.'

Dorothy was shocked. 'Really, Lucy! Pubs are no place for a lady! Where are your standards?'

'Things are different these days. Now I'm off.'

Dorothy stood on the doorstep as the girl set off down the drive bending her head against the rain. 'I know we Virgos are very fastidious,' she called out, 'not easy to please, but someone has to fly the flag for decency.'

Greta made a point of going down to Jubilee Terrace in the evening when Reginald was out and when she knew she would most likely find the girls at home.

The air was heavy with the scent of perfume and talc when Linda let her in. In a bathrobe and with a towel round her hair, the girl went back to varnishing her fingernails. Upstairs Greta could hear water splashing and Mandy's voice singing with gusto.

Greta leaned forward. 'So I felt I ought to have a word with you about it,' she said gently. 'You can understand that the neighbours might be concerned if they thought that strangers—'

317

'It was my birthday,' Linda cut in. 'We had a bit of a party.'

'Oh, I see,' said Greta. 'But apparently there was a lot of noise, and in these days when there are all sorts of peculiar folk roaming around ...'

The door opened and a bathrobed Mandy breezed in, surrounded by a fresh wave of aromatic fragrance. 'Oh hello,' she said in surprise. 'Didn't expect you.'

Linda looked up with a scowl. 'Seems the neighbours saw us with some fellows last week,' she muttered. 'Trying to make summat of it, they are.'

Mandy's jaw dropped. 'Nosy devils. They ought to mind their own business.'

Linda held out her fingernails and wriggled them. 'So I told her about me birthday,' she said, 'when we had your brother and his pal round for a drink.'

Mandy's bewildered face cleared. 'Oh aye, that's right. Good night, that were.'

Linda screwed the cap back on the varnish bottle. 'Now the neighbours are trying to make out as if it weren't right,' she grumbled. 'I don't know, some folk ...'

Greta stood up. 'I'm glad you've explained it, and I'm sorry. I do hope you enjoyed your birthday. Only I wouldn't want to think that anything might happen to you. I mean, you have to be so careful – this murderer fellow is still roaming loose.'

Linda stood up, pulling the robe tight about her waist and shaking her head. 'He'll never get to Hawksmoor. They'll catch him long before that. You've no need to worry your head about us.'

Mandy picked up the bottle of nail varnish. 'No,' she said, 'we can take care of ourselves.' She held the bottle up to the light. 'Hey Linda, you've gone and finished off me f— me Scarlet Passion!'

*   *   *

Hero sat waiting patiently on the doorstep. He leapt up, his stumpy tail wagging as he saw his mistress emerge, and he padded along beside her down the darkening street, keeping a weather eye open for any possible threat to her.

Greta was unaware of him, lost in thought about the recent conversation with Linda. The girl's explanation had seemed reasonable enough, so why did a tiny flicker of doubt keep wriggling in her mind?

She couldn't help remembering Matron, the one they'd sacked all those years ago for taking money in exchange for babies. She'd been fair of face, that one, and had a pleasing manner which had fooled the whole board for long enough.

What was it someone once said about the smile on the face of the tiger?

Chapter Twenty-eight

The café was seething with customers, every table filled and other would-be customers searching the place hopefully from the top of the stairs before giving up and leaving.

Rosa had taken off her jacket and stood up to her elbows in soapsuds at the kitchen sink. From there she could see Mandy, standing chatting to a couple of youths at a far table, completely oblivious to the clients still waiting to be served. Inwardly fuming, Rosa dried her hands.

'Mandy,' she called. The girl turned her head. Rosa beckoned sharply. The girl took her time.

'What's up?' she asked.

Rosa jerked her head towards the nearest table. 'Can't you see people are waiting?' she demanded. 'Those two must have been here for ages.'

Mandy shrugged. 'Is it my fault I've only one pair of hands? We ought to have more help.'

Rosa felt like thumping her. 'We'd manage perfectly well if you'd stop flirting and get on with the job,' she snapped. 'You're serving so slowly people are leaving.'

'There's more to life than making money,' the girl muttered as she turned away. Rosa heaved a sigh of frustration and went back to the sink. A moment later she heard raised voices and then Mandy's shrill tone.

'For heaven's sake. I can't stand here all day.'

'Mandy!'

The girl's sulky face appeared round the door. 'What is it now?'

Rosa grabbed her arm and drew her inside, glaring. 'You're sacked!' she hissed. 'Get your coat on now.'

Her timing couldn't have been worse, thought Rosa later as she scurried up and down, trying to serve and keep up with the dishes at the same time. Thank goodness it was nearing the end of the afternoon and things would soon quieten down. At the moment, however, all the tables were filled but for the one by the stairs, and another customer was just coming up.

The woman seated herself, then glanced back over her shoulder towards the kitchen, and in that moment Rosa felt a leap of half recognition. She'd seen that face somewhere before.

She served the couple in the window, then cleared the table alongside. She dumped the tray next to the pile of dishes accumulating in the sink then went over to the woman.

That face – it was familiar, but she was not a regular customer. She looked up at Rosa without speaking. Rosa took out her pad.

'Can I help you?'

She must have been frowning. 'Yes,' the woman said, inclining her head, 'you do know me. It was a long time ago now.'

And then, in a flash, it came. 'You,' Rosa gasped, 'you're the woman who sold my child.'

Her knees suddenly seemed to turn to rubber. Holyoak – that was her name. Behind her a voice spoke.

'Miss – is that coffee ready yet? We haven't got much time.'

Mrs Holyoak peered round Rosa's shoulder. 'You're very busy,' she remarked. 'Where's Mandy?'

321

'Gone,' snapped Rosa. 'I sent her packing this afternoon, but never mind that – I want to talk to you.'

'We'll have a talk later, but not now. I'll give you a hand.'

Mrs Holyoak pushed back her chair and went into the kitchen. Rosa followed, staring in amazement. 'What do you think you're doing?' she demanded. 'You can't come in here.'

The woman shrugged off her coat and laid it aside. 'I can't offer to wait at table but I've got a lifetime's experience of washing-up.' She began rolling up her sleeves. 'You see to your customers,' she said, 'before they disappear.'

The last customers finally left. Rosa returned to the kitchen bearing yet another tray-load of dishes which she set down alongside the sink. Greta dried her hands.

'Here,' said Rosa gruffly, holding out a clenched fist, 'this is your share of the tips.'

Greta shook her head. 'No, really,' she said, 'there's no need. I don't want payment.'

'I'm not going to pay you, but fair's fair. It's only one pound seventy.'

Greta looked down at the coins in her palm. 'Thank you,' she said quietly, folding her fingers around them, 'I shall treasure this. It's the first money I've earned with my own hands in many a long year.'

Rosa ignored the comment. 'Time for that talk,' she said curtly. 'Tea or coffee?'

The two women sat face to face in the deserted café. The coffee cups in front of them stood empty now and the place was silent except for the slow regular drip of the tap in the kitchen.

'So you see I knew nothing of what was going on at

322

Wood Lea,' Greta said softly. 'I should have, but I didn't. You do believe me, don't you?'

Rosa gave a disclaiming shrug. 'I only know you gave me money, can you blame me for thinking it was my share?'

Greta's hand reached out to touch hers. 'If it's any consolation to you, once we found out about it, the matron was sacked instantly without a reference.'

Rosa drew her hand away. 'Wasn't there a court case? Wasn't she punished?'

Greta smiled. 'I rather think she was; it must have been very hard for her to find a new post. Would you like to try and explain away a six-year gap in your working life with no reference to show for it?'

For a time Rosa said nothing, toying with the teaspoon. 'Angela was the most beautiful baby in the world when she was born, you know,' she murmured. 'Such a mop of hair and the tiniest fingernails you ever saw.'

Greta nodded. 'I know.'

'She was mine. She was perfect. I didn't want to let her go.'

'You did the best thing possible in the circumstances,' Greta soothed. 'You gave her a better chance in life.'

Rosa flipped the teaspoon over. 'I'd have managed,' she said brusquely. 'If I'd known what I know now I'd never have let you persuade me.'

'Perhaps not,' sighed Greta. 'With hindsight we're all wise.'

'Tell me,' said Rosa, 'if I check the records could I find out who adopted Angela?'

Greta took a deep breath. 'Even if it were possible, are you sure that would be wise, after all this time?'

'What's wise got to do with it? I'd like to know she's OK.'

323

Greta sighed. 'So much to explain – to her, and does your husband know?'

Rosa lowered her head. 'No. He mustn't know. We have no children and he thinks it's me. I can't tell him.'

'I see.'

Rosa looked up directly into her eyes. 'But I'd like Angela to know. I'd hate her to think she was abandoned.'

The older woman shook her head gently. 'Let me put it to you this way – would you want to upset her way of life, the only life she's ever known?'

Rosa wavered. 'I don't know. It's just that it all feels so, sort of unfinished, somehow.'

'You have a new life now,' Greta pointed out. 'My advice is concentrate on that. I can see you've worked hard and been successful here.'

'I could do better,' murmured Rosa. 'I'd like to expand into the room next door – it used to be part of this. See the partition there?' She turned to point to the far wall. 'It would make the place twice as big.'

'You've looked into it?' asked Greta.

'It's nowhere near as grotty as this place was when I got it.'

'So if it's empty, what's to stop you?'

'Planning permission, that's what. You wouldn't believe the delays and questions, but I won't give up.' Rosa glanced up at the clock. 'Look,' she said, holding out her hand, 'I've got to go. But thanks for your help. Thanks for coming.'

Mandy stamped defiantly along the high street. So what if she'd got the sack? It was a lousy job anyway, having to be nice to silly devils who kept changing their minds about what they wanted and then complained if the tea was too strong or the coffee not strong enough.

Daft old women they were, mostly, mean with their tips,

hardly ever a good-looking young fellow. The lads knew better than to come to a fuddy-duddy dump like Kadinski's. She'd be far better off working in a snack bar; at least she'd meet her own kind and it didn't really matter if the pay wasn't terrific. Not now Linda and her had found another way to earn real money.

At least that crabby Mrs Pearson had paid her off up to the end of the week. She had money jingling in her pocket. She could go and get those pink shoes she'd seen in Freeman Hardy and Willis to go with the clingy pink frock she bought on Saturday.

Maybe then that hunky Ben on the door down at the club would flirt with her again like he did that time he let her sneak in free. God, he was gorgeous! He looked like a wrestler with those huge shoulders, and she'd seen the way troublemakers suddenly shut up when Ben squared up to them.

She shivered at the thought of those big muscular arms about her, pulling her close. God, she'd take him down a back alley any time and give him a treat for free. It'd be a damn sight nicer than letting those clumsy breathless punters maul her about.

Yes, she decided, turning into Freeman Hardy and Willis's doorway, I'm going to pull out all the stops for Ben. He'll never know what hit him.

Greta made sure Reginald was not yet home before she picked up the telephone directory, flicked through the pages, then dialled a number. She stood, inspecting her fingernails, listening to the ring-ring until a man's voice answered.

'Hello?'

'Councillor Moxon? My name is Greta Holyoak,' she said with quiet confidence. 'Reginald Holyoak's wife. Tell me, are you still on the Planning Committee? ... You are? Good.'

She settled herself down on the hall seat. 'You may remember a petition, some time ago, which was brought to you by a lady called Betty Tasker. A large number of names protesting against the redevelopment of the Mafeking Street area. You may remember too that it enabled you to call a halt to that plan ... You do. Well, my husband never knew, but that petition was my doing, and now I'd like to ask a favour of you.'

She listened carefully to his reply, that if it was possible, if it was within his purview, if it wasn't breaking any code of conduct ...

'It's a very simple matter, Mr Moxon,' she cut in politely, 'just a matter of cutting through all the red tape and getting some planning permission speeded up. The applicant is a Mrs Rosa Pearson ...'

Lucy's mother sounded even more fretful than usual on the telephone.

'It's more than one person can handle alone,' she complained. 'I really do need help. This Overmeer fellow is a real trial.'

'Have you talked to Graham about it, Mother?'

Dorothy sounded distant. 'He doesn't want to know, I'm afraid. Too much happening in his life. To be honest, reading between the lines, I think there's a girl.'

Very possibly, thought Lucy. He was a good-looking boy, but it was more than that. Graham had never hidden his dislike of Daddy's business – trade, he called it.

'*When I graduate I want to do business management,*' he used to say to his father.

'*So why not manage Challis's?*'

Graham would tilt his head, looking as if there was a nasty smell under his nose. '*Real business, Dad, in a firm with corporate management structure, like IBM, with long-term projections and strategy planning. I want to organize executive personnel, not a blue-collar bunch.'*

Mother was still complaining '... and he won't let me,' she whimpered. 'Anyone would think he was the managing director, not me. I mean to say, bullying a lone woman like that. I never did trust foreigners.'

'If you mean Mr Overmeer, Daddy trusted him,' said Lucy, 'and he has a lot of experience. Maybe you should listen to him.'

She heard the long-drawn sigh. 'You haven't heard a word I've said, have you? That man's determined to thwart me.'

It was Lucy's turn to sigh. 'But why a bungalow?'

'It makes sense. This house was meant for a family and I haven't got a family any more.'

'You've got Graham and me.'

'You?' The word almost exploded down the line. 'You were always Daddy's girl, never mine!'

Lucy was stung by the viciousness of her tone. 'And whose fault was that?' she retorted. 'He loved me. You always made me feel like a cuckoo in the nest.'

'Because that's just what you were,' the voice hissed malevolently. 'Trying to push Graham out, getting the best of everything.'

'You malicious old bitch!' Lucy heard herself shouting. 'That's not true and you know it!'

For a moment there was a stunned silence and then the voice reverted to its old familiar whine. 'I might have known you'd turn against me too. All these years you've brought me nothing but misery.'

Lucy could feel the tears starting to sting. 'Well don't worry, Mother,' she said quietly. 'I won't bring you any more.'

And with that she replaced the receiver on the rest.

*   *   *

327

Lucy looked up as Neela bounced into the room. 'I've failed my medical care practical again,' she announced. 'That's twice now – if I don't get it next time I'm out.'

'You'll get it,' said Lucy. 'We'll make sure you do.'

Neela slumped on the bed beside her. 'Decided what you want to do for your speciality yet? Gynae-urinary?'

'No thanks! Maybe ophthalmic – only I can't spell it.'

Neela sprawled full-length, her hands behind her head. 'Only three years to go to SRN – if I can get through my practical. Hey, why are you looking so down? Your mother been on at you again?'

Lucy hitched up her knees. 'I've decided, I want to look for my real mother,' she said quietly. She sank her chin on her knees. 'I miss being somebody's daughter.'

'Mmm,' said Neela. 'That might not be easy.'

'I know she had me in Hawksmoor, in a private maternity home, and I've been checking. Only Wood Lea was open then. I wonder if I was to ask them to check the records ...'

Neela sat up. 'Hold on, I know someone who might be able to help. They won't tell you anything, but if I was to ask Sylvia ...'

Lucy gripped her hands. 'Would you? It means such a lot to me.'

'I know. Especially since you lost your dad. Leave it to me.'

It was Lucy's second day on the geriatric ward. The sister on duty watched her, frowning, as she plumped up and settled an old lady's pillows more comfortably.

'This isn't your first block ...?'

'No, Sister,' said Lucy. 'I've done my sixteen weeks on women's medical and I passed the aseptic practical on Friday.'

Sister looked her up and down appraisingly. 'Well, you'll find care of the elderly rather different from medical,' she sniffed. 'Come with me.'

She led the way to a side ward. Her hand on the doorknob, she paused. 'Ever laid out a dead body?' she asked.

'No, Sister.'

'You'll soon get used to it on this ward. Here's a patient who died in the night. Come and help me see to him.'

Lucy stood frozen at the foot of the bed. It was old Mr Harper, lying supine, eyes closed and his face waxy white, looking for all the world as if he were sleeping.

'Mr Harper,' she breathed. 'I was talking to him only yesterday. Such a nice old gentleman.'

Sister pulled off the sheets. 'Soap and water, Nurse,' she said crisply. 'A bed-bath first, then we'll do his hair and put in his teeth.'

It was with a strange feeling of unease that Lucy touched the translucent skin, so thin and fragile she almost feared it would tear like tissue-paper. This was no longer Mr Harper, but the shell which had once housed him. Nevertheless it felt like an intrusion to handle his body. She tried hard to bathe him with reverence and care.

'Now turn him over,' said Sister, and together they rolled him over. As they did so Lucy heard a softly exhaled groan.

'Don't worry,' Sister reassured her, 'it's only the last of the air being driven out of his lungs. I'll see to his teeth now and then leave you to comb his hair. All right?'

When she'd gone Lucy sat on the edge of the bed, combing the sparse grey hairs carefully into place.

I'd like to think someone cared for you like this, Daddy. I couldn't bring myself to go with Mother to see you in the chapel of rest, but I hope someone gave you these same last respectful rites and wished you Godspeed.

'Have you done?'

Sister was standing behind her. Lucy stood up. 'Then I'll put him in his shroud,' said Sister. 'Just watch how it's done.'

At last he lay enveloped in the thick white linen with his name taped to his chest. 'Funny,' murmured Sister, 'but until this moment he was Mr Harper for me, now it's a body ready for the mortuary.' She looked up at Lucy sharply. 'What are you doing?'

'Just opening the window, Sister.'

'Whatever for?'

Lucy bit her lip and shrugged. 'I don't know,' she muttered, then, turning to look out of the window at the glorious sunshine flooding across the car park, she added in an undertone, 'Just letting his soul go free.'

Chapter Twenty-nine

Dorothy sailed into her office and dumped her handbag on the desk. Miss Cherry followed her in with anxious steps.

'I wasn't expecting you this morning, Mrs Challis,' she said nervously. 'Would you like me to bring you some coffee?'

'Milky, and a few biscuits please.'

The secretary turned to go; Dorothy lowered herself gracefully into the depths of the leather executive chair behind the desk. 'Oh, and tell Mr Overmeer I'd like a word with him,' she added. 'If he doesn't mind.'

'I'm afraid he's with Mr Hedge at the moment, Mrs Challis. Shall I tell him when the meeting's over?'

Dorothy frowned. 'Mr Hedge? Who's he?'

Miss Cherry cleared her throat. 'He's from the bank – we always deal with him – he's in charge of corporate accounts.' She glanced over her shoulder. 'Oh, he's just leaving now. I'll give Mr Overmeer your message.'

As the door closed behind her Dorothy sat back, frowning and drumming her fingertips on the mahogany desk. She should have been told about this Hedge's visit. He was the man she needed to see.

She swung round slowly in the swivel chair, taking in the cosy fresh appearance of the room. She didn't come into the office very often, but it was nice to know the place now had a welcoming feel. It had looked far too spartan before;

Theo hadn't been a man for frills and fripperies but even he would admit it looked far more cheerful nowadays with the potted plant on a pretty jardinière under the window and a tasteful Chinese rug contrasting with the neutral carpet tiles. Dreadful things those beige tiles – they showed every footmark.

Miss Cherry came in carrying a tray of coffee and biscuits. 'Mr Overmeer says he'll be in directly,' she said, laying the tray within Dorothy's reach. 'Will there be anything else?'

'Not at the moment,' said Dorothy crisply. 'I'll ring if I want you.'

Be in directly, she thought crossly as she snapped off the end of a Garibaldi biscuit. The insolence of the man! If he believed his tactics could put her off, he had another think coming. She poured the coffee and sat back to wait for him, crossing her legs with purposeful precision.

'I wasn't married to a successful builder for all those years without learning something, you know,' Dorothy said. 'That plot won't wait for ever – for all we know someone else might already have a bid in. We can't afford to shilly-shally.'

She set the cup down. She wasn't going to offer coffee to Overmeer; it would appear too friendly, and he had to recognize that she was the superior.

He was no gentleman; he made no attempt to hide the pained look in his blue eyes. 'Mrs Challis,' he said patiently, 'as I've tried to explain, there are several factors to take into account. Money for one – the cash-flow situation has to be balanced with care.'

'Cash flow fiddlesticks!' she exclaimed. 'We can well afford the price they're asking.' She wagged a Bourbon biscuit at him. 'I've seen the books, remember.'

He shook his head gently. 'Flow, Mrs Challis, means the way money comes in and goes out. At any one time a great

332

deal of cash is tied up in materials in stock, and don't forget we don't receive payment for a building until it's complete. For quite a time we're out of pocket.'

Dorothy frowned. It didn't make sense. The profit came in eventually, didn't it? And there was always the bank ...

'You should have let me know Mr Hedge was here,' she remarked drily. 'We could have discussed a loan with him.'

Overmeer inclined his head. 'We could, but he'd have enquired how we intended to repay the interest on a loan of that size.'

'He knows we'll make a healthy profit when the bungalows are sold.'

'And until then? There's nothing coming in from that piece of land until they are sold. And that's assuming they will sell, and that the land is fit for building in the first place.'

Dorothy leaned forward. 'Ah, now that's something I do know. My husband used to say it paid to buy a flat plot because it saved the cost of excavation which I know can be very expensive. This is a beautiful plot, as flat as a billiard table.'

Overmeer folded his hands neatly together and sat back. 'With all due respect, Mrs Challis, I don't think you get my drift ...'

Dorothy's patience gave way. 'With all due respect, I think I do,' she snapped. 'Your plan is to thwart me, to stop me having my dream bungalow on my dream plot. And you can't bear the thought that a woman can pull off a deal at a bargain price. It's your pride that's hurt, Mr Overmeer, but let me remind you that this is my company, not yours.'

Overmeer inclined his head. 'So be it, but take my advice – at least let Carter get a surveyor in first. There could be a good reason for them cutting the price.'

'Like what?' she demanded.

He shrugged. 'It could be contaminated – who knows?'

'Rubbish. There's never been any industry of any kind up there.'

'That's not what I meant.'

'I want that site, Mr Overmeer, so there's no point putting up any further argument.'

Dorothy swung the chair round to face the window. Overmeer recognized the signal and rose, tight-lipped, to leave.

Carter, for all his uncouth ways, had been perfectly right. The woman was unquestionably a mad cow.

Greta just couldn't stay away. She felt compelled to go back to Kadinski's café to see Rosa Pearson again. By now she should have got the planning permission and things should be moving – not that Greta would dream of letting her know she'd had any hand in it. But she did feel she owed Rosa something. She'd been the one who'd persuaded her to give up her child all those years ago. She'd acted with the best of motives but maybe it was the wrong advice and maybe Rosa was right in saying she could have coped. The way things had turned out she might have managed very well.

Life is full of crossroads, Greta mused, but sometimes the route we choose affects others more deeply than we realize. How do we ever know whether we've made the right decision?

It was late afternoon when she entered the arcade. Business should have slowed down by now. The bell tinkled as she pushed open the shop door and went in. There was no-one behind the counter, but beyond it a hand-painted sign stood propped against the wall at the foot of the stairs: 'Café closed for alterations.'

She paused, hearing footsteps coming up from the cellar. The young man who ran the shop appeared.

'Isn't Mrs Pearson here?' she asked.

He smiled. He had a pleasant face, she thought, full of kindly good humour. 'She is – she's up there doing something. Shall I call her?'

'If it's all right with you I'll go up – I'm a friend.'

He moved the sign to one side to let her pass. As he did so Rosa came running down, her pretty face flushed.

'Mrs Holyoak, how nice to see you again,' she said. 'I'm afraid I can't offer you a coffee ...'

'No need,' said Greta. 'I was passing – I just wondered how you were getting on, that's all.'

'She's keeping me busy, that's for sure,' murmured the young man. Rosa laughed.

'He's been wonderful,' she said to Greta. 'I don't know what I'd have done without him. We're very nearly ready to open again. You know, it's ironic, straight after I was grumbling to you about that planning permission, it came through. Just a few days after. So we've been up to our eyeballs, Alex and me. It's going to be terrific when it's done.'

Greta smiled to see the girl's excitement. 'I look forward to seeing it.'

Rosa leaned her elbow on the balustrade. 'I'm going to get one of those microwave things,' she enthused, 'not to do any real cooking, just to heat up pies and do baked potatoes. Alex suggested that.'

'Sounds a great idea – I love baked potatoes.'

Alex excused himself and moved towards the back room. As he passed, Greta could see that his gaze was fixed on Rosa, and she could swear that the light in his eye was more than just admiration.

'Life's opening new doors all the time, it seems,' she murmured.

Rosa's face grew serious. 'Yes. You were right. There's no point dwelling on the past. I just wanted to feel Angela is happy and she's found whatever she wants from life, that's all.'

Greta smiled. 'If she's anything like her mother, she will.'

Rosa straightened. 'Ah well,' she said, 'it was a nutty idea anyway. A lot's changed since then.'

Greta touched her arm. 'Especially you,' she chuckled, 'I wouldn't know you for that slip of a girl I once met. An up-and-coming Hawksmoor businesswoman now, you've all but lost that lovely accent of yours.'

At last the shift was over. Lucy was making her way back to the nurses' home when she caught sight of Neela's uniformed figure striding ahead. She hurried to catch up with her.

Neela's dark eyes were shining. 'I made it, Lucy – third time lucky! I passed the practical!'

Lucy squeezed her arm. 'I knew you'd do it. There's no stopping you now. SRN, here we come.'

'My dad will be so pleased,' enthused Neela as she pulled open the door and went in, then suddenly her smile fell away. 'Oh, I'm sorry ...'

'Don't worry,' said Lucy quietly. 'My dad is always with me. Whatever I'm doing, he's there, sitting in the back of my head. It's as though, if I was to turn round suddenly, I'd see him.'

'Like he was sitting in the back seat of a car?'

'That's right. So you see, you don't have to avoid mentioning him, honest.'

Together the girls went into their room. Lucy tossed her cape over a chair. Neela picked up a piece of paper from the table and sat on the bed.

'Sylvia, Sheridan,' she murmured. 'Oh yes – that Wood Lea business you were on about, Lucy – Sylvia rang this

336

morning just after you'd gone. She said she's managed to check up on that year, the date you said.'

Lucy came close. 'And?' she asked eagerly. 'What did she find.'

Neela drew her down to sit beside her. 'Not a lot, I'm afraid. All she got was that the Challises adopted a baby girl, and the mother was called R. Sheridan.'

'Sheridan.' whispered Lucy. 'Lucy Sheridan.' She took hold of the Indian girl's arm. 'Didn't it give an address?'

Neela shook her head. 'No address here, only it said she was Irish. She must have just come over to England.'

'Because she was pregnant,' murmured Lucy. 'With me.'

There was a sharp rap on the door and a girl's voice called out. 'Challis, phone call for you.'

Lucy stood up. 'That'll be Mother again. I wonder what she wants now.'

'It's the third time I've rung today,' Dorothy complained.

'Why? What's the matter, Mother?'

Lucy heard the plaintive sigh at the other end of the line. 'As if I haven't got enough on my plate already, now this letter from Graham. It really is too much.'

'What's happened? I thought he was doing all right.'

'It's not his studies, it's this girl he talks about. She's not right for him, Lucy. I mean—'

'How can you possibly tell? She might be a very good influence for all you know.'

'But a black girlfriend, Lucy! What on earth would your father think?'

Lucy heard the harshness in her own voice. 'He'd give Graham his blessing, Mother, and that's what you should do.'

The voice sounded wistful. 'I wrote to tell him I

needed him here. All he talks about is this blessed girl.'

'Don't worry so much, he's bound to get interested in girls at his age. It's only natural.'

The voice took on a sly tone. 'Well, if Graham won't come back where he's needed, it falls on you, Lucy. I'm afraid it will mean giving up your nursing, but this is far more important as I'm sure you'll agree. Knowing I'm no longer well enough to manage on my own ...'

'You're not ill,' Lucy cut in quietly. 'You're headstrong and wilful and you've just talked yourself into believing you're ill, and that's dangerous. I'm not giving up nursing, for you or anybody else.'

She heard the quick hiss of indrawn breath. 'What do you mean, dangerous?' Dorothy demanded. 'I never thought the day would come when a child of mine would speak to me like that. Are you trying to say I'm mad?'

'No, Mother – irrational, confused maybe. I think you need help. Why don't you go and see Doctor—'

Lucy heard the abrupt burr as the telephone slammed down at the other end. With a sigh she retraced her steps along the corridor.

Linda slammed the front door and turned the key in the lock. Mandy started to giggle.

'Curtain's twitching next door again,' she whispered. 'It's that miniskirt of yours.'

'Listen who's talking!' retorted Linda. 'I can just about see your backside. Pink knickers, you got.'

'You saw me put 'em on.'

Their footsteps clattered along the pavement in unison. Mandy tugged at the hem of her skirt. 'Where we off to then?' she asked. 'I fancy the club.'

Linda snorted. 'There's nowt worth picking up there. Let's try The George cocktail bar again.'

Mandy pulled a face. 'Aw heck! We could be there all night and get nowt. You go if you like. I'm for the club.'

'Suit yourself,' said Linda. 'You'll end up getting Ben if you're lucky but you'll earn nowt. Still, whatever happens, I'll meet you back at the taxi rank same as usual. OK.'

Mrs Kadinski pored over the spread of playing cards fanned out on the kitchen table. Betty Tasker watched the old lady's face closely, trying not to show her curiosity.

Mrs Kadinski laid a plump finger on the nine of diamonds. 'Money,' she murmured. Betty sat up. 'Somebody is looking to you for money.'

Betty slumped back in her seat. 'Who isn't?' she muttered. 'If it isn't the rates or the gas it's the blooming electric. Never mind about money – can't you see owt more interesting?'

Mrs Kadinski chewed her bottom lip, tapping the three of hearts. 'A journey?' she hazarded. 'Over the water, perhaps.'

Betty snorted. 'Seems to me them cards know nowt, else they'd know I never go further than Skegness. Two feet on terra firma, that's me.'

Mrs Kadinski's pudgy face was a little troubled as she traced a finger over the jack of spades. 'A man,' she murmured, and when Betty didn't leap in she went on rather more confidently. 'There's definitely a dark-haired man – he seems to be waiting for you.'

Betty folded her arms and shook her head vigorously. 'There's nowt like that going on,' she rumbled, 'nor is there likely to be. I don't want no man, dark or fair. Our Fred'll do me a while yet.'

'Your husband – what colour was his hair when he still had hair?'

339

Betty rubbed her chin thoughtfully. 'Do you know, it's been that long I've quite forgot.' She looked up at the clock on the mantelshelf. 'Eeh, is that the time? I'd best get off now or I'll be late for me bingo. I promised our Fred I'd meet him there at eight.'

Mrs Kadinski's plump face creased into a smile as she scooped the cards together. 'So I am right,' she said complacently. 'There is a man waiting for you after all.'

A shadow stirred in the darkness under the railway arch. Someone was coming – a woman, judging by the clip-clop of her heels ringing out in the deserted street.

She appeared at last under the lamplight, her heavy body swaying from side to side like a matelot. She was old; she was fat; she wouldn't do. It was early yet. He could wait.

On silent, crêpe-soled feet the shadow sidled back, melting into the darkness of the sombre stone.

Chapter Thirty

Dan Pearson drove blindly up out of the town, heading instinctively towards the moors. He was halfway to Rochdale before he realized where he was. He pulled in on the grass verge and sat staring out over the rolling acres of heather mingled with wiry cotton grass.

He still felt numb. It was hard to take in, even though he'd known for months that he wasn't going to get well. He hadn't told Rosa; no point in worrying her any further. She'd accepted that he hadn't been able to work for the past eighteen months, but she still fervently believed that he was going to get better.

While she was at work it had been easy to hide from her the times he'd been up to the hospital for those tests. But now . . .

'I'm sorry,' the doctor had said. 'There's no resolution. I'm afraid you'll have to break it to your wife.'

So that was it and he'd have to face it. He was dying. A couple more months and then his world would stop, but the irony was that the rest of the world would go on without him. Rosa would go on without him; he choked at the thought of her grieving alone.

He'd watched her last night in the bath, humming to herself as she dipped the sponge in the bubbles and then lifted and squeezed it over her breasts. Her thick dark hair scraped up on top of her head and her eyes shining with enthusiasm as she talked eagerly about the café, she'd looked like a child. In seventeen years she'd never changed, never grown older. And now, he thought wistfully, he would never see her grow old.

He couldn't bring himself to tell her. It was too final. She'd always been a woman to cope with any problem so long as she could find a way to get to grips with it. This one was too implacable even for her. She mustn't know – not yet.

He couldn't go home for a while. She'd guess all too soon that something was up. He needed time to collect his thoughts and plan just how and when he was going to break it to her.

His moor, that's where he'd go, to the cliff edge overlooking the valley where he'd taken all his troubles as a boy. Up there he could sit and think, and the clean cold air would blow away the debris cluttering his brain. His moor had never failed him in the past.

Reginald felt edgy all through dinner. Greta chatted on easily, apparently unaware, about the developing plans for the hospice, but he couldn't concentrate. He fidgeted with his dessert spoon until at last she got up to fetch the pudding.

It had been a lousy day, one way or another; a flat tyre on the way to the office, an hysterical typist spilling tears over her boyfriend as well as over the letters he was waiting to sign, and then that dolt of a burglar he was trying to defend had blurted out enough in the dock to talk himself into six months. Reginald wasn't used to losing cases and he wouldn't have lost this one if the idiot had remembered what he'd been coached to say.

Greta came back and leaned over him to put a bowl on the table. The smell of her perfume, soft and earthy, made him glance up. He hadn't really noticed how her hair, once

342

mousy-brown, was now a pretty silvery shade, almost like a platinum blonde; her skin looked nice and her bearing was that of a lady with poise. Odd, he thought, how a woman could look more attractive at sixty than she did at forty-five. It was almost as though she'd only learned how to become a woman in her later years.

A woman ... That's what he needed – Madame Zara. An hour with her would calm his nerves.

'What do you think?' Greta asked.

He jerked back to life. 'Sorry – I was miles away,' he murmured. 'I didn't catch what you said.'

She smiled. She had a nice smile. 'Mind on other things?' she enquired. 'Council business?'

He needed to ring Zara. 'You read my mind,' he smiled. 'Housing Committee again – we've had a few problems. I'll have to go tonight, I'm afraid.'

It wasn't a bad story, on the spur of the moment, and it wasn't entirely untrue. There had been complaints about the newly completed flats on the ring road.

'Fine,' she said. 'I've got plenty to occupy me.'

He took his coffee into the lounge and sat in his armchair staring at the television screen but not taking in a word of what the investigative reporter had uncovered. Greta must be absorbed with her chores in the kitchen by now. It should be safe to ring Zara.

He rose and hurried to the door, but as he stepped out into the hall he saw his wife, sitting on the telephone seat and nodding at what the unseen person at the other end of the line was saying. She covered the mouthpiece.

'Did you want to use the phone?' she asked. 'I won't be long.'

He waved a dismissive arm as he turned away. 'Don't worry,' he said airily, 'I only wanted to find out which

343

committee room we're in tonight – I'll find out when I get there.'

Dammit, he thought as he reversed the car out of the drive. Madame Zara doesn't like people turning up without an appointment, but needs must when the devil drives.

He was halfway to Leeds before it occurred to him to stop and use a public telephone, clear proof that his nerves were bad, he thought as he pushed coins into the slot. Where now was the crystal clarity for which he was renowned in court?

For long minutes he stood staring out of the kiosk into the darkened street, letting the telephone ring, but there was no answer. He finally gave up and put the receiver down. Just because she didn't answer it didn't prove she wasn't at home. She could be busy with another client. Anyway, he wasn't going to turn back now. He'd press on and hope.

The dancehall was heaving with sweating bodies and the blare of the rock music over the huge amplifiers made her ears ring. Mandy pushed her way through the gyrating bodies to the stairs leading up to the club entrance.

She could feel the cool night air brushing her cheek as she reached the top. Ben stood by the open door. Christ, he was big! Either his jacket was getting too tight for him or his muscles bulged bigger than ever.

He caught sight of her. 'Back again?' he said. 'Can't take it, eh?'

'Need a breath of air,' she explained. 'It's stinking hot down there.'

He grinned. 'Good job I don't have to stamp your hand every time you go out or you'd be covered. You've been in and out like a yo-yo all night.'

'Ooh,' she simpered. 'I should be so lucky.' She came up close, running her fingers lightly down his thigh.

'Knock it off,' he growled. 'I'm supposed to be working.'

'It's quiet enough now,' she murmured softly. 'Fancy coming outside with me for a bit?'

The fingers were insinuating their way higher. Ben glanced around. 'OK – but not for long,' he muttered. 'I don't want the sack.'

They'd only walked twenty yards away from the club when he pulled her into the dark entry. It was smelly in here, with tin cans and rubbish littered about their feet. He stopped suddenly and reached for her, breathing hard, fumbling, pressing ...

There was no kiss. She couldn't even see his face as he pinned her against the cold stone wall and her face was pressed hard against his chest. She could see nothing, only smell the sour sweat of his armpit as he panted and groaned.

This wasn't the way she'd meant it to be. This was no better than a hasty punter. 'An Englishman takes time' – what a joke.

And then he was pulling away, refastening his jacket and smoothing his hair. 'Better get back now,' he grunted.

She reached up to touch his face. 'Oh Ben, we haven't been here two minutes. Let's have a cuddle first, eh?'

He brushed her hand away. 'Don't be daft. I can't spend all night shafting silly little bitches like you – I got to get back to me job.'

Mandy felt stung. 'I'm not a silly little bitch. I thought you fancied me.'

He sighed. 'Look, you been asking for it all night, now you got it.' He stood in the entrance, under the lamplight. 'You coming?'

'No,' she replied sulkily.

'Suit yourself.'

And he was gone. For a few moments Mandy stood in the dark, feeling the tears start to sting. He'd treated her like dirt, the sod! Who did he think he was, just because he was good-looking and built like a bull? To hell with him!

She flicked the tears away, pushed her hair back into shape, and in the gloom did her best to touch up her lipstick. When she emerged at last into the street, she hesitated. She ought to turn right, away from the club, but somehow her feet turned to the left.

Twenty yards down the road a pretty brunette with long legs stood by the railings outside the club doorway. She'd seen her earlier in the dancehall and the way the lads' eyes fastened on her as she passed. Ben stood behind her on the doorstep as she scribbled on a piece of paper.

As Mandy reached them the girl folded the slip of paper, then turned and handed it to Ben.

'There you are,' she said brightly. 'Give me a ring – any time.'

Ben glanced at the slip before tucking it into his breast pocket. 'I will,' he grinned. 'Tomorrow.'

Burning with rage, Mandy swept on by.

Reginald had been ringing Madame Zara's doorbell off and on for over two hours now, sitting waiting in the car between attempts. There was no light he could see inside the flat, but then the curtains were thick velvet and she often used candles.

It was late by the time he had to admit it was useless and gave up. With the engine switched off it was cold in the car and somehow it had quenched the fire in his belly, but his nerves felt even more frayed as he turned the car about and headed for home.

On the outskirts of Hawksmoor he slowed. He was in no state to confront Greta right now. If he waited just a little longer she'd be sure to be in bed by the time he got back. Near the gaunt arches of the viaduct he turned into a side-street, drew up and switched off the engine.

For a time all was quiet, just the odd car passing now and again. Then suddenly the stillness of the night was broken – a bunch of noisy kids were spilling out of a doorway up the road. He watched them, couples linking arms and scattering, laughing and teasing, small knots of youngsters drifting away into the darkness.

It was well past midnight. Time to go home. Sighing, he reached for the ignition.

Dan was beginning to feel the cold wind biting into his bones. With so little flesh on his frame he felt the cold easily these days.

He left the cliff edge and went back to sit in the car on the roadside. For a long time he sat slumped, watching the passing headlights as an occasional car droned by. Those people were unaware of him and the threat hanging over him.

He couldn't explain the anger which burned in him, the frustration of being forced to leave life when others, with less to live for, lived on. Maybe Rosa would understand.

He laid a hand on his stomach. Somewhere in there the disease was eating its remorseless way through his organs, gnawing away like a rat at the shreds of his life.

It was no use. However hard he mulled it over, phrasing and rephrasing the speech in his head, he still couldn't come up with the right words to break the truth to her. There was just no way to make it easier for her. There is little kindness in the word cancer, and even less in the word death.

*   *   *

Up the narrow entry twenty yards from the club a shadow stirred and stretched. It was a vile, evil-smelling alley and he'd been crouching here for a long time, ever since the couple had come in.

Their business had been far too pressing for them to notice a shadow. He'd crouched there, motionless, until they grunted their way to a squalid conclusion.

He saw what happened next, the big fellow abandoning the slut and walking off. She hung about for only a moment before she left, and he watched from the entry as she made her way down the street towards the viaduct. Making sure no-one else was about, he slipped across the street and set off to follow her.

She was what he'd been looking for, undeniably a harlot, with that mass of peroxided hair trailing down her back and a skirt which barely covered the pert little buttocks peeping out like an open invitation. She was filth, like the voices said, carrying infection from man to man like a medieval plague. Between those narrow little hips, swaying along provocatively in front of him, lay a maggot-ridden mass of putrefaction.

She had to be purged. Evisceration, the voices said. Like a surgeon – neat, swift and clean. He could feel the steel blade lying snug against his thigh.

She was nearing the viaduct now. He quickened his step. It was easy to catch up with her, teetering along on those ridiculous pink high-heeled shoes.

At the corner she paused and looked back. Under the lamplight he could see her face, her painted mouth showing black in the sodium light. She was a whore all right and no mistake. Then, as luck would have it, she played right into his hands.

She evidently hadn't heard his footsteps behind her because, instead of carrying on to the main street, she took a short cut through an archway under the railway line. On silent feet he followed. The place had evidently once been used as a warehouse of some kind, littered with rubbish and open on both sides to the night. Her heels were clattering over the flagstones to the far end when he stumbled against something in the dark.

He saw the pale blur of her face as she looked back, startled. He heard her thin frightened voice. 'Who's that?'

He moved out of the shadows to where she could just see him in the half-light. Neat, clean and quick – no need for her to suffer ...

'Got a light?' he murmured, moving in closer.

Chapter Thirty-one

Rosa stretched out sleepily and yawned. Her fingers touched warm flesh and she opened her eyes.

Dan lay sleeping, his arm curled over his head and his expression as innocent as a child's. Filling with tenderness for him, she touched a finger to his hollow cheek. With a soft moan he stirred, but his eyes remained closed.

She wouldn't wake him, not yet. He'd been out very late last night. She'd bring him a cup of tea when she had dressed and was ready for work.

His eyes were still closed when she came back with the tea. She set the cup down quietly on the bedside table.

'Hi,' he murmured, raising himself on one elbow. 'Ready to go?'

'You're awake?' She sat down on the edge of the bed. 'Yes – I've got to make an early start. I've got those two new girls starting today so I'll have to keep an eye on them. I was surprised how many replies I got to my advert. I only hope to God these two are better than Mandy.'

He gave a sleepy smile as he leaned over to pick up the cup. How thin his arms looked, and she could make out his ribs beneath the flesh. 'You have a lie-in, you need it,' she murmured, standing up to go. 'You were out very late last night.'

He nodded, swallowing a mouthful of tea, but said nothing. Rosa went on. 'It was gone midnight when I

350

settled down and you still weren't back. Did you go round to Ted's?'

'No.'

'Then where were you till that time?' She hadn't meant it to sound like an accusation but she saw his cheeks redden. 'Or shouldn't I ask?' she said banteringly, trying to pass it off. 'Maybe you had a secret date I oughtn't to know about.'

'I have not,' he said quietly. 'I was up on the moors.'

She bit her lip. 'Sorry,' she muttered. 'That was a silly thing to say. Look – I've got to be off. See you at six.'

Bending, she kissed his forehead and hurried from the room.

The minute she'd left the house Dan threw back the sheets and got out of bed. Walking slowly to avoid bringing on another attack of giddiness he made his way to the bathroom to wash and shave. Then, dressed at last, he adjusted his tie in front of the living-room mirror and picked up the car keys.

He was a man with business to attend to, and it was business which couldn't wait.

He parked the car close to the arcade. There wasn't far to walk to the café but it was odd how the slight incline made his legs feel weak. He reached the shop at last and, leaning his weight on the ledge, he peered through the window.

Alex was alone behind the counter. He saw Dan and gave a cheery wave. Dan pushed open the door and went inside. The scent of coffee which greeted him was tantalizingly delicious.

He jerked a thumb towards the stairs. 'Is she in?' he asked.

Alex came round the counter, smiling. 'Why yes, but she's rather busy right now. The place is packed.'

'It's you I want to see anyway,' said Dan. 'I wanted a private word with you.'

On hearing the seriousness in the other man's tone, Alex's smile slipped away. 'Private?' he repeated. 'Perhaps you'd best come in the back.'

When his guest was seated in the pokey little back room Alex perched on the high stool. 'What is it, Dan?' he enquired. 'You look down.'

Dan gave a sigh. 'I wish to God that's all it was,' he murmured, 'only it's far worse than that. I haven't had the heart to tell Rosa yet.'

He looked up into Alex's eyes. 'I've got to tell you, Alex, but swear you won't let anything slip to Rosa – I've got to tell her myself.'

Alex felt apprehension trickle down his spine. 'Why? What's happened?' he asked. 'Nothing to be ashamed of, surely?'

Dan gave a slow shake of the head. 'Nowt I can control, more's the pity. I'm dying, Alex. There isn't long to go.'

For a long time neither man spoke. Alex stared down in numb disbelief. Dan sat slumped, elbows on widespread knees, his hands locked together. He looked so fragile with his gaunt features and his thin shoulders and he was so enveloped in an air of utter defeat that Alex felt overcome with compassion for him. This was the man who'd once been as big and powerful as himself. Unambitious for himself, he'd been so eager to help Rosa realize her dream.

Dan was muttering quietly. 'I don't know how I'm going to break it to her, Alex, but I'll have to do it soon. I don't know how she'll manage.'

'She will,' murmured Alex. 'She's tough.'

'I've nowt to leave her – no cash, that is. Not that Rosa would ever starve. I know my lass. But she'll need comfort and support. She hasn't that many friends.'

352

'She's been busy with the café.'

'There's Ted and Kitty, I know, but they have their own business.' He looked up directly into Alex's eyes. 'The one person she's close to is you.'

Alex nodded, swallowing hard. 'I'll be here,' he said.

Dan rose wearily to his feet. 'I'd best be off.' He made slowly for the door, then stopped and turned. 'Take care of her for me when I'm gone, lad,' he said in a tight voice. 'Somebody needs to.'

Alex came close and laid a hand on his shoulder, feeling the bone beneath the skin. 'You can count on me,' he said quietly. 'I won't let you down.'

Dan clapped a hand over his and for a moment both men stood silent and motionless. Then Dan broke away and headed out into the shop.

Rosa kept an eagle eye on the new girls as they hurried in and out of the kitchen. They both looked smart in their navy and white but they couldn't be more different in personality. Sally, the taller one, moved about her work with quiet efficiency while Barbara was a small blonde bubble of enthusiasm. So far they promised well.

Barbara came in waving an order. 'Baked potato with cheese for number four,' she said, then as Rosa turned to open the new microwave she added, 'and coffee for the man at the next table on his own – he doesn't look very well at all.'

'Really?' Rosa peered through the open door. Only two weeks ago there'd been that old lady who suffered an angina attack and needed an ambulance. Over the heads of chatting customers she could see him, a smartly dressed man, his face partly obscured by the menu, but she recognized him at once.

'Dan!' She dropped the tea towel and hurried over to

join him. 'Hello, love,' she said warmly. 'What are you doing here?'

He gave a slow smile as she slipped into the chair opposite. 'I fancied being a customer for once,' he said. 'You've told me that much about how good the place looks now, I had to come and see it for myself.'

'And what do you think?' she said, sitting back to let him see the whole expanse of the enlarged area.

His gaze roved appreciatively over the room and he nodded. 'You've done a grand job, lass. I'm proud of you.'

She laid a hand over his. 'Thanks, Dan – that means a lot to me. Look, I've got to get on. We'll talk tonight, OK?'

He looked into the deep blue eyes searching his. She knew him too well to be easily fooled. She knew damn well there was more to this than just an inquisitive visit.

'Are you all right?' she asked as she stood up. 'You must be dead beat.'

He snorted. 'Nowt a good cup of coffee wouldn't put right. God, the service is slow around here.'

When he finally left the café, Rosa stood watching him go. He took the stairs cautiously, one by one, unaware of the anxious speculation in her eyes. There was something on his mind, she knew.

Linda hurried home from work, anxious to see if Mandy had come home. When she hadn't turned up at the taxi rank Linda had waited impatiently for over half an hour for her, then decided she could damn well pay for her own flaming taxi if she couldn't be on time.

When she hadn't come home all night Linda had begun to worry, but then it occurred to her that maybe for the first time a punter had paid for a whole night's fun. The lure of big money might have been more than Mandy could resist.

354

Even so, she could have found a telephone to let her know. When she finally did show up she was going to get a right rollicking and no mistake. She wouldn't do that again in a hurry.

Mandy wasn't in the house when Linda arrived back at Jubilee Terrace, nor was there any sign that she'd been home during the day. Linda began to feel uneasy. Something was up, but what?

She was debating what to do when there was a loud knock at the front door. Mandy – maybe she'd lost her keys! Linda opened the door to find a burly policeman standing on the step and, behind him, the slighter figure of a policewoman.

Linda's heart leapt. Police always spelled trouble.

'What's up?' she asked fearfully.

'Do you live here, miss?' asked the constable.

'Yes.'

'Do you know a girl called Amanda Affleck?'

'Mandy? She lives here with me. Why?'

The policewoman held out a photograph and spoke for the first time. 'Is this her?'

Linda stared down at the little snap, one of the set Mandy had had taken in a photo booth not long ago. 'That's her,' she murmured. 'What's happened?'

The constable ignored the question. 'I think we'd best come inside for a minute.'

Dumbly she let them into the living-room. 'Are you the owner of this house?' said the policeman, taking out a notebook.

'No, Mrs Holyoak owns it. I rent it. Why?'

'Your name?'

'Linda Mason.' He wrote in his notebook.

'When did you last see your friend, Linda? Were you with her last night?'

Linda's apprehension was turning to irritability. 'Look, what is this?' she demanded. 'Where is Mandy? I've been worried sick about her. Has something happened to her?'

'I'm afraid so,' said the policewoman, coming forward to take Linda's arm. 'We need to trace her family. You see, she's been found dead.'

It took some time before Linda's uncontrollable sobbing began to quieten down. Each time she dabbed her eyes and went to sip the tea the policewoman had made for her, a sudden memory would trigger off a fresh outburst.

'Them's her slippers down there,' she wept, pointing to the pair of fur-trimmed slippers beside the hearth. 'She took 'em off last night to put on some new pink shoes she got to go with her new frock. She were that pleased with 'em.' She began sobbing again.

The policewoman's voice was gentle. 'Have you any idea where she was going, love?'

Linda blew her nose noisily. 'Could be anywhere, depending on who she met. If she met some friends, she'd go to whatever pub or club they were going to.'

The policewoman took the cup from her shaking hand. 'And you say she was supposed to meet you at eleven-thirty to take a taxi home? Can you think of any reason why she didn't come?'

Linda shrugged. 'Maybe if she saw Ben – she's got a crush on him.'

'Ben? Who's he?'

'He's a nice enough bloke, I reckon. Not my type, but Mandy's nuts about him.'

The policewoman took out a notebook. 'Any idea what his surname is or where he lives?'

'No. Only that he's the doorman at the Kingfisher Club.'

356

'Right.' The policewoman closed her notebook and rose to go. 'You'll be all right now, will you?'

Linda nodded and rose to see her out. In the doorway the policewoman turned. 'She was on the game, wasn't she, your friend?'

Linda looked startled. 'No!' she cried. 'Whatever makes you say that?'

A faint smile crossed the policewoman's face. 'We're not daft, love,' she murmured. 'We keep an eye on things. We've noticed the two of you the last few weeks.'

Greta was sitting with a gin and tonic in her hand, reading the *Examiner* when Reginald came home from the office.

'Have you seen this?' she said, nodding down at the page. 'Another girl's been found murdered; in Hawksmoor this time.'

'In Hawksmoor? The Ripper again?' Reginald asked.

'It doesn't say,' murmured Greta. 'Only that the body was found down by the viaduct. The identity of the victim is not being revealed until the family has been informed.'

Reginald opened the cocktail cabinet. 'Freshen your drink?' he enquired, waving the bottle of gin.

'No thanks. Isn't it dreadful? Poor thing – and poor family when they find out.'

Reginald poured a stiff whisky and sat down. 'If she's a Ripper victim she's probably no better than she ought to be. No great loss.'

Greta looked shocked. 'That's a heartless thing to say. Just because it was near the viaduct – she could have been walking home quite innocently.'

Reginald's glass paused halfway to his lips. 'Where did you say?'

'Down by the viaduct. Why?'

He waved his arm. 'There you are then – notorious

red-light district. No nice girl would be down there at night.'

Greta consulted the newspaper again. 'The police are anxious to contact anyone who was in the area between eleven and twelve last night.' She lowered the newspaper. 'Switch the television on, Reginald – let's see if there's anything about it on the news.'

Ben was visibly shaken when he joined his mate Trev in the pub. Trev shoved a pint in front of him.

'Here, get that down you,' he muttered. 'What did the fuzz want then? Was it about that gear you sold for Ronnie?'

Ben sank a mouthful of beer. 'Wish to God it was,' he growled. 'Know that girl in the papers who got knifed last night? It was Mandy Affleck.'

'Mandy? The little blonde tart – she was hanging about last night.'

Ben nodded gloomily. 'Somehow they found out I was with her; they say I'm the last person to see her alive.'

Trev's mouth opened wide. 'They can't think you done that to her though – stabbing her, I mean.'

'It's not easy telling a copper you only had a quick shag up the alley.'

'But everybody knows she's an easy lay. A nice enough kid, but a slag for all that.'

Ben wiped the froth from his upper lip. 'That's what I told 'em. They said I could go, but I have to stay in Hawksmoor in case they need me again.'

Trev shook his head sadly, then went to fetch another pint.

Dorothy Challis jumped out of her chair and switched off the television. Nothing but riots and drugs and murders on the news these days, and if she heard another word about the Ripper and the way he mutilated his victims she'd be sick.

She reached for the bottle of pills. If ever anybody needed their nerves calming, she did. What with Graham, not only turning his back on the business, but also insisting that his silly infatuation with this black girl was true love. Lucy was also too self-engrossed to give her a helping hand. What with all that, and the supercilious Overmeer constantly telling her that buying the plot was crazy, she didn't know whether she was coming or going.

It hadn't been like this before Theo died. The world used to run smoothly then. He'd done it on purpose to spite her, she was sure of it; he'd always had a malicious sense of humour, but that little voice in her head kept telling her to be strong. Be bold, it said, don't let that dictatorial Overmeer ruin your dream.

So she wouldn't. If he wouldn't agree to raise the money, she'd do it on her own. The bank would be happy to accept the house as security. It would be a fair exchange: this place, which was far too big for her on her own, for the dream bungalow she'd always craved. And Overmeer needn't know a thing about it – not yet.

She smiled to herself, visualizing his reaction when he discovered he'd been outmanoeuvred. Suppressed fury, that's what it would be, a phlegmatic face controlled by his infuriating Dutch impassiveness.

Now, had she taken that pill or not? She held the bottle up to the light, then, to be sure, she popped another into her mouth and washed it down with gin and tonic.

Dan was reading the newspaper when Rosa arrived home. He laid it aside to make her a cup of tea, then picked it up again as he sank into his chair.

'Dreadful business, this,' he remarked, 'this latest girl the Ripper's killed. She was only a kid.'

'I heard the girls talking about it,' said Rosa. 'I don't know any details.'

'They reckon it must be him – "Another brutal murder in the Terror Triangle", it says.'

'He gets around,' remarked Rosa. 'I've heard it said he could be a commercial traveller.'

'"Body badly mutilated, and there were signs of recent intercourse."'

'Bastard!'

'I don't know,' sighed Dan, 'we all have our time to go, but not like that. We have no choice when it comes down to it.'

Rosa sat forward in her chair and pulled down the newspaper hiding his face. 'Dan,' she said quietly, 'this isn't like you. Come on, out with it. I can tell there's something wrong.'

She could see his face tighten, the misery in the shake of his head. 'It's hard, lass,' he muttered.

'Whatever it is, it's best out in the open.'

His voice became small, defeated. 'I'm not going to get better, lass. There's nowt they can do.'

Rosa squeezed his hand. 'Nonsense. It's depression talking, and I'm not surprised after what you've gone through.'

'It's cancer, lass. Terminal.'

Rosa sat stunned. At last she found her voice. 'Why didn't you tell me before?'

He gave a weary shrug. 'No point dragging us both down. You had enough on your plate as it was.'

'Oh Dan!' Rosa fell on her knees before him, hugging his body to her, gripping him tightly as though she could shield him from death. She could feel his hands stroking her hair.

'Don't fret, lass,' he murmured. 'We've had a good innings, thee and me. We've nowt to complain about.'

At that moment came a thunderous knocking at the door. Rosa didn't look up. 'Go away,' she muttered. 'Go away.'

The loud knocking went on, and voices called out. 'Better go,' said Dan, taking her face in his hands. 'It sounds urgent.'

Chapter Thirty-two

Rosa was startled by the appearance of the two policemen, but Dan seemed unperturbed.

'Sit yourselves down,' he said. 'What can I do for you?'

The sergeant took out a notebook. 'Routine enquiry, sir. We're hoping to gain some information which might help us.'

Dan nodded. 'To do with that murder, I take it?' He saw Rosa start up from her seat. 'Fair enough,' he said. 'You have to do it.'

The sergeant cleared his throat. 'Can you tell us where you were last night, sir? From, say, ten o'clock onwards?'

Dan rubbed his chin thoughtfully. 'I was out,' he murmured.

'Can you tell us where?'

'Not exactly. I drove around for a while – quite a long time, in fact. I was thinking.'

'I see. Did you stop at all?'

'I filled up with petrol, then I drove up onto the moors.'

'Whereabouts was this petrol station?'

'That garage downtown near the viaduct – I can't recall its name.'

The sergeant and constable exchanged glances. 'What time would that be, sir?'

Dan spread his hands. 'God knows. It must have been about tennish, I guess. After I'd filled up I parked the car round the corner in a side-street and had a smoke.'

'Had a smoke?' the sergeant repeated.

'I needed to think.'

'I see. Did you notice anybody else? Anyone hanging about, anything unusual?'

'No, sorry, I can't say I did.'

'And then you say you drove up onto the moor? Did anyone see you up there?'

Dan shook his head. 'Not that I know of. I wasn't really taking notice.'

The sergeant snapped his notebook shut and pushed it into his breast pocket. 'I think that's all for the moment, sir,' he said, rising to his feet. The constable followed him to the door, and then he turned. 'You won't be going anywhere in the near future, will you, sir?'

Dan shook his head with a wry smile. 'I'm afraid I can't guarantee that, sergeant.'

The sergeant adjusted his cap. 'If you do, you will let us know where you are?'

Dan glanced across at Rosa. 'I'm sure somebody will,' he said.

Reginald had dumped his briefcase on the chair in the hallway and was just shrugging off his overcoat when he caught sight of the uniformed figures in the living-room.

'What's this?' he demanded as he strode in. Greta did not move from her chair. Hero made a token growl and slumped on his belly again.

'What's going on?' Reginald persisted. 'It's not that dratted dog is it ...?'

The sergeant turned to him. 'Not the dog, sir. Just a little matter about the house in Jubilee Terrace, but Mrs Holyoak has cleared that up for us now. She assures us she knew nothing about what was going on.'

Reginald's jaw dropped open. 'Jubilee Terrace?' he repeated. 'What on earth has that to do with us?'

'Not you, sir, your wife. As the owner it could appear she knew of the activities there. If she had, there might well have been charges brought against her.'

Reginald turned pale. 'Charges? Whatever are you on about, sergeant? What kind of activities? What is all this?'

Greta's voice was low and subdued. 'I'll explain later.'

'It was the house where the murdered girl Amanda Affleck lived,' the sergeant answered. 'She and another girl were carrying on a trade there as prostitutes.'

Reginald's face turned purple. 'And you think my wife was involved?' he exclaimed.

'Not any more, sir. We're satisfied on that point. Now we'll be on our way and leave you in peace.'

After they'd gone Reginald strode to the cocktail cabinet, but after downing two stiff whiskies he was still outraged.

'You, the madam of a whore-house!' he raged. 'Didn't you give a thought to my good name?'

'No, Reginald,' Greta said quietly, 'I'm not a madam. You heard the sergeant say I was cleared.'

'Even so, how could you be so stupid as to let it to a pair of call-girls? That could have blackened my reputation, ruined my career!'

'I didn't know what they were up to. I thought Linda was really nice.'

'You thought,' he sneered. 'Just goes to show what kind of judge of human nature you are. Anyone can take you in, you're such a simpleton. Anyway,' he went on, thumping his glass down on the coffee-table, 'what about this house?

I didn't even know you had a house in Jubilee Terrace. You never consulted me about it.'

'No more than you consulted me about the new car,' she replied. 'They probably cost about the same.'

He stared at her, bewildered. This wasn't the dutiful wife of years. Picking up his glass he slumped back in his chair, grumbling.

'I don't know you any more, Greta,' he muttered. 'Slow-witted you might be, but I'd never have taken you for a sly deceitful woman, acting without a thought to the consequences. And selfish too – you risked ruining my reputation.'

Greta's voice was quiet but firm. 'Reginald, that's enough.'

The glass paused halfway to his lips, and he stared. 'What?'

'I said that's enough. You've sneered at me long enough over the years and I'm not taking it any more.'

He set the glass down and leaned forward in his chair. 'Do my ears deceive me?' he enquired. 'I cannot believe that any wife of mine would speak to me like that. I think this little contretemps has addled your wits.'

'On the contrary,' she said calmly, 'it seems to have cleansed my brain. I can see things more clearly now than I have ever done.'

Reginald was nonplussed. He found himself struggling for words. Precise turns of phrase seemed to come easily when confronted with a truculent witness in the courtroom, but not now.

'I suggest you have a long hard think about your conduct, Greta,' he said with a sad shake of the head, 'otherwise, if this strange, schizophrenic behaviour continues, you're no wife of mine.'

She laid her glass aside and stood up. Hero shook himself

and sat at her feet. 'As you wish, Reginald,' Greta said smoothly. 'As it happens I've been thinking along the same lines. I'll see a solicitor tomorrow.'

Then she swept from the room, Hero trotting along at her heels.

A stiff morning breeze was blowing across the hospital quadrangle but even so there was a hygienic scent of antiseptic about Neela when Lucy met her.

'What a night!' Neela breathed. 'I'll be glad to get to my bed. Did you have a good weekend?'

Lucy gave a dry laugh. 'Home and good weekend don't go together, Neela. My mother's getting worse.'

'Bad time? Quarrelling again?'

Lucy shrugged. 'Not really. She goes on with a long monologue most of the time. It doesn't really matter who's listening. To be honest, I think she's going round the bend.'

Neela cocked her head to one side. 'Could be grief, I suppose. It takes some funny forms.'

Lucy shook her head. 'It's more than that. She keeps taking pills all the time without even looking at the bottle. I found hundreds of Soneryl tablets all over the house so I took them away.'

'Maybe you should have a word with her doctor about it,' suggested Neela. 'Sounds dangerous.'

'I did. He's promised to ring me back when he's talked to her. Look, I'll have to hurry or Sister will have my guts for garters. See you later.'

Reginald had just finished dictating replies to the morning's mail when the police officer showed up in the office. The secretary was clearly intrigued when she showed the chubby-faced young constable in.

'What is it, Constable?' Reginald demanded irritably. 'I thought your colleagues sorted out that little matter with my wife the other day.'

The constable shook his head. 'Nay, it's you I want a word with, sir. Routine enquiries – nowt to fret about. Now then,' he said, taking out his notebook with a smile, 'the night of Tuesday the eighth – could you tell me where you were that night?'

Reginald stared in disbelief. 'The night of that grisly murder?'

'Between ten and twelve o'clock?'

Reginald gasped. 'Do you know who I am, Officer?'

The policeman consulted his notebook. 'Reginald Vernon Holyoak, solicitor, of The Firs, Edgerton – is that correct?'

'That is so,' replied Reginald, folding his hands. 'So why are you questioning me?'

The constable gave a cheery shrug; 'Like I said, sir, routine enquiries. We're talking to everyone who might be able to shed some light on the matter.'

'Well I'm very sorry but I can't help you.'

The chubby face grew serious. 'If you were out and about that night you might have seen something which meant little to you but could mean a lot to us.'

Reginald shook his head firmly. 'I can assure you, I know nothing. Much as I'd like to, I can't help you, Officer.'

The young constable wasn't to be deterred. 'All the same would you mind telling me where you were that night?'

Reginald took a deep breath. 'As a matter of fact I was at a Council meeting,' he said. 'At the Town Hall. Housing Committee – I'm the chairman.'

'And that went on till after midnight, did it, sir?'

'Long after. It was an emergency meeting.'

The constable nodded and grinned. 'Thank you, sir.' He

scribbled in his notebook then tucked his pen away. 'I don't think I need trouble you any longer.'

Greta made her way purposefully down Jubilee Terrace, its cobblestones glistening under the lamplight after the rain. She was deep in thought, mulling over just the words to choose. Stricken or not by what had happened, Linda had to face facts and she wasn't going to like what Greta had to say.

But to her surprise there was no light burning in the window and no answer to her knock. She took the key from her handbag and let herself in.

The house was silent, the only evidence of Linda being the heavy aroma which hung in the air: those joss-sticks she burned. Greta switched on the light in the living-room and gasped. The room, usually so neat and tidy, was in total disarray, with a litter of paper and cardboard boxes everywhere. No fire burned in the grate, no curtains hung at the window, and the mantelpiece and sideboard had been stripped of ornaments.

It looked as if the girl were packing to leave. Well, thought Greta as she put her handbag down on the table, that would save a deal of hassle. She made her way upstairs. On the landing she paused. Facing her was the door to the smaller bedroom, the one Mandy had occupied. With tentative fingers she turned the knob.

The room was bare save for the naked dressing-table and the single bed stripped of its bedding. After the police had finished here someone from the girl's family must have been to clear her things away. A wave of sadness swept over Greta. The room was as barren as the dead girl's life had been, she thought, devoid of any meaning or achievement. A good-time girl, the newspapers had called her, a pin-money prostitute. She closed the door and turned to Linda's room.

The wardrobe was bare and the bedroom had been stripped of all Linda's belongings. In the bathroom a toilet bag stood on the window-sill, crammed to the brim with the girl's toiletries, a face flannel and bottles of shampoo and lotion. Satisfied, Greta turned to go downstairs.

As she reached the little vestibule a key grated in the lock and the front door opened. Linda stepped inside and, seeing Greta, she caught her breath.

'You're leaving, I take it?' said Greta.

Linda followed her into the living-room. 'I am,' she muttered in embarrassment. 'I hope you don't mind me not giving a month's notice like we agreed, only I couldn't stay here on me own, not now.'

'You'd cope,' Greta replied quietly. 'You'll always cope.'

The girl gave an apologetic half smile. 'I know you won't want me here after what's happened.'

Greta folded her arms. 'I'm disappointed in you, Linda. You let me down. You and your friend – you took advantage of me, using my house so disgracefully behind my back. I bet the two of you had a darned good laugh together over the way you conned me. Silly old woman, daft as a brush.'

Linda bit her lip. 'I'm sorry. I'll never do owt like that again, honest.'

'I'm sure you won't,' agreed Greta, 'but I've learned a lot from you nevertheless. I'll never trust anybody quite the same again. Where are you going?'

Linda hung her head. 'Me mam says I can go home, I'll be better off there.' A car horn sounded outside the window. Linda jerked a thumb. 'That's me stepdad – he's waiting out there for me in the car.'

'It wasn't true about him either, was it?' said Greta. 'He never interfered with you.'

The girl's face turned scarlet. 'He might a done,' she blustered. 'I don't know why but men fancy me, old 'uns and all. Look, I'll fetch the rest of me stuff tomorrow. OK?'

'You've got till midday,' Greta said sternly. 'Whatever's left after then I'll put out on the street.'

Greta turned away from the window as the car pulled away from the pavement edge. The girl's clutter lay everywhere, marring the room just as her lewd behaviour had defiled the house.

She felt sickened. To think how full of joy she'd been when she first bought the place, her little haven of peace. She'd sworn then only to let in people who would bring the right kind of vibrations – 'vibes', the young people said.

But the only vibrations in the air tonight were foul-smelling emanations which turned the stomach. The house had to be cleansed before its infection spread. Starting with those bloody joss-sticks.

Greta flung all the windows wide, letting in the cold night air and ignoring the rain which was beginning to fall again, splashing the wooden window-sills with huge droplets. Rain was pure; it would help to wash away the lingering scent of deceit.

Tomorrow the house would be hers again. Her new life here was going to be happy and wholesome.

Reginald watched his wife carefully as she brought in the supper. He didn't know this new woman in his house, and he was wary about how he should handle her.

She had poise and dignity, this stranger; he'd learned to his cost that she had to be tackled with respect. Somehow he had to find a way to erase from her mind the scornful way he'd treated her.

The old trick, implying that the fault was on the other side and then building on that basic premise – that might well work. He'd give it a try, in his most gracious charming manner.

He waited his moment, until she brought in the coffee and settled down in a fireside chair. He sank into its twin on the other side of the hearth just as the dog came to squat beside Greta. She poured the coffee and handed a cup to Reginald. He smiled as he took it.

'Greta, my dear,' he said gently, 'I'm not looking for an apology, but I'm sure that now you've had time to think things over you regret those unpleasant words the other evening.'

Greta gave him a grave look. 'As I recall,' she said quietly, settling back in her chair, 'it was you who spoke unpleasant words. I said nothing I regret.'

She wasn't taking the bait. Reginald took a more direct route. 'I mean when you spoke rashly of seeing a solicitor. I know you were upset and nervy but I'm willing to talk things over – there really is no need for anything so drastic.'

Greta lifted the cup to her lips. 'I think there is,' she said calmly. 'I see no reason for us to stay together.' She let her free hand fall on the dog's head. 'I've more in common with Hero here than I have with you.'

The dog wagged his tail as if he recognized the compliment. Reginald grew uneasy. The paternal tone of patient humouring wasn't going to work. He set his coffee cup down.

'You wouldn't want to harm my reputation, I know,' he said. 'And what about you – you're sixty, for heaven's sake – you can't manage alone at your age.'

Greta gave a faint smile. 'Who says I'll be alone?'

Reginald grew flustered, spreading his hands in a gesture of helplessness. 'But why buy a house in Jubilee Terrace of all places? It's a slum – it's not your style.'

'You forget, Reginald, I grew up just round the corner in Mafeking Street. They're my people down there.'

He was getting nowhere. He leaned across to touch her knee. 'Look,' he said quietly, 'I've worked for over thirty years now. I could take retirement – at least semi-retirement – and we could find a nice little cottage somewhere, in the Lake District, perhaps. You'd like that – you could go there whenever you wanted, and I could tell people you were at our place in the country. What do you say?'

He gazed into her eyes, composing his features into as appealing an expression as he could manage.

With delicate fingers she removed his hand from her knee. 'I can see your point,' she remarked. 'It doesn't have quite the same flourishing ring about it, does it, saying our place in the slums? No matter, Reginald, I'm moving to Jubilee Terrace just as soon as I can arrange it.'

There was no doubting the quiet determination in her tone; she meant every word.

Chapter Thirty-three

Dorothy was surprised when the receptionist rang from the surgery to say that the doctor would like to call to see her. She hadn't reported any of the unpleasant symptoms plaguing her, the headaches and dizzy spells, the sudden bursts of panic or the sleepless nights.

Maybe it was normal practice to keep an eye on the recently bereaved. After all, lots of people must find it hard to cope after an unexpected death in the family. Theo had been gone for some time now, but it was common knowledge that it took a long time to get over a blow like that.

'How's the family?' the doctor asked cheerily as soon as he'd put his bag down on the table.

She gave him tea and told him about Graham at university, 'Such a clever boy,' she murmured, 'Always the apple of his father's eye. I'd be so proud of him if it wasn't for ...'

The doctor was listening and nodding. There was something in the sympathetic way he inclined his head which she found encouraging, and before long she found herself pouring out her fears.

'I don't know what's got into him, Doctor,' she said with a sad shake of the head. 'I don't know what it is about children, but after all you've done for them they seem determined to thwart you and go their own way. I mean, Graham, now he won't give me a hand with the business, and on top of that he's gone and got himself entangled with a black girl!

Would you credit it, after the way he's been brought up? You devote your whole life to them, trying to teach them some principles, and then they turn round and slap you in the face. I don't know what I've done to deserve it, I'm sure. I've dedicated my life to my family.'

'I'm sure you did,' murmured the doctor, 'but now you have the time—'

Dorothy hadn't finished. 'I suppose it could be because I'm a Virgo,' she went on mournfully, 'not that I hold with such stuff, you know, but the magazines all say Virgo is the sign of service to others. It's an in-built characteristic, I suppose, but it hurts to realize your good nature has been exploited. No gratitude at all.'

'Well,' said the doctor, snatching the moment when she paused to draw breath, 'you can rest easy knowing you've done your duty, but now the fledglings have flown, why not turn your mind to other things? You've got time for yourself; take up a hobby – golf, perhaps, or bridge.'

Her nostrils flared. 'Hobby?' she echoed. 'When I'm up to my ears trying to manage the business on my own, with that slimy creature Overmeer doing his level best all the time to find ways to stab me in the back? Honestly, I feel the whole world is against me – nothing goes right.'

'Come now,' said the doctor, 'it's not that bad. You have no money worries, have you?'

'How little you know,' she said darkly. 'Customers never pay up on time.'

'But that's part of the ebb and flow of any business. It isn't done to spite you.'

'You think so? It's playing havoc with my nerves and no-one wants to help, that's for sure.'

The doctor smiled. 'Well I do, Mrs Challis. That's what I'm here for.'

Dorothy gave him a searching look. 'Those pills seem to

374

help, but I seem to be running out. Can I have a prescription for some more?'

The doctor hesitated, then leaned forward and took her hand. 'You know, Mrs Challis, you need more than pills. Maybe a little talk with a colleague of mine would help to ease the strain for you. He specializes in your kind of problem. Will you let me make an appointment for you?'

Dorothy sat up. 'A specialist?' she said. 'A consultant?'

'One of the very best.'

He gathered up his bag and made for the door. 'You haven't mentioned your daughter,' he remarked. 'How is Lucy?'

Dorothy snorted. 'She's too busy with her training in Hawksmoor to bother about me. She's always been wilful and selfish, that one, not a bit like me. But then,' she added with a sigh, 'she's not my real daughter, you know. She's adopted.'

After the shop had closed for the night Rosa hurried down the café stairs. She'd just reached the foot when Alex came out from the back room.

'Rosa, don't go yet,' he said. 'Stay a minute.'

She hesitated, her hand on the latch. All she wanted to do right now was get home to Dan. He'd not been at all well when she left him this morning.

'I'm in a bit of a hurry, Alex,' she murmured.

'Only a minute,' he said. 'You look bad. Even the customers must notice you're not your usual bouncy self. Come on now.'

She eased herself round the counter and sank onto the stool with a sigh. 'It's Dan, Alex. He's far worse than I thought. Until the other night I honestly believed it was just an ulcer, something they could operate on, but now ...'

Her voice tailed away. Alex stood, arms folded, looking down at her. He could read the pain in every line of her body, and he ached to comfort her. 'I'm sorry,' he muttered. 'If there's anything I can do ...'

Dumbly she nodded her thanks. He could see she was fighting hard to keep back the tears. 'It's going to be tough,' she said in a croak, 'watching him, not being able to help him. He won't be able to stay at home much longer.'

'They'll be able to help him in hospital,' Alex murmured.

'For how long?' she cried. 'It could be next week, next month – God knows how long he's got. But I can see in his eyes he doesn't want to go on like this. Oh, Alex!'

She slithered off the stool and buried her face in his shoulder. 'I only pray I'm strong enough for him,' she mumbled. 'I'm afraid I'll weaken.'

'Not you,' said Alex, stroking her shoulder. 'You'll be strong for his sake, for as long as it takes. And I'll always be here for you.'

She stood back and gave a faint smile. 'Thanks, Alex. I've got to go now.'

And flicking away a threatening tear she hurried from the shop.

When Reginald arrived home he found his wife sitting with her feet propped up on the coffee-table and a gin and tonic in her hand. She was watching *Coronation Street* on television; at one time he'd have reprimanded her for wasting her time on such a plebeian programme, but tonight he held his tongue.

She didn't look round when he came into the room. She waved an airy hand. 'I've left you some dinner in the oven,' she said, 'but do bear in mind that before long you'll either have to cook it for yourself or get a housekeeper.'

He poured himself a drink in silence. As he touched the

glass to his lips he heard the sound of a car engine outside, and then a loud ring at the doorbell.

'Now who the devil can that be?' he exclaimed testily, slapping the whisky glass down.

On the doorstep stood the same chubby-faced young constable who'd called at his office the other day. The constable took off his helmet as he followed Reginald into the lounge. He declined his invitation to take a seat. Greta sipped her drink and eyed him thoughtfully, watching him as he stood, hands clasped behind his back.

'About the night of Tuesday the eighth,' he said gravely.

Reginald seated himself comfortably. 'Yes? What about it?'

'You didn't exactly tell me the truth, did you sir?'

Reginald felt his cheeks begin to burn. The young pup should know better than to challenge a solicitor. 'Are you doubting my veracity, Officer?' he demanded.

'There was no Housing Committee meeting that night, sir. We've checked. Where were you?'

Reginald felt the hairs on the back of his neck stiffen. Greta was watching in silence, twirling her glass between her fingers.

'I can't remember now – it was ages ago.'

The constable took out his notebook. 'Your car was seen late that night near the viaduct, at the time you said you were at that meeting.'

Reginald could feel his hands shaking. Not for the world could he reveal where he went that night. The fear and tension in the air about him was so tangible even the policeman must be able to sense it. He was trapped.

He looked helplessly across to Greta. She gave a quiet chuckle. The young constable turned to her. 'What's so funny, Mrs Holyoak?'

She lay back in her chair and pointed her glass at Reginald, still chuckling. 'He was probably seeing the woman who smacks his bottom,' she giggled. 'He can probably show you the evidence.'

The doctor's tone over the telephone was gentle and reassuring, but his words were not. Lucy clutched the receiver to her ear and listened.

'I called to see your mother the other day as I promised,' he said. 'I certainly think she's in need of help as you suggested.'

'How was she?'

'In a very negative frame of mind, I'm afraid. It could be depression, of course, brought on by your father's death. She's totally self-orientated and displaying some rather worrying symptoms.'

'Such as what?'

'Well, she does seem to see herself as a victim of circumstance, a martyr even. With these paranoid tendencies, she needs specialist advice.'

'So what do you suggest?'

'I'm recommending her to see a consultant psychiatrist here in Leeds. I'm arranging an appointment as soon as I can.'

Dorothy had another name for him when Lucy rang home.

'I'm to see a nerve specialist soon,' she said proudly.

'That's good,' said Lucy. 'He'll be able to help you.'

'It's high time somebody realized I am ill,' her mother went on. 'Nobody takes any notice when you don't complain but just struggle on.'

'No, Mother.'

'And I never do complain. Virgos don't, you know, but Doctor Lewis made a point of coming to see me at home although I hadn't asked for a visit. He spotted straight away what was wrong without me having to tell him.'

'He's a good man,' said Lucy.

'You didn't, for all your medical training. Still, Doctor Lewis forgot to give me any more pills so, you see, even he's not infallible.'

Dan was lying on the settee when Rosa came home. The television was on, dancing girls pirouetting around a sequin-clad youth who was singing, but Dan's eyes were closed.

Rosa bent over him. 'You all right, love?' she whispered.

He opened his eyes. 'Not so bad. I could do with a breath of air.'

'Didn't you go out today?'

He rolled his head from side to side. 'Didn't feel up to driving. Would you take me while it's still light?'

She smiled. 'Of course I will, if you can put up with my kangaroo-jump start. Where to?'

He levered himself slowly into an upright position. 'Same as usual,' he murmured.

Rosa did not speak as she drove up to the moor. It was clear Dan wanted to be quiet. She pulled up near the ridge and he wound down the window. They sat unmoving, but she saw his eyes rove over the distant horizon, then down to the valley below with its greying spread of villages and mill chimneys.

It was growing darker. Black night clouds were stealing across the sky, obscuring the last glow of the setting sun. She watched them glide stealthily on, as inexorably as the cancer.

She turned to glance back at Dan. He looked pale and haggard in the dusk, his cheeks hollow with pain. She would not speak, not intrude on his reflection. His would be deep thoughts, filled with death and eternity, and she felt angry. She longed to hug him to her, to cry out that she desperately wanted to keep him. If love could withstand death, he'd live for ever.

At last he looked away from the scene and stared ahead into the darkness. His hand reached out to cover hers.

'All right, lass,' he said gruffly. 'I'm ready now.'

Lucy lay supine on the bed in the nurses' home, staring up at the ceiling. In ten minutes she was due to start the new block of sixteen weeks in the men's medical ward, but her mind still kept fluttering back to her mother's phone call.

Paranoid tendencies, the doctor had said. She was talking of voices now, or at least a voice which had long been urging her to turn a deaf ear to the financial director's advice. Lucy hadn't been able to gather from her rather garbled conversation just what it was she had done, but it seemed to have given her pleasure that she'd outwitted the man.

'He's going to have rather a shock when he discovers he hasn't succeeded in spoiling my dream,' she said triumphantly. 'And I shall crow even more when we make a fat profit.'

'Profit on what, Mother? What have you done?'

The voice turned wily. 'Ah, that's my secret. It won't be long now ...'

'Ready?'

Neela's bright tone woke Lucy from her reverie. She held out Lucy's cap. 'You'd better get a move on,' she warned. 'I've worked with that Sister Fleming – she can be a sweetie, but I know from experience what a sod she can be if you're late.'

Once Greta had concluded the formalities with the solicitor she headed for Kadinski's. She needed a cup of coffee.

It gave her pleasure to sit among the chatting ladies, surveying the scene. Rosa Pearson was a gutsy girl who'd done well and she couldn't help admiring her. It wasn't easy for a girl from a country village to come to a strange land, pregnant, and make a new life for herself, but she'd done it. Twenty years younger than herself she might be, but Greta would dearly like to make a friend of her.

'Can I help you?'

A dark-haired waitress stood before her, notepad in hand. Greta glanced back towards the kitchen. Rosa stood in the doorway, watching the two young waitresses.

'I'd like to have a word with Mrs Pearson if she has a moment,' said Greta. The girl nodded and went to speak to Rosa. Greta saw her look along the tables, then smile and come towards her.

'Mrs Holyoak!'

'Greta, please. Do sit down a minute.'

The girl looked pale as she slid into the seat opposite, as if she'd been working too hard. 'How are things?' Greta asked.

Rosa shrugged. 'Could be better. My husband's very ill.'

'Oh, my dear. I'm sorry to hear that.'

'In fact he's dying.' The words were spoken in a quiet, matter-of-fact way, but there was no doubting the pain in the girl's eyes.

'I'm so sorry,' said Greta. 'If there's anything I can do ... If you need to take time off, I can still wash up.'

'You're very kind,' murmured Rosa. 'I might take you up on that. It wouldn't be for long. Next week, next month at the latest.'

'So soon?' Greta's hand reached gently to touch hers. Life was cruel, taking a man so young. 'What can I say?'

she murmured, 'except that I'll do anything you want. Any time. You won't be alone.'

Rosa bowed her head. 'Thanks,' she murmured. 'It's odd, you know, he's always been the focus of my life, not having a child to care for.'

'I know.'

'You never had a child, did you?'

'I did. I lost him at birth. I've been paying for it ever since.'

'I'm sorry – I didn't know that.'

'But not any more. Like you, I'm facing a new life on my own. You see, I'm leaving my husband.'

Rosa looked up in surprise. 'Leaving him? Why?'

Greta smiled wryly. 'It must seem odd to you, choosing to live without a husband, but I didn't choose as wisely as you did. I should have done it long ago.'

Rosa thought for a moment. 'That's a brave thing to do.'

'At my age? Oh yes, I'm a pensioner I know, much older than you. You can't be forty yet. You've many years of life ahead of you. You can't waste them just because you feel full of anger.'

Rosa searched her eyes. 'How do you know that?'

'Because it happened to me – I raged against fate for a long time for robbing me of my son. It was so cruel, so unfair. But life went on.'

The corners of Rosa's mouth twitched into an attempt to smile. 'You understand, don't you?' she said softly. 'Thanks.'

Greta opened her handbag. 'I'll give you my new address.'

Chapter Thirty-four

'... a judicial separation only,' Greta told Reginald. 'I see no need for a divorce as I don't plan to remarry.'

Reginald sat quiet, his hands clasped, conscious that he was in no position to argue. Ever since that Madame Zara business had come to light ...

'It could soon be changed to divorce, however,' Greta went on, 'if at some future date you decide you want your freedom.'

'I see no need for a separation,' he muttered. 'Can't we leave things as they are?'

Greta shook her head firmly. 'It's too late now. I've made up my mind and the legal process is already under way.'

He knew he was beaten; he had no grounds to contest it. 'Greta,' he said hoarsely, 'I don't want you to go. You're a fine woman – I want you here.'

She sighed. 'What a pity. You've had almost forty years to tell me that, but now it's too late.'

'It's never too late, Greta – there's still time to reconsider.'

'I'm moving to Jubilee Terrace on Monday.'

He looked up, startled. 'Monday? So soon?'

'It's all arranged,' she said smoothly. 'I shall take the little writing bureau and my favourite chair, the pembroke table from the hall and several of the vases and ornaments I've collected over the years. And of course my own bedroom furniture. I'm sure you won't object.'

'Take what you want,' he mumbled. 'I'm not a hard man.'

'No,' sighed Greta, 'I'm sure you honestly believe that.'

Dorothy sat behind the big office desk glaring up at the two men before her. Overmeer clutched a file tightly to his chest, his usually pallid face red and his lips set tight. Carter was shuffling uncomfortably from foot to foot.

'But why can't we build on the land?' Dorothy demanded. 'Three acres for a hundred thousand in a perfect spot like that – it's a bargain in anybody's book.'

'With planning permission, yes,' agreed Overmeer, 'but you haven't got the OK from the Engineer's Department, or Planning or Highways. You've gone ahead with no discussion – you've committed us. It was an extremely rash move.'

Dorothy waved a hand. 'Surely there'll be no planning restriction for a residential development?'

Carter spread work-roughened hands. 'As I've tried to explain, Mrs Challis, they've done a ground test on the land and it's contaminated. It's not fit for building.'

'How can it be contaminated?' she demanded. 'It baffles me – there's been no chemical works there, no nuclear power station, nothing to pollute it.'

Carter looked helplessly at the financial director. Overmeer tried to sound patient. 'It doesn't necessarily mean contaminated in that sense. There's been open mining on that land, replaced with infill over the years which is unstable. We couldn't put down a foundation. There could be subsidence if we built on it. Upgrading it would be financially prohibitive.'

'Upgrading?'

384

'Making the land viable for use.'

Dorothy looked at Carter. 'That's right,' he said. 'Our own preliminary tests with a JCB show a high concentration of sulphur and asbestos in what's been dumped there.'

Dorothy bit her lip thoughtfully. 'Does that mean it can be put right?'

Carter cleared his throat. 'Well it could, if we took off the vegetable layer to a depth of maybe four metres, replaced it with a clay cap and then vibro-compacted it.'

'There you are then,' said Dorothy. 'Problem solved.'

'No,' said Overmeer. 'It would be far too costly. A year's work at least just to prepare the land, and then the local authority and building control will want to ground-test it again. Could take another year or more. It's out of the question.'

Carter nodded in agreement. Dorothy thought hard. The two of them were in collusion, closing in on her, trying to beat her down, but she wasn't going to give in that easily.

'You're being very short-sighted,' she said. 'The cost will surely be met by the profit we make on the other houses.'

Overmeer gave a deep sigh. 'You really don't understand.' Dorothy felt her resistance harden. He wasn't going to win by treating her like a backward child. 'In order to recoup the outlay, just to break even,' he went on patiently, 'you'd need to sell a house valued at, say seventy thousand, for more than twice that. Now who in their right mind would pay that kind of money? You won't be able to sell.'

Dorothy shook her head, her lips compressed. 'It doesn't matter what you say,' she said firmly. 'Even if you argue till the cows come home, I'm going ahead with this. Those bungalows are going to be built. Nothing you can say is going to stop me.'

Overmeer glanced at his colleague, then laid his file down on the desk. 'Mrs Challis,' he said quietly, 'it seems you either

385

cannot or will not recognize the situation. If you insist on flying in the face of my advice, you leave me no choice but to offer my resignation.'

'I accept,' said Dorothy. 'The meeting is over.'

Overmeer turned on his heel and marched out. Carter watched him go, bewildered, then, with a worried look, hurried out after him.

Dorothy sat back with a smile of triumph.

Rosa picked her way through the small bodies hopping from one chalked square to another on the pavement. Reaching her own front door, she let herself into the house quietly in case Dan was sleeping.

He wasn't lying on the sofa where he usually lay. As she set down her bag on the living-room table he came in from the backyard. She could see at once by his haggard face that he'd had a bad day.

'How are you feeling, love?' she asked. 'Did you manage to eat something today?'

She searched his eyes as he shook his head. His eyes told her so much more than he did. 'I tried,' he said, 'but I couldn't keep owt down.' He gave a weak smile. 'I bet it'd stay down if it was a pint of good ale, though.'

He was trying to make light of it. 'Have you been bringing up blood again?' she asked anxiously.

She heard him sigh as he sank into a chair. 'On and off.'

She came close and knelt before him. 'Have you got pain?' she asked gently.

The corners of his mouth twitched. 'I feel a bit rough, lass, and that's a fact.'

That settled it. For Dan to admit to pain, it must be bad. She'd better get the doctor right away.

*　　*　　*

386

The doctor had no hesitation in calling the ambulance.

'Your husband will be far better off in hospital,' he assured Rosa. 'You can't help him any more. They'll have all the means there to give him some sustenance and at the same time alleviate his pain.'

Rosa watched the men help Dan out to the ambulance. *'You can't help him any more.'* The words sounded so final, so inexorable. She turned to the doctor. 'Can I go with him?' she asked.

'Of course. In view of his condition they'll probably allow you to stay with him.'

Rosa caught her breath. She heard her own voice, no more than a tentative whisper. 'Are you saying ... it's the end?'

The doctor took her arm. 'My dear, you'll have to be brave,' he murmured. 'It can't be very far away now.'

Greta hummed to herself as she moved the little china figurine to a higher shelf in the display cabinet, out of the reach of Hero's wagging tail. It was surprising how much joy she derived from arranging and rearranging her possessions in the little house. Most of Mrs Clancy's old furniture dating from the 1930s had now gone, and the place was taking on a much more personal feel with Greta's favourite pictures on the walls, her own satin quilt and counterpane on the bed, and her perfume spray and other pretty bottles decorating the dressing-table. Every last trace of Linda and Mandy was now gone, the scent of joss-sticks replaced by the mingled aroma of bleach and polish upstairs, and by fresh herbs in the kitchen and delicately scented freesias in the living-room.

This house, which had so often been a brief haven of peace in the past, whenever she could escape here for a few hours, was now her permanent sanctuary. She stretched her arms happily above her head. She was free now to do whatever she pleased. Cooking for one would be a pleasure, free to sample any new taste which took her fancy. In fact, she thought with a surge of joy, she was free to do anything which took her fancy. She was her own woman at last.

She picked up the shaggy little dog gambolling around her feet and hugged him close to her chest. 'Greta Kaye,' she smiled to the face in the mirror over the fireplace, 'you've come home.'

Any moment now Alex would be home from work. Ivana Kadinski sat in her backyard, peeling potatoes for supper. It was pleasant out here, soaking up the last of the evening sun before it sank behind the slate roof of the carpet factory.

Through the open kitchen door wafted the tantalizing aroma of roasting brisket in the oven. Alex, like his father, enjoyed a good bit of beef. She smiled as she watched the knife slide into the white flesh of the potato, remembering how Feodor used to say her roast beef was the tenderest and juiciest in the whole of Yorkshire. In the whole of Cracow, he used to say in the early days of their marriage, she reflected, before the enemy drove them from their home. Even now it gave her a shudder to remember the long cold weeks they'd spent hiding in the dank vaults of the church. She could still feel the cold stone under her feet and Alex's little body huddled against her own for warmth under her shawl.

She held up a long gleaming coil of potato peel and watched it fall into the bowl of water. They'd prayed, my God how they prayed in the darkness of the crypt for deliverance, almost fearing to hope too much. She could still recall the fierce determination in Feodor's eyes, fading gradually over the weeks to a kind of stoic resignation. She'd seen death in his eyes, and felt only sadness for her son, who would never know the joys they had shared.

388

But then suddenly came escape and a new life here in England. Joyfully she and Feodor had snatched at life and savoured every moment, till he died. Ivana shaded her eyes against the setting sun.

'I watched the sun go down with you, Feodor,' she murmured, 'and I gave thanks for the life you gave us.'

She groped round in the muddy water in the bowl and fished out the last potato. Would Alex be going out tonight? He had many friends, she thought proudly, men and women, and sometimes they came to the house, laughing and joking, and he'd go out with them to the wine bar or the bowling-alley. At other times he just wanted to sit and read or walk in the woods alone.

If only he would find the right woman and settle down, she'd be content. A man his age ought to have a wife, and she should have grandchildren by now. The knife paused in her hand as a sudden thought occurred to her: maybe she was in the way – maybe that was why he often spoke of buying another house!

A tiny fluttering movement caught her eye. A single white feather floated down from the pigeon loft over the wall and settled on the cobblestones.

'Blotty birds,' she muttered, then she caught sight of a pair of feet. Alex stood in the kitchen doorway, smiling down at her.

'I keep telling you we could move away from here,' he said, 'and then you'd be rid of the blotty birds. But I know I'm wasting my time – you're too fond of Betty and Winnie, whatever you say.'

'Aye,' she murmured, wiping her hands on her apron and getting up off the stool, 'they're a rough lot, but they'll do.'

*   *   *

Sister Fleming sat at the desk in her cramped little office. Lucy stood before her with the two other nurses while Sister finished her briefing.

'There's still Mr Blake, acute nephritis, in bed four,' said Sister, reading from her notes, 'medication unchanged. Two admissions – Mr Curtis, aged sixty-seven, down from intensive care after a heart attack, under observation. Forty milligrammes of Frusemide once a day and Slow K potassium tablets three times a day. The second admission is Mr Pearson in bed seven, aged forty-one, carcinoma of the stomach and liver. Ten milligrammes Maxolon three times a day and terminal routine.'

Cancer. Poor old fellow, thought Lucy. Tender loving care and painkillers would be all they could do for him.

'Mr Pearson has a saline drip,' Sister went on, 'and he's on diamorphine elixir four-hourly, so long as the Maxolon helps him keep it down. Mrs Pearson can have unlimited access. Right, that's all. You'd better make a start on the bedpans.'

Sunshine poured in through the window across the dining table where Dorothy sat with a large sketch-pad, drawing rough plans of her ideal home. It was important to let the architect know exactly what she had in mind, otherwise a mere man might draw up something totally unsuitable. Since it was always a woman who ran a home, goodness knew why they didn't employ women to design them.

Theo had always acknowledged that she knew best in these matters. He'd never tried to stop her when he knew she was right. That utility room, for instance – it would never have been built but for her. Theo hadn't been at all keen on the idea at first, but he'd been obliged to admit that it made good sense since it added considerably to the value of the house.

Yes, she'd made a good job of the house. She'd be quite

sorry in a way to leave it, but the bungalow would be perfect, everything on one floor for convenience, with one bathroom *en suite* with the master bedroom, of course. Plenty of wardrobes and storage space and built-in bookshelves. And outside she'd have a sizeable but manageable garden. Lots of patio and no lawns to mow, a little pond with fish and a bird-bath.

It would be a ranch-style bungalow, she thought with pride, with a small conservatory on the side, like the bungalow Mr and Mrs Wallace had had specially built in Berkshire for their retirement, complete with a long verandah where she could sit out whatever the weather. Dorothy had pored over the photographs so long she knew every detail, and now the Wallaces had gone they need never know how she'd copied their ideas.

They knew about the land, of course, since it was Mrs Wallace who'd tipped her off about the bargain.

'Wonderful spot,' she'd said. *'For a friend of ours I'm sure they'd be willing to let it go at a knock-down price.'*

She'd have been a fool not to grab the opportunity, Dorothy reflected, whatever that miserable Overmeer said. Carter had agreed the land could be put right even if the contamination story was true.

She doodled on, her fingers flying back and forth like her thoughts. Graham had rung last night. He would have been home this coming weekend but for the fact that he wanted to bring that black girl with him. She'd had to tell him she couldn't lower her standards just to accommodate his juvenile infatuation. He hadn't sounded very pleased, but he would come round. Graham always did. One day, when he realized the error of his ways, he'd thank her for it.

Her fingers were outlining a sketch of how the bungalow would look – an elevation, Overmeer would call it. Old-world shutters – now how would they look on a ranch-style bungalow?

'Go on,' said the little voice in her head, 'be daring, be different, have the shutters. They'll add a touch of class.'

From the hallway came the shrill sound of the telephone. With a sigh Dorothy laid down the pencil and got to her feet. The voice at the other end of the line was coldly official.

'Concerning your application for a loan, the bank has given a great deal of thought to the matter and I'm afraid I have to tell you that we cannot advance the money.'

Dorothy frowned. 'Can't advance? But you've already agreed – I came in to see you ...'

'Agreed in principle, Mrs Challis. Taking into account your husband's record with us, we were prepared to look on your application favourably. But it was a conditional offer pending further investigation.'

Anger boiled in her. Dorothy gripped the phone fiercely. 'You didn't tell me that,' she raged. 'You can't go back on your word – I need that money – I've already told the vendors I'm buying that plot!'

'A little prematurely,' the cool voice replied. 'Our preliminary report was unfavourable, and after further advice revealing certain information about the project we've come to the conclusion that this investment would be unwise ...'

'You mean you're not going to lend me the money?'

'I would recommend that you put the whole matter on hold for the time being.'

She slammed the receiver down, her brain reeling, then sank onto the bottom step of the stairs, her head in her hands.

How could they do this to her? They'd been happy enough when she spoke to them about the land. They'd let her down, going back on their word. Bastards! It seemed as if they too were determined to see her fail. Well damn you, she raged.

I'll do without your money. I'll find some other way, and do you out of the interest you'd have charged me.

'*Further advice*,' the voice had said, '*certain information . . .*' She leapt to her feet. That bloody Overmeer! It had to be him – the devil was still determined to bring her down! It was his way of wreaking his revenge because she hadn't listened to him, because she'd got one over on him and he'd been forced to resign. The treacherous bastard – what a sneaky, spiteful thing to do! She'd been right all along; she'd kept telling Theo you could never trust these devious foreigners.

But he wasn't going to get away with it that easily, no, by God he wasn't.

Chapter Thirty-five

It was Mrs Overmeer's silvery voice which answered the telephone.

'I'm sorry, Mrs Challis, my husband isn't here at the moment. Can I give him a message?'

She needn't put on that sweetie-pie tone with me, thought Dorothy angrily. He's there, all right; he just doesn't want to face up to what he's done. He's put his mealy-mouthed wife up to this subterfuge.

'Second-hand messages won't do,' she insisted. 'I want to speak to him personally.'

'Ah,' she heard the woman exclaim, 'he's just come back. Hold on a moment.'

That's more like it, thought Dorothy grimly. Persistence pays off. She could hear murmured words, and then the sound of the receiver being picked up.

'Hello?'

She took a deep breath and launched into the attack. 'Just what do you think you're playing at?' she demanded. 'Is this your idea of getting your own back? Because, if so, let me tell you it won't wash. You're a mean deceitful man, Overmeer, and—'

'Hold on,' he cut in quietly, 'what's this all about?'

'The bank – you know damn well – you told them the land was unfit so that they withdrew my loan, that's what,' she snapped. 'They promised me the money, but you couldn't bear to see me go ahead, could you? You made them go back on their word.'

'Mrs Challis,' he replied smoothly, 'the bank's decision has nothing whatsoever to do with me.'

'Oh no?' she sneered. 'How else would they know about the contamination if it wasn't from you?'

She could hear his weary sigh. 'My dear lady, banks are not stupid,' he said. 'They make it their business to find out whether a proposition is a sound investment or not. If they have decided not to grant you a loan, I assure you, it had nothing whatsoever to do with me. Now please ring off.'

'You expect me to believe that?' Dorothy snorted, 'After you—'

'You can believe whatever you wish, but that is the truth. Now please ring off and do not bother me again.'

She heard a click and then the line went dead. Fuming, she turned and went back into the lounge. She didn't believe him, not for an instant. Overmeer was a smooth and cunning devil; he wouldn't miss out on a God-given opportunity to plague her.

Everyone, it seemed, was hell-bent on destroying her. Even the children didn't care; they didn't want to know her any more since they'd gone into the outside world. For them, she'd outlived her usefulness. She wouldn't mind so much if she wasn't so painfully aware of how the curtains in the avenue twitched when she passed, eyes following her, and how they were all talking about the widow and her ungrateful children.

She was on her own now against the world. All she wanted to do was to creep away from all the persecution into the sanctuary of her bungalow, to close the front door, shutting out the rest of the world so no-one could plague her any more. Safe in a haven where no-one could get at her ...

But why the devil should she let them beat her? Damn

them – she'd beat the bastards at their own game. She only had to find a way to raise the money. She'd set fire to the house if need be, use the insurance money …

'Why not?' said the little voice. 'The house is insured for far more than you need for the new place. Set fire to it – claim on the insurance, and to hell with the bank.'

Dorothy bit her lip. 'I'd like to get the better of the bank, but what about my things?'

'All replaceable,' said the persuasive little voice. 'Just make sure you hide your jewellery first.'

'Why, yes,' Dorothy said eagerly. 'I could give it to someone to mind – Lucy, perhaps.'

'She's too honest to be trustworthy,' warned the voice. 'There's the safe in the cellar, built in the stone – the fire will never harm that.'

It was a brilliant idea, killing two birds with one stone. All it needed was some careful planning; nothing must go wrong. Chuckling to herself, she headed upstairs to the bedroom where her jewellery box lay in the dressing-table drawer.

She smiled craftily at the face in the mirror. You'll see, Mr Clever Clogs Overmeer, I'm not beaten yet.

Greta yawned as the ten o'clock news came to an end. Five more minutes while Hero had his last run out in the back alley, and then she'd make her bedtime cup of cocoa. While she sipped it she would mull over what she might do tomorrow.

The backyard could do with livening up, she thought as she let Hero out. Maybe she could plant a few small shrubs in terracotta pots, or buy a couple of hanging baskets to fill. She could hang out a line of washing like everyone else and feel she belonged to the community. Or she could go out. There was a good film on at the Ritz, according to Betty

Tasker, or she could go up to Wood Lea, or maybe offer her help with the hospice appeal – a deserving cause if ever there was one. The possibilities were endless.

She was waiting on the step for Hero to come romping back into the yard when she heard the knock at the front door. Frowning, she went through to the hall. Whoever could it be at this time of night?

Rosa Pearson stood on the doorstep, her pretty face pale and anxious. Greta led her inside.

'I'm sorry to bother you so late,' said Rosa. 'I've only just left the hospital.'

Greta took her hand. 'Your husband?'

The girl nodded. 'They say I can stay with him. I keep dashing back to see they're all right at the café, but it's difficult—'

'You want me to take care of things there? Of course I will,' said Greta. 'I told you – anything I can do.'

'I'd be so grateful. Barbara and Sally can cope – they're good girls – and there's Alex downstairs, but if you could keep an eye on things and see to the money ...'

'Certainly. I'll be there in the morning. Just tell me what you want me to do.'

Rosa gave a pinched smile. 'You're very kind. I've got a cheek really – I hardly know you.'

Greta squeezed her hand. 'Sometimes you only need to know someone a short time to know they're a friend. You can trust me.'

'I know that. Thanks.' Rosa made for the door. 'I'm going to grab an hour or two's sleep now and then get back to Dan.'

Greta stood in the doorway, watching the slight figure hurry away into the darkness. 'My thoughts and prayers are with you,' she murmured. 'God bless.'

* * *

397

The men's medical ward was in darkness except for the pool of light spilling out from the open doorway of Sister's office. The only sounds to break the silence were the irregular snoring of sleeping men and the occasional cough from the bronchitic in bed eight.

Strange how the night shift seemed so long, thought Lucy, with none of the daytime chores to fill the hours. Sister would be going off any minute for her coffee break.

At that moment Sister Fleming appeared in the doorway, clipping her pen into her pocket. 'I'll be five minutes,' she said crisply. 'Keep an eye on the drips, and don't forget it's almost time to turn Mr Pearson.'

She turned briskly on her heel and walked out. For all her curtness, thought Lucy, Sister Fleming was a kindly woman under that starched exterior. Care of the terminally ill was a high priority with her. Discomfort and pressure sores would never be permitted in her ward.

Lucy slowly walked the length of the room, flicking on a pencil torch to check each patient, every one sleeping peacefully. Reaching the sixth and last bed, she turned to bed seven on the other side. Mr Pearson lay in a pool of moonlight. His eyes were wide open, staring up at the drip.

She came close. 'Let me turn you,' she whispered, 'and then maybe you'll sleep.'

As she bent to pull back the sheets she saw the hint of a curve on his lips. 'Nay lass,' he murmured, 'I shall soon be sleeping sound enough.'

She took hold of the emaciated body to turn him gently, taking care not to disturb the drip. It was a crying shame, she thought. He was still only a young man. The pretty wife she'd seen by his bedside couldn't be more than thirty-odd. Death was for the elderly, those in the geriatric ward, not these people. Fate could be

398

so unfair at times, and she couldn't help the feeling of anger.

She tucked the sheets in around him, not too tightly. He gave that faint smile again. 'You're a bonny lass,' he mumbled. 'What's your name?'

'Lucy,' she answered. 'Lucy Challis.'

'Sit with me a bit.'

She pulled the hard plastic chair close to the bed. He reached out a bony hand and took hers. For long minutes they sat in silence, caught in the shaft of moonlight like two lead actors centre stage in a drama. And this was real drama, thought Lucy, a tragedy of life and death. Again the anger burned.

'Look after her for me,' a thin voice whispered. Lucy leaned over him to listen.

'What?'

'Rosa – my wife. She'll take it hard when I'm gone.'

Lucy squeezed the thin hand. 'Come now, don't talk like that,' she said softly.

The eyes glinted in the moonlight. 'Don't try and flannel me, lass,' he murmured. 'I know. Just see to her, try and ease her.'

Lucy nodded, filled with guilt. 'I'm sorry,' she muttered. 'I'll do my best, I promise.'

With a sigh he drew his hand away. 'Good lass. I reckon I'll sleep now.'

He closed his eyes just as the ward doors swung open and Sister Fleming's tall figure appeared. She stopped short when she caught sight of Lucy in the moonlight.

'Everything all right?' she asked.

Lucy padded quietly back down the ward. 'Yes, Sister. I was just making Mr Pearson a bit more comfortable.'

Sister's glance swung to bed seven. 'Good,' she nodded.

*   *   *

Dorothy felt pleased with the progress of her plans. Half her jewellery now lay in a velvet-lined box in Theo's safe in the cellar, and the other half in a security box in the bank.

It had given her a thrill of malicious pleasure, arranging to hire the box. The bank hadn't wanted to know what she was going to put into it.

'Just so I know where my personal papers are,' she'd told the cashier airily, 'like my passport, birth and death certificates, a few shares and things.'

They would never know they held in safe keeping in their vaults, not only her jewellery, but also the deeds to her house which wouldn't be there much longer. Right under their very noses. She couldn't help chuckling at her own cunning.

She would plan the fire with military precision and detail; she'd already discovered a way from that timely television programme on arson. And shrewdly she'd had the foresight to realize she'd need somewhere to stay while the insurance was sorted out. The next move was to plan, not only a refuge, but also an alibi.

She picked up the telephone and dialled a long-distance number. Mrs Wallace sounded politely surprised.

'Well yes thanks, we've settled in very nicely,' she said. 'We're building up quite a pleasant social circle in the neighbourhood. But tell me, my dear, how are you going on?'

Dorothy told her in some detail about Graham away at university and Lucy gone to Hawksmoor. 'And to tell the truth, I could do with a break after all the ups and downs of the past year,' she concluded.

Mrs Wallace oozed sympathy. 'I'm sure you could. A break away from it all would do you good. Have you ever thought of going on a cruise?'

'Well actually,' said Dorothy, 'I was wondering – you know you said I'd be welcome to come and stay with you any time ... ?'

Minutes later she replaced the receiver with a contented smile. Another piece of the jigsaw had fallen into place.

Bright morning sunlight streamed across the café floor and almost every seat was filled. Greta stood in the kitchen doorway watching the two waitresses at work.

Rosa was right; they were good girls. Sally's tall slender figure wove busily among the customers, a smile on her lips for everyone. Barbara, the smaller, fair-haired one, didn't have Sally's brisk pace but she worked methodically and conscientiously. She was over in the far corner now, at table nine in the window, taking the order from two women.

The younger one looked up and Greta started as their eyes met. It was Linda Mason. She saw the girl colour up before looking quickly away. Greta turned to the cash desk. Embarrassing or not, the girl would have to come and pay her bill before she left.

For the next forty minutes Greta was fully occupied dealing with customers. There seemed to be an almost continuous queue to hand over bills and money. At last a hand laid a bill numbered table nine in front of her, and she looked up.

The face smiling down at her was an older version of Linda Mason, unmistakably her mother. The girl herself hovered at the head of the stairs.

'You was our Linda's landlady, she tells me.'

The woman cocked her head to one side in query. She had a pleasant face, once as pretty as her daughter's. 'That's right,' said Greta.

'I didn't know you worked here. You the owner?'

'I'm just keeping an eye on things for a friend. Your change.'

The woman pushed the coins into her purse. 'It's nice to have our Linda back home again,' she said. 'My Jack looks on her like she was his own. She's probably told you about Jack.'

'Yes,' said Greta.

'He were that upset when she ran off. He used to chase after her to stop her messing about. She could have been the one that Ripper got, not Mandy.'

'Yes,' agreed Greta, 'she was very lucky.'

'Nobody's safe till they catch him. I make sure she doesn't go anywhere now on her own.'

'Very wise,' said Greta. And as she watched the two, mother and daughter, descending the stairs, she added mentally, I only wish to God you'd done it sooner.

Alex dropped Greta off at the bank so she could put the takings in the night safe, then drove her home to Jubilee Terrace.

'I'm only round the corner in Mafeking Street,' he said. 'I'll pick you up in the morning.'

'I know,' said Greta; 'you live in the house where I was born.'

'Small world,' he smiled, and she couldn't help noticing once again how attractive his smile was. She climbed out of the car and, as she was about to close the door, Alex leaned across. 'If you happen to see Rosa before I do,' he murmured, 'tell her I'm here for anything she wants of me. I wish I could help.'

Greta smiled. 'I think she knows that. Good night, Alex.'

She slammed the car door and watched him drive away. He was a good man, that Alex Kadinski. A world of solidity and strength lay behind his gentle exterior. Now if only she'd met a man like him ...

With a sigh she unlocked the front door and let herself in. From out of nowhere a small furry body hurled itself at her in delight. She bent to stroke the shaggy little back and felt her face plastered with moist frenzied licks.

It was good to feel welcome.

Dorothy's heart was beating fast. Everything was in place. Her suitcase already in the car parked in the back lane. Theo's car, of course – it was far more powerful and more comfortable than her little Mini. Anyway, if the fire were to spread as far as the garage it would be a crying shame for the big car to go up in flames.

Now all that remained was to set light to the rolls of scrim she'd soaked in paraffin and carefully laid throughout the house, then race down the garden to the lane and drive away. The neighbours wouldn't hear – the back gardens were long and the big car's engine no more than a whisper. With any luck she'd be well away from Hawksmoor before anyone discovered the fire.

From the habit born of years of nightly routine she put the milk bottles out on the back doorstep, unplugged the television and switched off all the lights. Stepping carefully over the trail of white scrim she returned to the kitchen and opened the back door, then took the box of matches from her pocket.

She stood in the open doorway, looking back at the pale trail snaking away into the gloom of the hall and up the staircase, and she sighed. She'd taken such care to see that the washing and ironing were all done; what a pity that paraffin was soaking into the carpet and leaving a stain. It offended her sense of systematic orderliness, but then, she reflected as she struck a match, needs must . . .

Chapter Thirty-six

Mrs Kadinski was sitting by the fire, reading the *Examiner* when Alex came home from work. Betty Tasker came in from the kitchen carrying a pot of tea.

'I've just brewed a cuppa for your mother,' she explained. 'She wasn't feeling too clever.'

Alex looked at his mother in concern. She waved a hand.

'It's nothing – just a giddy turn, that's all. Did you take your lady home again?'

'Greta? Yes.'

Betty Tasker poured tea and handed a cup to Mrs Kadinski. 'She's a good woman, is that,' she pronounced. 'Do a good turn for anybody, I know. Not many like her these days. How long is it now since the owner's husband took ill?'

'He's been in hospital a couple of weeks,' said Alex.

'Not expected to come out, I hear?'

'That's right, I'm afraid.'

Betty shook her head. 'It's a bad do, is that, dying so young. Just goes to show, you got to make the most of what time you have.'

Mrs Kadinski nodded agreement. Alex said nothing. Betty carried on, unopposed.

'Every time you switch on the news you hear more accidents and muggings, people popping off before they expect. You never know when your time's up.'

'True,' murmured Mrs Kadinski. 'Very true.'

'So it's up to us to pull our socks up and get on with it before it's too late,' declared Betty. 'Never mind putting things off. It gets you nowhere.'

'I'm sure you're right,' murmured Alex, 'but—'

'Never mind your ifs and buts,' Betty cut in. 'It's high time you found yourself a woman and settled down. You're going to leave it too late at this rate. Don't you know what it means to your mother?'

Alex glanced at his mother and saw her face redden in embarrassment, and she lowered her eyes to avoid meeting his gaze.

'I have found the woman I want, Mrs Tasker,' he said in a low voice. 'She is everything I ever wanted in a woman.'

His mother looked up, surprise in her grey eyes. Betty too stared at him, speechless for a moment. Then she found her voice again.

'Well where is she then? Why haven't you brought her home? Your mam would be that pleased ...'

'All in good time,' he replied quietly. 'I'll make a move when the time is right. Until then you'll have to be patient.'

Dorothy manoeuvred the car carefully through the busy teatime traffic in Leeds city centre. Outside the Queen's Hotel she hesitated for only a second. No, better not book a room yet, just in case anyone were to check on her movements. She'd best not be seen to have arranged a bed for the night before she'd even discovered the tragedy.

Excitement fluttered as she drove out of the town towards home. She'd had plenty of time on the long journey north to rehearse in her mind just how she was going to behave when she discovered the burned-down house. Shock and horror, of course, then running wailing to Mrs Whiteley's next door. They would explain how they'd been unable to reach her, not knowing where she was, and they'd give her a cup of tea to restore her nerves.

A decent cup of tea, she thought, not that dishwater stuff they sold in the motorway services. How they had the nerve to serve that up, at such an outrageous price too, was beyond comprehension. The cost certainly wasn't justified; no waitress service, horrid thick cups and plastic teaspoons, ghastly Formica tables spattered with squashed chips and tea stains, not to mention those revolting ashtrays overflowing with ash and cigarette stubs. Those places were really quite disgusting. What a come-down after a week of Mrs Wallace's delicate bone china and linen table napkins. And not an ashtray in sight. Nicotine ruined the decor, Mrs Wallace said. True – Theo's cigars used to make the net curtains filthy and she was forever washing down the woodwork. There'd be no smoking, no nicotine stains in the new bungalow.

'Never mind all that,' said the little voice. 'Concentrate on the matter in hand.'

Yes of course. Let's see now – she'd be inconsolable over Mrs Whiteley's cup of tea, distraught to the point of being unable to think coherently. She bit her lip. What if she offered to put her up?

'Oh no,' warned the little voice. 'You couldn't keep up the pretence of grief in front of her. She'll be watching you like a hawk.'

All right then, after a little while she'd ask if she could make use of their telephone to ring the Queen's.

She was nearing the avenue now, and she could feel an erratic fluttering under her ribs. The car nosed gently round the corner, down the tree-lined road to where her house had once stood behind that clump of elms.

'Easy now,' said the little voice, 'into the driveway, then comes the shock ...'

She pulled on the handbrake and switched off the engine out of habit, but her brain could barely register what she saw. The house sat, four-square and solid as ever, exuding tranquillity in the late-afternoon sun. She sat dumb and motionless, unable to believe it. It should have been a heap of blackened ruins. She couldn't have dreamed all that business with the scrim and the paraffin, could she?

Leaving the car, she walked up to the front door. Everything looked normal, even down to a leaflet sticking out of the letter-box. In a daze she walked slowly round the garage to the back.

The first thing she registered was how the flower-beds were all awry, shrubs trampled and flattened, broken glass glinting in the grass. Then she saw the boards roughly nailed over the kitchen window and the upper part of the door, the stonework around them darkly stained with soot. She reached into her handbag for the back-door key.

The kitchen was in darkness, a gaping black hole. She stepped gingerly inside, reluctant to place the soles of her new shoes on the sludgy floor.

'Well,' said the little voice, 'the scrim clearly did its work here and no mistake.'

The pale blue of the tiled walls was now a grimy grey-black, and the wooden kitchen cabinets burned to a cinder, the copper-bottomed pans she used to polish so lovingly now hung blackened on the ceiling rack or lay scattered on the floor. From the ceiling strange black strings of cobwebs hung everywhere. The far door leading into the hall was closed.

She picked her way cautiously through the debris to open it. There was no sign of the scrim she'd trailed so carefully through the house, no sign of any damage beyond the dirty marks and lingering acrid smell of smoke.

Suddenly she had a strange sensation that eyes were watching her, and her body stiffened. Then from behind she heard a quiet movement. She spun round. In the open doorway stood a uniformed figure framed by the sunlit garden.

'Mrs Challis?' he said, stepping into the room. 'I saw your car in the drive.'

'I've – I've just got back,' she stammered. 'I don't know what's happening.'

'Lucky the fire was confined to the kitchen,' the constable remarked, 'otherwise the whole house could have gone up.'

She looked helplessly around her, then stared into the hallway. Whatever had gone wrong? Where was the scrim? The police constable nodded.

'We took it away, love,' he said. 'Could have been a bit dangerous, could that.'

Dorothy could feel her knees buckling under her. 'I don't feel very well,' she said weakly. 'I need a cup of tea.'

'Course you do,' he agreed, 'but you can't brew up in this mess. Let me take you down to the station – they make a real good cuppa there.'

And taking her gently by the arm he led her out into the sunlight.

'Councillor Holyoak!'

Reginald turned to look back. Councillor Moxon came hurrying down the corridor towards him. Reginald frowned. He was anxious to get away out of the Town Hall, forget the Housing Committee meeting. The news was bad enough; Moxon would be sure to make the most of it.

'Well now,' said Moxon, slightly out of breath, 'what a carry-on over them flats, eh? Maybe it wasn't such a good idea after all, bringing in a company we'd never heard of. Heads are going to roll over this.'

'Not necessarily,' said Reginald airily. 'Things may not be as bad as they look.'

Moxon raised his eyebrows as he followed him down the ornate staircase. 'Not bad?' he echoed. 'Those flats are running with damp, cracks as wide as your fist – I've seen 'em. If the building inspectors say they're unsafe and unfit for occupation, there'll be a government inquiry sure as eggs is eggs. Mark my words, there will. And what's more,' he added as they reached the entrance hall, 'if them tower blocks have to come down – well, God help Systembuild and God help them who engaged 'em.'

Grinning, he ran down the steps and away up the street to where his car was parked. Reginald glared after him, anger mingling with anxiety in his chest. Government inquiry. The words rang like a tolling bell in his brain. If it came to that, he was done for.

Rosa hurried out of the infirmary and across the darkness of the car park. Her eyes burned from lack of sleep. If only she'd passed her test before Dan was taken so ill she could have driven home now. As it was . . . She glanced at her wrist-watch, twisting her arm to catch the light from the lamp.

A car horn beeped. She looked up. A man was climbing out of his car, and with a surge of relief she recognized Alex.

'You've missed the last bus,' he said as he came across to her.

She gave a rueful smile. 'I lost track of the time.'

He gazed into her face, and she knew he was taking in the eyes, red-rimmed and sore. 'Come on,' he said quietly. 'I'll take you home.'

'What are you doing here anyway?' she asked as she climbed into the car. 'It's nearly midnight.'

'I guessed you'd miss the bus.'

She sighed. 'I could have gone home with Ted and Kitty – they left when visiting was over – but I didn't want to leave him.'

'You've been there all this time on your own?'

'No,' she said wearily, leaning her head back on the upholstery. 'The nurse sat with me – Lucy – she's a lovely girl. She looks after him like he was her own flesh and blood. Dan seems fond of her too, the way he tries to smile at her. I'm glad. They say it can't be long now.'

Alex drove in silence. When he reached the house he pulled up and turned to Rosa. 'Greta's doing a grand job with the café,' he said quietly. 'She says you're not to worry.'

Rosa nodded. 'She's very kind to me.'

'She says if you'd like to go and stay with her when this is all over, stay as long as you like ...'

Rosa shook her head firmly and snatched the door handle. 'I can't think about that, Alex,' she muttered, 'not yet, but tell her I'm grateful for the thought.'

And before he could go round to help her out of the car she'd vanished into the house.

Alex sat in the car for some time, watching the house. No lights came on at the windows. She must be sitting alone in the dark. Was she weeping? Maybe not. Rosa was as strong as they came, but she must be feeling desperately alone in her grief, and his heart ached for her.

If only he could go to her, try to comfort her. But he wasn't very good at this sort of thing. Words came awkwardly. And she wouldn't welcome it – she needed to be alone with her struggle. God give her strength, he prayed. One day, God willing, he'd be able to help her find peace.

*   *   *

'You're very quiet,' said Neela. 'Penny for 'em.'

She turned from the mirror to look at Lucy as she lay on the bed, staring up at the ceiling, arms curled behind her head.

'I wasn't thinking of anything special,' she murmured. 'Just one of the patients.'

'The terminal cancer, I bet,' said Neela, turning back to brushing her glossy dark hair. 'You've talked about little else lately.'

'You haven't met him or you'd understand. He's such a lovely man, sort of gentle and dignified. In a way he reminds me of Daddy.'

Neela lowered the hairbrush and turned with a frown. 'You know what we've been taught – we haven't to get involved, not like that. I know he's young to die but it happens. Wait till we get on children's ward.'

Lucy still stared up at the ceiling, unhearing. 'And his wife is lovely too,' she went on. 'They hold hands and say nothing, but you can see the love. Daddy and I had that too.'

'Listen,' said Neela, and Lucy could hear the impatient tone, 'he's dying – you said Sister told you it's near. Think of the living, for God's sake; think of that good-looking student in ophthalmics who keeps eying you. But stop this obsession with Mr Pearson before it takes you over.'

Lucy sat up slowly. 'It isn't an obsession, Neela. It's just that it's made me think. It's those left behind who suffer most. I know. Poor Mrs Pearson – she's got the worst part still to come.'

Reginald was feeling flustered enough when he reached the office. Since Greta had left nothing had gone right. The house was a mess; there were no clean shirts and socks left in his drawer, no food in the fridge beyond a

411

slab of greening cheese and a mulch of salad stuff in the bottom, the kitchen waste bin was full to overflowing and the stench was overwhelming.

So far he'd closed his eyes to it all in the vain hope she'd come back. He'd eaten out at the beginning, but solitary dining was no pleasure. Since he had no idea how to operate the washing-machine he'd soon be forced to go to one of those dismal-looking laundrette places, where once again he'd be baffled by the technicalities. He'd better see about getting a woman in.

And as if domestic discomfort wasn't enough, there was this other anxiety preying on his mind. The building inspectors were insistent that the high-rise flats built by Systembuild had to come down and, though there'd been no further word, there was still the fear that a government inquiry might ensue. Then all the business of the money he'd received as non-executive director of the company would inevitably come to light.

His secretary came in, placed a pile of letters on his desk, and went out again without a word. Reginald picked up the top sheet. Yesterday's letters – he hadn't come back in the afternoon to sign them. Miss Holroyd's silence was her form of mute rebuke. He growled to himself. He could do without that. His head ached enough as it was. Thank God he didn't have to appear in court today.

The door opened again and Miss Holroyd swept in. 'Mr Hetherington has left a message for you,' she said icily. 'He's had to go into Leeds so he can't keep his meeting with you this afternoon.'

Reginald grunted. Miss Holroyd hovered, clearly wanting to say more. 'It seems he met a nurse up at the infirmary while his father was in with his prostate last week,' she said confidentially. 'Her mother's up on an arson charge, and Mr Hetherington's offered to take it on.'

'At the hospital? So we're turning into ambulance-chasers now like the Americans, are we?' grumbled Reginald. 'Arson, indeed.'

Miss Holroyd ignored the jibe. 'He reckons he can get her off – he thinks the woman's deranged.'

Reginald waved his hand. 'I really couldn't care less about him,' he muttered. 'I've got problems of my own.'

Miss Holroyd blushed. 'Sorry, Mr Holyoak,' she murmured, 'I was forgetting. I'll leave you in peace.'

Reginald scowled at her disappearing back. So the office had got to know about Greta leaving. Still, it was the other matter which was causing his stomach to tie itself in knots.

He craned his neck to peer through the glass partition. Miss Holroyd was not at her desk. He consulted his notebook, lifted the receiver and dialled an outside line.

'Systembuild. Can I help you?'

'I want to speak to Frank Crawshaw.'

'I'm sorry, Mr Crawshaw is not to be disturbed.'

Reginald could feel the panic rising from his guts. 'Tell him it's urgent,' he shouted. 'Tell him it's Holyoak, from Hawksmoor.'

For a time there was silence on the line. He sat chewing his fingernail anxiously.

'Hello?'

With relief he recognized Crawshaw's voice. 'I had to ring,' he muttered. 'Those flats – you've heard – what are we going to do?'

Reginald gripped the telephone, waiting for a miracle. 'Don't panic,' Crawshaw said quietly. 'I've got it all in hand.'

A trickle of relief began to flow in Reginald's veins. 'How?' he asked cautiously.

'I'll talk to you later. Let me just say there's a Member

413

of Parliament, one of our consultants. He'll see to things. There'll be no inquiry.'

So that was it. Another well-paid non-executive director in Crawshaw's pocket. He'd recognize quickly enough that it would be in his interests to see to it that the inquiry never came to anything.

'So you see,' Crawshaw said smoothly. 'There is absolutely no cause for alarm. Goodbye, Holyoak.'

Reginald took a deep breath as he replaced the receiver. He felt a whole lot easier now the wily Crawshaw had the matter in hand.

Chapter Thirty-seven

Rosa hurried into the ward. A nurse blocked her way, handing out morning cups of tea from a trolley. Rosa edged round her, then stopped short. Dan was no longer lying in bed seven where she'd left him last night.

She turned anxiously towards the office just as Sister Fleming came out. 'Where is he?' Rosa asked, almost afraid to hear the answer.

'Ah, Mrs Pearson,' said Sister, 'we've put your husband in the side ward. I felt he'd be more comfortable there.'

She led the way to the small room. Rosa followed, her heart bumping. As she went in she saw Dan, his eyes closed, and bending over him a nurse she recognized. Lucy straightened and smiled.

'How is he?' whispered Rosa.

'Sleeping peacefully,' replied Lucy. 'He's in no pain.'

Sister Fleming left and Rosa seated herself on the edge of the chair. She understood – there was no need to spell it out. The end was near.

Dan looked still and deathly pale, like a ghost already. She followed the line of the life-giving drip attached to his arm, bringing him peace in the shape of morphine. Over the last few days they'd increased the dose so that he slept more and more. He'd probably slip away in his sleep, they said, and she prayed he wouldn't wake in the meantime. He'd had enough; he was ready to go. If he woke and was capable of thinking lucidly he'd only worry about her.

She looked down on his shrunken frame, wondering vaguely why no tears came. This husk wasn't Dan, not the burly fellow she first set eyes on all those years ago, filling the width of the gangway with his magnetic presence. This puny body wasn't big enough to contain the gentle strength and generosity of him.

You've been so strong, she said silently, the way you've accepted this thing. You've never once complained. You were always there to hold my hand, to help me do what I wanted. You've been my rock. You never wanted much from life, never anything for yourself. I wish I had your strength, your contentment.

The nurse standing at the foot of the bed looked down with compassion on the suffering woman. What a strong woman she is, she thought. It takes great courage to sit helplessly by for so long watching your husband, waiting for death to release him.

Rosa became aware of the girl still standing by the bed. 'It won't be long now, will it?' she murmured.

Lucy shook her head. 'Hours at the most.'

Rosa gave a thin smile. 'I'm glad you're here,' she said softly. 'I know how he took a shine to you.'

The girl smiled shyly. 'I asked Sister if I could stay with him,' she murmured. 'He makes me remember my dad.'

Rosa looked up, startled. 'You lost your father?'

The girl bent her head. 'Last year. We were very close.'

'Oh, my dear – I'm so sorry.'

Lucy blinked away a tear. 'It's all right, like I say to my friend Neela, he's never really left me, he's still sitting in the back of my mind. I sometimes feel that if I turned round suddenly I could see him.'

Rosa smiled. 'I like that. But you still have your mother, don't you?'

She saw the girl's eyelids flicker. 'I never really knew her,' she murmured.

Rosa felt a stab of compassion for the child. So young, and no mother or father to turn to. She reached up and touched the slim hands clasped in front of the starched apron.

'I had a daughter once,' she said gently. 'She'd be about your age. I like to think she'd have been a lot like you.'

'You're very kind,' said Lucy.

'I mean it,' murmured Rosa. 'I don't want this to be the last time I see you. I'd like to think we're going to meet again after—' She glanced down at the figure in the bed and covered the bony fingers with hers. 'He'd like that, I know.'

Reginald was beginning to feel easier about the flats. They'd still have to come down, of course, but at least no-one was talking of an official inquiry any more. Crawshaw's puppet in the House of Commons must have done his stuff.

He was passing through the general office when Hetherington breezed in. Reginald greeted him genially.

'How are things going?' he enquired. 'Dealt with that arson case in Leeds yet?'

Hetherington nodded. 'Case adjourned,' he said briefly. 'They've ordered the woman to be remanded in custody pending psychiatric reports.'

'Barmy, is she?' smiled Reginald. 'She could get off then if you can show the balance of the mind was disturbed.'

'Very possibly she'll be unfit to plead,' said Hetherington. 'She's clearly paranoid. Tells me everyone hates her, even her children and her doctor, and what's more, she says she hears voices.'

'No problem then,' said Reginald, waving his arm. 'They

417

won't jail her – long stretch in a psychiatric hospital, that's all.'

Hetherington nodded gloomily. 'She's there now – I went to see her. Ordering the nurses about like they were her personal servants. She's convinced it's some sort of convalescent home for the genteel.'

Reginald was still chuckling to himself as he went back into his office. Women. Unpredictable, capricious creatures at best; untrustworthy and unstable at the worst. The loony-bin was the best place for the lot of them.

Dorothy laid the paperback novel down on her lap and stretched her bare feet out on the stool. The book was yawningly boring, with a heroine predictably arguing non-stop with the lantern-jawed man she was clearly destined to fall in love with. Why did people waste their time writing such trash? And why did the home offer nothing better in its limited library? Theo's books back at home – now there was a collection to be proud of; leather-bound classics and beautifully illustrated art books, not slushy romances. No-one with their head screwed on right believed in romance anyway.

She looked around at the comfortable room. The decor was quite pleasant, even if the seascape pictures on the walls weren't exactly her cup of tea. It was a mercy those people had recognized how deeply she was suffering from strain and found this convalescent home for her to spend a little time recuperating.

Lucy should have done that. After all, she was in the medical profession, wasn't she? Fat lot of use she'd turned out to be. Her and Graham – neither one of them had come near. For all they cared she could be dead and gone. To think of all the years she'd wasted caring for that ungrateful pair.

That Mr Hetherington showed more interest than they did. He'd been to visit her several times. He said he'd been sent by Lucy, but she hadn't fallen for that, not for a minute. Lucy would never show such consideration. They'd had some nice chats about the weather and the decor in the home. Mind you, his eternal questions about the fire did become a little tiresome at times.

The fire? She sat up abruptly and the paperback slid from her lap to the floor. Maybe he was a spy from the insurance company! Damn Lucy – why wasn't she here to protect her? Was it because she really had sent Mr Hetherington to harass her?

Dorothy pushed her feet into the satin slippers and hurried out into the corridor. A tall figure came striding towards her, and with a smile she held out her hands.

'Graham! I should have guessed you'd come!' She glanced down at her dressing-gown and waved a gracious hand. 'Oh, ignore the robe, my dear. I haven't got round to dressing yet.'

'It doesn't matter,' he replied. 'It's not important.'

Her glance slid to the figure waiting patiently behind him, a pretty girl with skin as black as coal. Dorothy recoiled visibly.

'Oh no!' she cried, covering her face with her hands. 'You haven't had the gall to bring her here! Graham, how could you? Knowing how I feel about coloured people! You can't – you mustn't marry her! I won't have black grandchildren!'

She could feel the blood rushing to her head, her body shaking with rage. 'Get out of here!' she yelled. 'I won't see you – or her! You disgust me!'

Without a word to her he turned to the black girl. 'I think another ten milligrammes is called for, nurse,' he said coolly. 'Intramuscular.' He turned back to Dorothy.

'Let nurse take you back to the ward, Mrs Challis. She'll get you a nice cup of tea.'

Dorothy gave the girl a suspicious look, but his words and soothing tone allayed her fears. 'Earl Grey, remember,' she muttered. 'I never drink anything else.'

'That's what we always say back home in Jamaica,' smiled the nurse as she took her arm. 'There's nowt else to touch it.'

Reginald signed the last of the letters Miss Holroyd had placed before him, then laid down his pen and stretched his arms above his head. Heavens! It was five o'clock already. He pushed back his chair and turned to take his coat from the peg.

As he went through the outer office he placed the pile of letters on Miss Holroyd's desk. She was nowhere in sight. He pushed open the swing door and set off down the stairs. At the bottom his secretary was standing, a package in her hand.

'Special delivery for you, Mr Holyoak,' she said crisply. 'Just arrived by special messenger.'

He looked down at the envelope in her hand. Without doubt it would be from Greta's solicitors, queries relating to the separation. He didn't want to know about it right now; the day had gone quite well so far and he was damned if he was going to have his evening with the Robsons spoilt by worrying about Greta's demands.

'Leave it on my desk,' he said tersely. 'I'll deal with it in the morning.'

'Very well.'

Miss Holroyd watched him swing away out of the front door before she turned and climbed the stairs back to the office. Thank goodness he was being less irritable these days than he had been of late. There'd been days he'd almost had her in tears with his vexatious ways, and she wasn't a woman who cracked easily.

She looked down at the envelope before she placed it on her desk. She'd seen the look on his face down there. He hadn't wanted to deal with this tonight – he evidently knew what it was. She picked up the envelope again, turning it over thoughtfully. She could leave it until morning; on the other hand, it was her duty as secretary to open Mr Holyoak's mail . . .

Picking up the brass letter opener she slit the envelope and glanced at the single sheet of paper with its impressive heading.

Oh dear. Mr Holyoak was being summoned to appear before a tribunal, a formal inquiry, it said, instituted by Her Majesty's Government into those defective tower blocks. Miss Holroyd smiled to herself as she fished in her handbag and applied a touch of lipstick to her thin lips.

Poor Mr Holyoak – he wasn't going to like this at all.

'Your friend is here to see you, Mrs Pearson.'

Rosa looked up in surprise. The nurse in the doorway stood back to let her pass. Lucy nodded.

'You go – I'll stay with him.'

Greta was waiting in the corridor. 'What are you doing here?' asked Rosa. Greta took her hand.

'It's gone closing time,' she said softly. 'Alex insisted we should call round on the way home to see you were all right. I didn't want to intrude, only I bet you've not eaten all day.'

Rosa felt numb as she shook her head. 'I'm not hungry,' she muttered, and then her lips began to tremble. 'God, I'm going to miss him, Greta. I never really knew love till I met Dan.'

Greta slipped an arm around her shoulders. 'At least you've known it now, my dear.'

Rosa laid her head against the comforting shoulder. 'But it seems that those I love are always taken from me.'

The gentle voice flowed over her like a warm shower. 'What is it the poet says? "'Tis better to have loved and lost, than never to have loved at all." You've had something very special, my dear, but it's not the end. There's always something else there in the shadows you haven't seen yet. Believe me, I know.'

Rosa broke away with a muffled sob. 'I must get back to him now,' she croaked. 'He needs me – he's never failed me.'

With a sigh Greta watched her slim figure hurry away along the echoing corridor. When it's all over, Rosa, come home to me, she breathed. There is so much love in me to give.

From her easy chair Dorothy watched with sullen suspicion as the nurse served cups of hot chocolate. She was beginning to revise her opinion of this place. Convalescent home or not, she could feel the eyes furtively watching her, turning away abruptly whenever she caught them at it, unwilling to meet her gaze. They were hiding something.

She wasn't born yesterday. There was some sort of conspiracy going on between them, she was sure of it, a plot to keep her in the dark about something. They were spying on her too, like that wily Mr Hetherington. She wasn't taken in by his smiles, not for a minute.

'Drinking chocolate, Mrs Challis?'

The nurse handed her the cup with a smile. Her uniform crackled as she bent. Dorothy sniffed.

'My daughter's in the medical profession, you know.'

'Is she now?' said the nurse. Dorothy felt her head begin

to swim. She was getting confused. She had no daughter. Whatever was she thinking of?

She took a sip from the cup, and then frowned. The stuff clung bitter around her tongue. She was about to protest, but on second thoughts she bit back the words. Had they deliberately put something in her drink? She wouldn't put it past them. Far wiser not to let them know she'd rumbled them.

She waited until the nurse had left and then surreptitiously poured the thick brown liquid into the potted fern alongside her chair. The poor neglected thing looked dehydrated anyway.

She must think coolly. What reason could they have for wanting to drug her? Was it because she'd so strenuously refused to let them put any more needles into her arm this afternoon? They hadn't liked that at all – she'd seen the icy look in their eyes.

A sudden thought alarmed her. They could be trying to poison her, or dope her in order to keep her prisoner? But why? Acting on someone else's orders – not Graham or Lucy, surely? Hetherington must have something to do with it, acting for the real persecutor, but who could that be?

That murderer they called the Yorkshire Ripper? He was still at large and, according to the newspapers, that girl in Bradford made no fewer than seven murders now, all of which could be his work. No, it wouldn't be him. His victims had all been young women, waylaid in the dark, and most of them no better than they ought to be.

Overmeer! Dorothy almost started out of her chair. That was it! Why hadn't she tumbled to it before? The evil bastard was planning to get his revenge by seeing to it that she never built her dream bunga- low. Kill her or keep her prisoner – the result was the same. She'd always known, whatever Theo thought of him, that the Dutchman was a cunning malicious swine.

'Ready for bed now, Mrs Challis?'

The nurse was standing at her elbow, holding out a hand. Dorothy declined to notice it, gathering her robe about her as she stood up. Through the mist in her head she heard the little voice.

'You aren't going to let that foreign bastard get away with it, are you? You're not going to let him beat you.'

'Indeed I'm not,' she muttered, a crafty gleam in her eye. 'I'll get my way if it's the last thing I do.'

'Of course you will, Mrs Challis,' soothed the nurse. 'Would you like a hot-water bottle tonight?'

The shadows of the hospital lengthened across the car park. With the dying of the day Dan Pearson slipped away just as the evening sun went down. Wife and nurse sat silent on either side of the bed, each gripping the other's hand across the still body.

Rosa felt numb, drained of emotion, as she gazed down on his beloved face. Her free hand clutched a string of rosary beads long hidden away in a drawer. Dan had a gentle look about him now, his white face no longer contorted but composed in peace at last. She felt at the same time overwhelmed and desperately alone. He was setting out on a journey where she could not follow.

She tried to think of those others she'd loved who'd gone before, now lining up to welcome him: Maggie Malone, Oona, Grandma Sheridan, and gentle Daddy Kerrigan. Not to mention the generations of Pearsons spanning back over the centuries. She could visualize Dan's soul, freed from the flesh at last, winging its way to his beloved moor ...

The scrape of a chair pulled her back to the moment. Lucy was rising to her feet. Rosa felt agitated.

Don't, for God's sake, cover his face – not yet!

She watched as the girl crossed to the window and stood there for a moment in silence, looking out into the dusk. Then she raised her arm and threw back the casement. The cool evening breeze fanned her hair.

Rosa's gaze turned back to the motionless figure on the bed. 'Thanks,' she muttered.

Lucy came back to stand beside her. 'What for?' she asked.

Rosa lifted her tear-misted gaze to look directly into the girl's eyes. 'For letting his soul go free.'

Alex sat in the darkening car park, his fingers tapping the steering-wheel in rhythm to the music on the radio. In the hospital windows lights were beginning to appear, one by one.

He leaned down to switch the radio off, feeling the cramp starting to seize his calves, but he was reluctant to leave the car and go for a walk. From this vantage point he could watch the colonnaded entrance to the infirmary and see her the moment she appeared. She'd be terribly vulnerable tonight. She'd come out, bruised and bleeding, but not broken. Women like Rosa Pearson were not easily broken.

He'd keep his promise to Dan. He'd be proud to be at her side when she took her first steps into the new life stretching ahead. And if she'd let him stay on ...

Then suddenly he saw the distant door swing open and the slight figure emerge under the arched colonnade and pause to look up. She was still standing there when he reached her side. A slight rain was beginning to fall and he saw the tiny spots flecking her face.

'He's gone, Alex,' she murmured.

He could find no words. Instead he laid a hand on

her elbow, wondering whether he was intruding where he shouldn't. She turned sorrowful eyes to him.

'I was never so glad to see anyone, Alex.'

He drew her gently away, along the colonnade towards the car. At the end she pulled her arm free and looked up, raindrops mingling with the tears on her cheeks. Alex looked down at her, puzzled.

'What is it, Rosa?'

A faint smile curved her lips. 'I was remembering what you told me once,' she said softly, 'about the harvest festival. Remember? The arch covered with fruit?'

'The Succoth? What about it?'

'You said something I need to remember.'

'I did? What was that?'

For a moment she stared up at the heavens, and he barely heard her low reply. 'You have to be able to see the sky,' she murmured.

Rain was spattering against the windscreen in huge, spider-like blobs. The young man eased the car round the bend and then glanced down at the girl beside him.

'No chance of the woods tonight,' he said, 'unless you fancy a soaking. We'll have to stay in the car.'

She looked out at the wooded country lane. 'I don't know,' she said with a nervous giggle, 'there's a phone box over there. We've never—' She broke off suddenly. 'Oh my God! What the hell's that?'

There was a squeal of brakes as the car scraped to a halt. Ahead of them, on an open expanse of land, caught in the glare of the headlights, the white-robed figure of a woman seemed to be dancing a frenzied waltz alone. Her flimsy robe floated in rhythm with her wild movements. Like a whirling dervish she twisted and dipped, every now and again touching the ground.

426

'Christ!' muttered the young man.

The girl's voice was a timid whisper. 'Is it a ghost?'

'Don't be daft,' he growled. 'She's as real as you and me, but what the hell is she up to?'

The woman suddenly ceased her frenetic dance and crouched down, scrabbling at the earth with bare hands, seemingly unaware of the headlights and the rain soaking her hair, plastering it to her face.

'She's digging,' whispered the girl. 'What shall we do? Just drive on and pretend we haven't seen her? Or will you go and ask her what's up?'

The young man bit his lip, then made up his mind. 'I'll go to that phone box and call the police. You stay here.'

It took only minutes for the patrol car to arrive. Dorothy looked startled when the young officer took her arm, preventing her from throwing any more rocks and stones into the trees.

'Mrs Challis?' he enquired politely. 'We had word you was missing. It's doing you no good, out in this rotten rain and all.'

Dorothy looked down at her hands, then held them out. 'Look at my nails,' she whimpered. 'They're broken! I always have perfect nails.'

'We'll get them fixed for you,' he assured her, taking her arm again. 'You just come on home with me.'

'Don't be insolent,' she yelled, trying to wrench her arm free from his grip. 'You're not going to keep me prisoner! This is my land and I'm going to clear it. It's not contaminated, whatever he says!'

'Of course not,' the officer agreed, 'only your daughter's been worried sick about you. She's here with us now. She's waiting in the car.'

Dorothy's face blanched with rage. 'You're lying – just

427

trying to lock me up again,' she screamed. 'I have no daughter, and I never had!'

Lucy felt utterly weary as she crossed the lawn to the nurses' home. One way and another it had been a hell of a day.

First there'd been Dan Pearson's death, and that wonderfully close feeling with his wife Rosa. Then Mother.

'I have no daughter ...'

She'd heard the words clearly from the back of the patrol car. It should have hurt like hell, but maybe Dan Pearson's death had robbed her of feeling, because she felt no hurt. Instead she felt only a glow, a sense of being honoured to know the kind of love that couple had shared, to have been allowed to take part in the last few precious weeks of Dan's life. Their love restored one's faith in mankind.

She dug a hand in her pocket for the key and pulled out a piece of paper. On it, in hastily scrawled handwriting, were Rosa Pearson's address and telephone number. Lucy smiled. She looked forward to seeing her again soon, and as she pushed the door open she sighed.

'I wish I had a mother like you.'

THE END

THE JERICHO YEARS
by Aileen Armitage

Jericho Farm, high in the Pennines, had been in the Hemingway family for generations. Life on the farm was hard, yet the place had a rugged compulsion for those who lived and worked there. But now James Hemingway was thinking of breaking with tradition and selling up. With his wife tragically dead, David, his son, making a separate career as an artist, and his daughter, Ellen, a strange, withdrawn and troubled girl, there seemed little point in staying on at Jericho.

Then David, the beloved and only son, was struck by a fatal illness and with Lisa, the girl he wanted to marry, came back to Jericho, to the house and land that he loved. As the new family coped with fresh tragedy and began to try and weld together once more, so an entirely unexpected and unconventional relationship exploded into their lives, one that offered hope to James, to Lisa, and to Jericho Farm.

0 552 14049 X

CEDAR STREET
by Aileen Armitage

May Turnbull had been born and raised in Cedar Street. When the chance came for her to better herself in Rose's soft furnishing workroom, she seized it with everything she had. At home was a father crippled in a mine accident, a mother who kept the family together by taking in laundry, and two sisters. May was determined that she was going to succeed.

When Aaron Rose, wealthy young heir to Rose's Furniture Emporium, saw May for the first time, he realised that she was different, special. Adroitly, with all the skills of an experienced charmer, he set out to win her, half promising a lifetime's love and marriage. It was – almost – to be the end of May's dreams.

But through the cruel times that followed, May and her family drew on all the gutsy strength of Cedar Street to go forward to a new life.

Cedar Street – a novel of the tough, vibrant people of Hawksmoor.

0 552 14229 8

THE BELLS OF SCOTLAND ROAD
by Ruth Hamilton

To the Liverpool of the 1930s came Bridget O'Brien, a young widow with two children, about to be forced into marriage with a man she had never met. Her destination was the infamous Scotland Road, with its noise, its colour, its poverty and humour, where the people lived lives of deprivation and courage backed by rich tradition and a folklore they had themselves evolved.

For Bridget, straight from Ireland, fleeing from a brutal and bigoted father, Scotland Road was, at first, noisome and terrifying. Her sense of isolation was made worse when she met her bridegroom, Sam Bell, a middle-aged pawnbroker whose twin sons were older than she was. Grimly, thankful that at last she and her daughters had a roof over their heads, she settled to make the best of it she could.

It was the rough and vibrant Costigan family who first made her welcome. Diddy, a huge warm-hearted Liverpudlian and Billy, her docker husband, did their best to ease the young widow into her new life. Anthony, one of her so-called stepsons, also held out the strong hand of friendship, but Liam, the favourite of his father, had the power to terrify her. Liam was cold, compelling, mysterious and antagonistic. He was also a priest.

Against the backdrop of a unique culture, through the depression of the 30s and the savagery of WWII, the story of Bridie, her daughters, and the two men who were to shape her destiny was played out.

0 552 14385 5

A SELECTED LIST OF NOVELS
AVAILABLE FROM CORGI BOOKS

THE PRICES SHOWN BELOW WERE CORRECT AT THE TIME OF GOING TO PRESS. HOWEVE
TRANSWORLD PUBLISHERS RESERVE THE RIGHT TO SHOW NEW RETAIL PRICES ON COVER
WHICH MAY DIFFER FROM THOSE PREVIOUSLY ADVERTISED IN THE TEXT OR ELSEWHERE.

14060 0	MERSEY BLUES	Lyn Andrews	£4.9
14049 X	THE JERICHO YEARS	Aileen Armitage	£4.9
14229 8	CEDAR STREET	Aileen Armitage	£4.9
14514 9	BLONDE WITH ATTITUDE	Virginia Blackburn	£5.9
14309 X	THE KERRY DANCE	Louise Brindley	£5.9
13313 2	CATCH THE WIND	Frances Donnelly	£5.9
14442 8	JUST LIKE A WOMAN	Jill Gascoine	£5.9
14382 0	THE TREACHERY OF TIME	Anna Gilbert	£4.9
14097 X	SEA MISTRESS	Iris Gower	£5.9
14537 8	APPLE BLOSSOM TIME	Kathryn Haig	£5.9
14385 5	THE BELLS OF SCOTLAND ROAD	Ruth Hamilton	£5.9
14529 7	LEAVES FROM THE VALLEY	Caroline Harvey	£5.9
14297 2	ROSY SMITH	Janet Haslam	£4.9
14486 X	MARSH LIGHT	Kate Hatfield	£6.9
14220 4	CAPEL BELLS	Joan Hessayon	£4.9
14262 X	MARIANA	Susanna Kearsley	£4.9
14397 9	THE BLACK BOOK	Sara Keays	£5.9
14045 7	THE SUGAR PAVILION	Rosalind Laker	£5.9
14332 4	THE WINTER HOUSE	Judith Lennox	£5.9
14002 3	FOOL'S CURTAIN	Claire Lorrimer	£4.9
13737 5	EMERALD	Elisabeth Luard	£5.9
13910 6	BLUEBIRDS	Margaret Mayhew	£5.9
14498 3	MORE INNOCENT TIMES	Imogen Parker	£5.9
13904 1	VOICES OF SUMMER	Diane Pearson	£4.9
14124 0	MAGNOLIA SQUARE	Margaret Pemberton	£4.9
14400 2	THE MOUNTAIN	Elvi Rhodes	£5.9
14466 5	TOUCHED BY ANGELS	Susan Sallis	£5.9
13299 3	DOWN LAMBETH WAY	Mary Jane Staples	£4.9
14296 4	THE LAND OF NIGHTINGALES	Sally Stewart	£4.9
14118 6	THE HUNGRY TIDE	Valerie Wood	£4.9

All Transworld titles are available by post from:

Book Service By Post, P.O. Box 29, Douglas, Isle of Man IM99 1BQ

Credit cards accepted. Please telephone 01624 675137,
fax 01624 670923 or Internet http://www.bookpost.co.uk
or e-mail: bookshop@enterprise.net for details.

**Free postage and packing in the UK. Overseas customers: allow
£1 per book (paperbacks) and £3 per book (hardbacks).**